VAULT

PUBLISHER
DAMIAN A. WASSEL

EDITOR-IN-CHIEF
ADRIAN F. WASSEL

ART DIRECTOR
NATHAN C. GOODEN

BRANDING/DESIGN
TIM DANIEL

MANAGING EDITOR
REBECCA TAYLOR

DIRECTOR OF PR & MARKETING
DAVID DISSANAYAKE

PRODUCTION MANAGER
IAN BALDESSARI

PRINCIPAL
DAMIAN A. WASSEL, SR.

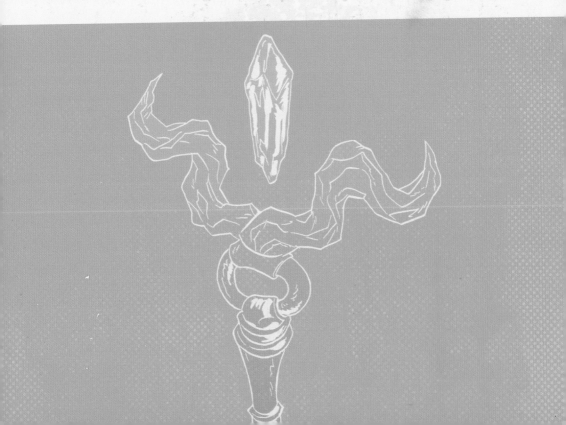

JON TSUEI
WRITER

AUDREY MOK
ARTIST

RAÚL ANGULO
COLORIST

JIM CAMPBELL
LETTERER

KARINA PLAJA
ASSISTANT COLORIST

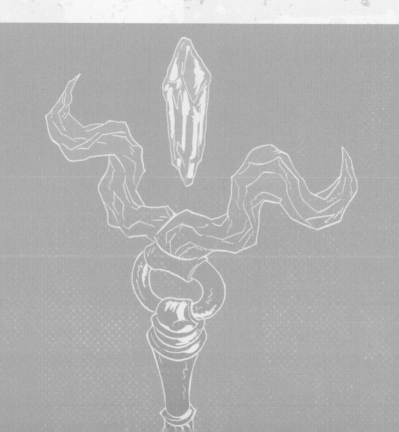

VAULT COMICS
PRESENTS

SERA
AND THE ROYAL STARS

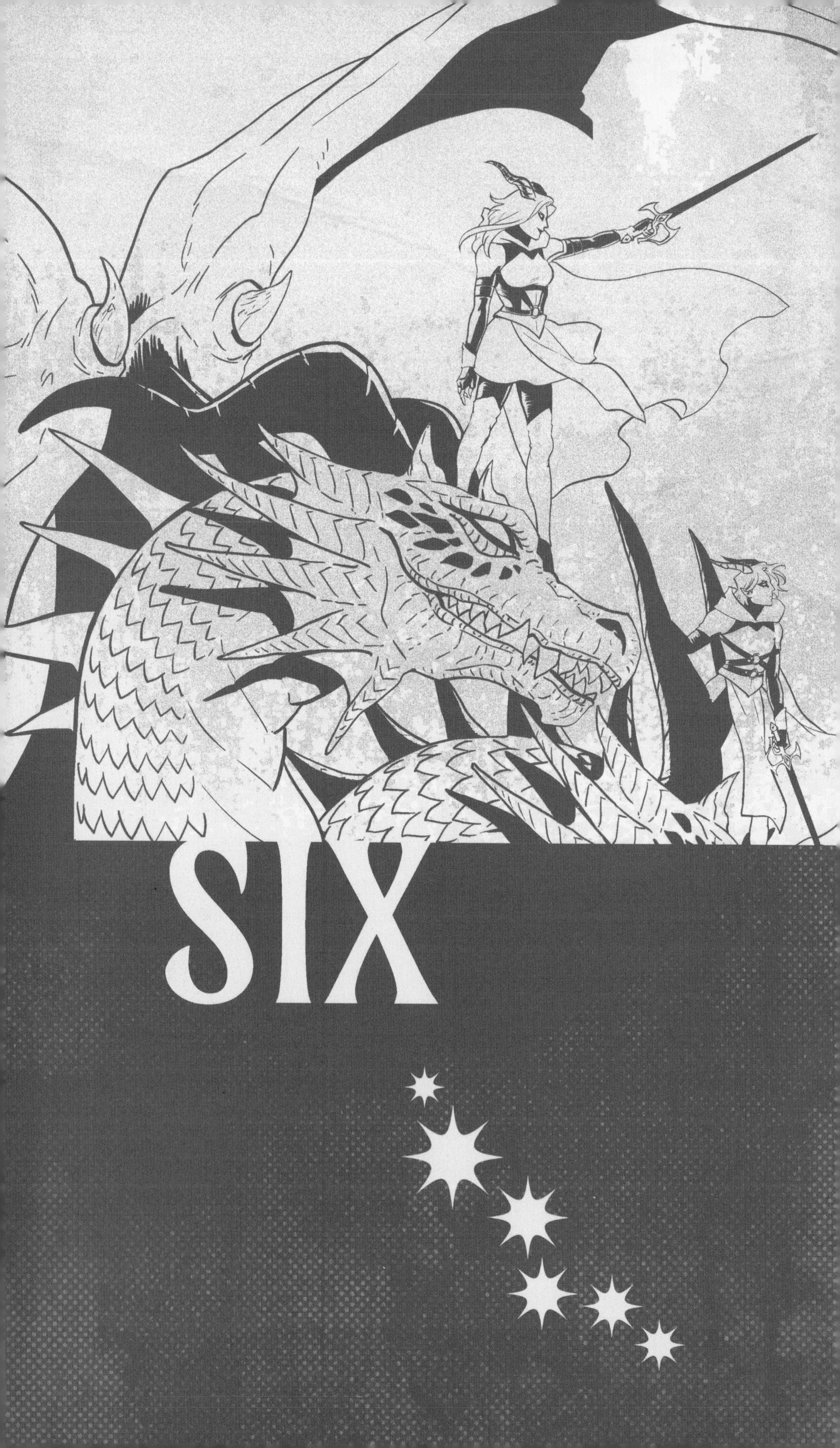

SIX

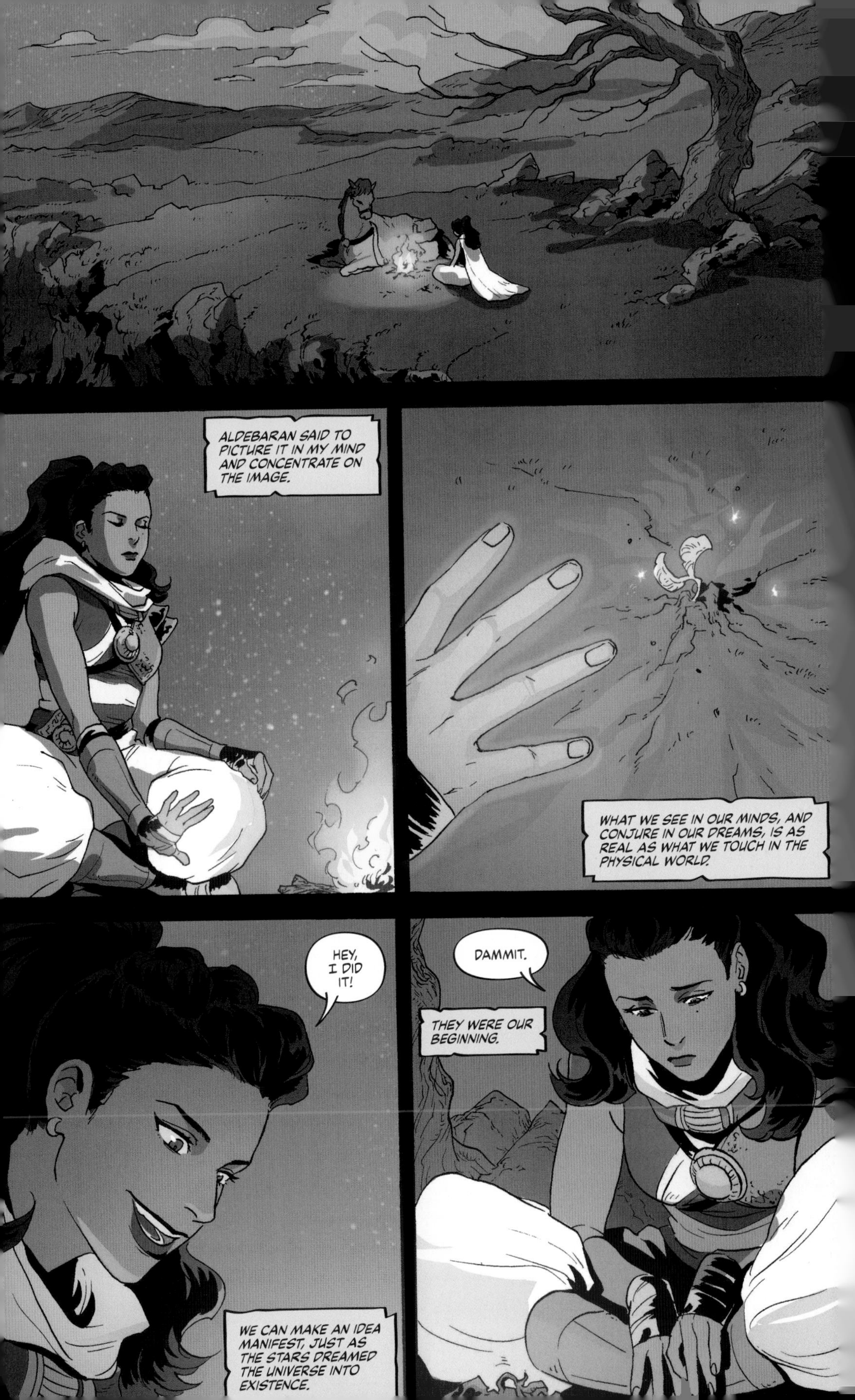
ALDEBARAN SAID TO PICTURE IT IN MY MIND AND CONCENTRATE ON THE IMAGE.
WHAT WE SEE IN OUR MINDS, AND CONJURE IN OUR DREAMS, IS AS REAL AS WHAT WE TOUCH IN THE PHYSICAL WORLD.
HEY, I DID IT!
WE CAN MAKE AN IDEA MANIFEST, JUST AS THE STARS DREAMED THE UNIVERSE INTO EXISTENCE.
DAMMIT.
THEY WERE OUR BEGINNING.

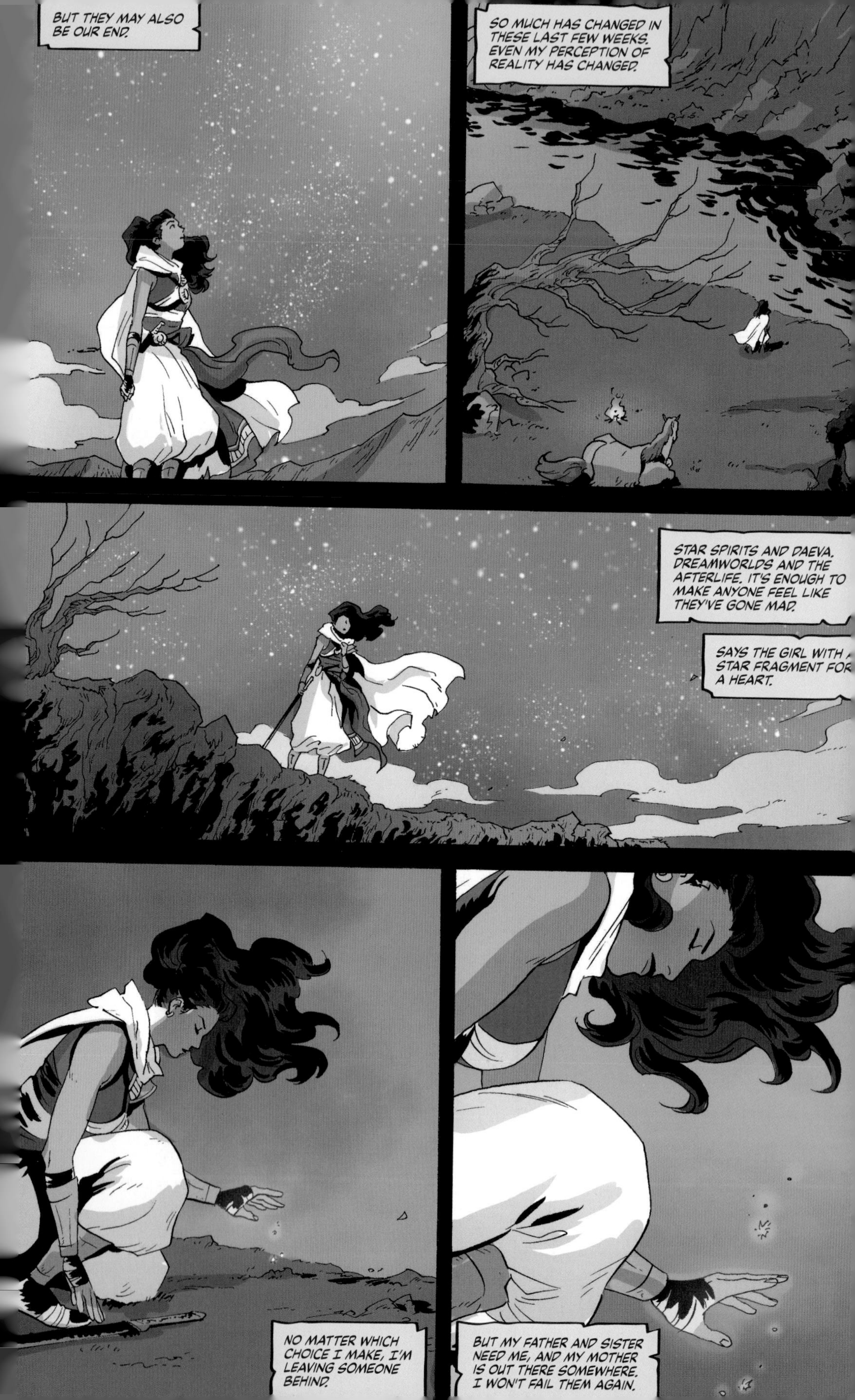
BUT THEY MAY ALSO BE OUR END.
SO MUCH HAS CHANGED IN THESE LAST FEW WEEKS. EVEN MY PERCEPTION OF REALITY HAS CHANGED.
STAR SPIRITS AND DAEVA. DREAMWORLDS AND THE AFTERLIFE. IT'S ENOUGH TO MAKE ANYONE FEEL LIKE THEY'VE GONE MAD.
SAYS THE GIRL WITH A STAR FRAGMENT FOR A HEART.
NO MATTER WHICH CHOICE I MAKE, I'M LEAVING SOMEONE BEHIND.
BUT MY FATHER AND SISTER NEED ME, AND MY MOTHER IS OUT THERE SOMEWHERE. I WON'T FAIL THEM AGAIN.

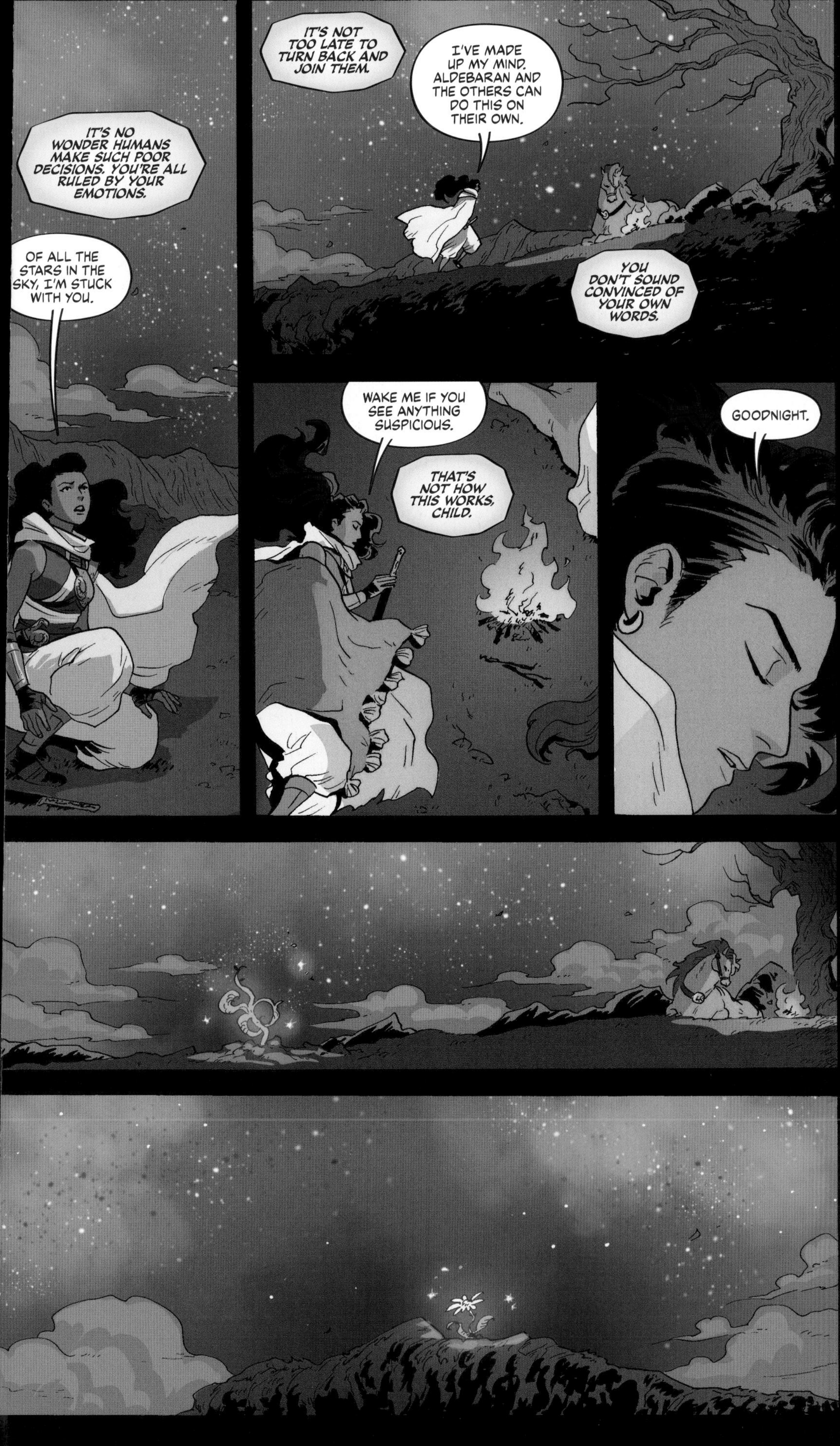

IT'S NO WONDER HUMANS MAKE SUCH POOR DECISIONS. YOU'RE ALL RULED BY YOUR EMOTIONS.
OF ALL THE STARS IN THE SKY, I'M STUCK WITH YOU.
IT'S NOT TOO LATE TO TURN BACK AND JOIN THEM.
I'VE MADE UP MY MIND. ALDEBARAN AND THE OTHERS CAN DO THIS ON THEIR OWN.
YOU DON'T SOUND CONVINCED OF YOUR OWN WORDS.
WAKE ME IF YOU SEE ANYTHING SUSPICIOUS.
THAT'S NOT HOW THIS WORKS, CHILD.
GOODNIGHT.

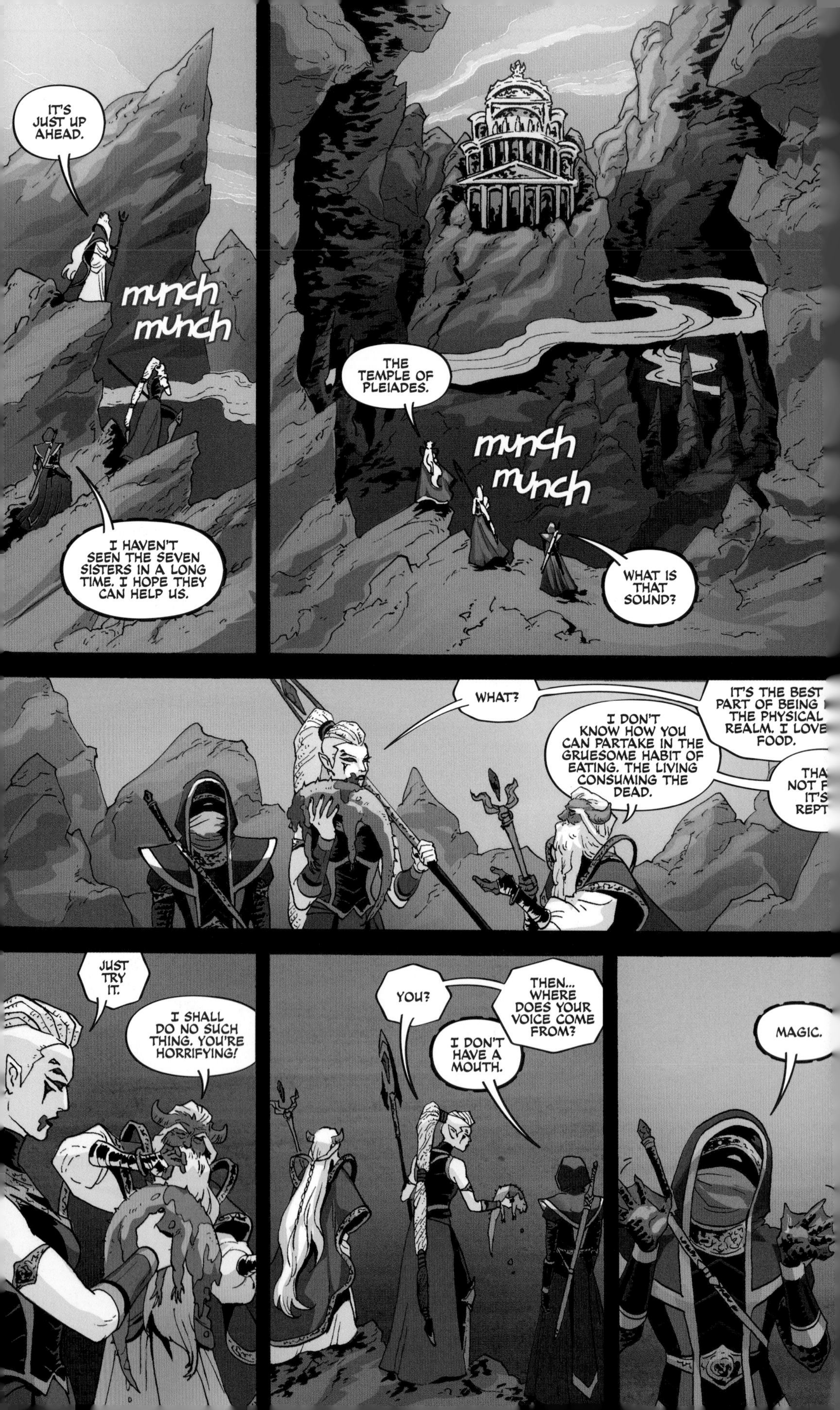
IT'S JUST UP AHEAD.
munch munch
I HAVEN'T SEEN THE SEVEN SISTERS IN A LONG TIME. I HOPE THEY CAN HELP US.
THE TEMPLE OF PLEIADES.
munch munch
WHAT IS THAT SOUND?
WHAT?
I DON'T KNOW HOW YOU CAN PARTAKE IN THE GRUESOME HABIT OF EATING. THE LIVING CONSUMING THE DEAD.
IT'S THE BEST PART OF BEING THE PHYSICAL REALM. I LOVE FOOD.
JUST TRY IT.
I SHALL DO NO SUCH THING. YOU'RE HORRIFYING!
YOU?
I DON'T HAVE A MOUTH.
THEN... WHERE DOES YOUR VOICE COME FROM?
MAGIC.

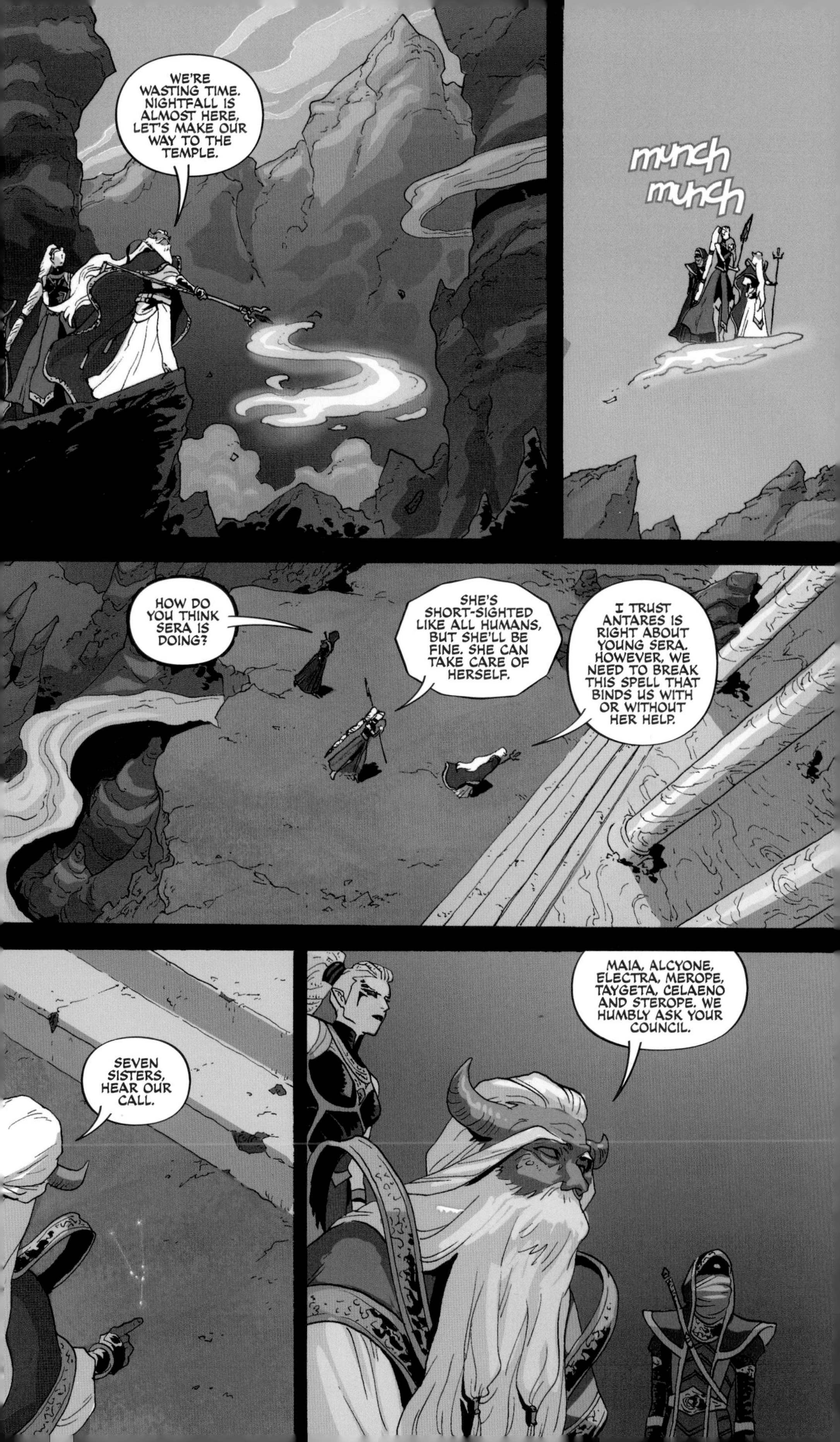
WE'RE WASTING TIME. NIGHTFALL IS ALMOST HERE, LET'S MAKE OUR WAY TO THE TEMPLE.
munch munch
HOW DO YOU THINK SERA IS DOING?
SHE'S SHORT-SIGHTED LIKE ALL HUMANS, BUT SHE'LL BE FINE. SHE CAN TAKE CARE OF HERSELF.
I TRUST ANTARES IS RIGHT ABOUT YOUNG SERA. HOWEVER, WE NEED TO BREAK THIS SPELL THAT BINDS US WITH OR WITHOUT HER HELP.
SEVEN SISTERS, HEAR OUR CALL.
MAIA, ALCYONE, ELECTRA, MEROPE, TAYGETA, CELAENO AND STEROPE. WE HUMBLY ASK YOUR COUNCIL.

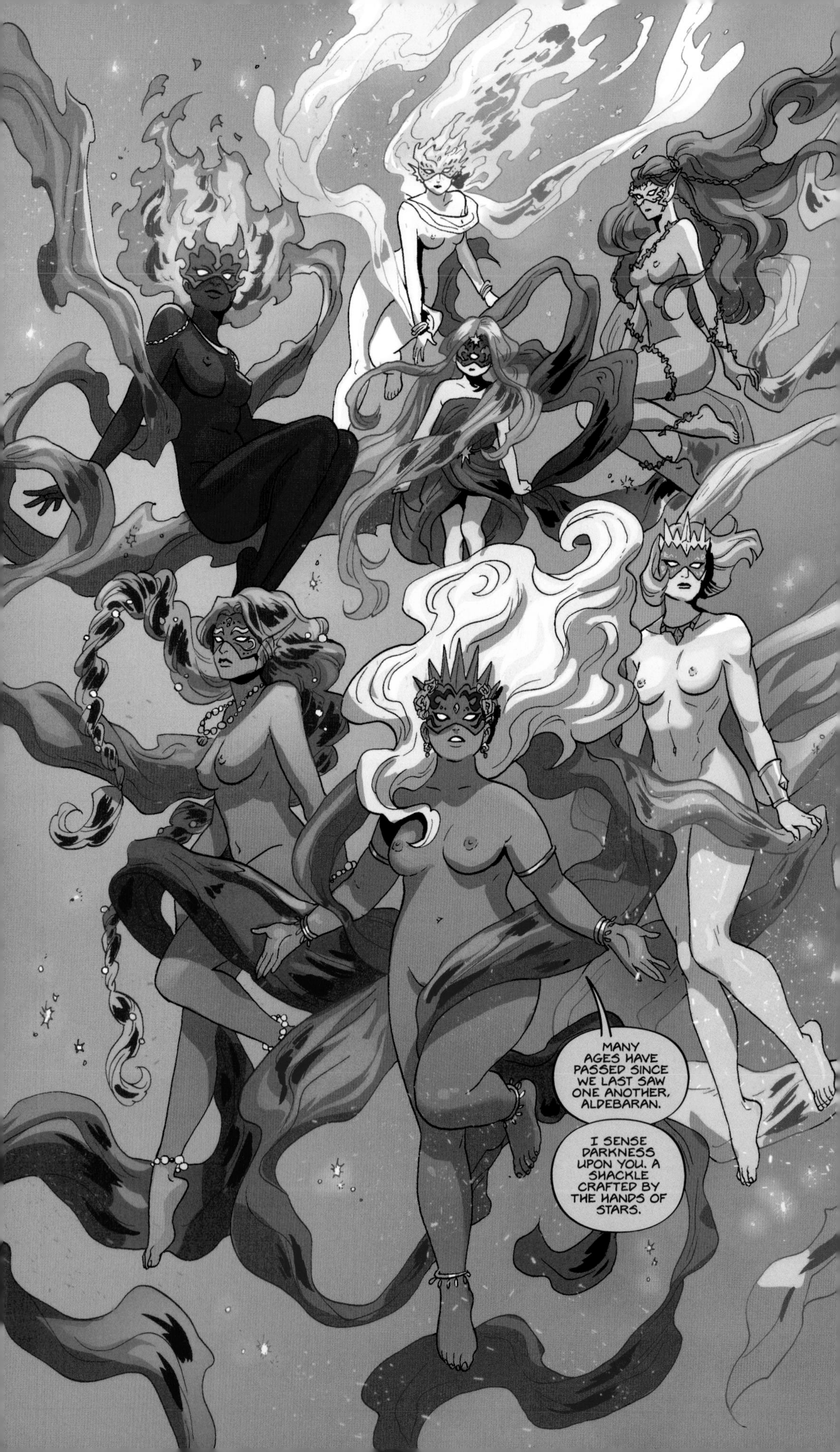
MANY AGES HAVE PASSED SINCE WE LAST SAW ONE ANOTHER, ALDEBARAN.
I SENSE DARKNESS UPON YOU. A SHACKLE CRAFTED BY THE HANDS OF STARS.

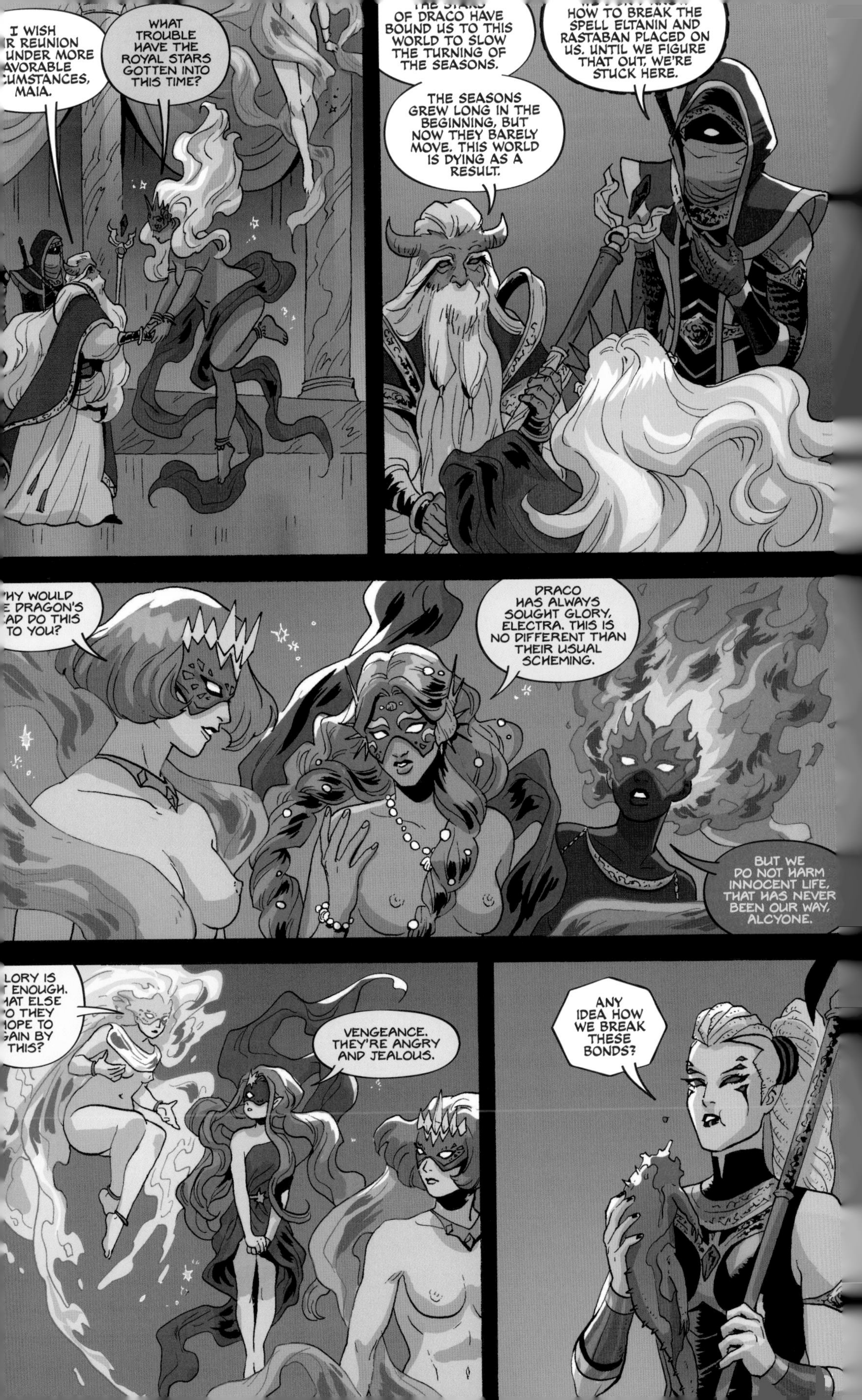
I WISH R REUNION UNDER MORE AVORABLE CUMSTANCES, MAIA.
WHAT TROUBLE HAVE THE ROYAL STARS GOTTEN INTO THIS TIME?
OF DRACO HAVE BOUND US TO THIS WORLD TO SLOW THE TURNING OF THE SEASONS.
THE SEASONS GREW LONG IN THE BEGINNING, BUT NOW THEY BARELY MOVE. THIS WORLD IS DYING AS A RESULT.
HOW TO BREAK THE SPELL ELTANIN AND RASTABAN PLACED ON US. UNTIL WE FIGURE THAT OUT, WE'RE STUCK HERE.
HY WOULD E DRAGON'S AD DO THIS TO YOU?
DRACO HAS ALWAYS SOUGHT GLORY, ELECTRA. THIS IS NO DIFFERENT THAN THEIR USUAL SCHEMING.
BUT WE DO NOT HARM INNOCENT LIFE. THAT HAS NEVER BEEN OUR WAY, ALCYONE.
LORY IS T ENOUGH. HAT ELSE O THEY HOPE TO GAIN BY THIS?
VENGEANCE. THEY'RE ANGRY AND JEALOUS.
ANY IDEA HOW WE BREAK THESE BONDS?

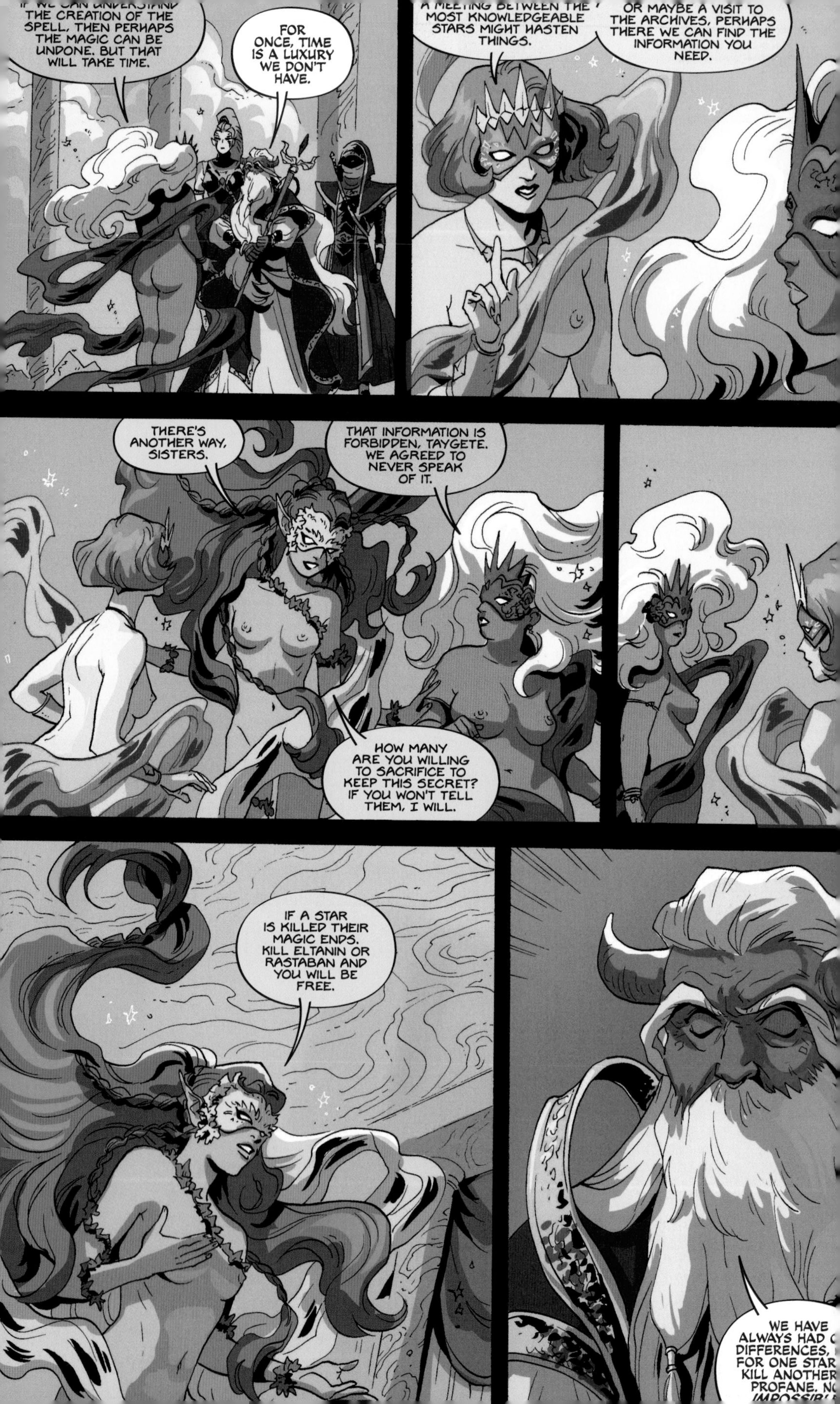
IF WE CAN UNDERSTAND THE CREATION OF THE SPELL, THEN PERHAPS THE MAGIC CAN BE UNDONE. BUT THAT WILL TAKE TIME.
FOR ONCE, TIME IS A LUXURY WE DON'T HAVE.
A MEETING BETWEEN THE MOST KNOWLEDGEABLE STARS MIGHT HASTEN THINGS.
OR MAYBE A VISIT TO THE ARCHIVES, PERHAPS THERE WE CAN FIND THE INFORMATION YOU NEED.
THERE'S ANOTHER WAY, SISTERS.
THAT INFORMATION IS FORBIDDEN, TAYGETE. WE AGREED TO NEVER SPEAK OF IT.
HOW MANY ARE YOU WILLING TO SACRIFICE TO KEEP THIS SECRET? IF YOU WON'T TELL THEM, I WILL.
IF A STAR IS KILLED THEIR MAGIC ENDS. KILL ELTANIN OR RASTABAN AND YOU WILL BE FREE.
WE HAVE ALWAYS HAD DIFFERENCES, FOR ONE STAR KILL ANOTHER PROFANE.

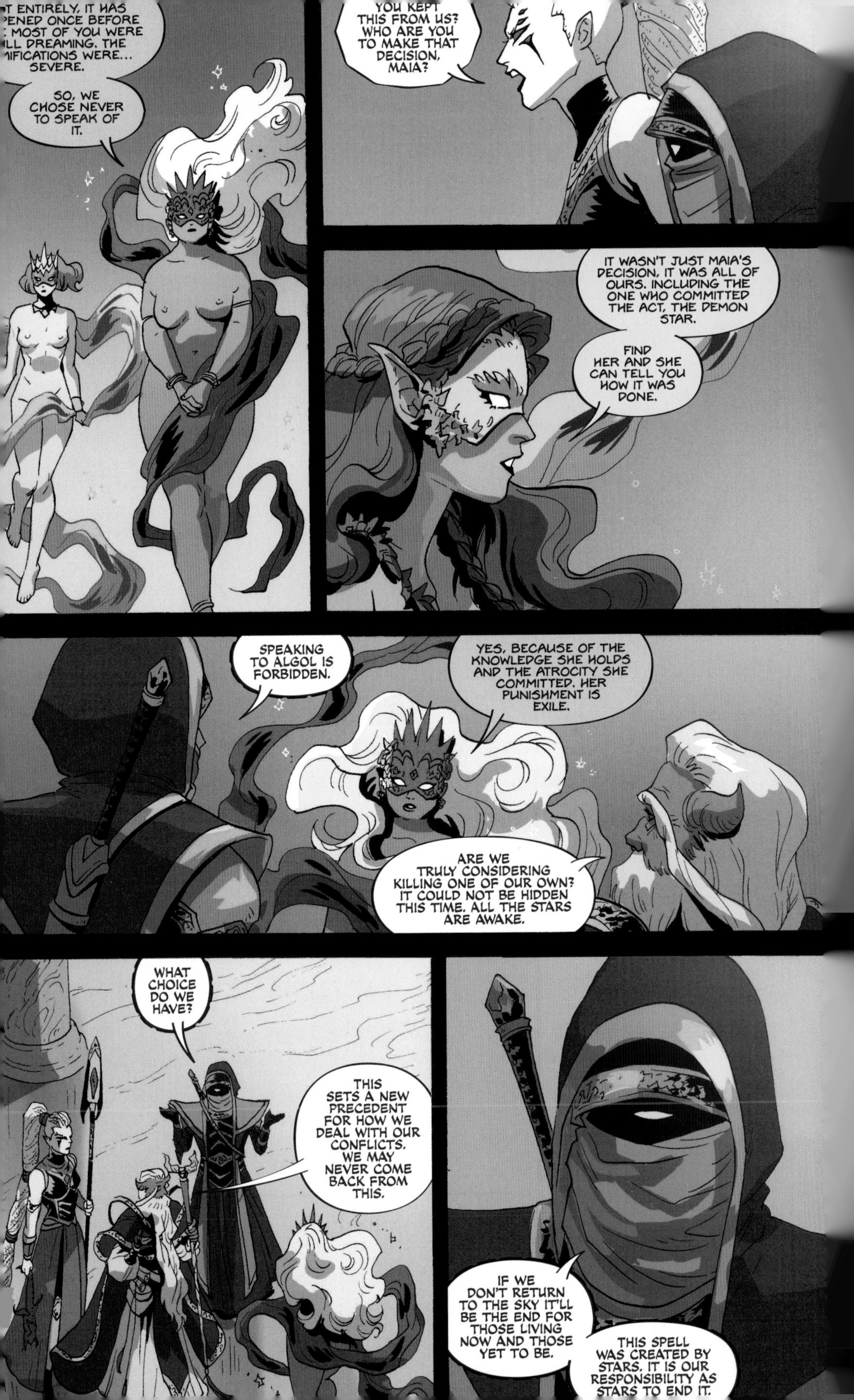
T ENTIRELY, IT HAS PENED ONCE BEFORE MOST OF YOU WERE LL DREAMING. THE MIFICATIONS WERE... SEVERE.
SO, WE CHOSE NEVER TO SPEAK OF IT.
YOU KEPT THIS FROM US? WHO ARE YOU TO MAKE THAT DECISION, MAIA?
IT WASN'T JUST MAIA'S DECISION, IT WAS ALL OF OURS. INCLUDING THE ONE WHO COMMITTED THE ACT, THE DEMON STAR.
FIND HER AND SHE CAN TELL YOU HOW IT WAS DONE.
SPEAKING TO ALGOL IS FORBIDDEN.
YES, BECAUSE OF THE KNOWLEDGE SHE HOLDS AND THE ATROCITY SHE COMMITTED. HER PUNISHMENT IS EXILE.
ARE WE TRULY CONSIDERING KILLING ONE OF OUR OWN? IT COULD NOT BE HIDDEN THIS TIME. ALL THE STARS ARE AWAKE.
WHAT CHOICE DO WE HAVE?
THIS SETS A NEW PRECEDENT FOR HOW WE DEAL WITH OUR CONFLICTS. WE MAY NEVER COME BACK FROM THIS.
IF WE DON'T RETURN TO THE SKY IT'LL BE THE END FOR THOSE LIVING NOW AND THOSE YET TO BE.
THIS SPELL WAS CREATED BY STARS. IT IS OUR RESPONSIBILITY AS STARS TO END IT.

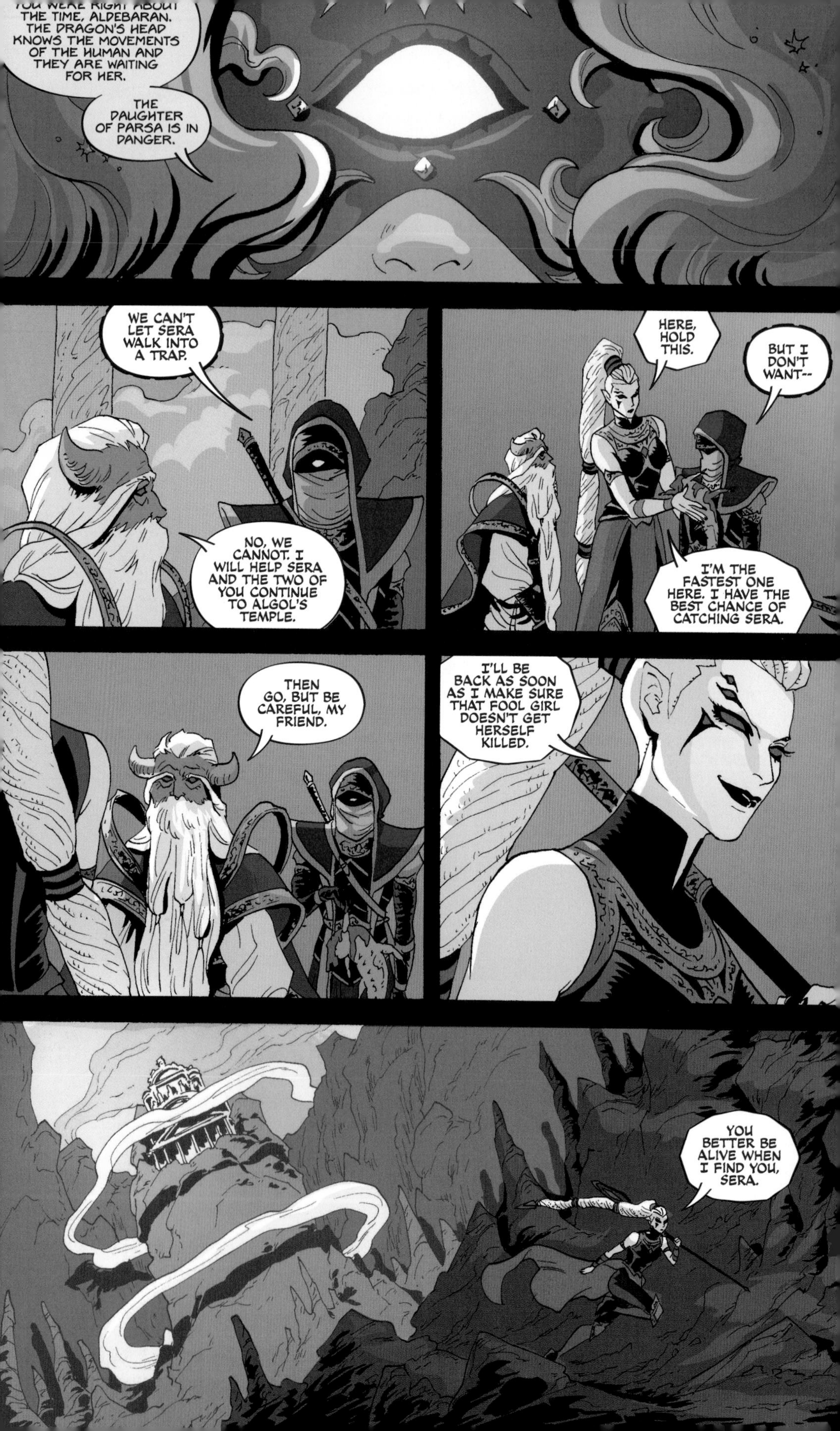

YOU WERE RIGHT ABOUT THE TIME, ALDEBARAN. THE DRAGON'S HEAD KNOWS THE MOVEMENTS OF THE HUMAN AND THEY ARE WAITING FOR HER.
THE DAUGHTER OF PARSA IS IN DANGER.
WE CAN'T LET SERA WALK INTO A TRAP.
NO, WE CANNOT. I WILL HELP SERA AND THE TWO OF YOU CONTINUE TO ALGOL'S TEMPLE.
HERE, HOLD THIS.
BUT I DON'T WANT--
I'M THE FASTEST ONE HERE. I HAVE THE BEST CHANCE OF CATCHING SERA.
THEN GO, BUT BE CAREFUL, MY FRIEND.
I'LL BE BACK AS SOON AS I MAKE SURE THAT FOOL GIRL DOESN'T GET HERSELF KILLED.
YOU BETTER BE ALIVE WHEN I FIND YOU, SERA.

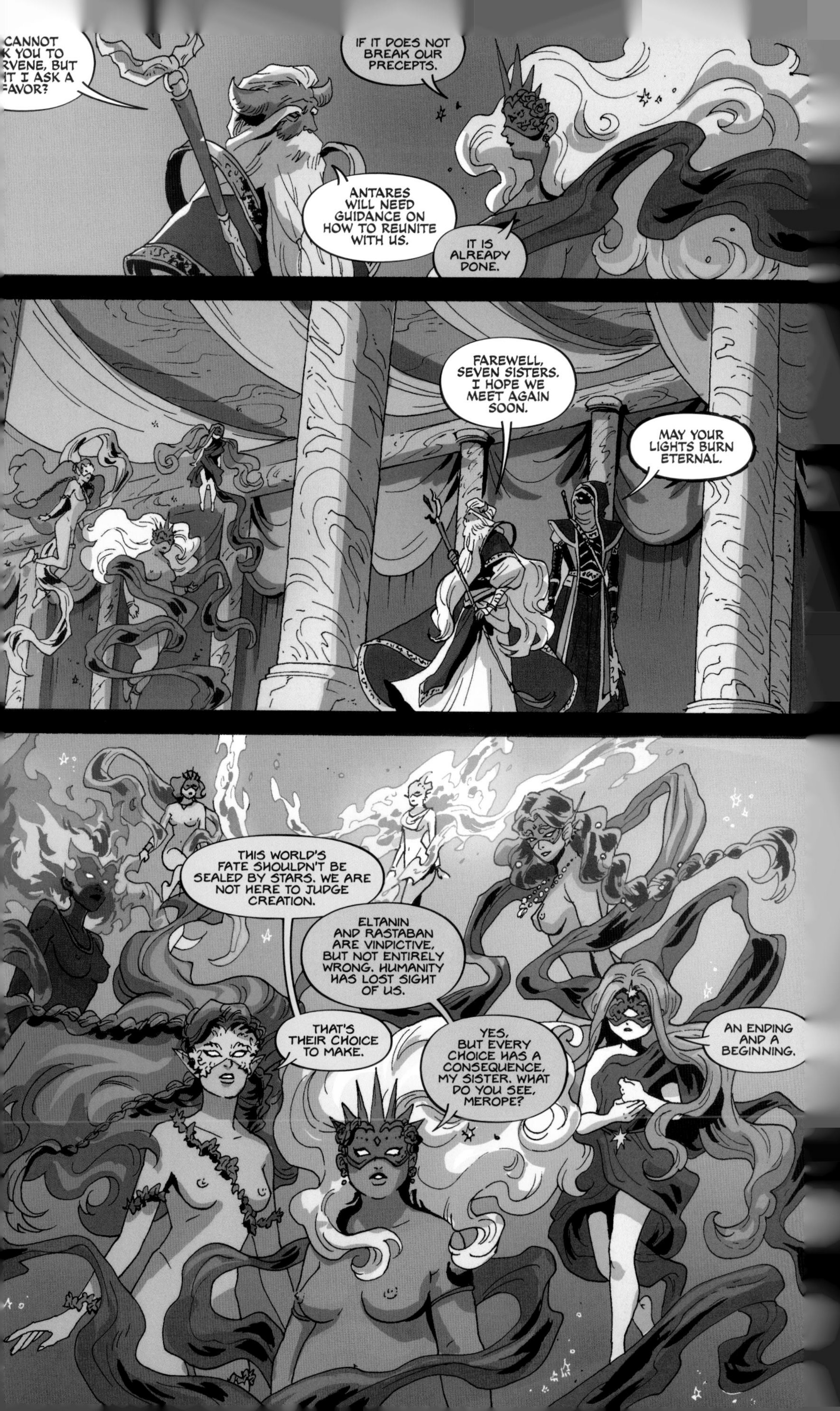
CANNOT
K YOU TO
RVENE, BUT
IT I ASK A
FAVOR?
IF IT DOES NOT BREAK OUR PRECEPTS.
ANTARES WILL NEED GUIDANCE ON HOW TO REUNITE WITH US.
IT IS ALREADY DONE.
FAREWELL, SEVEN SISTERS. I HOPE WE MEET AGAIN SOON.
MAY YOUR LIGHTS BURN ETERNAL.
THIS WORLD'S FATE SHOULDN'T BE SEALED BY STARS. WE ARE NOT HERE TO JUDGE CREATION.
ELTANIN AND RASTABAN ARE VINDICTIVE, BUT NOT ENTIRELY WRONG. HUMANITY HAS LOST SIGHT OF US.
THAT'S THEIR CHOICE TO MAKE.
YES, BUT EVERY CHOICE HAS A CONSEQUENCE, MY SISTER. WHAT DO YOU SEE, MEROPE?
AN ENDING AND A BEGINNING.

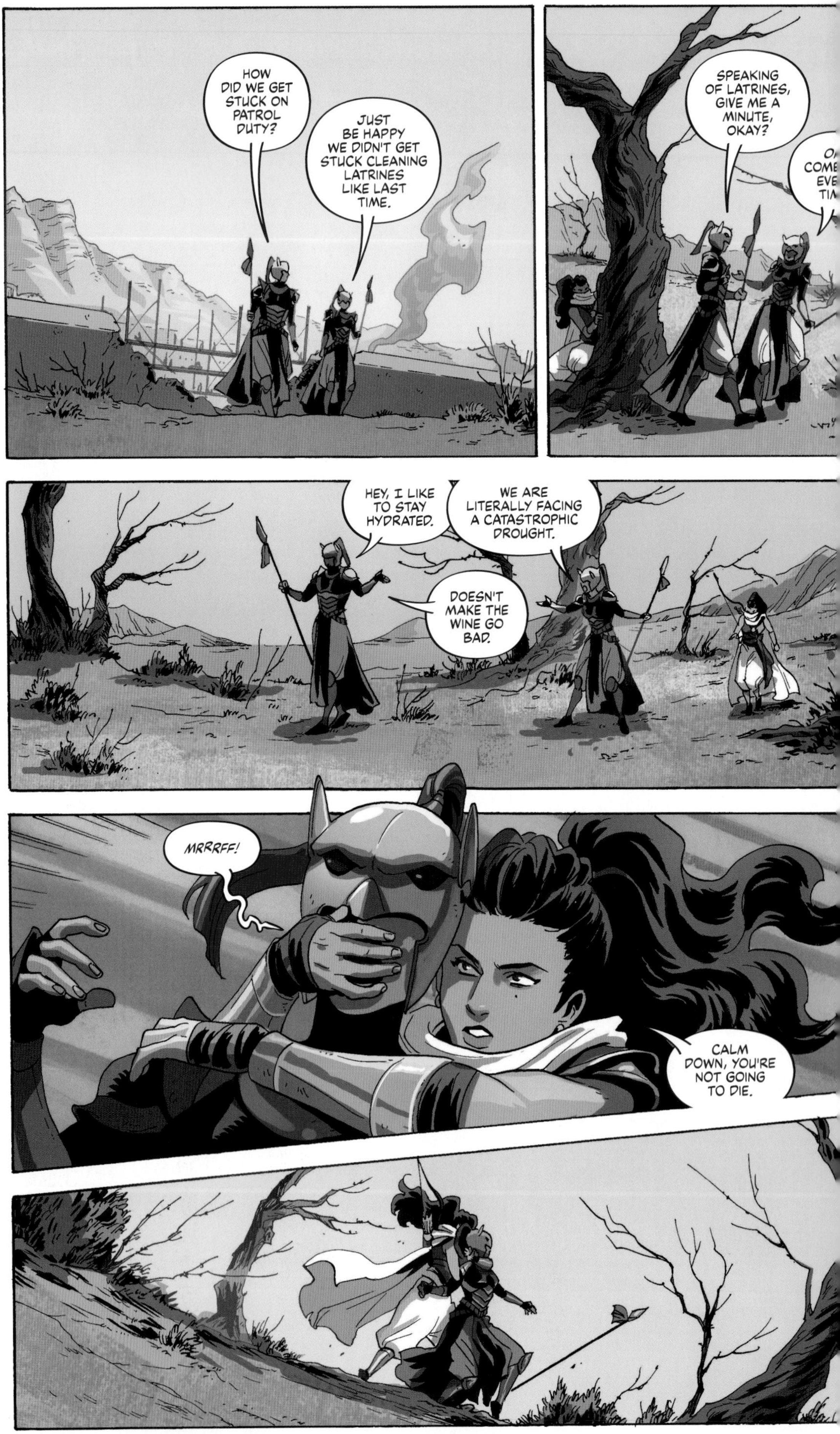
HOW DID WE GET STUCK ON PATROL DUTY?
JUST BE HAPPY WE DIDN'T GET STUCK CLEANING LATRINES LIKE LAST TIME.
SPEAKING OF LATRINES, GIVE ME A MINUTE, OKAY?
HEY, I LIKE TO STAY HYDRATED.
WE ARE LITERALLY FACING A CATASTROPHIC DROUGHT.
DOESN'T MAKE THE WINE GO BAD.
MRRRFF!
CALM DOWN, YOU'RE NOT GOING TO DIE.

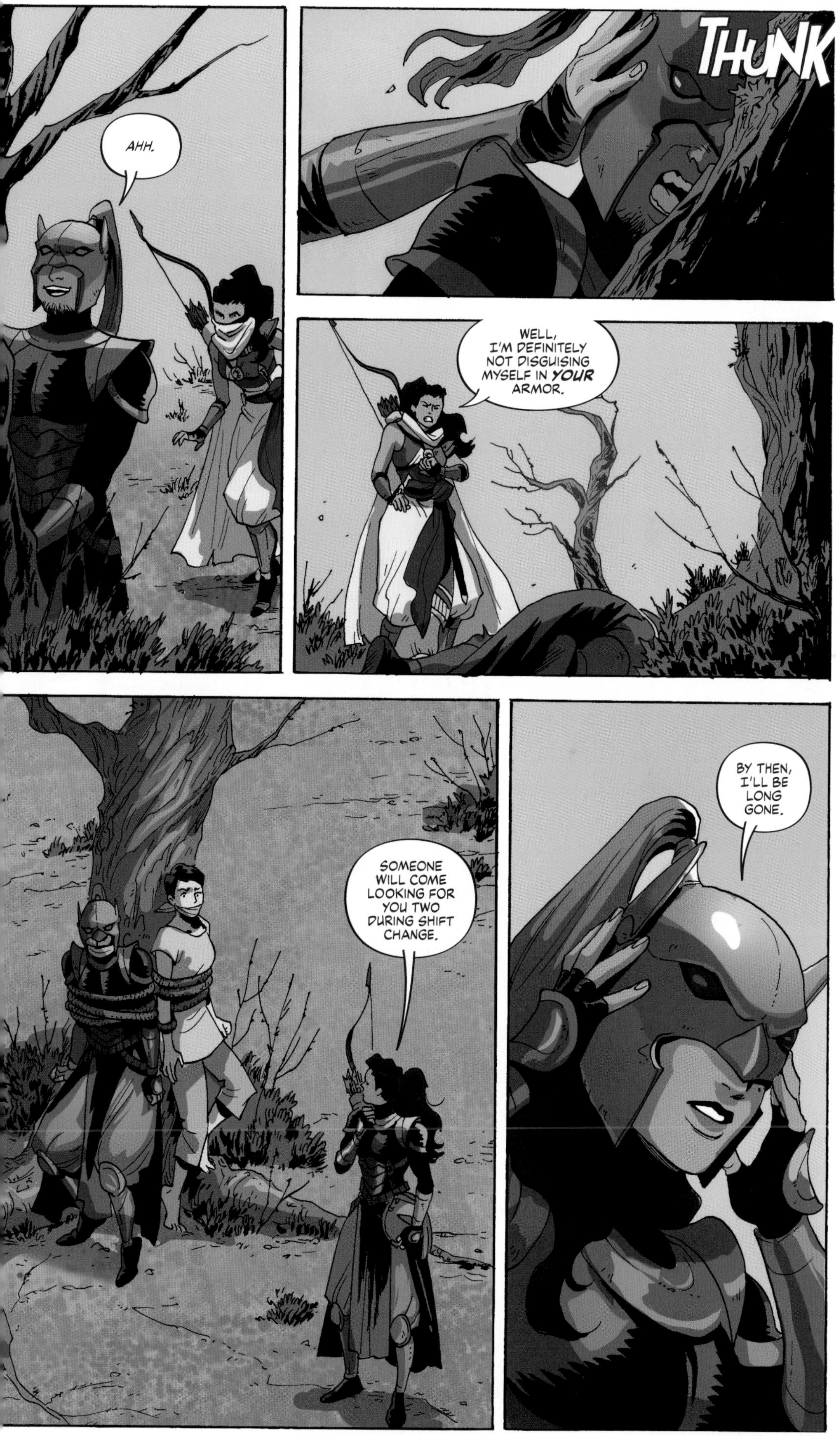
AHH.
THUNK
WELL, I'M DEFINITELY NOT DISGUISING MYSELF IN YOUR ARMOR.
SOMEONE WILL COME LOOKING FOR YOU TWO DURING SHIFT CHANGE.
BY THEN, I'LL BE LONG GONE.

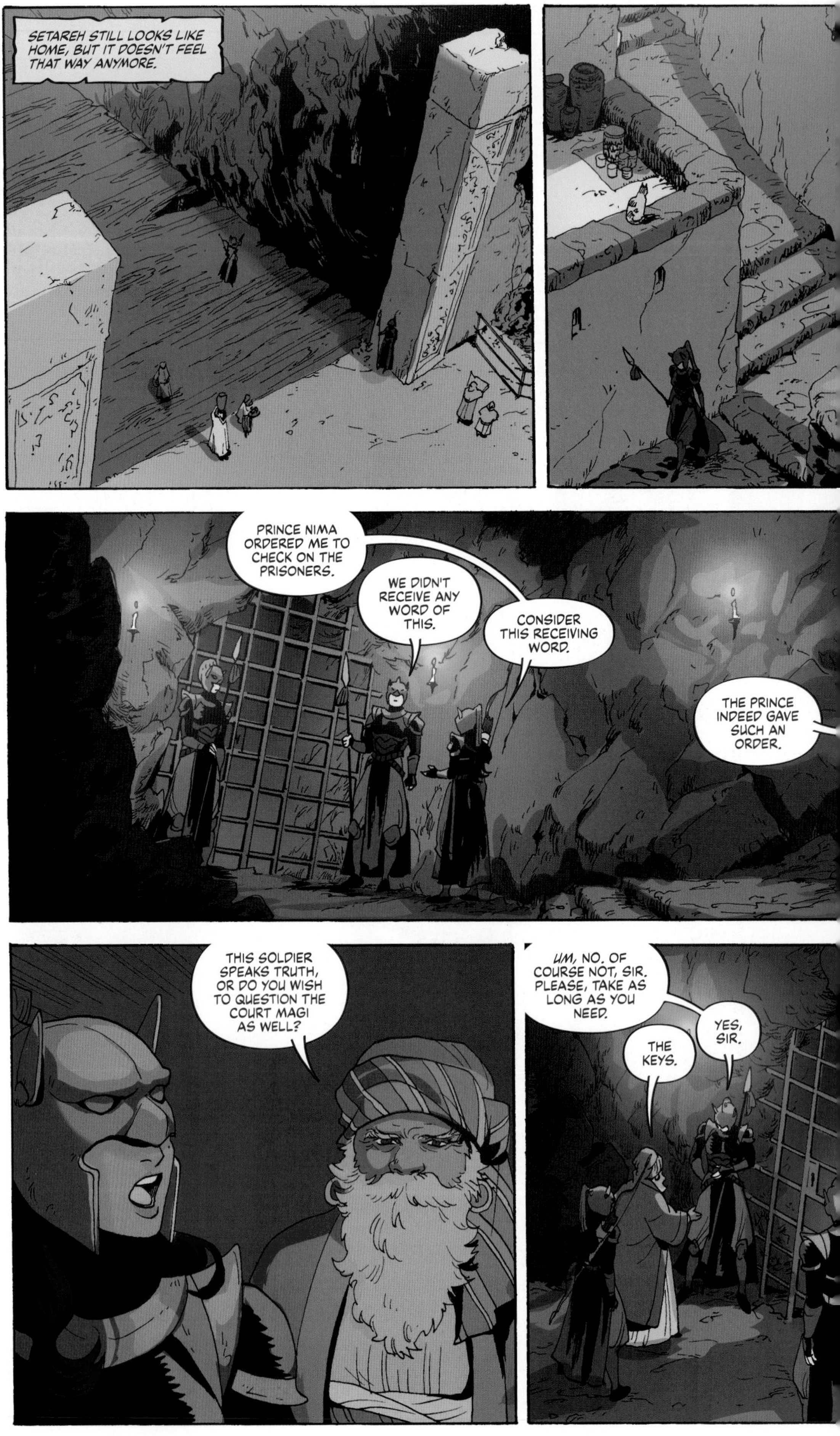
SETAREH STILL LOOKS LIKE HOME, BUT IT DOESN'T FEEL THAT WAY ANYMORE.
PRINCE NIMA ORDERED ME TO CHECK ON THE PRISONERS.
WE DIDN'T RECEIVE ANY WORD OF THIS.
CONSIDER THIS RECEIVING WORD.
THE PRINCE INDEED GAVE SUCH AN ORDER.
THIS SOLDIER SPEAKS TRUTH, OR DO YOU WISH TO QUESTION THE COURT MAGI AS WELL?
UM, NO. OF COURSE NOT, SIR. PLEASE, TAKE AS LONG AS YOU NEED.
THE KEYS.
YES, SIR.

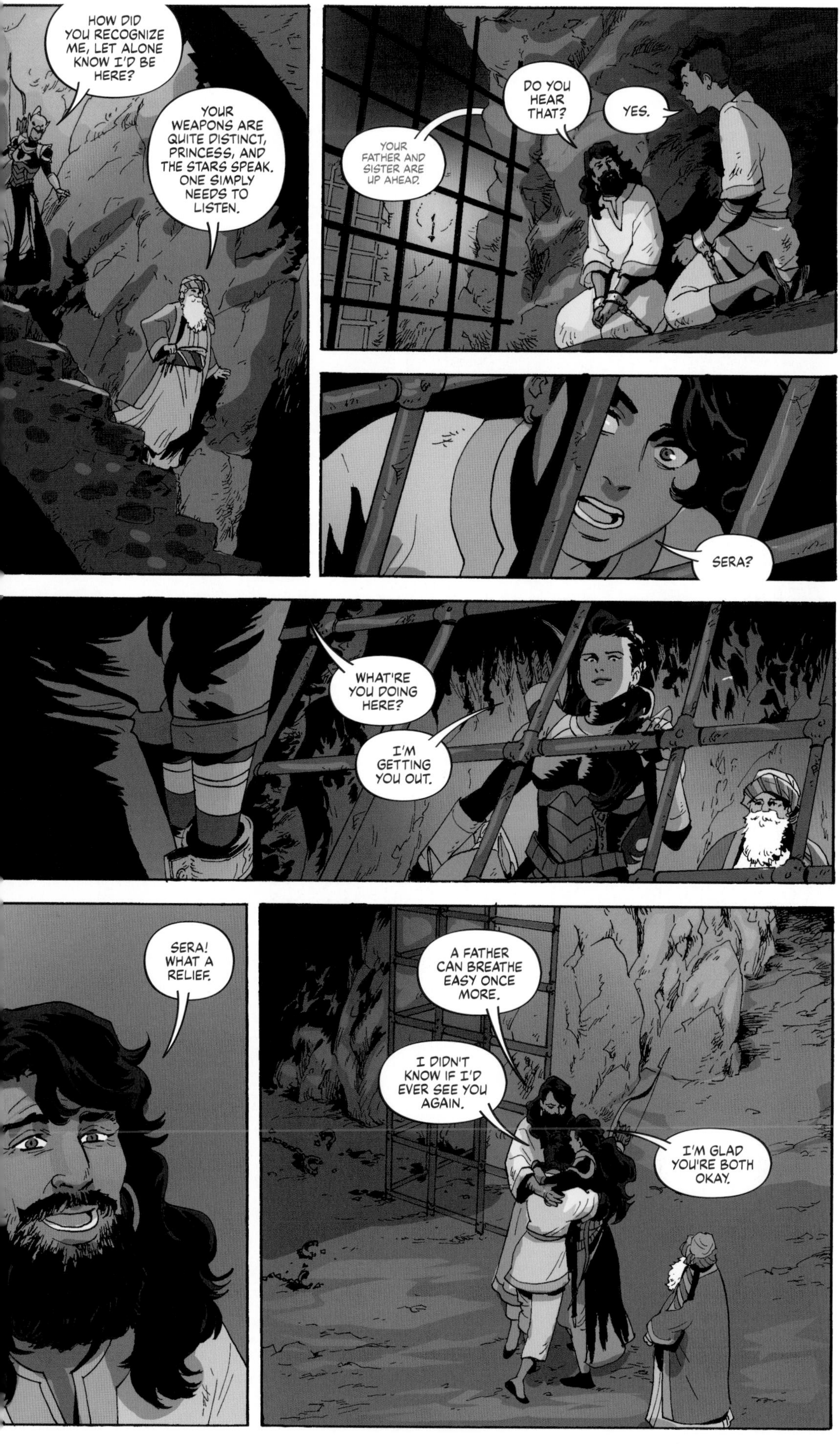
HOW DID YOU RECOGNIZE ME, LET ALONE KNOW I'D BE HERE?
YOUR WEAPONS ARE QUITE DISTINCT, PRINCESS, AND THE STARS SPEAK. ONE SIMPLY NEEDS TO LISTEN.
YOUR FATHER AND SISTER ARE UP AHEAD.
DO YOU HEAR THAT?
YES.
SERA?
WHAT'RE YOU DOING HERE?
I'M GETTING YOU OUT.
SERA! WHAT A RELIEF.
A FATHER CAN BREATHE EASY ONCE MORE.
I DIDN'T KNOW IF I'D EVER SEE YOU AGAIN.
I'M GLAD YOU'RE BOTH OKAY.

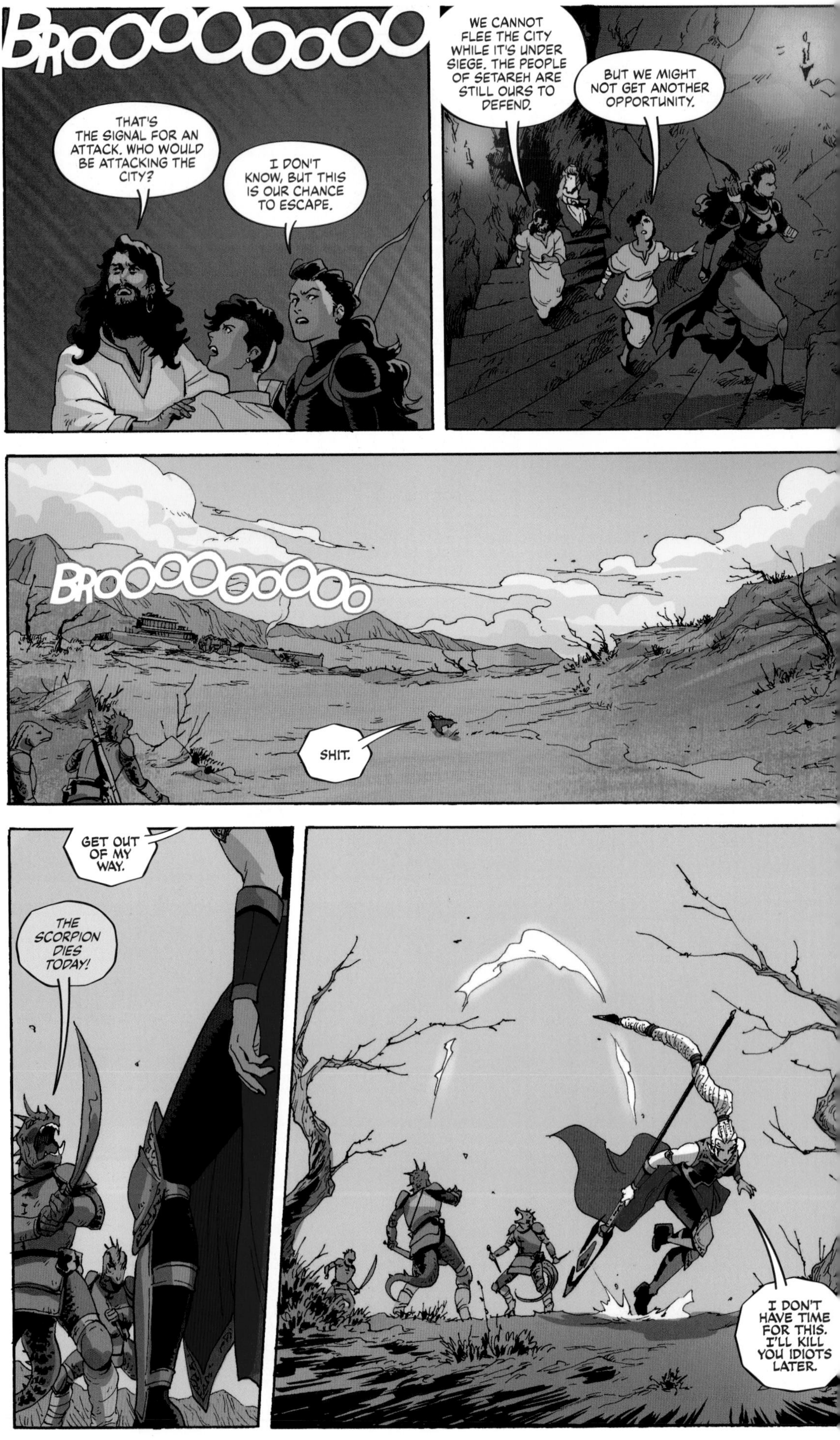
BROOOOOOOOO
THAT'S THE SIGNAL FOR AN ATTACK. WHO WOULD BE ATTACKING THE CITY?
I DON'T KNOW, BUT THIS IS OUR CHANCE TO ESCAPE.
WE CANNOT FLEE THE CITY WHILE IT'S UNDER SIEGE. THE PEOPLE OF SETAREH ARE STILL OURS TO DEFEND.
BUT WE MIGHT NOT GET ANOTHER OPPORTUNITY.
BROOOOOOOOOO
SHIT.
GET OUT OF MY WAY.
THE SCORPION DIES TODAY!
I DON'T HAVE TIME FOR THIS. I'LL KILL YOU IDIOTS LATER.

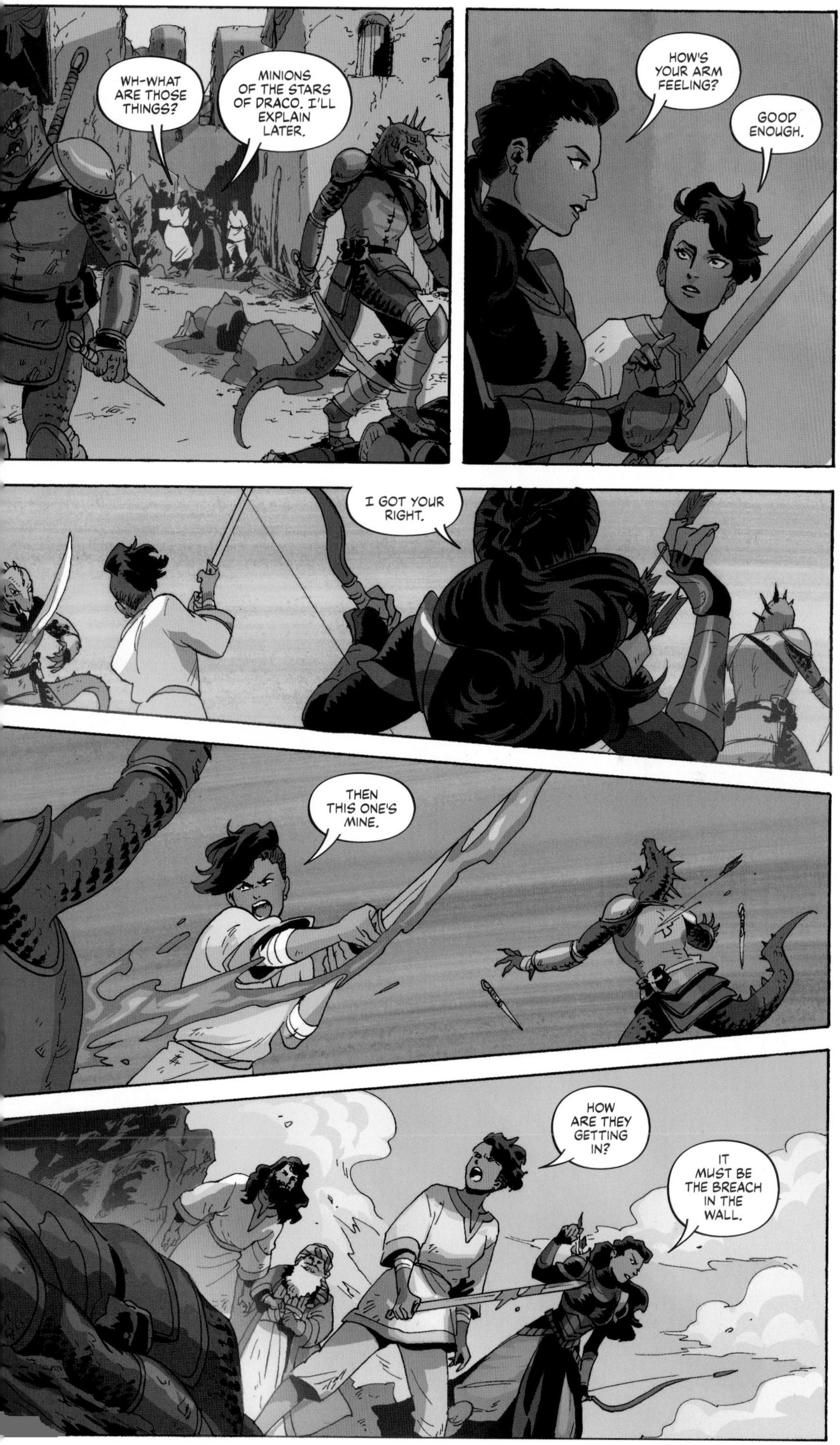
WH-WHAT ARE THOSE THINGS?
MINIONS OF THE STARS OF DRACO. I'LL EXPLAIN LATER.
HOW'S YOUR ARM FEELING?
GOOD ENOUGH.
I GOT YOUR RIGHT.
THEN THIS ONE'S MINE.
HOW ARE THEY GETTING IN?
IT MUST BE THE BREACH IN THE WALL.

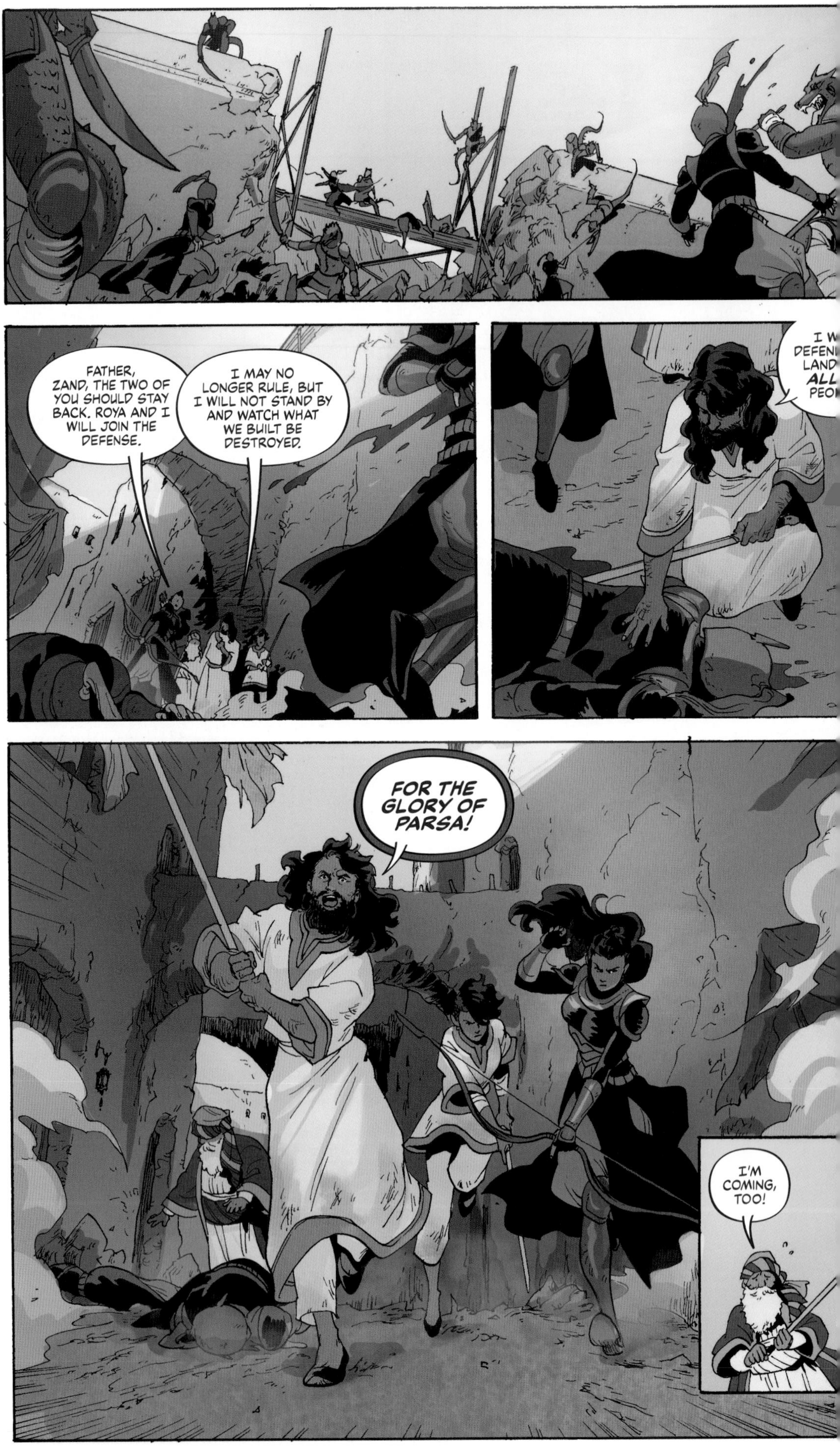
FATHER, ZAND, THE TWO OF YOU SHOULD STAY BACK. ROYA AND I WILL JOIN THE DEFENSE.
I MAY NO LONGER RULE, BUT I WILL NOT STAND BY AND WATCH WHAT WE BUILT BE DESTROYED.
FOR THE GLORY OF PARSA!
I'M COMING, TOO!

RAAAAH!

BEHIND YOU!

AAAH!

GET OFF OF HER!

WHO ELSE WAS GOING TO SAVE YOUR ASS?

RES?
UGHT
ERE ON
AY TO
MPLE.

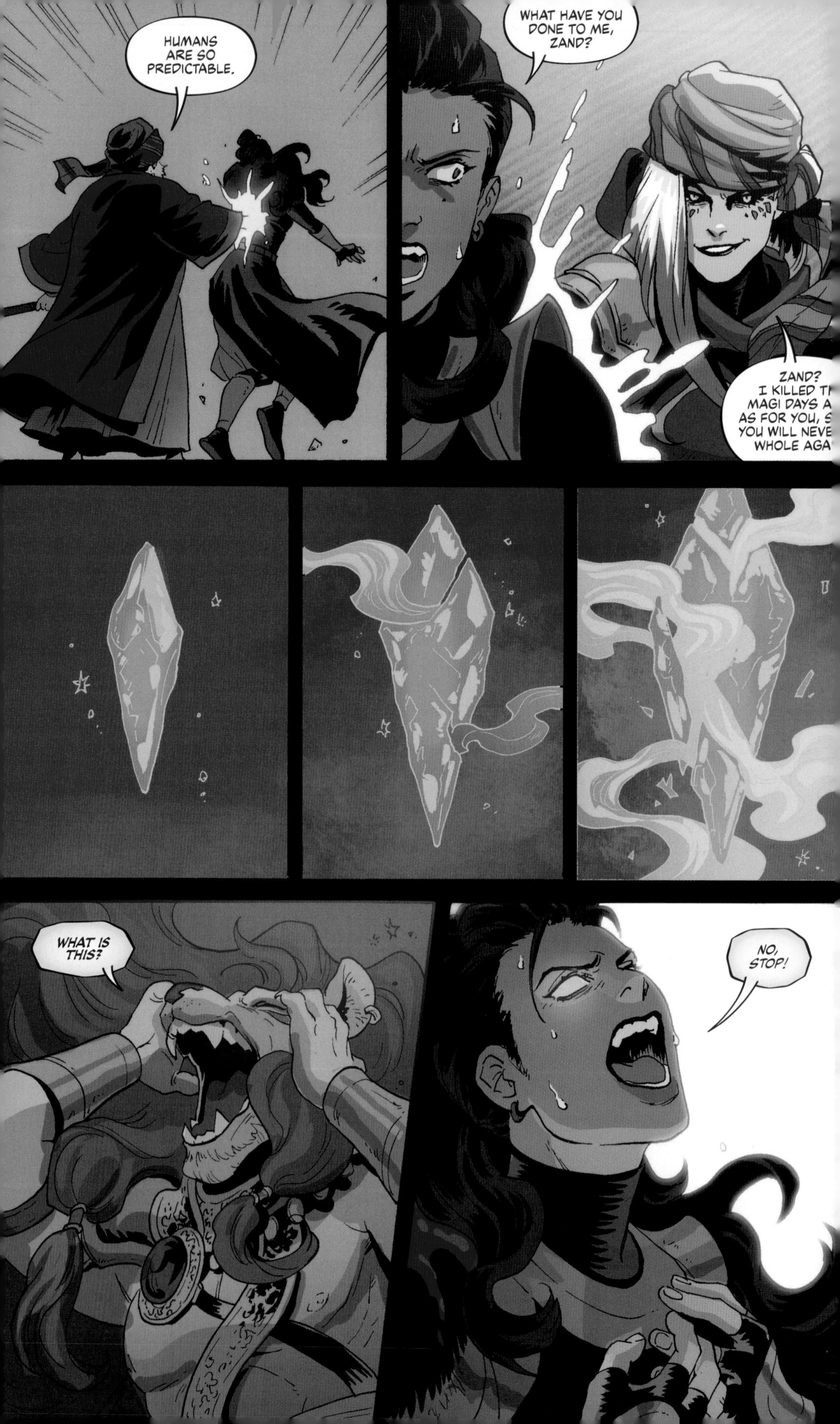
HUMANS ARE SO PREDICTABLE.
WHAT HAVE YOU DONE TO ME, ZAND?
ZAND? I KILLED TH MAGI DAYS A AS FOR YOU, S YOU WILL NEVE WHOLE AGA
WHAT IS THIS?
NO, STOP!

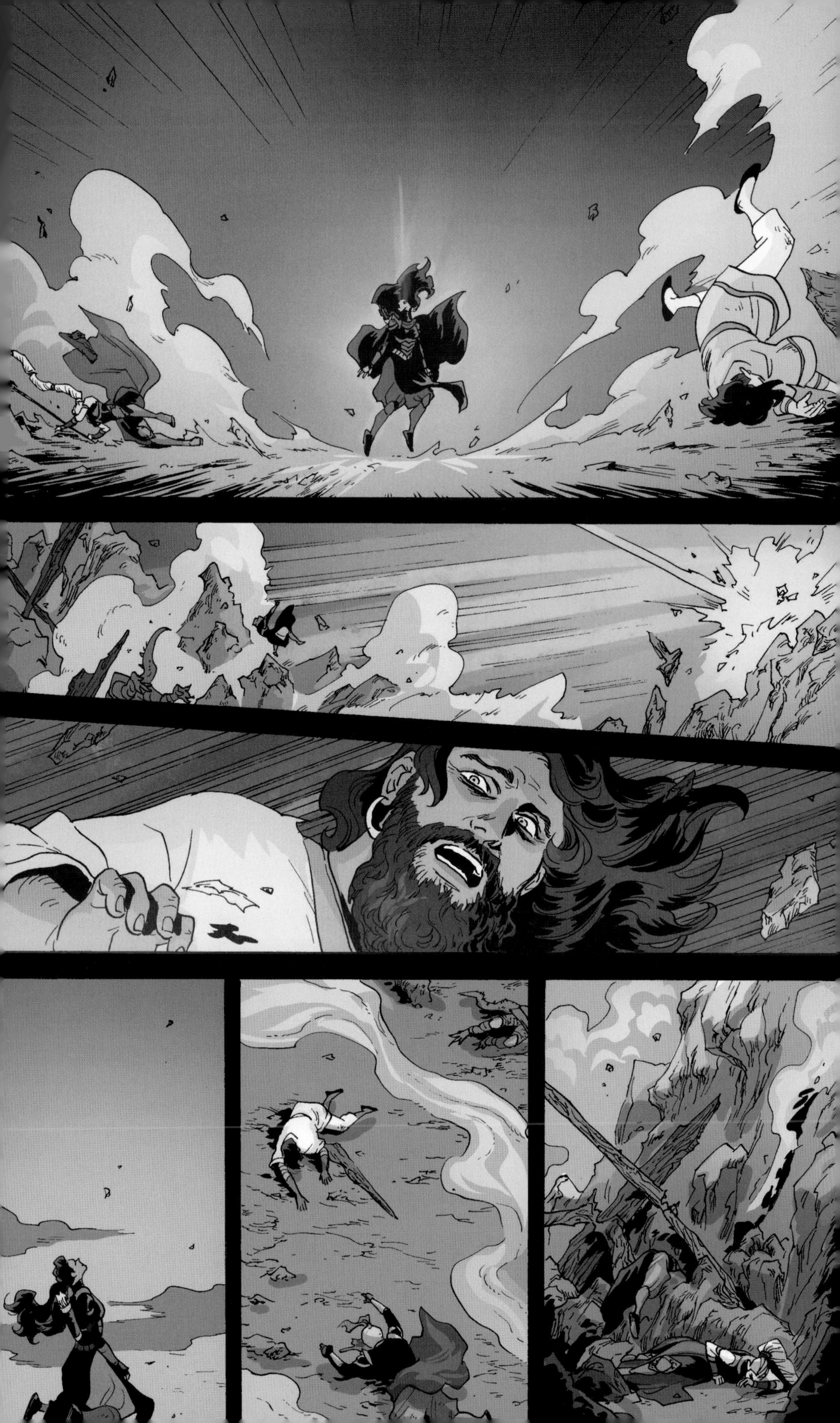

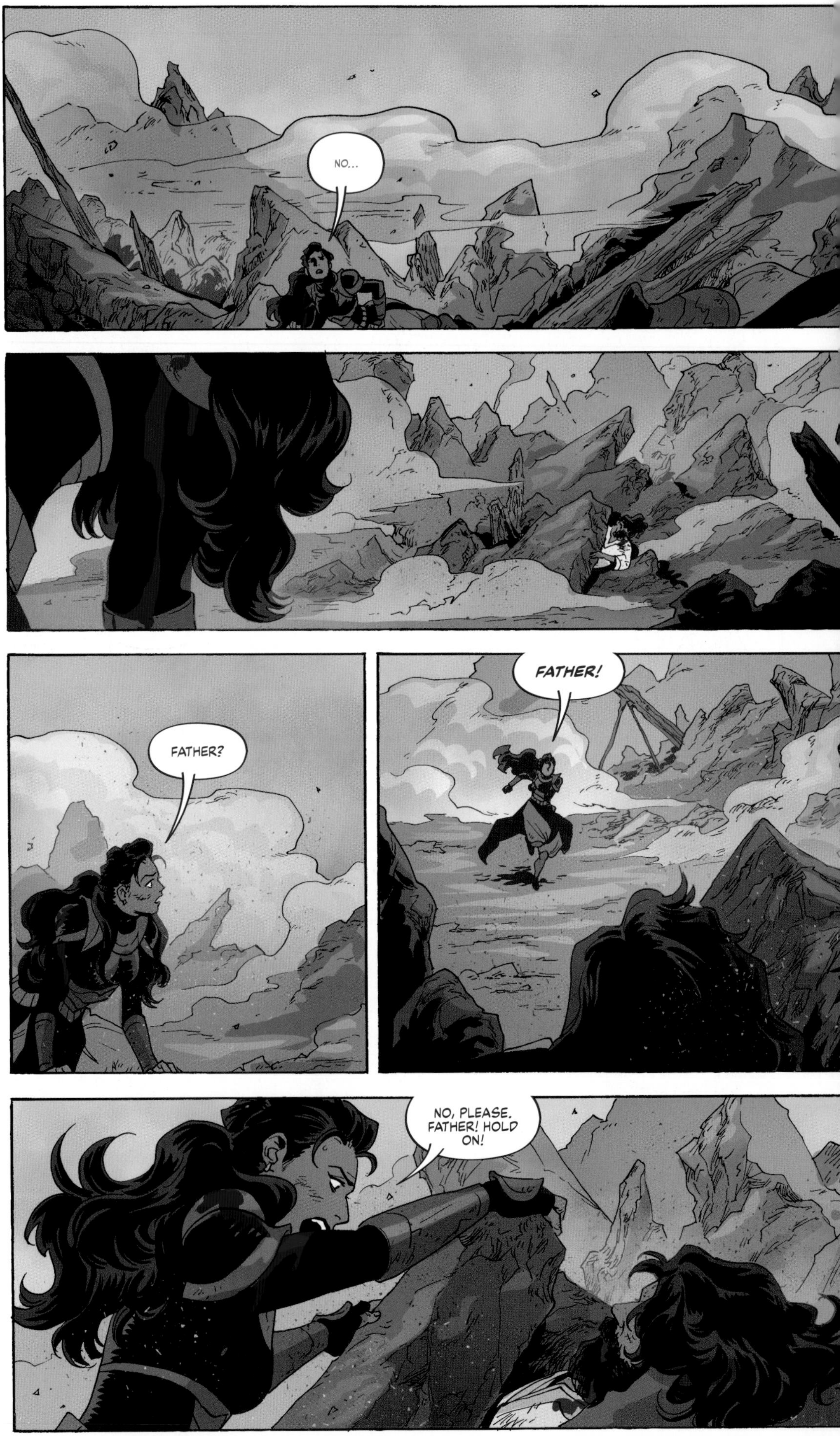
NO...
FATHER?
FATHER!
NO, PLEASE. FATHER! HOLD ON!

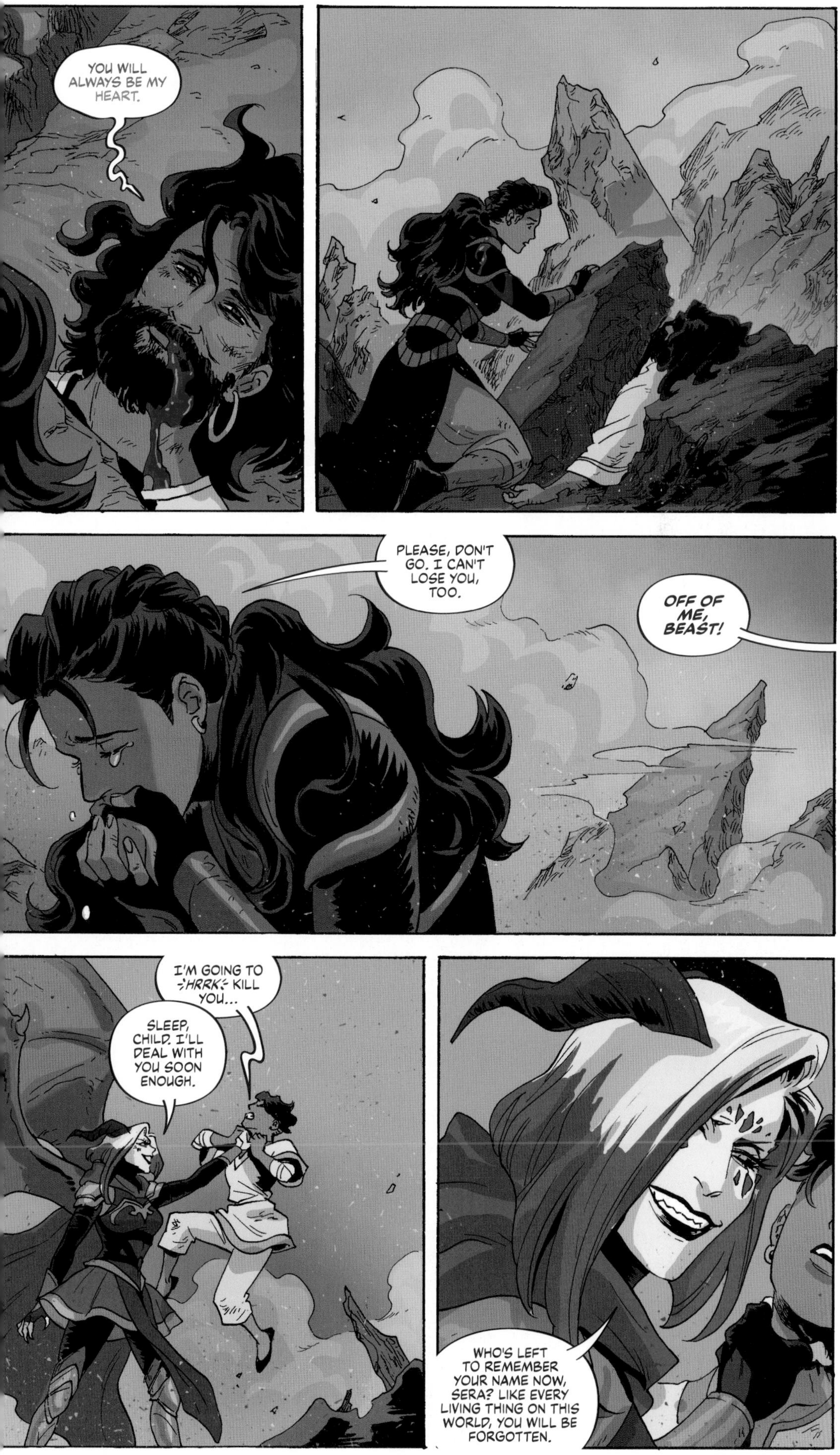
YOU WILL ALWAYS BE MY HEART.
PLEASE, DON'T GO. I CAN'T LOSE YOU, TOO.
OFF OF ME, BEAST!
I'M GOING TO -HRRK- KILL YOU...
SLEEP, CHILD. I'LL DEAL WITH YOU SOON ENOUGH.
WHO'S LEFT TO REMEMBER YOUR NAME NOW, SERA? LIKE EVERY LIVING THING ON THIS WORLD, YOU WILL BE FORGOTTEN.

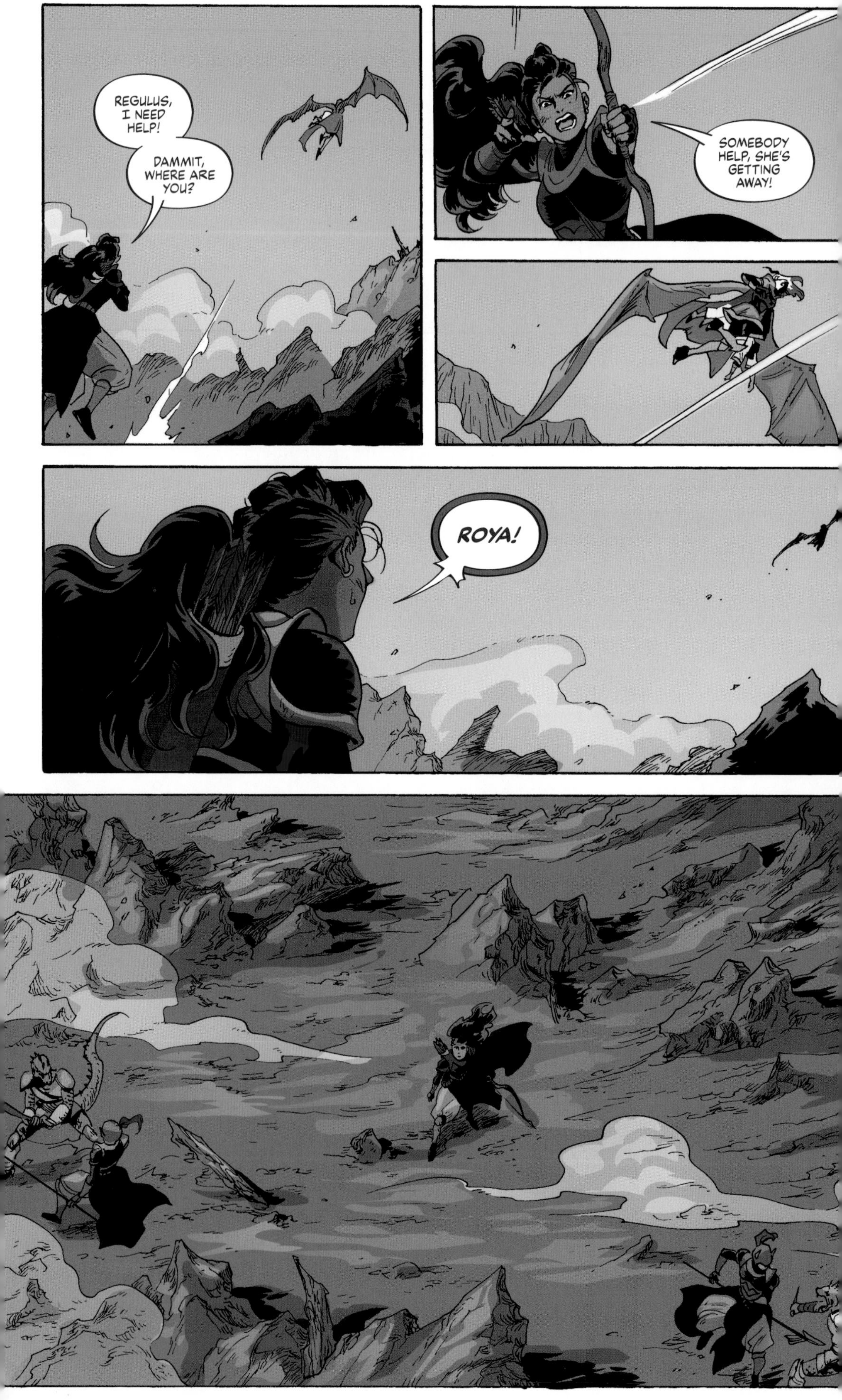
REGULUS, I NEED HELP!
DAMMIT, WHERE ARE YOU?
SOMEBODY HELP, SHE'S GETTING AWAY!
ROYA!

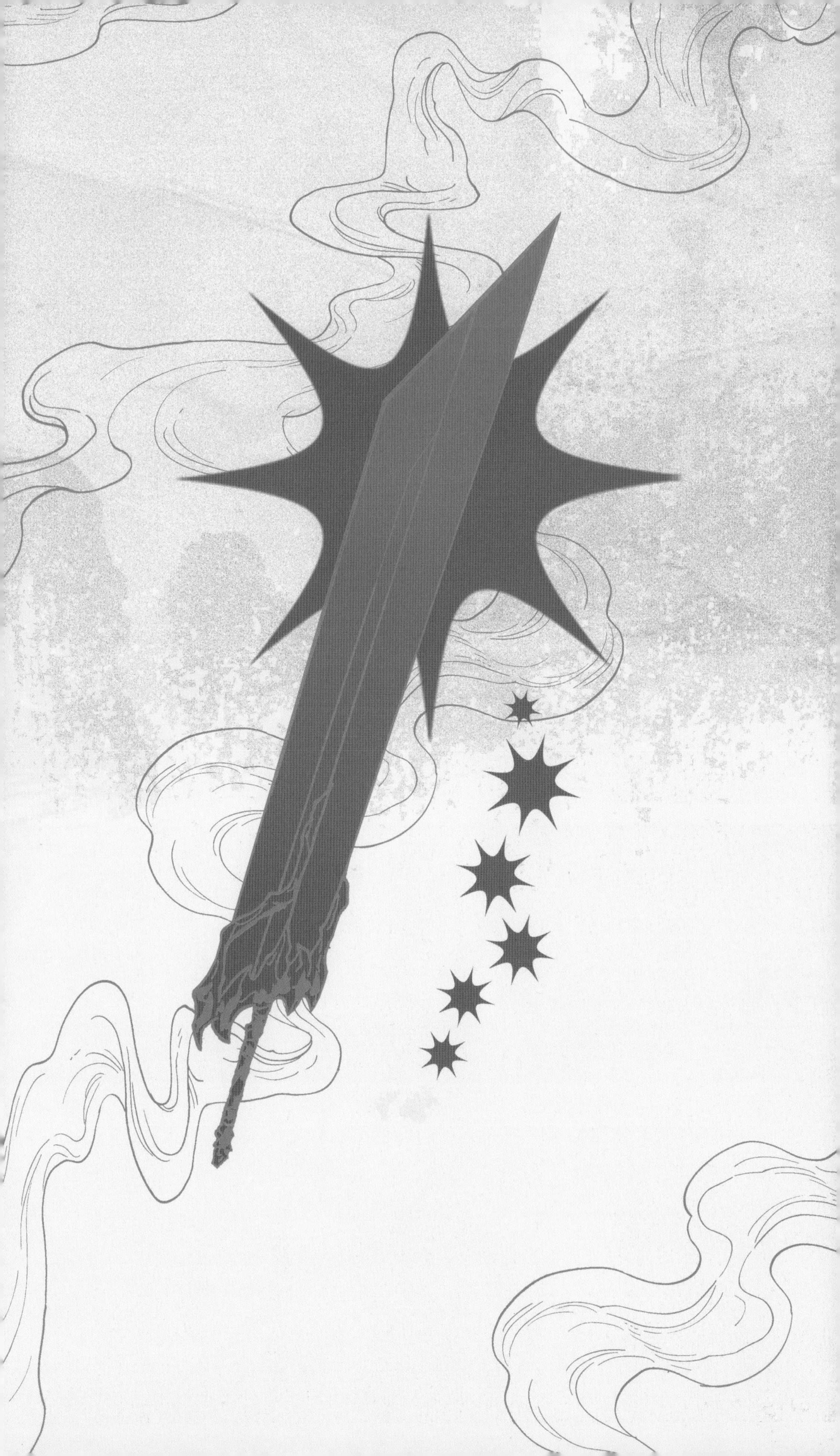

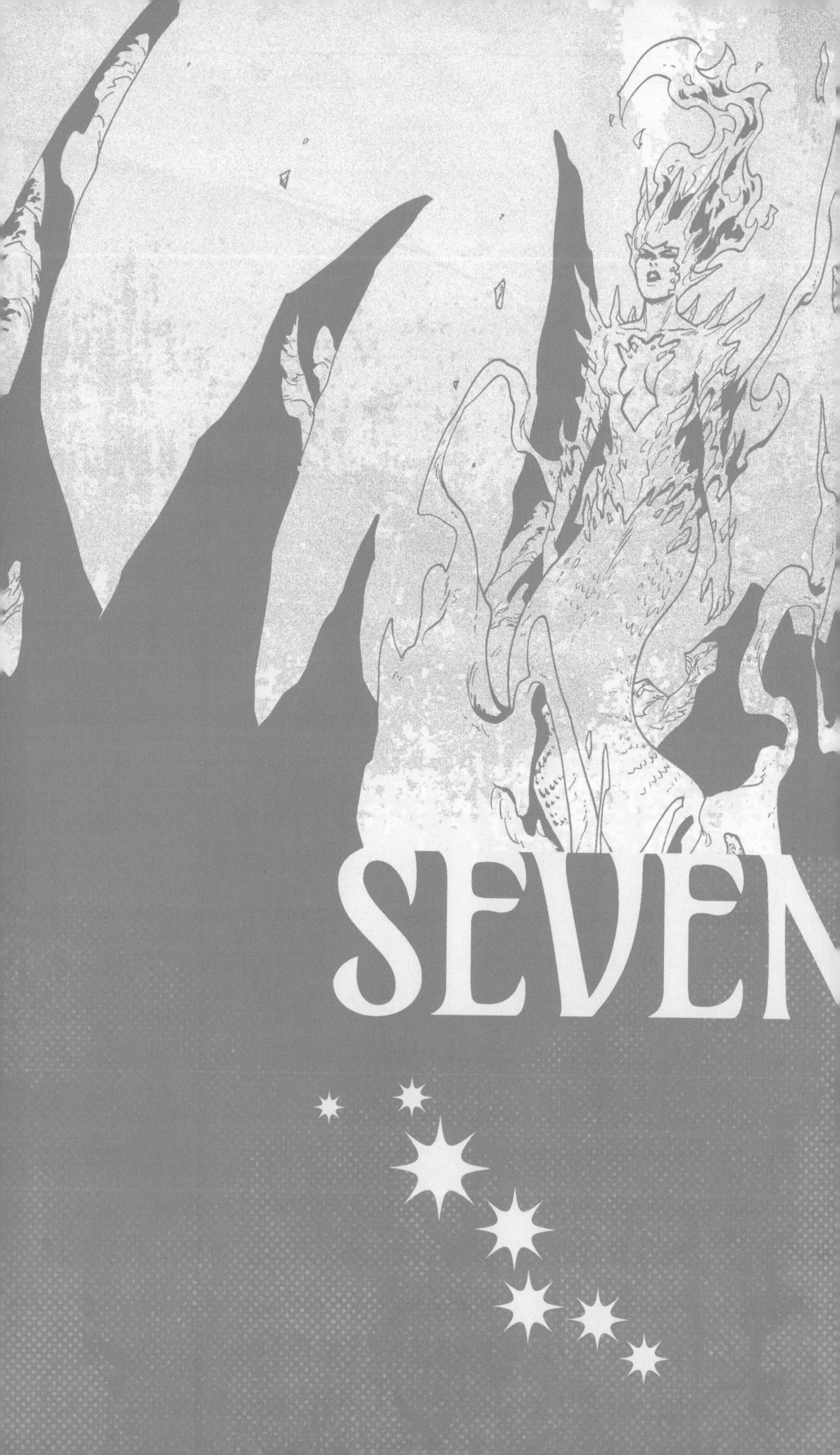
SEVEN

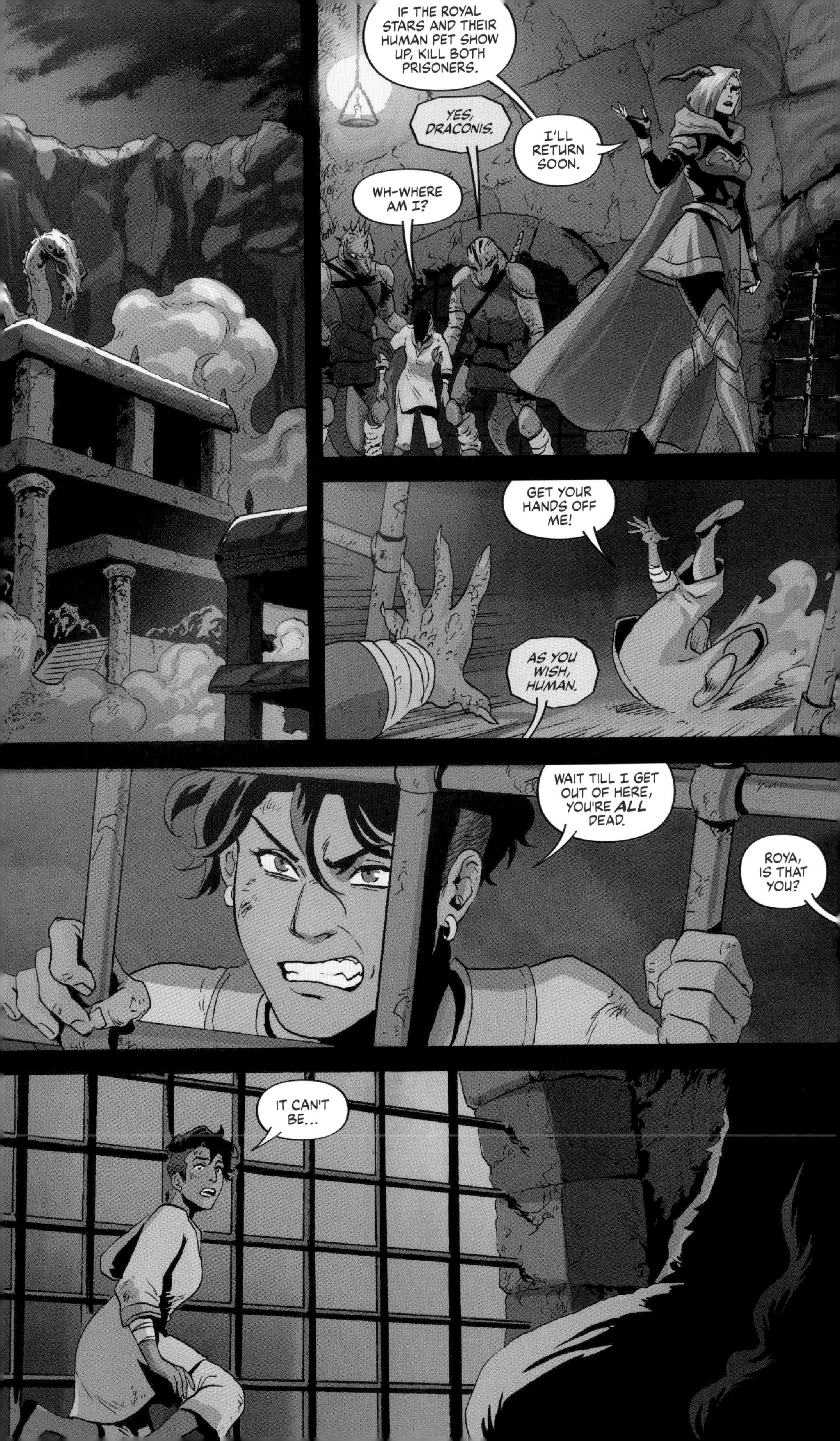
IF THE ROYAL STARS AND THEIR HUMAN PET SHOW UP, KILL BOTH PRISONERS.
YES, DRACONIS.
I'LL RETURN SOON.
WH-WHERE AM I?
GET YOUR HANDS OFF ME!
AS YOU WISH, HUMAN.
WAIT TILL I GET OUT OF HERE, YOU'RE ALL DEAD.
ROYA, IS THAT YOU?
IT CAN'T BE...

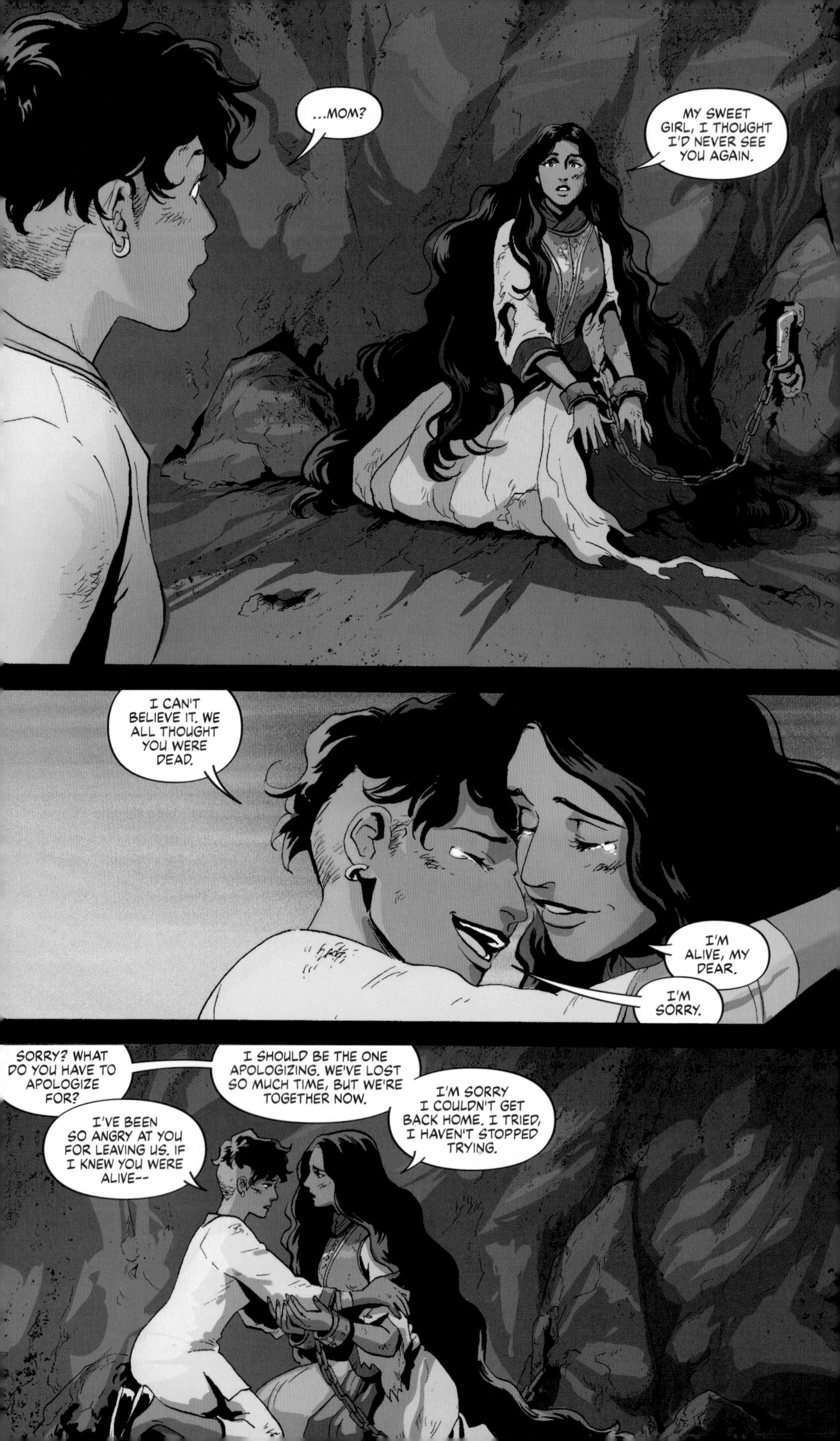
...MOM?
MY SWEET GIRL, I THOUGHT I'D NEVER SEE YOU AGAIN.
I CAN'T BELIEVE IT. WE ALL THOUGHT YOU WERE DEAD.
I'M ALIVE, MY DEAR.
I'M SORRY.
SORRY? WHAT DO YOU HAVE TO APOLOGIZE FOR?
I SHOULD BE THE ONE APOLOGIZING. WE'VE LOST SO MUCH TIME, BUT WE'RE TOGETHER NOW.
I'VE BEEN SO ANGRY AT YOU FOR LEAVING US. IF I KNEW YOU WERE ALIVE--
I'M SORRY I COULDN'T GET BACK HOME. I TRIED, I HAVEN'T STOPPED TRYING.

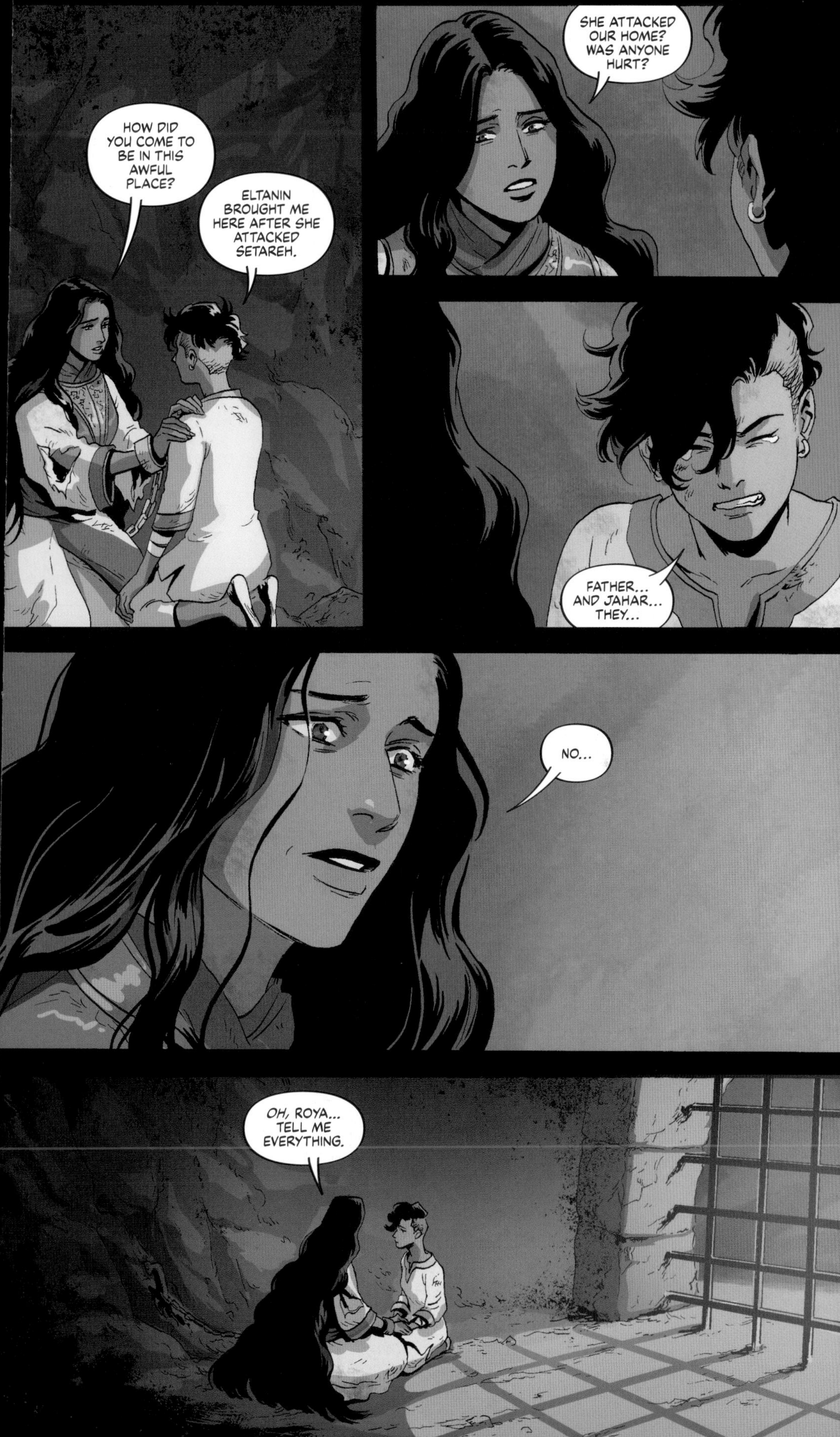
HOW DID YOU COME TO BE IN THIS AWFUL PLACE?
ELTANIN BROUGHT ME HERE AFTER SHE ATTACKED SETAREH.
SHE ATTACKED OUR HOME? WAS ANYONE HURT?
FATHER... AND JAHAR... THEY...
NO...
OH, ROYA... TELL ME EVERYTHING.

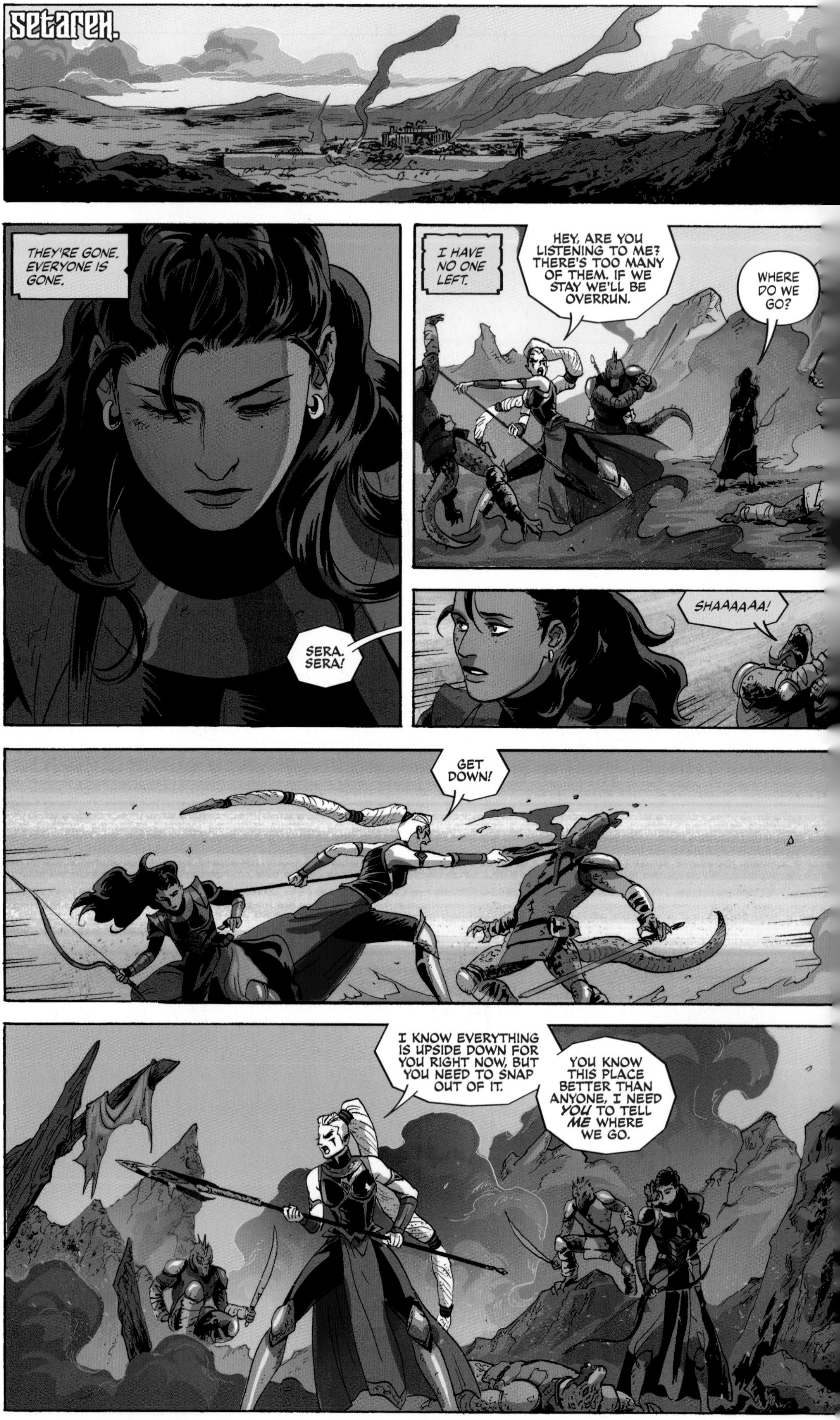
SETAREH.
THEY'RE GONE. EVERYONE IS GONE.
SERA. SERA!
I HAVE NO ONE LEFT.
HEY, ARE YOU LISTENING TO ME? THERE'S TOO MANY OF THEM. IF WE STAY WE'LL BE OVERRUN.
WHERE DO WE GO?
SHAAAAAA!
GET DOWN!
I KNOW EVERYTHING IS UPSIDE DOWN FOR YOU RIGHT NOW, BUT YOU NEED TO SNAP OUT OF IT.
YOU KNOW THIS PLACE BETTER THAN ANYONE, I NEED *YOU* TO TELL *ME* WHERE WE GO.

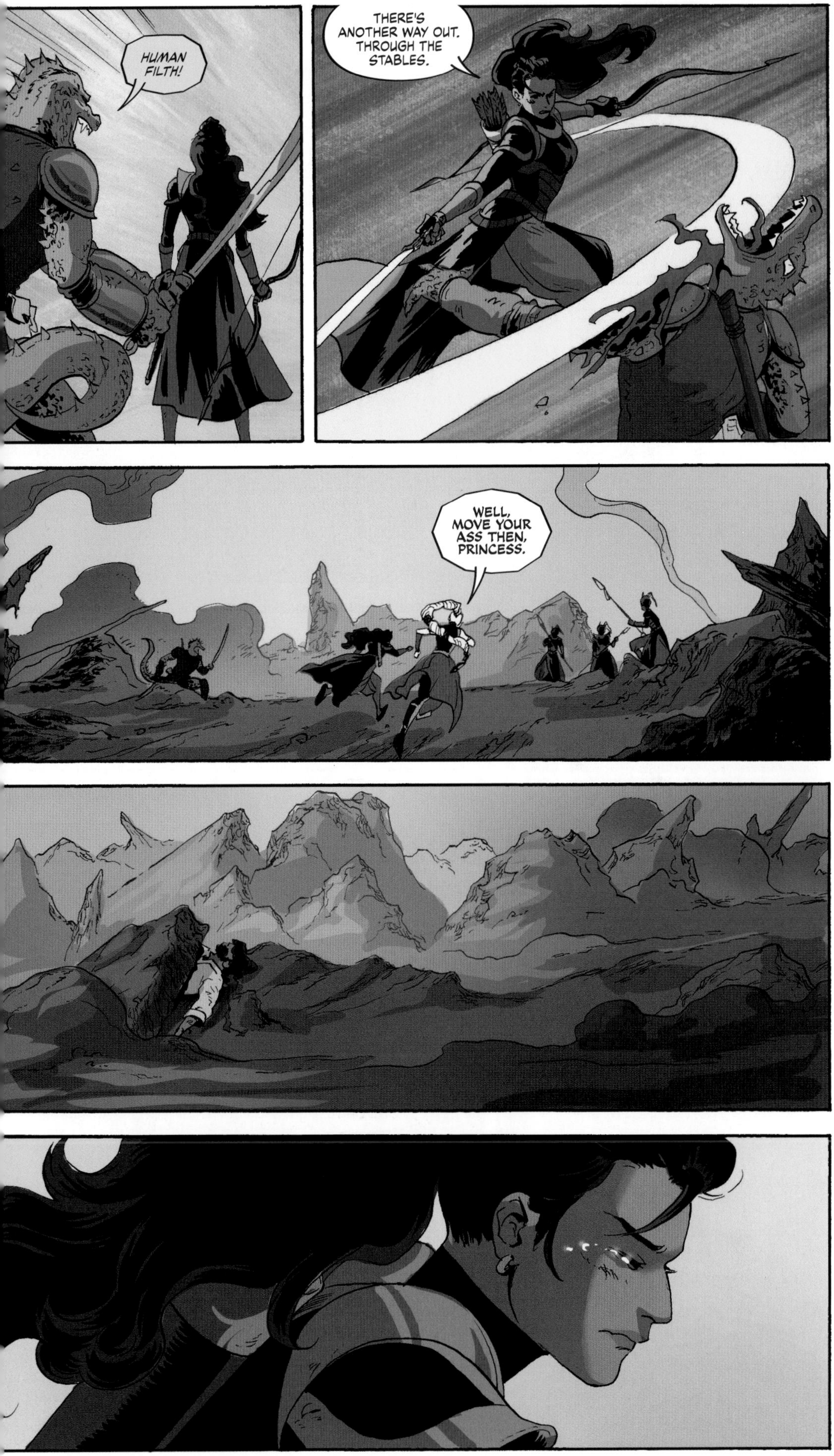
HUMAN FILTH!
THERE'S ANOTHER WAY OUT. THROUGH THE STABLES.
WELL, MOVE YOUR ASS THEN, PRINCESS.

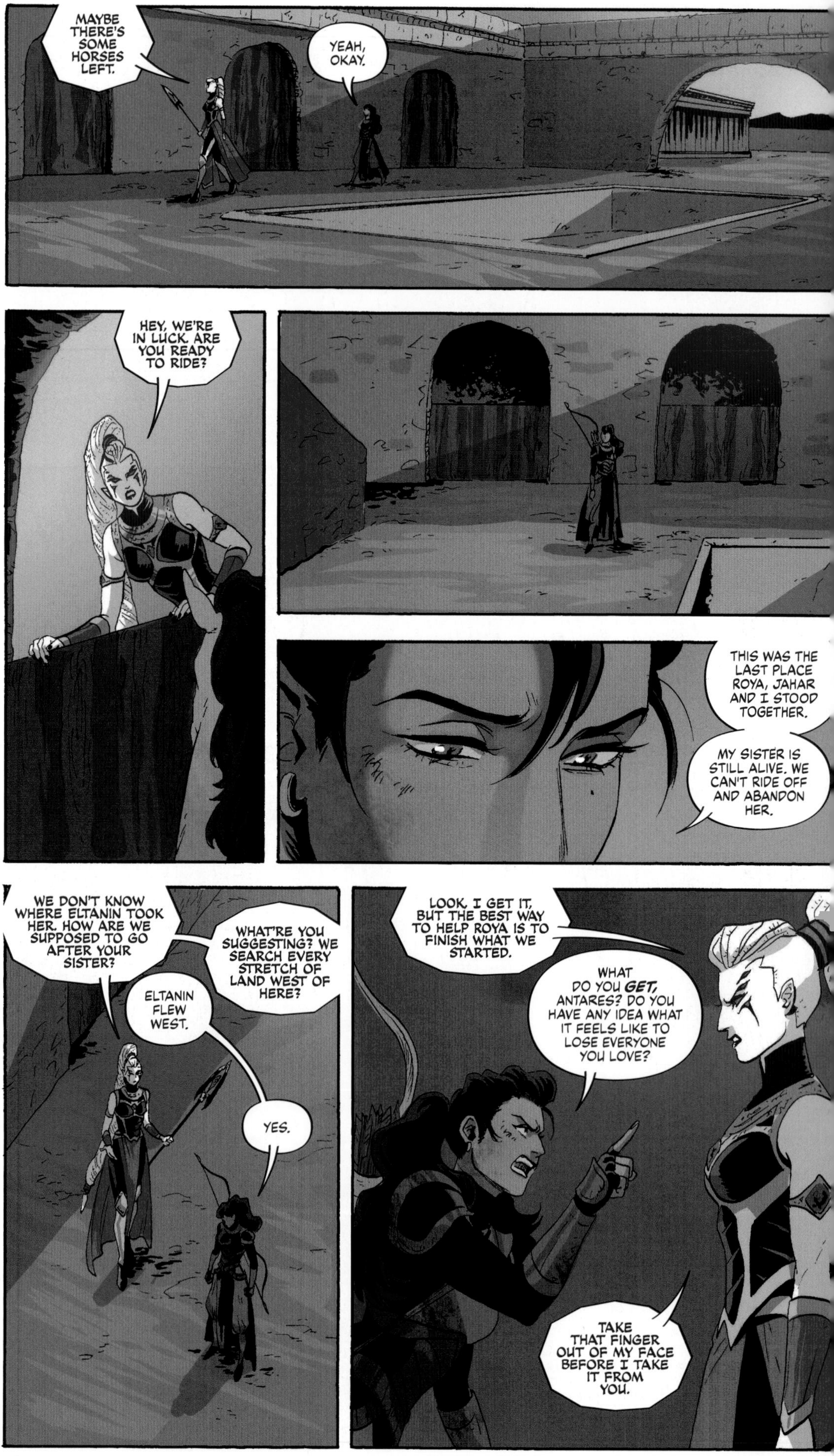
MAYBE THERE'S SOME HORSES LEFT.
YEAH, OKAY.
HEY, WE'RE IN LUCK. ARE YOU READY TO RIDE?
THIS WAS THE LAST PLACE ROYA, JAHAR AND I STOOD TOGETHER.
MY SISTER IS STILL ALIVE. WE CAN'T RIDE OFF AND ABANDON HER.
WE DON'T KNOW WHERE ELTANIN TOOK HER. HOW ARE WE SUPPOSED TO GO AFTER YOUR SISTER?
ELTANIN FLEW WEST.
WHAT'RE YOU SUGGESTING? WE SEARCH EVERY STRETCH OF LAND WEST OF HERE?
YES.
LOOK, I GET IT, BUT THE BEST WAY TO HELP ROYA IS TO FINISH WHAT WE STARTED.
WHAT DO YOU GET, ANTARES? DO YOU HAVE ANY IDEA WHAT IT FEELS LIKE TO LOSE EVERYONE YOU LOVE?
TAKE THAT FINGER OUT OF MY FACE BEFORE I TAKE IT FROM YOU.

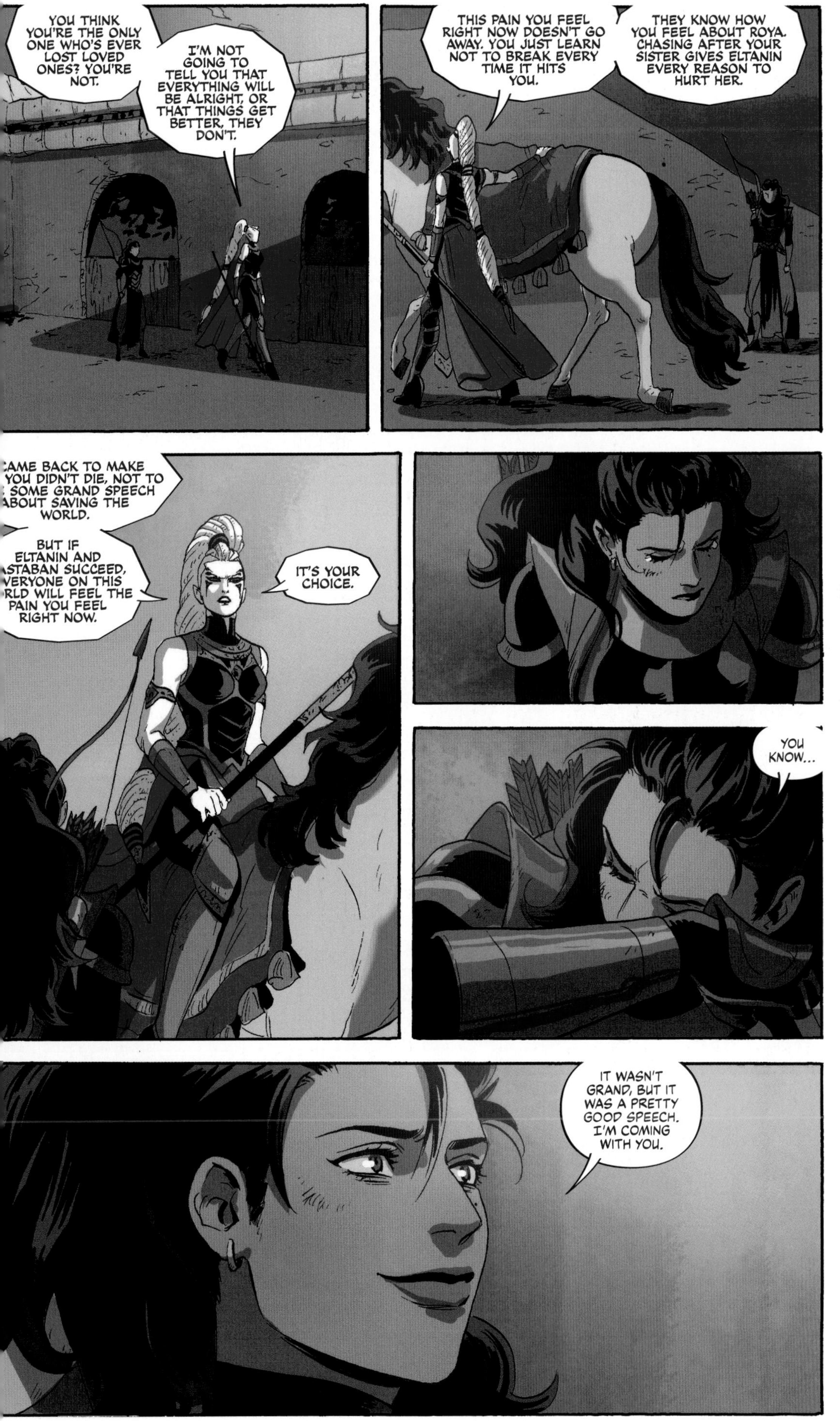
YOU THINK YOU'RE THE ONLY ONE WHO'S EVER LOST LOVED ONES? YOU'RE NOT.
I'M NOT GOING TO TELL YOU THAT EVERYTHING WILL BE ALRIGHT, OR THAT THINGS GET BETTER. THEY DON'T.
THIS PAIN YOU FEEL RIGHT NOW DOESN'T GO AWAY. YOU JUST LEARN NOT TO BREAK EVERY TIME IT HITS YOU.
THEY KNOW HOW YOU FEEL ABOUT ROYA. CHASING AFTER YOUR SISTER GIVES ELTANIN EVERY REASON TO HURT HER.
CAME BACK TO MAKE YOU DIDN'T DIE, NOT TO SOME GRAND SPEECH ABOUT SAVING THE WORLD.
BUT IF ELTANIN AND STABAN SUCCEED, VERYONE ON THIS RLD WILL FEEL THE PAIN YOU FEEL RIGHT NOW.
IT'S YOUR CHOICE.
YOU KNOW...
IT WASN'T GRAND, BUT IT WAS A PRETTY GOOD SPEECH. I'M COMING WITH YOU.

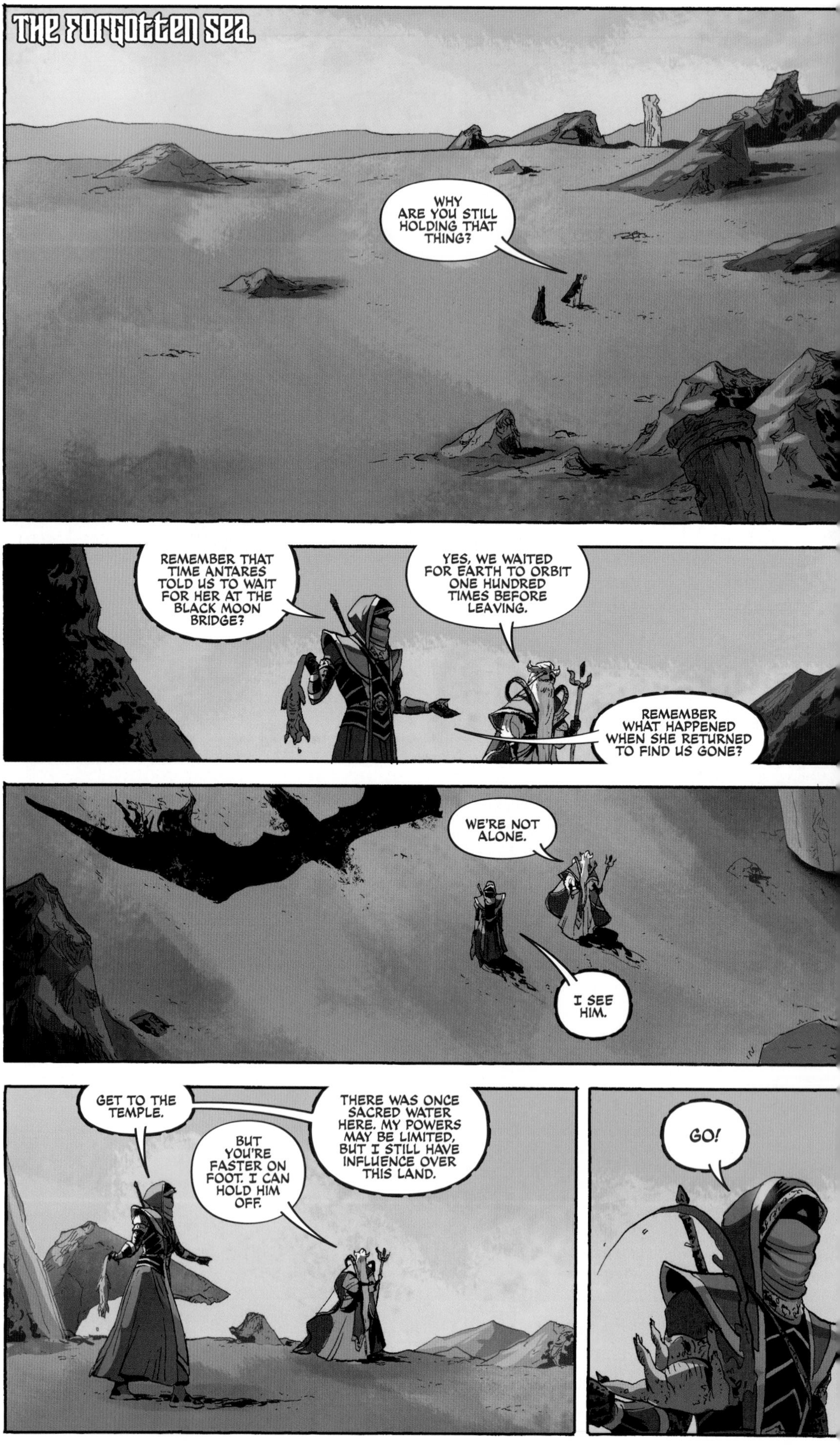
THE FORGOTTEN SEA.
WHY ARE YOU STILL HOLDING THAT THING?
REMEMBER THAT TIME ANTARES TOLD US TO WAIT FOR HER AT THE BLACK MOON BRIDGE?
YES, WE WAITED FOR EARTH TO ORBIT ONE HUNDRED TIMES BEFORE LEAVING.
REMEMBER WHAT HAPPENED WHEN SHE RETURNED TO FIND US GONE?
WE'RE NOT ALONE.
I SEE HIM.
GET TO THE TEMPLE.
BUT YOU'RE FASTER ON FOOT. I CAN HOLD HIM OFF.
THERE WAS ONCE SACRED WATER HERE. MY POWERS MAY BE LIMITED, BUT I STILL HAVE INFLUENCE OVER THIS LAND.
GO!

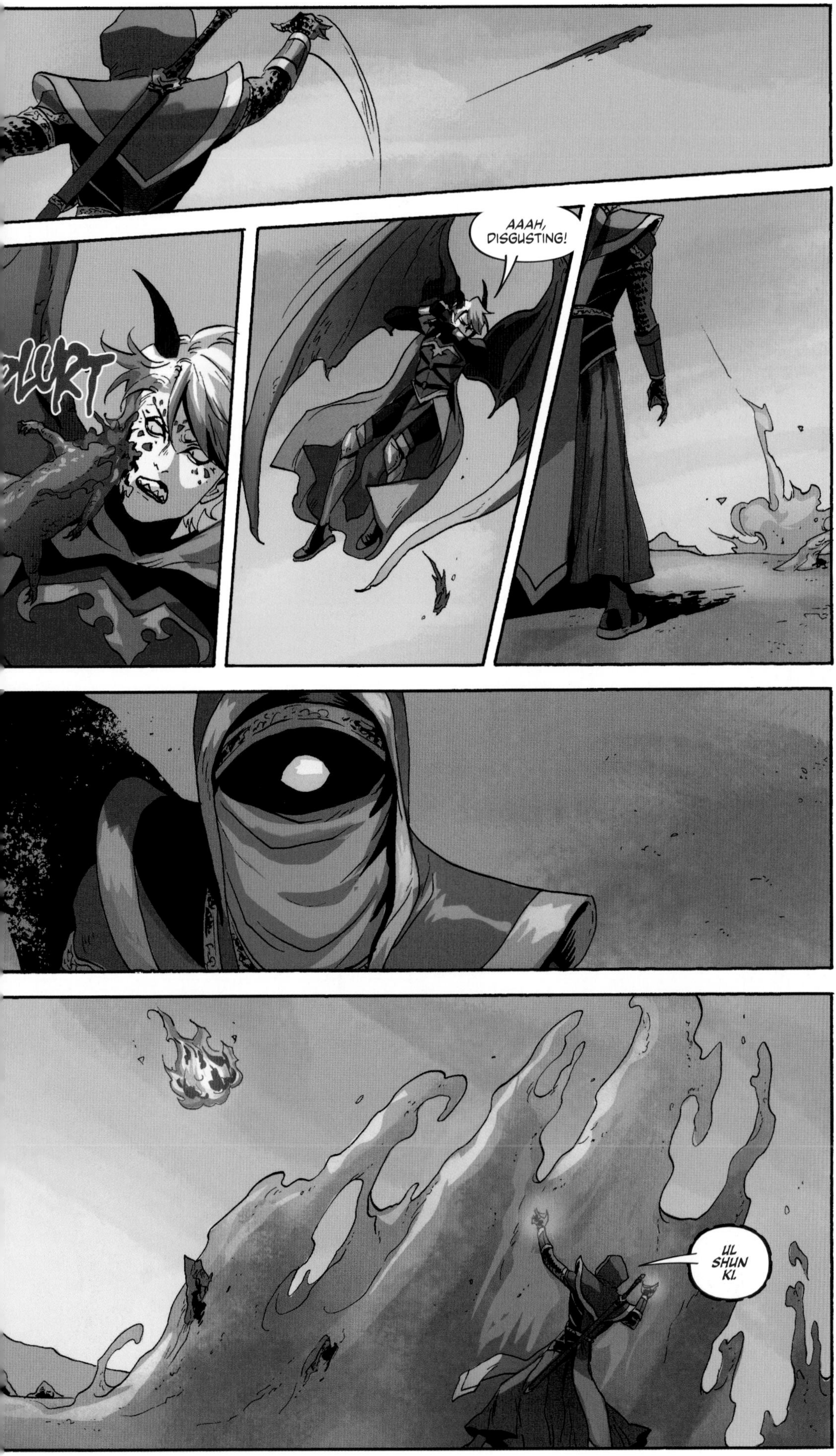
SPLURT
AAAH, DISGUSTING!
UL SHUN KI.

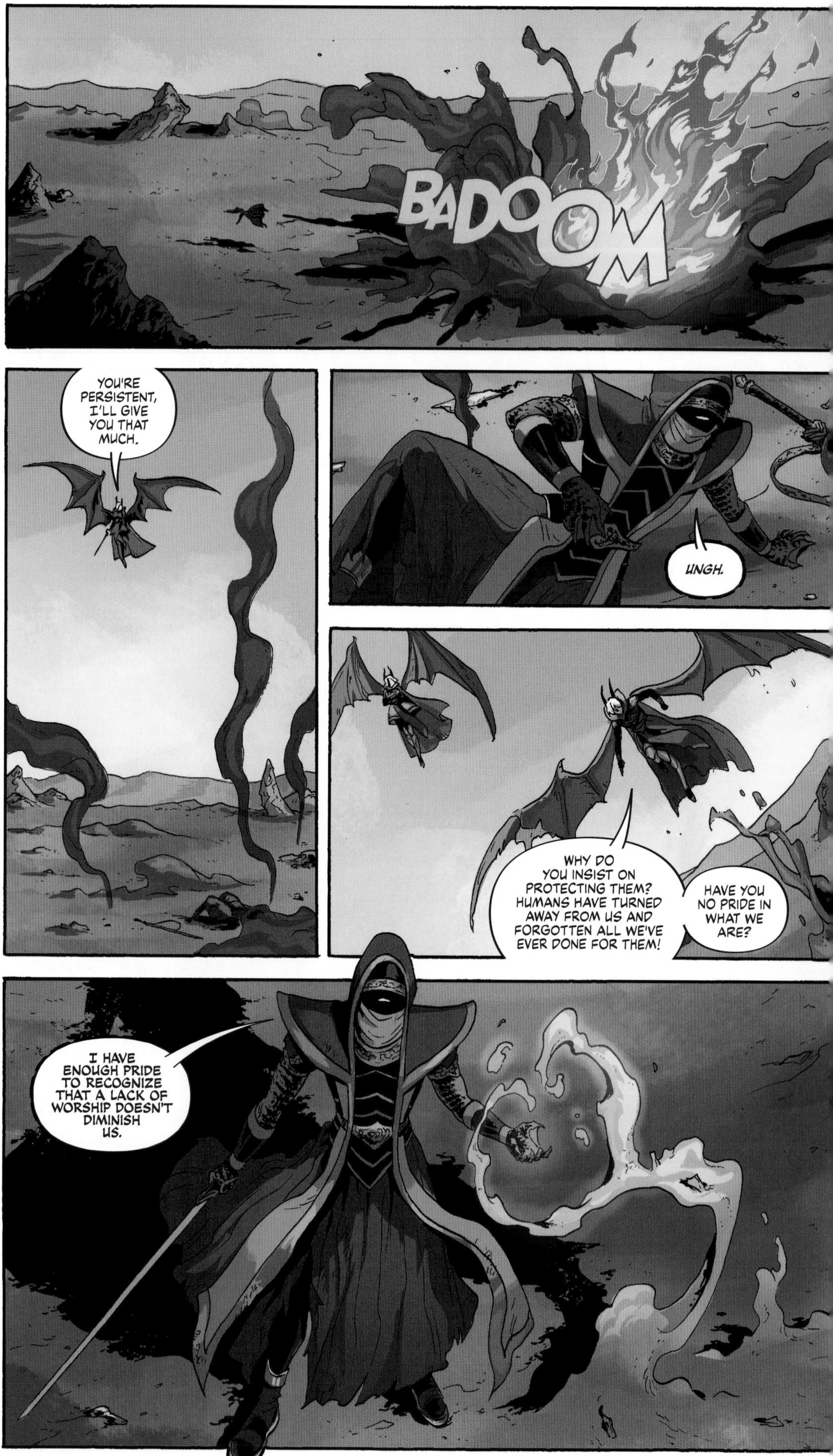
BADOOOM
YOU'RE PERSISTENT, I'LL GIVE YOU THAT MUCH.
UNGH.
WHY DO YOU INSIST ON PROTECTING THEM? HUMANS HAVE TURNED AWAY FROM US AND FORGOTTEN ALL WE'VE EVER DONE FOR THEM!
HAVE YOU NO PRIDE IN WHAT WE ARE?
I HAVE ENOUGH PRIDE TO RECOGNIZE THAT A LACK OF WORSHIP DOESN'T DIMINISH US.

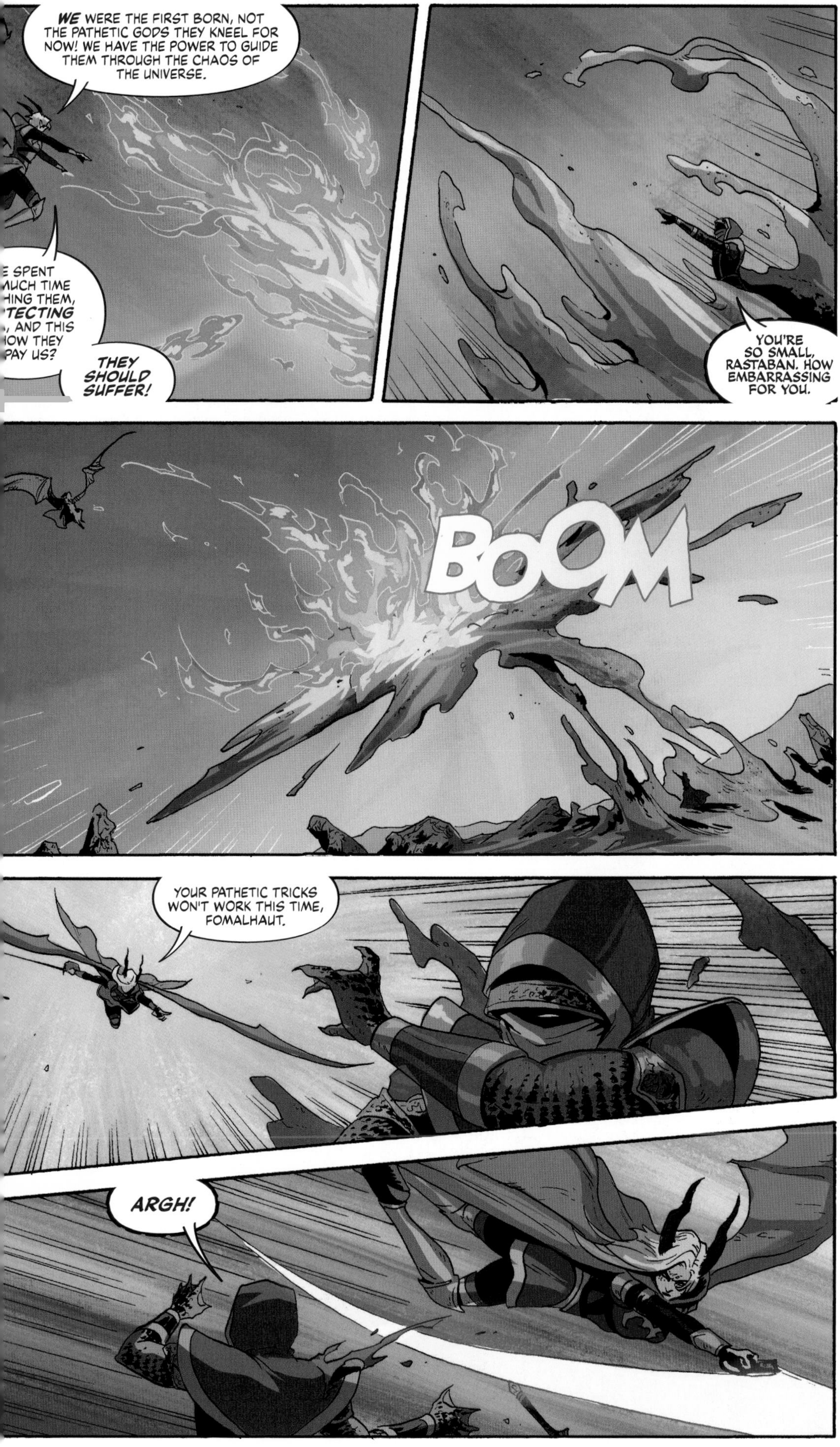
WE WERE THE FIRST BORN, NOT THE PATHETIC GODS THEY KNEEL FOR NOW! WE HAVE THE POWER TO GUIDE THEM THROUGH THE CHAOS OF THE UNIVERSE.
E SPENT MUCH TIME HING THEM, TECTING , AND THIS HOW THEY PAY US?
THEY SHOULD SUFFER!
YOU'RE SO SMALL, RASTABAN. HOW EMBARRASSING FOR YOU.
BOOM
YOUR PATHETIC TRICKS WON'T WORK THIS TIME, FOMALHAUT.
ARGH!

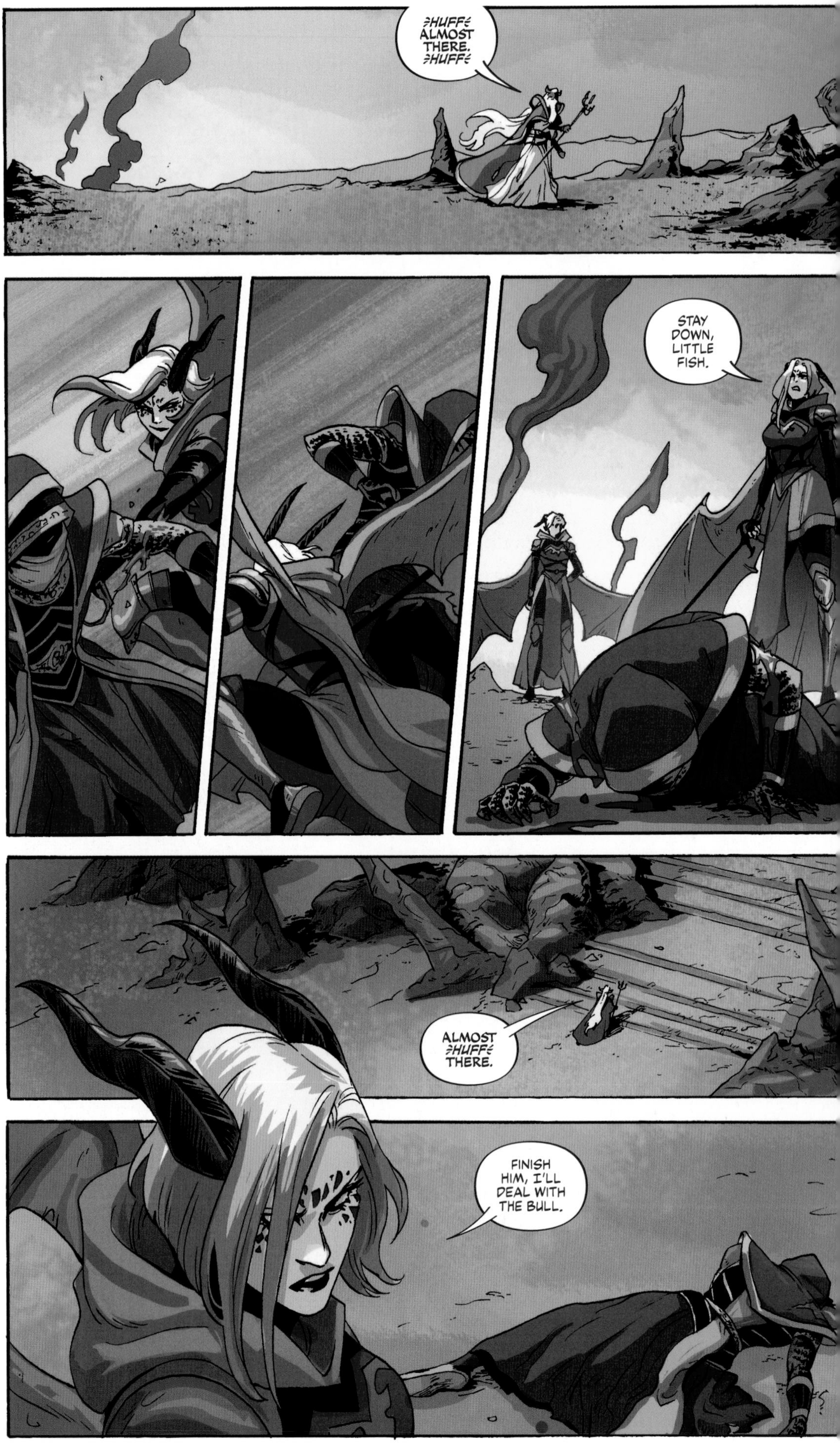

HUFF ALMOST THERE. HUFF
STAY DOWN, LITTLE FISH.
ALMOST HUFF THERE.
FINISH HIM, I'LL DEAL WITH THE BULL.

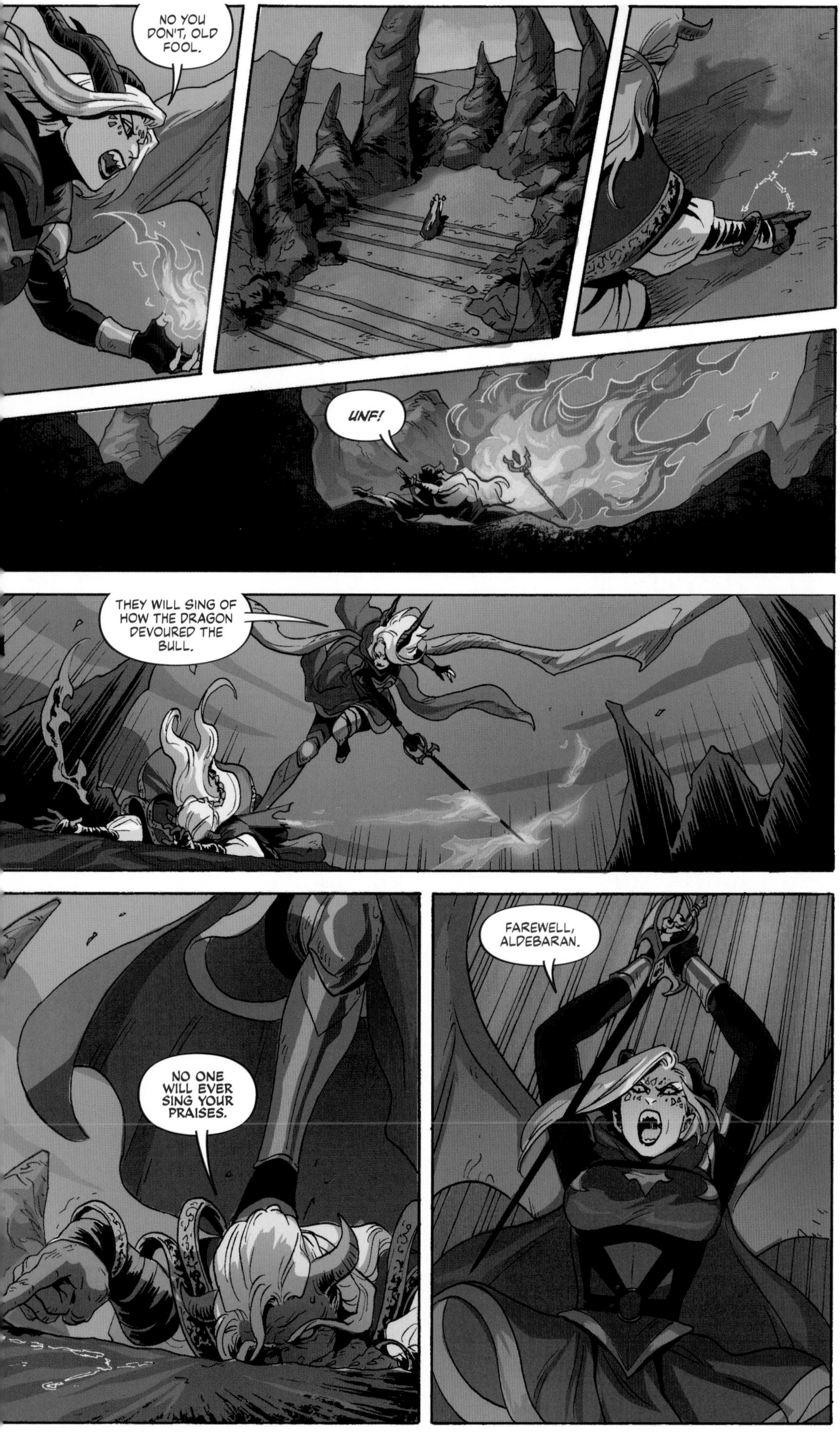
NO YOU DON'T, OLD FOOL.
UNF!
THEY WILL SING OF HOW THE DRAGON DEVOURED THE BULL.
NO ONE WILL EVER SING YOUR PRAISES.
FAREWELL, ALDEBARAN.

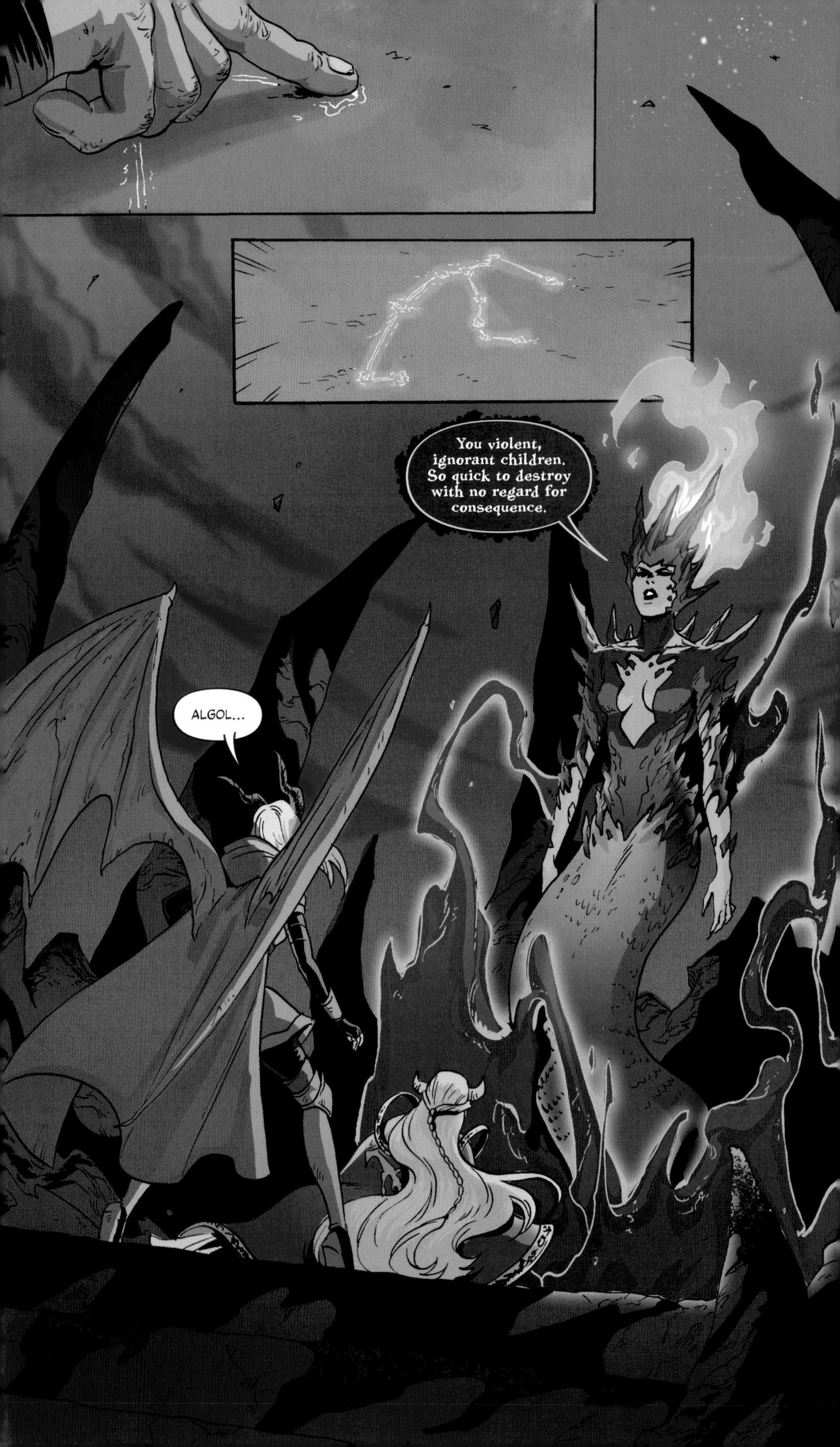
You violent, ignorant children. So quick to destroy with no regard for consequence.
ALGOL...

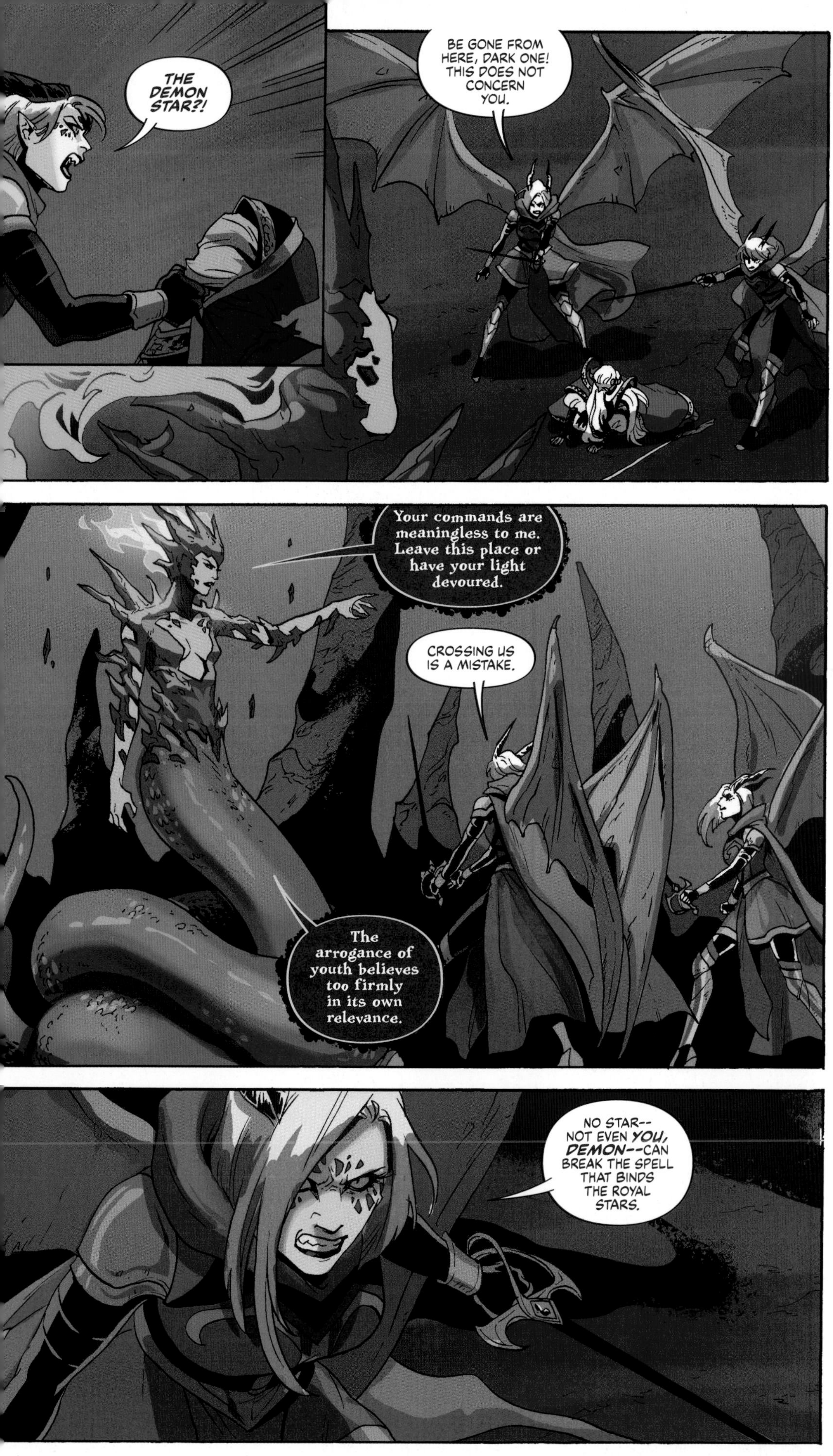
THE DEMON STAR?!
BE GONE FROM HERE, DARK ONE! THIS DOES NOT CONCERN YOU.
Your commands are meaningless to me. Leave this place or have your light devoured.
CROSSING US IS A MISTAKE.
The arrogance of youth believes too firmly in its own relevance.
NO STAR-- NOT EVEN *YOU, DEMON*--CAN BREAK THE SPELL THAT BINDS THE ROYAL STARS.

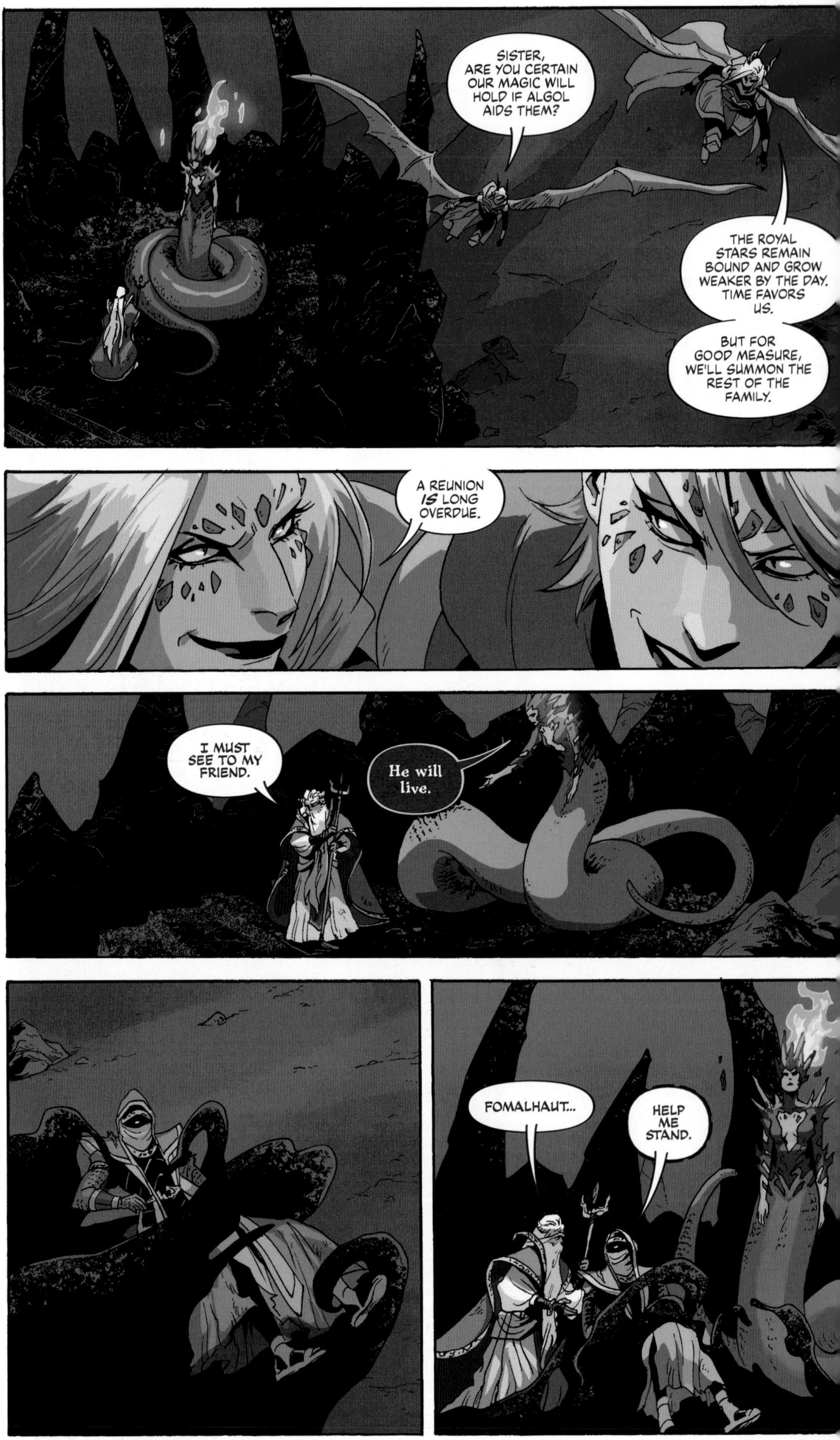
SISTER, ARE YOU CERTAIN OUR MAGIC WILL HOLD IF ALGOL AIDS THEM?
THE ROYAL STARS REMAIN BOUND AND GROW WEAKER BY THE DAY. TIME FAVORS US.
BUT FOR GOOD MEASURE, WE'LL SUMMON THE REST OF THE FAMILY.
A REUNION *IS* LONG OVERDUE.
I MUST SEE TO MY FRIEND.
He will live.
FOMALHAUT...
HELP ME STAND.

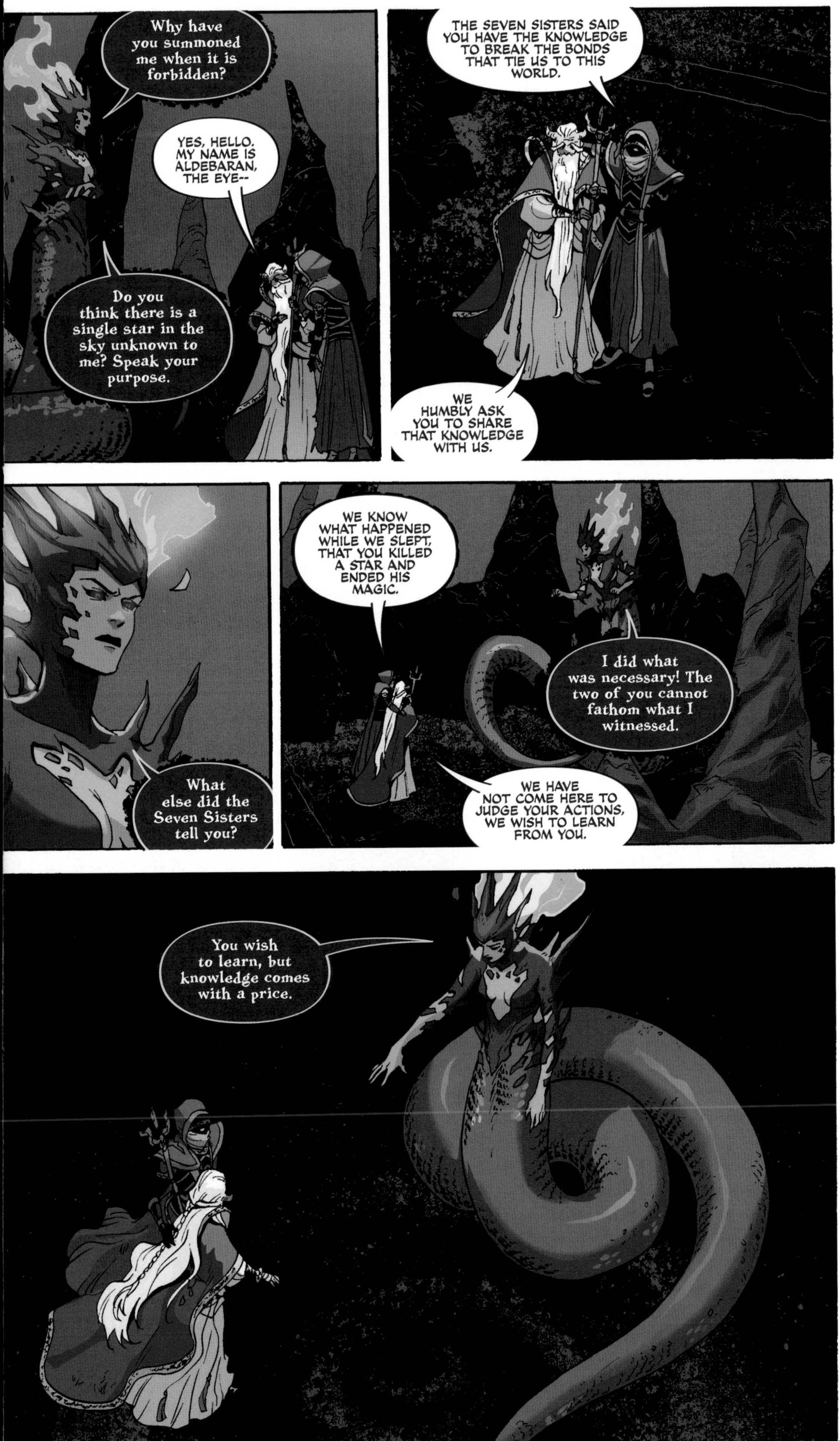
Why have you summoned me when it is forbidden?
YES, HELLO. MY NAME IS ALDEBARAN, THE EYE--
Do you think there is a single star in the sky unknown to me? Speak your purpose.
THE SEVEN SISTERS SAID YOU HAVE THE KNOWLEDGE TO BREAK THE BONDS THAT TIE US TO THIS WORLD.
WE HUMBLY ASK YOU TO SHARE THAT KNOWLEDGE WITH US.
What else did the Seven Sisters tell you?
WE KNOW WHAT HAPPENED WHILE WE SLEPT, THAT YOU KILLED A STAR AND ENDED HIS MAGIC.
I did what was necessary! The two of you cannot fathom what I witnessed.
WE HAVE NOT COME HERE TO JUDGE YOUR ACTIONS, WE WISH TO LEARN FROM YOU.
You wish to learn, but knowledge comes with a price.

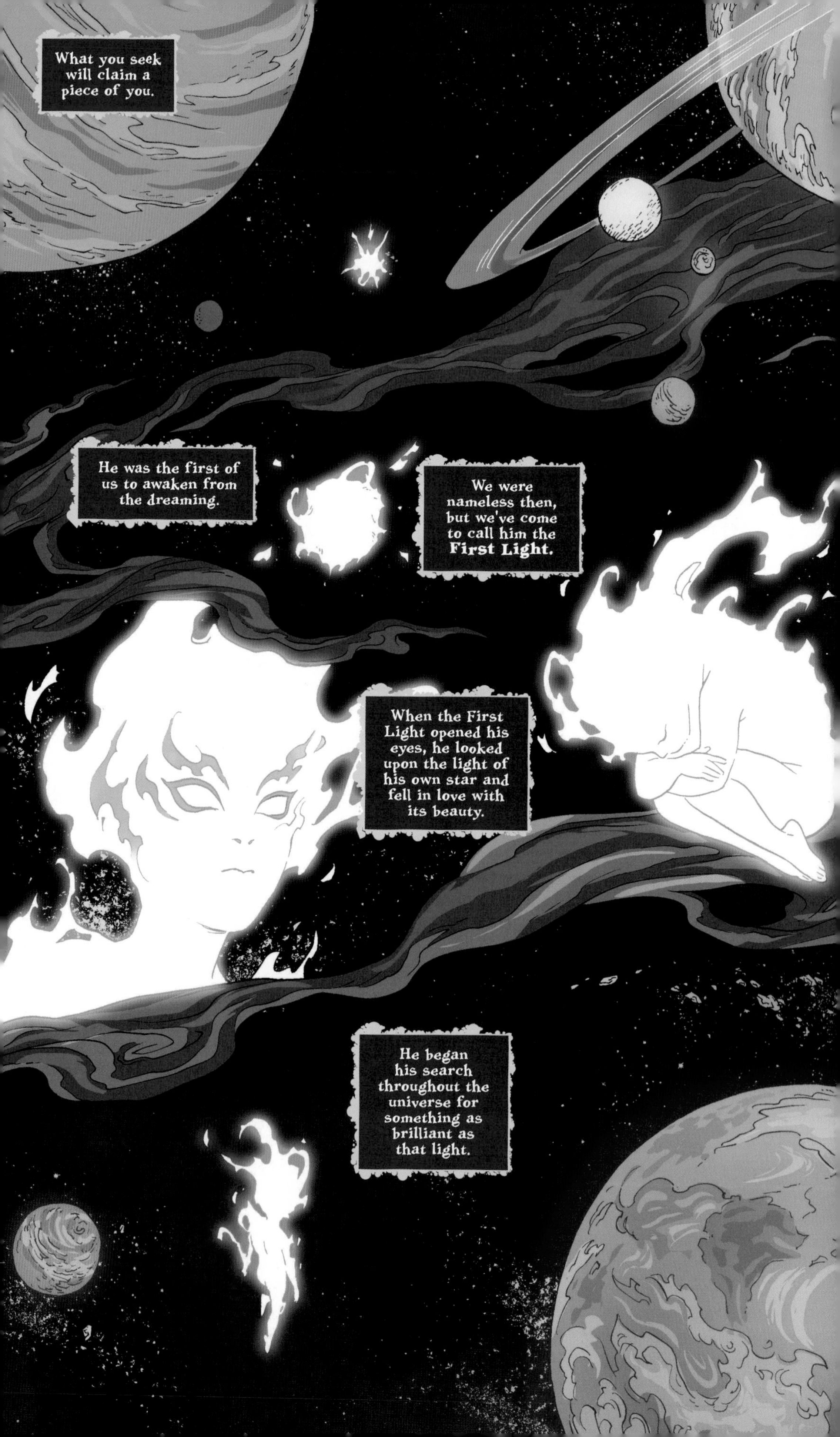
What you seek will claim a piece of you.
He was the first of us to awaken from the dreaming.
We were nameless then, but we've come to call him the **First Light.**
When the First Light opened his eyes, he looked upon the light of his own star and fell in love with its beauty.
He began his search throughout the universe for something as brilliant as that light.

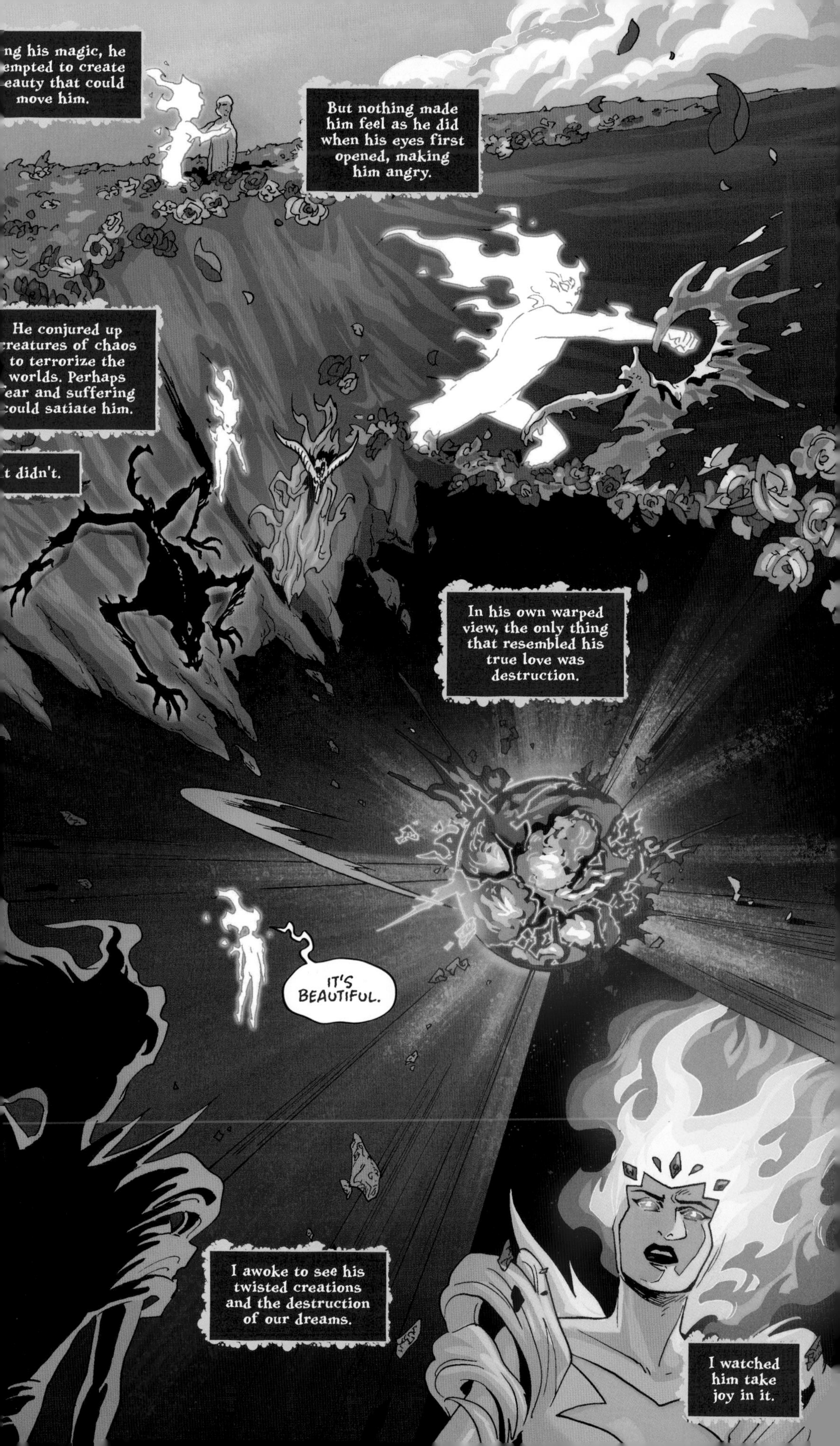

ng his magic, he
empted to create
eauty that could
move him.
But nothing made him feel as he did when his eyes first opened, making him angry.
He conjured up
reatures of chaos
to terrorize the
worlds. Perhaps
ear and suffering
ould satiate him.
t didn't.
In his own warped view, the only thing that resembled his true love was destruction.
IT'S BEAUTIFUL.
I awoke to see his twisted creations and the destruction of our dreams.
I watched him take joy in it.

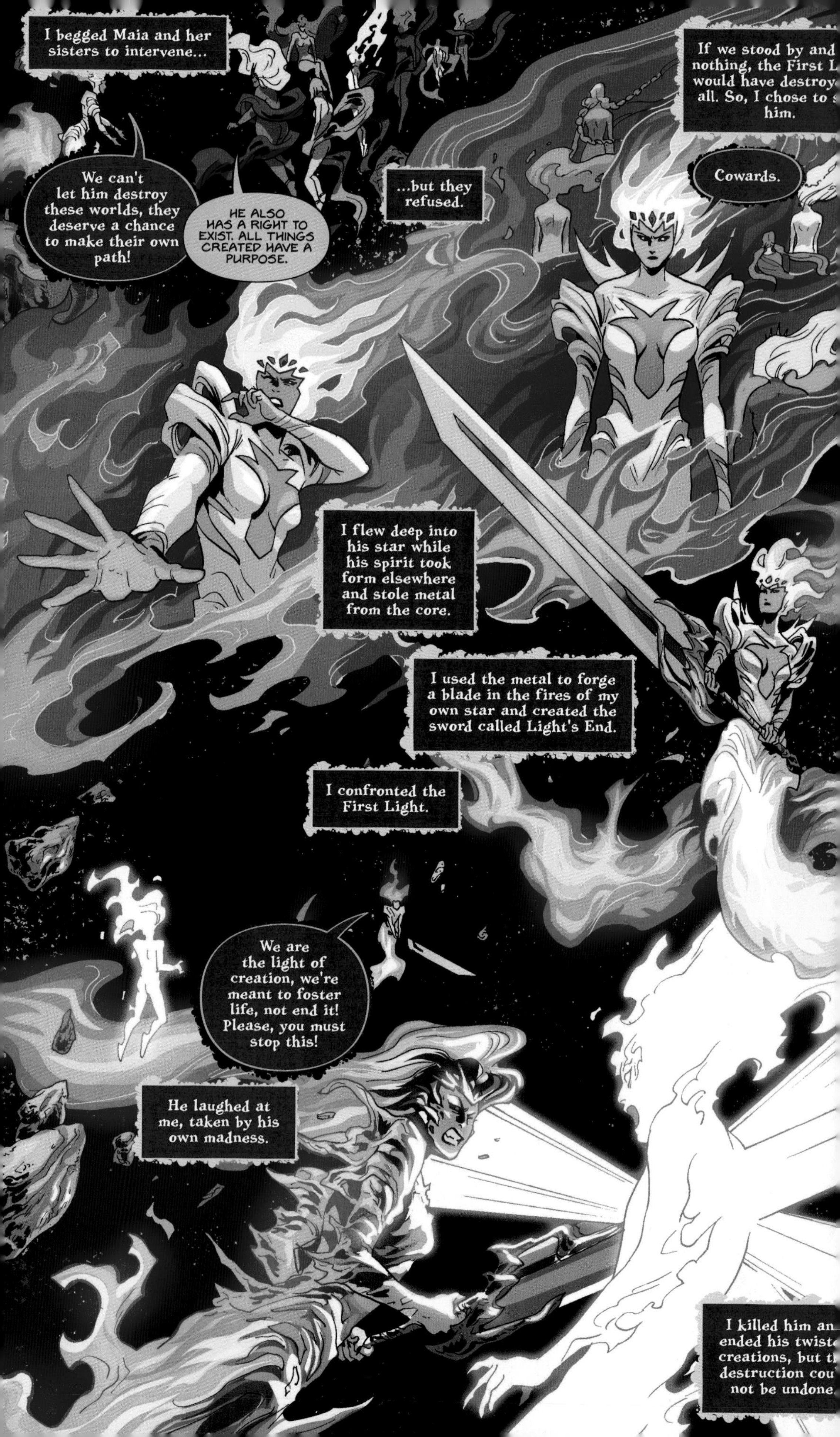
I begged Maia and her sisters to intervene...
We can't let him destroy these worlds, they deserve a chance to make their own path!
HE ALSO HAS A RIGHT TO EXIST. ALL THINGS CREATED HAVE A PURPOSE.
...but they refused.
If we stood by and nothing, the First L would have destroy all. So, I chose to him.
Cowards.
I flew deep into his star while his spirit took form elsewhere and stole metal from the core.
I used the metal to forge a blade in the fires of my own star and created the sword called Light's End.
I confronted the First Light.
We are the light of creation, we're meant to foster life, not end it! Please, you must stop this!
He laughed at me, taken by his own madness.
I killed him an ended his twiste creations, but t destruction cou not be undone.

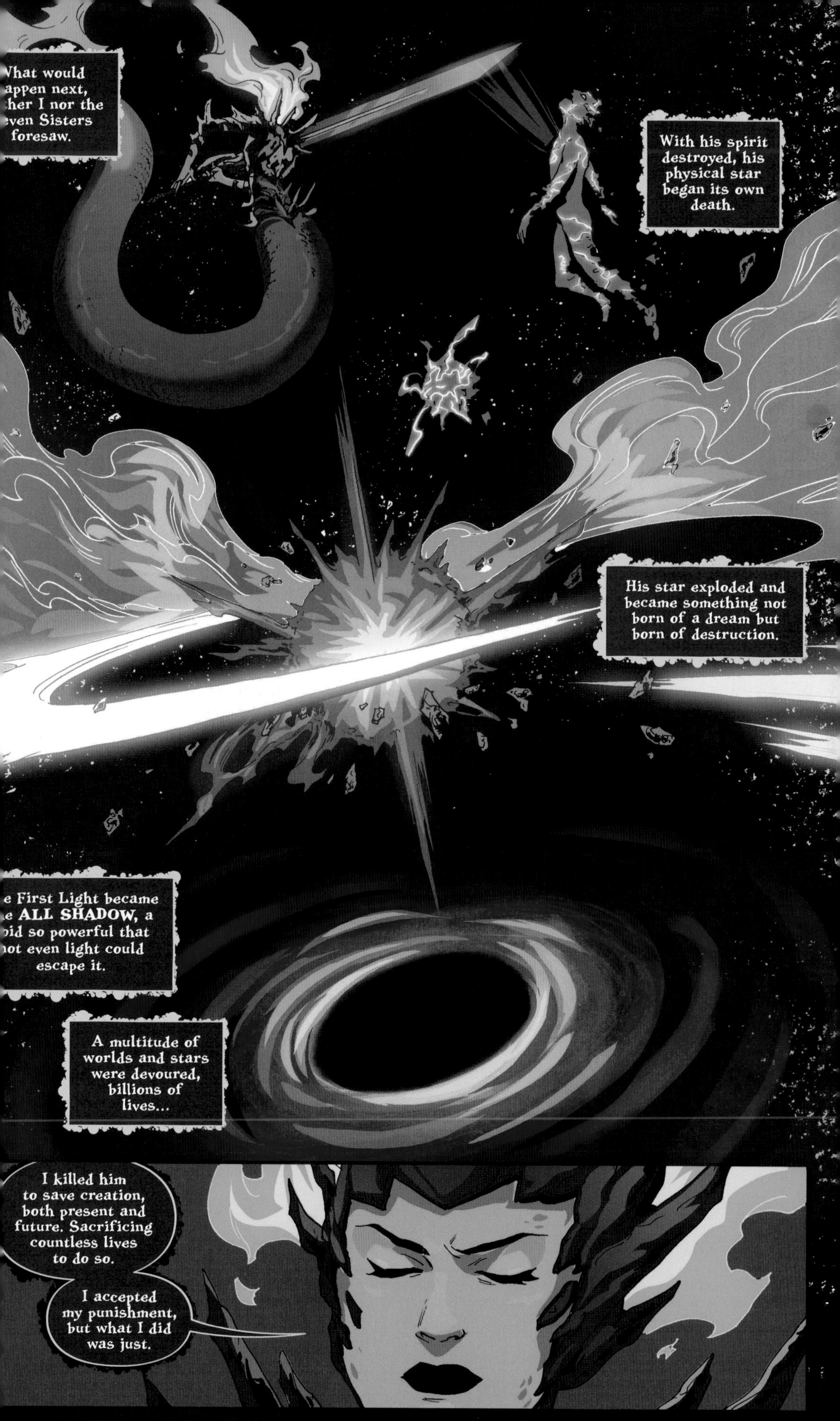
Vhat would appen next, her I nor the even Sisters foresaw.
With his spirit destroyed, his physical star began its own death.
His star exploded and became something not born of a dream but born of destruction.
e First Light became e ALL SHADOW, a oid so powerful that not even light could escape it.
A multitude of worlds and stars were devoured, billions of lives...
I killed him to save creation, both present and future. Sacrificing countless lives to do so.
I accepted my punishment, but what I did was just.

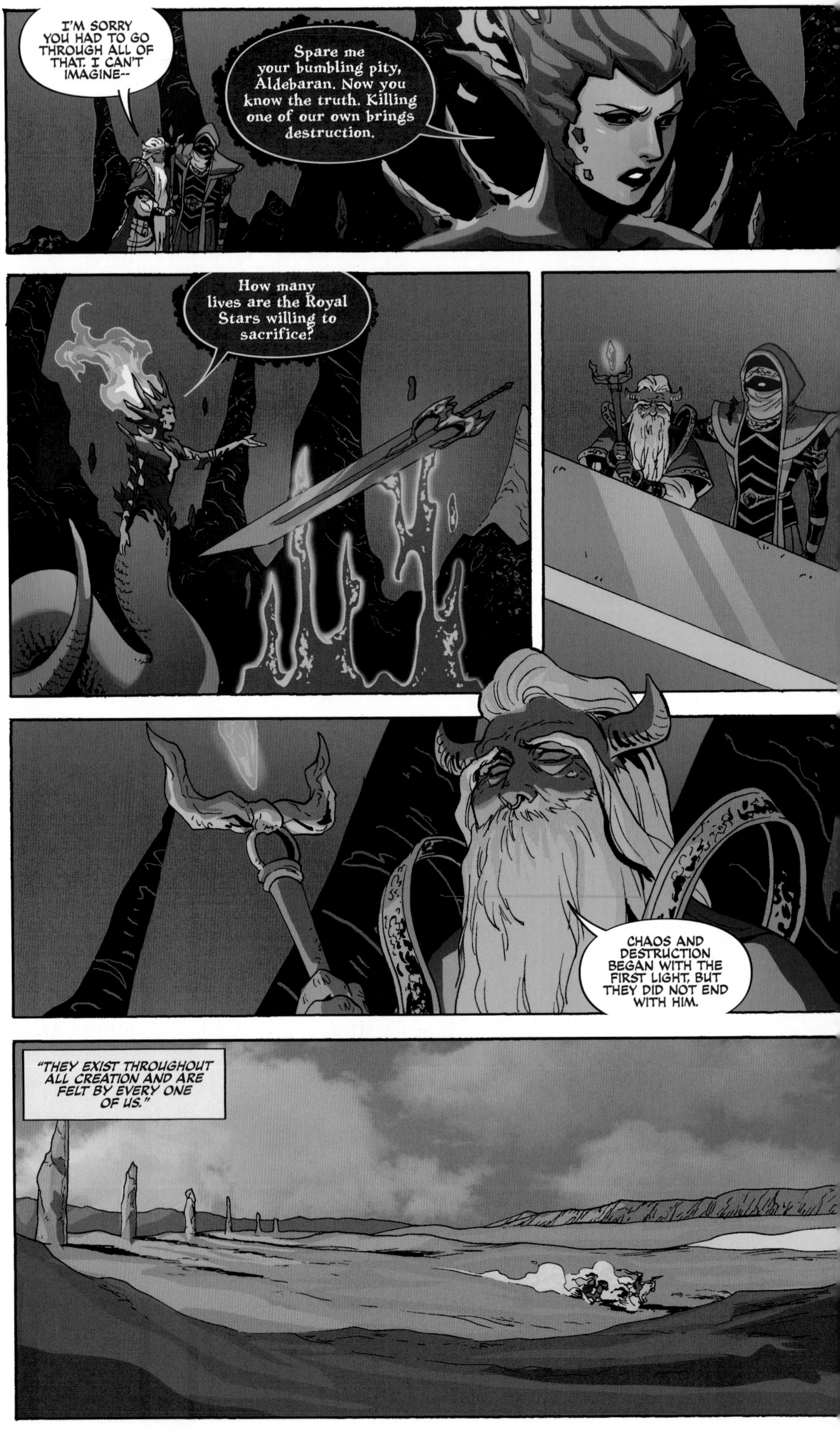
I'M SORRY YOU HAD TO GO THROUGH ALL OF THAT. I CAN'T IMAGINE--
Spare me your bumbling pity, Aldebaran. Now you know the truth. Killing one of our own brings destruction.
How many lives are the Royal Stars willing to sacrifice?
CHAOS AND DESTRUCTION BEGAN WITH THE FIRST LIGHT, BUT THEY DID NOT END WITH HIM.
"THEY EXIST THROUGHOUT ALL CREATION AND ARE FELT BY EVERY ONE OF US."

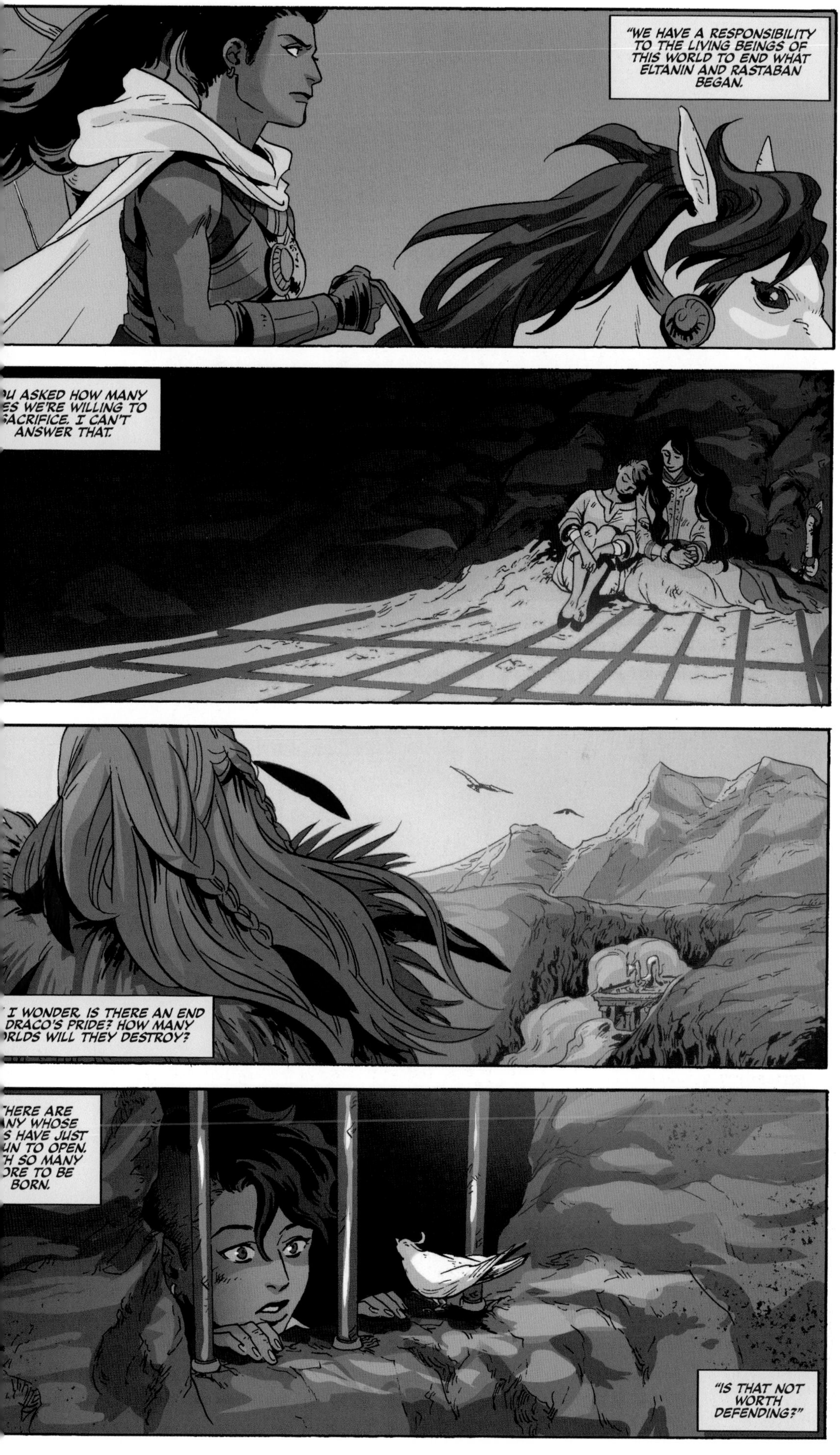
"WE HAVE A RESPONSIBILITY TO THE LIVING BEINGS OF THIS WORLD TO END WHAT ELTANIN AND RASTABAN BEGAN.
OU ASKED HOW MANY ES WE'RE WILLING TO SACRIFICE. I CAN'T ANSWER THAT.
I WONDER, IS THERE AN END DRACO'S PRIDE? HOW MANY ORLDS WILL THEY DESTROY?
HERE ARE NY WHOSE S HAVE JUST UN TO OPEN. H SO MANY ORE TO BE BORN.
"IS THAT NOT WORTH DEFENDING?"

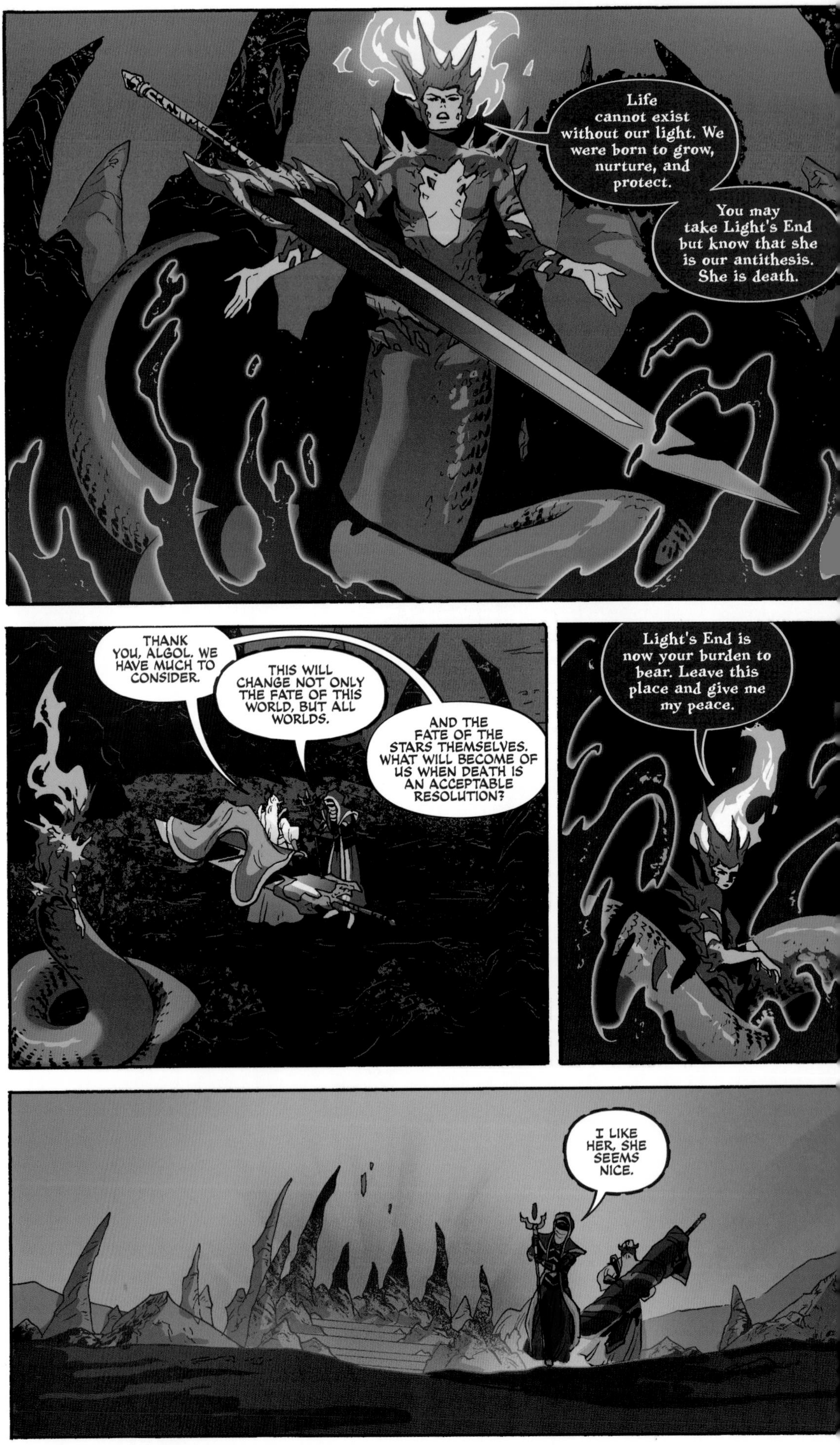
Life cannot exist without our light. We were born to grow, nurture, and protect.
You may take Light's End but know that she is our antithesis. She is death.
THANK YOU, ALGOL. WE HAVE MUCH TO CONSIDER.
THIS WILL CHANGE NOT ONLY THE FATE OF THIS WORLD, BUT ALL WORLDS.
AND THE FATE OF THE STARS THEMSELVES. WHAT WILL BECOME OF US WHEN DEATH IS AN ACCEPTABLE RESOLUTION?
Light's End is now your burden to bear. Leave this place and give me my peace.
I LIKE HER, SHE SEEMS NICE.

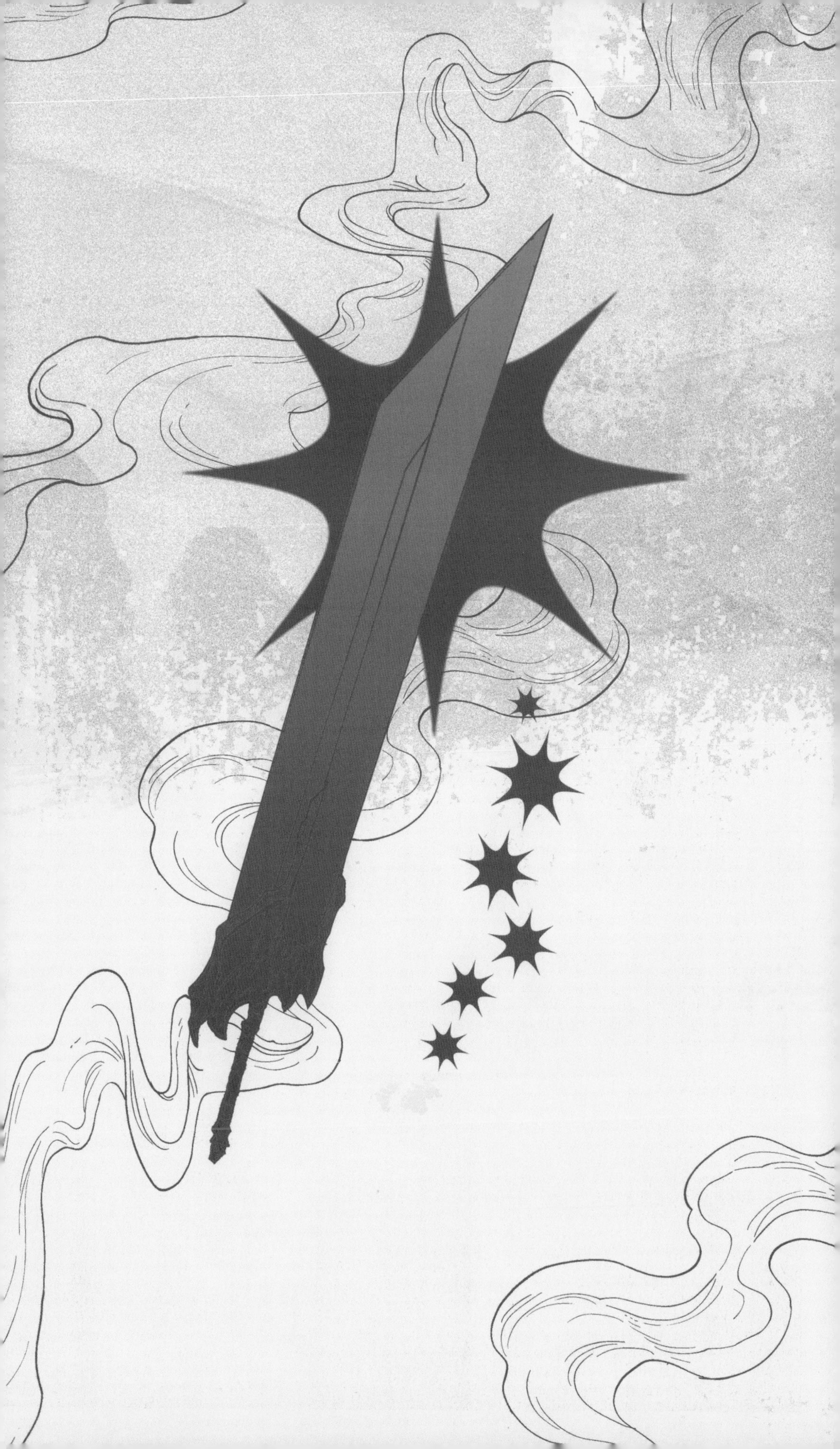

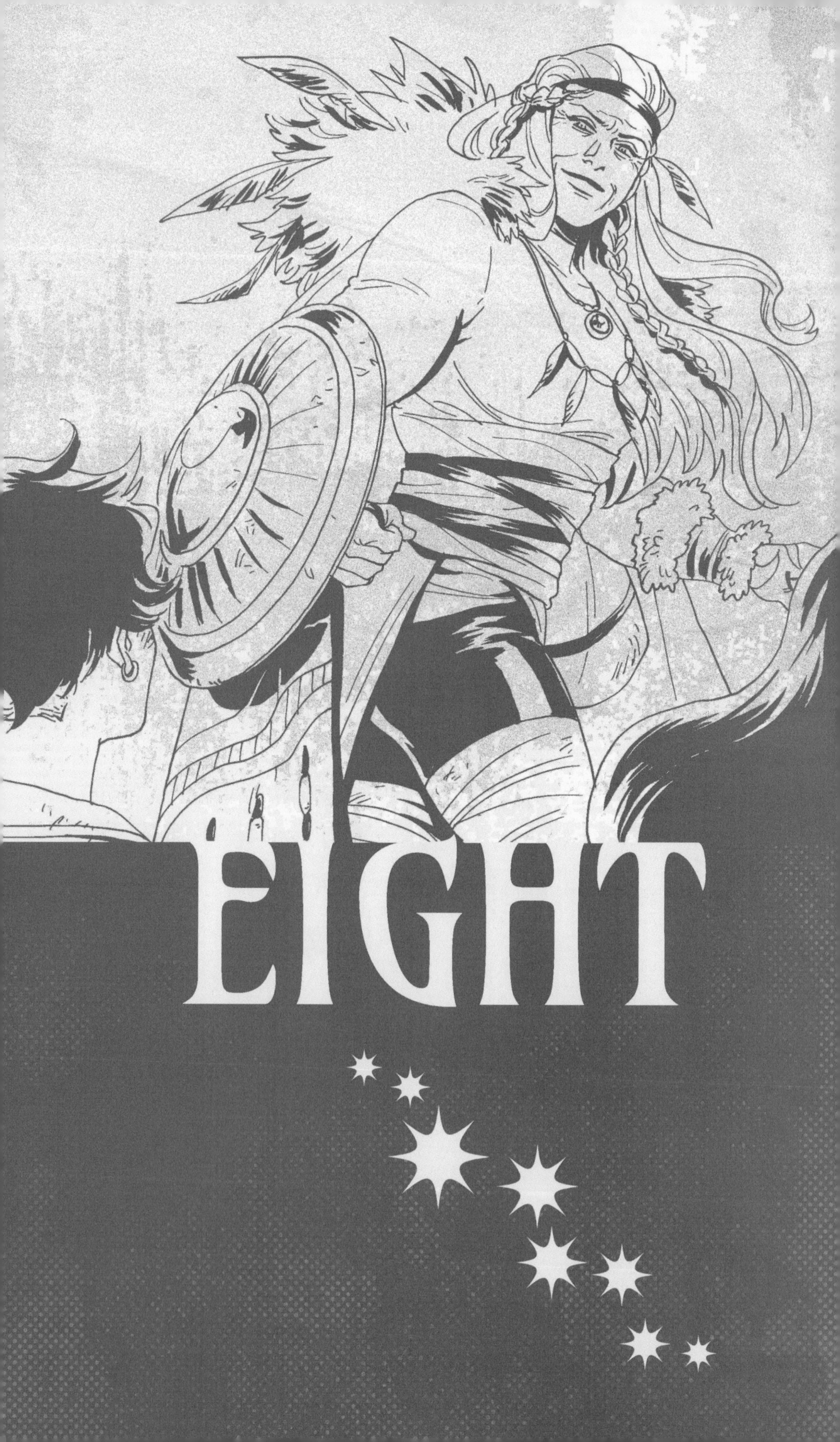
EIGHT

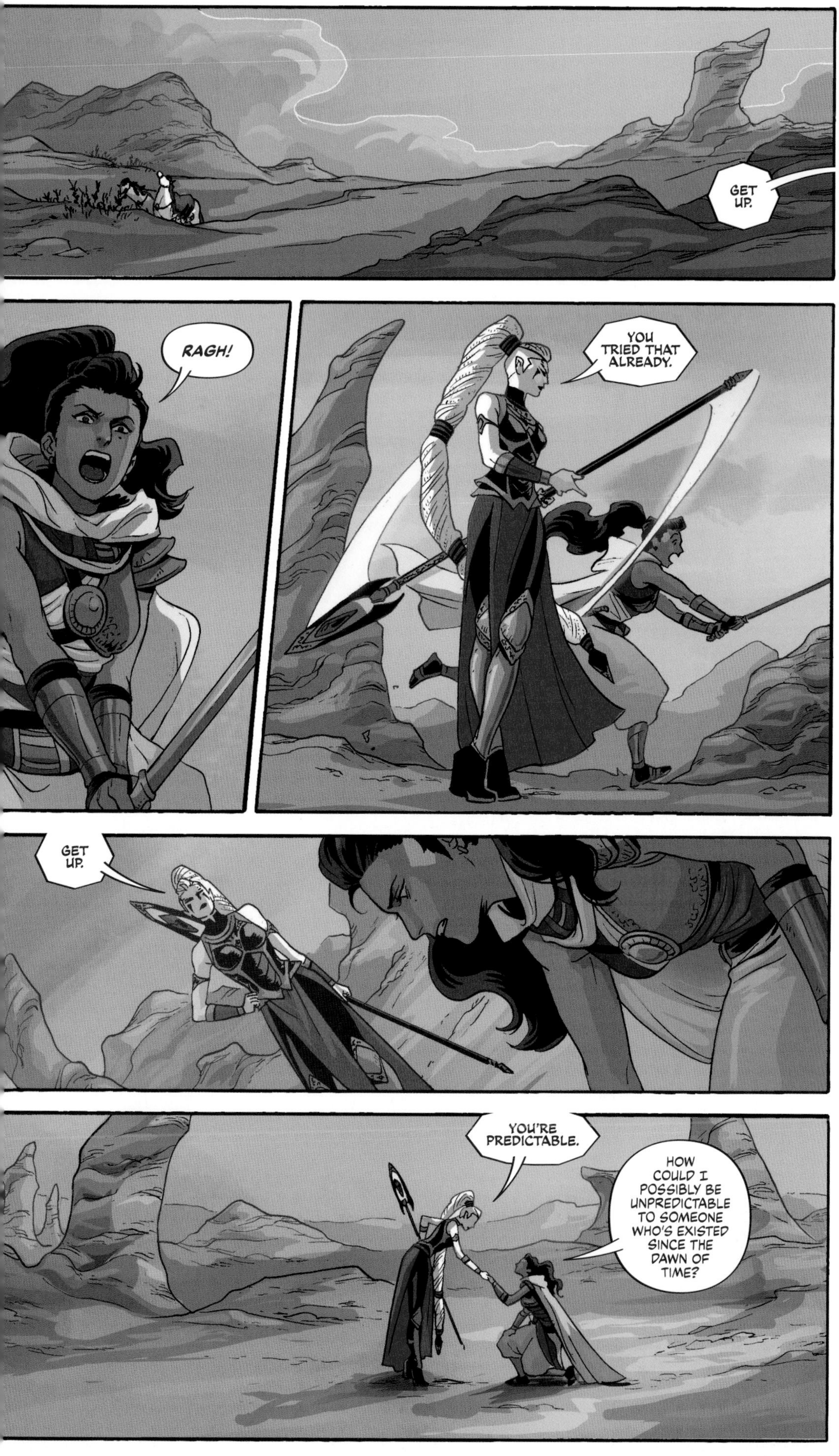
GET UP.
RAGH!
YOU TRIED THAT ALREADY.
GET UP.
YOU'RE PREDICTABLE.
HOW COULD I POSSIBLY BE UNPREDICTABLE TO SOMEONE WHO'S EXISTED SINCE THE DAWN OF TIME?

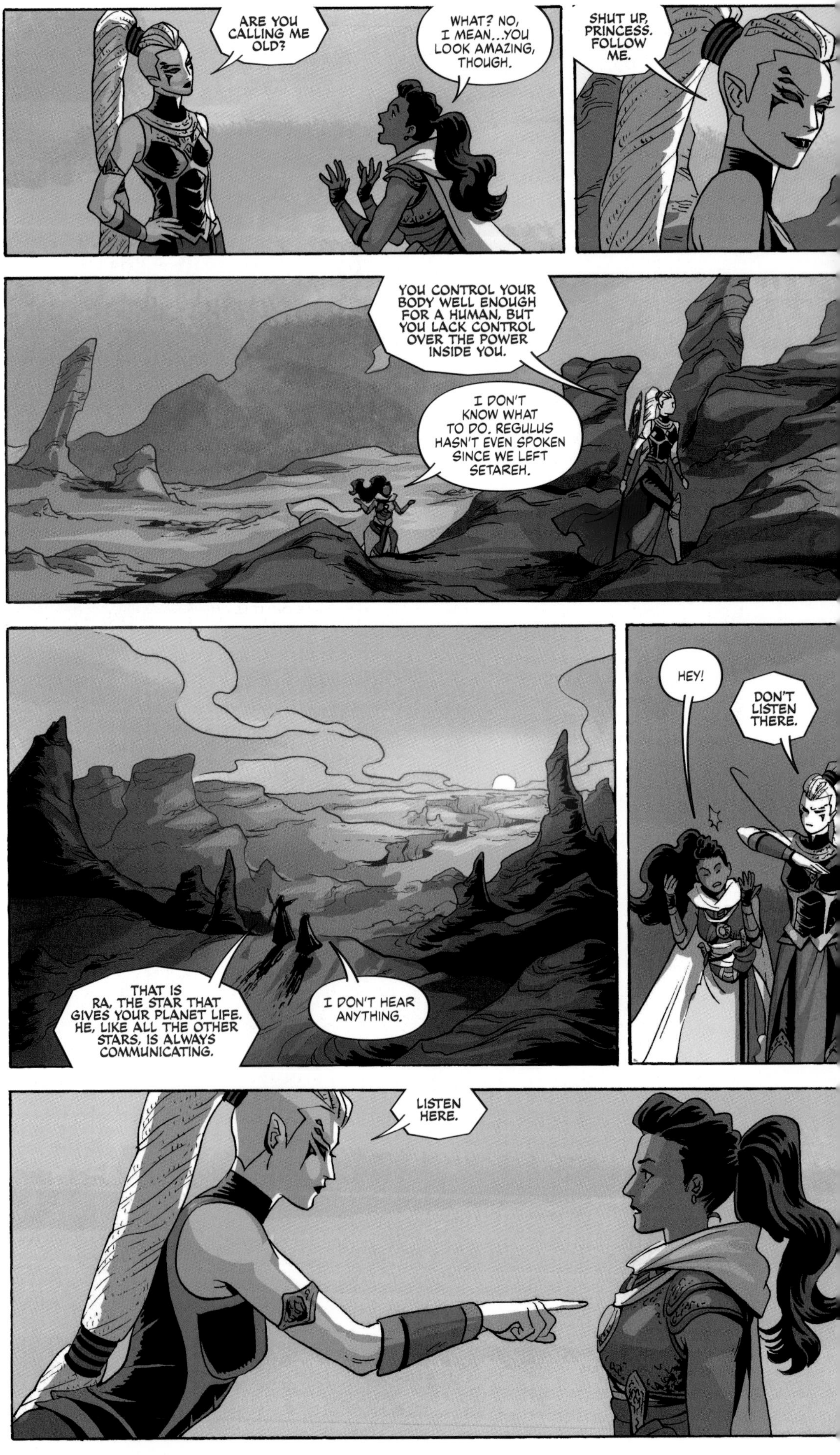
ARE YOU CALLING ME OLD?
WHAT? NO, I MEAN...YOU LOOK AMAZING, THOUGH.
SHUT UP, PRINCESS. FOLLOW ME.
YOU CONTROL YOUR BODY WELL ENOUGH FOR A HUMAN, BUT YOU LACK CONTROL OVER THE POWER INSIDE YOU.
I DON'T KNOW WHAT TO DO. REGULUS HASN'T EVEN SPOKEN SINCE WE LEFT SETAREH.
THAT IS RA, THE STAR THAT GIVES YOUR PLANET LIFE. HE, LIKE ALL THE OTHER STARS, IS ALWAYS COMMUNICATING.
I DON'T HEAR ANYTHING.
HEY!
DON'T LISTEN THERE.
LISTEN HERE.

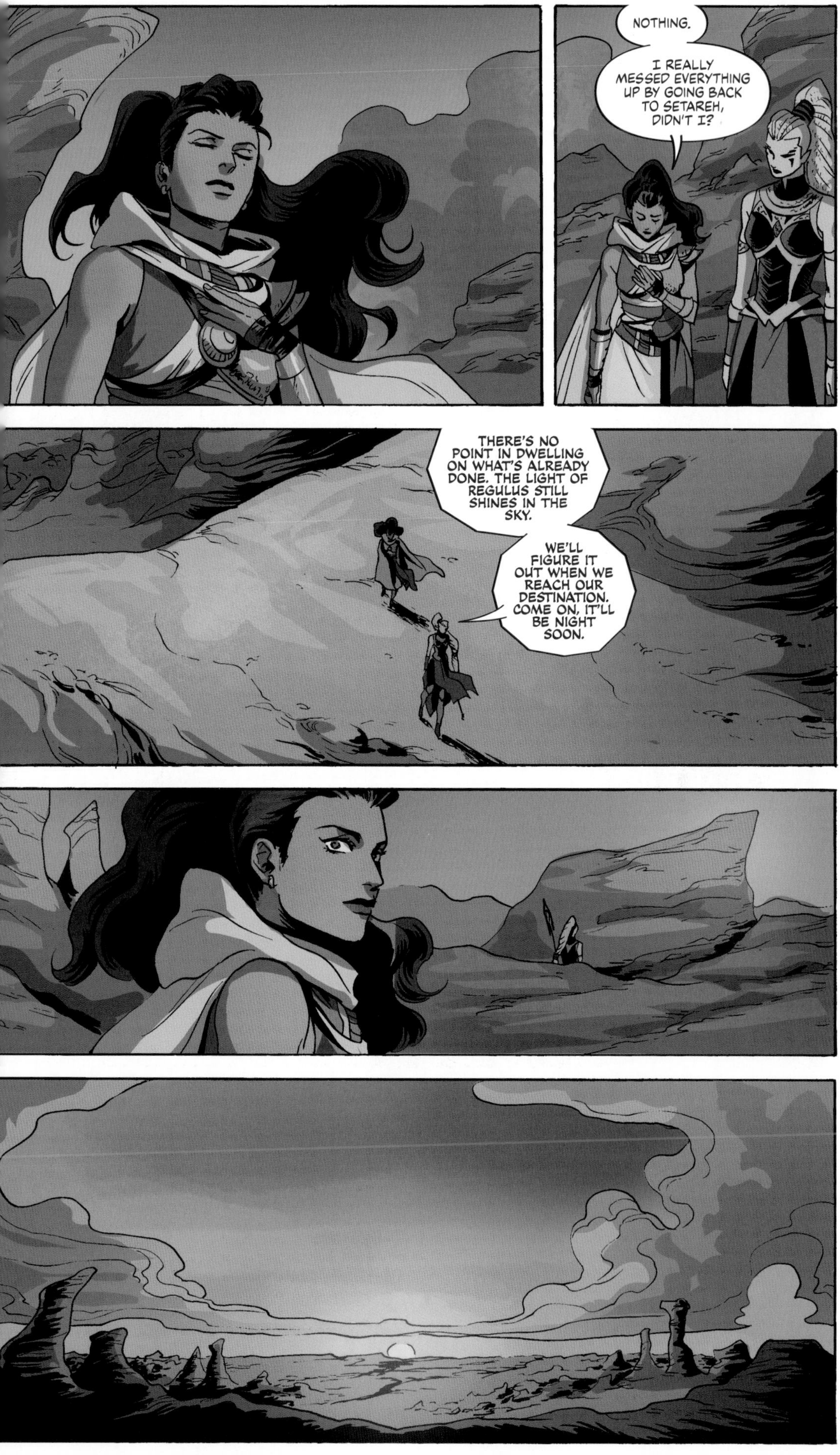
NOTHING.
I REALLY MESSED EVERYTHING UP BY GOING BACK TO SETAREH, DIDN'T I?
THERE'S NO POINT IN DWELLING ON WHAT'S ALREADY DONE. THE LIGHT OF REGULUS STILL SHINES IN THE SKY.
WE'LL FIGURE IT OUT WHEN WE REACH OUR DESTINATION. COME ON, IT'LL BE NIGHT SOON.

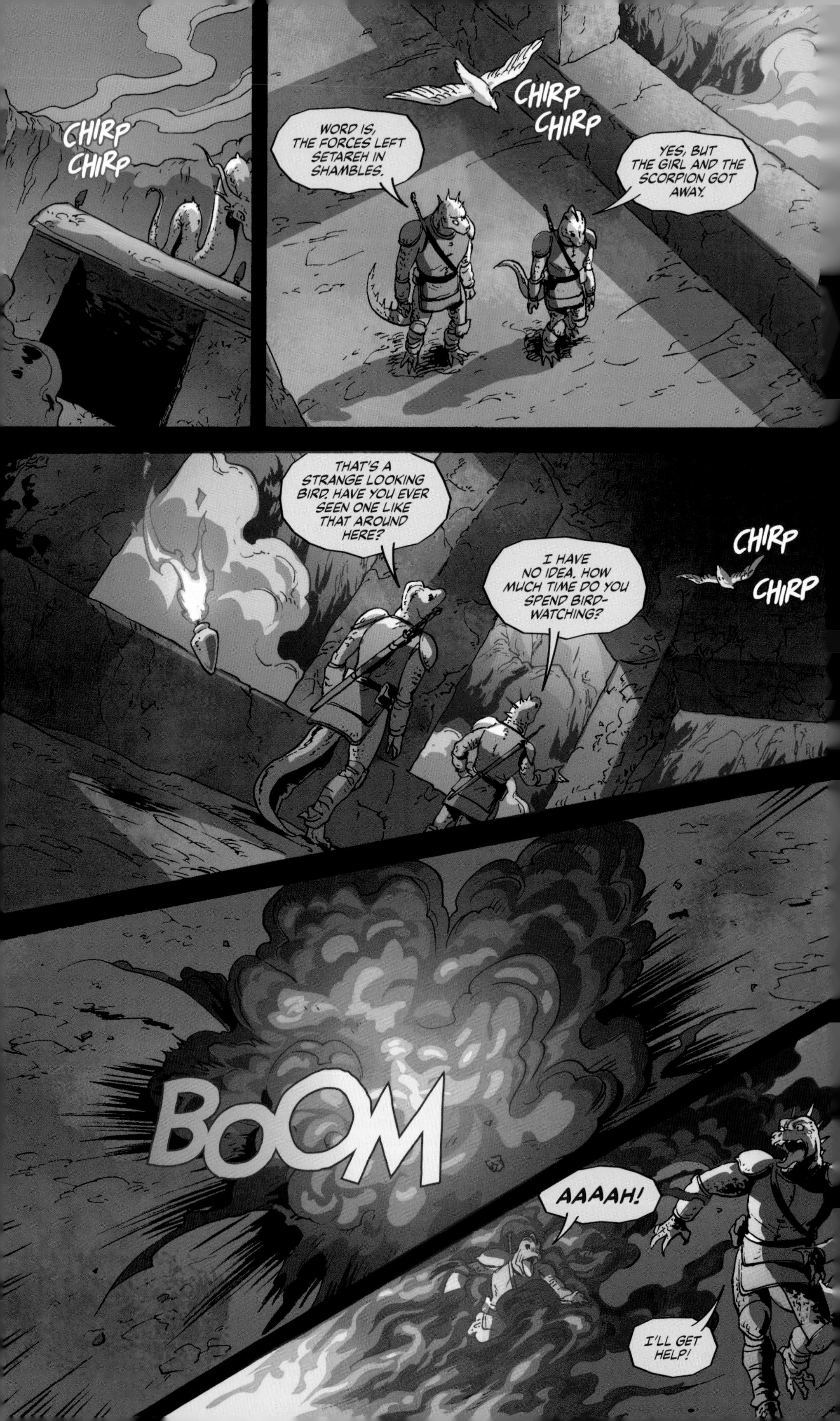
CHIRP
CHIRP
WORD IS, THE FORCES LEFT SETAREH IN SHAMBLES.
CHIRP
CHIRP
YES, BUT THE GIRL AND THE SCORPION GOT AWAY.
THAT'S A STRANGE LOOKING BIRD. HAVE YOU EVER SEEN ONE LIKE THAT AROUND HERE?
I HAVE NO IDEA. HOW MUCH TIME DO YOU SPEND BIRD-WATCHING?
CHIRP
CHIRP
BOOM
AAAAH!
I'LL GET HELP!

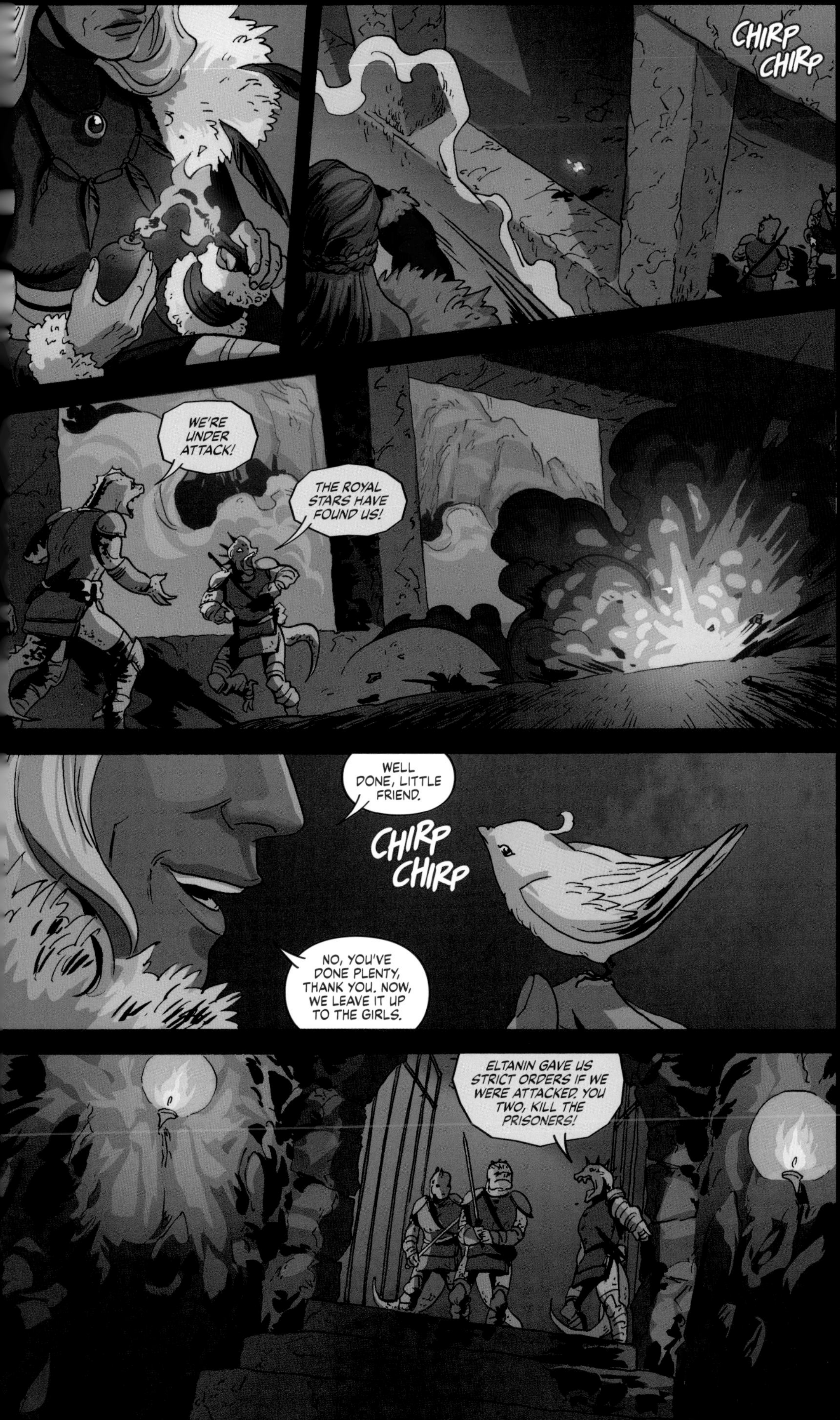
CHIRP CHIRP
WE'RE UNDER ATTACK!
THE ROYAL STARS HAVE FOUND US!
WELL DONE, LITTLE FRIEND.
CHIRP CHIRP
NO, YOU'VE DONE PLENTY, THANK YOU. NOW, WE LEAVE IT UP TO THE GIRLS.
ELTANIN GAVE US STRICT ORDERS IF WE WERE ATTACKED. YOU TWO, KILL THE PRISONERS!

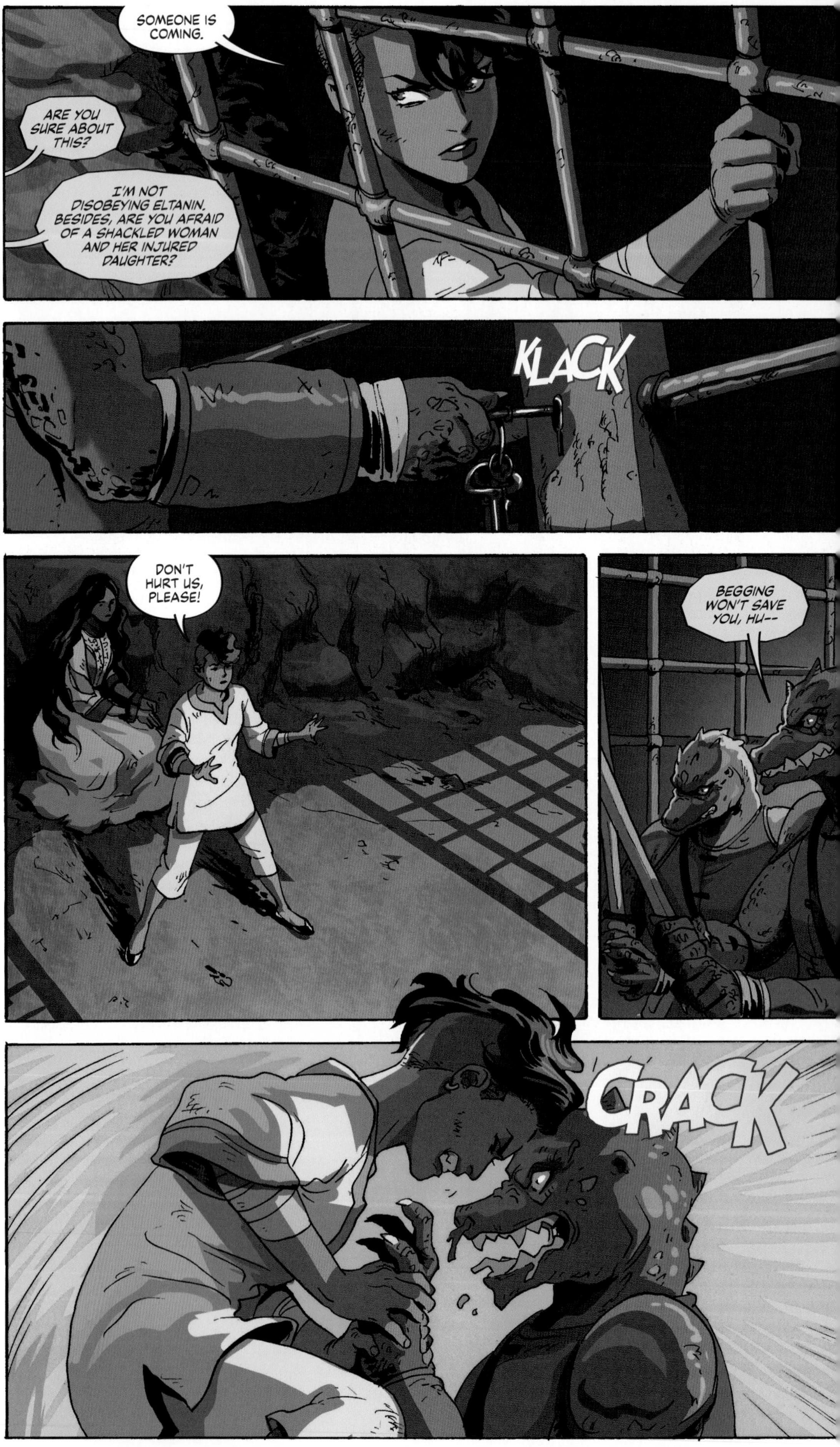
SOMEONE IS COMING.
ARE YOU SURE ABOUT THIS?
I'M NOT DISOBEYING ELTANIN. BESIDES, ARE YOU AFRAID OF A SHACKLED WOMAN AND HER INJURED DAUGHTER?
KLACK
DON'T HURT US, PLEASE!
BEGGING WON'T SAVE YOU, HU--
CRACK

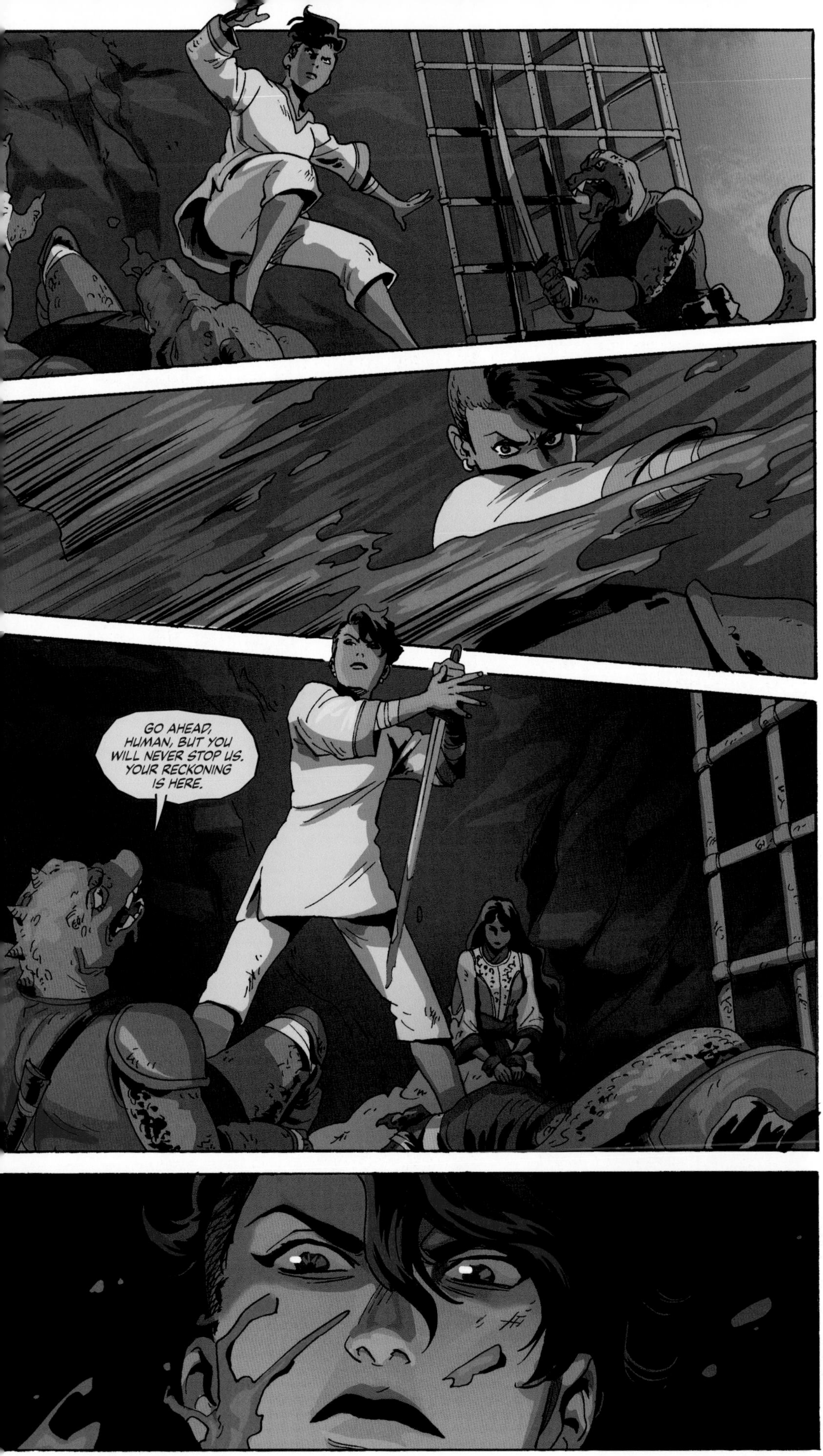
GO AHEAD, HUMAN, BUT YOU WILL NEVER STOP US. YOUR RECKONING IS HERE.

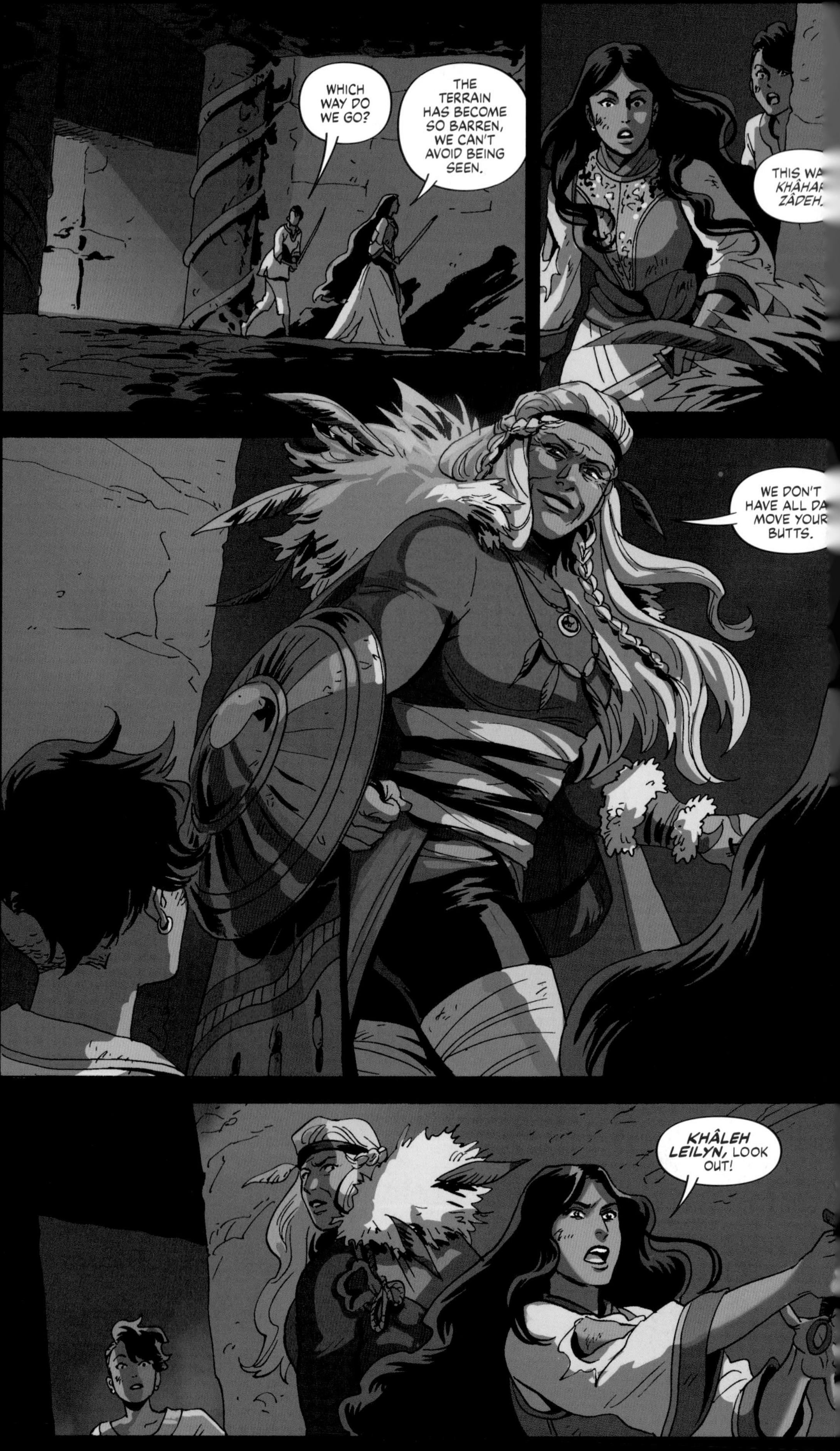
WHICH WAY DO WE GO?
THE TERRAIN HAS BECOME SO BARREN, WE CAN'T AVOID BEING SEEN.
THIS WA
KHÂHAR ZÂDEH.
WE DON'T HAVE ALL DA
MOVE YOUR BUTTS.
KHÂLEH LEILYN, LOOK OUT!

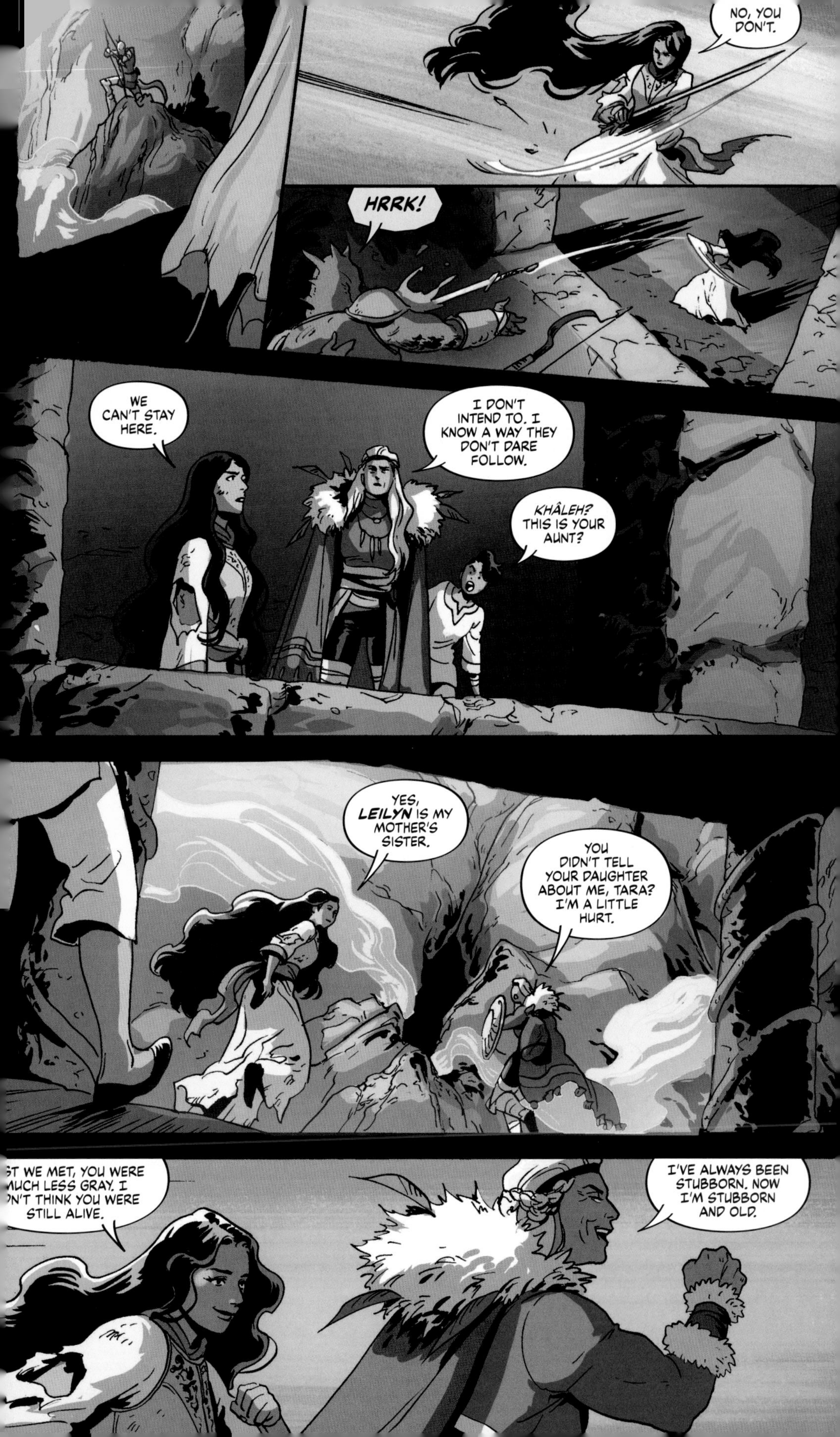

NO, YOU DON'T.
HRRK!
WE CAN'T STAY HERE.
I DON'T INTEND TO. I KNOW A WAY THEY DON'T DARE FOLLOW.
KHÂLEH? THIS IS YOUR AUNT?
YES, **LEILYN** IS MY MOTHER'S SISTER.
YOU DIDN'T TELL YOUR DAUGHTER ABOUT ME, TARA? I'M A LITTLE HURT.
ST WE MET, YOU WERE MUCH LESS GRAY. I N'T THINK YOU WERE STILL ALIVE.
I'VE ALWAYS BEEN STUBBORN. NOW I'M STUBBORN AND OLD.

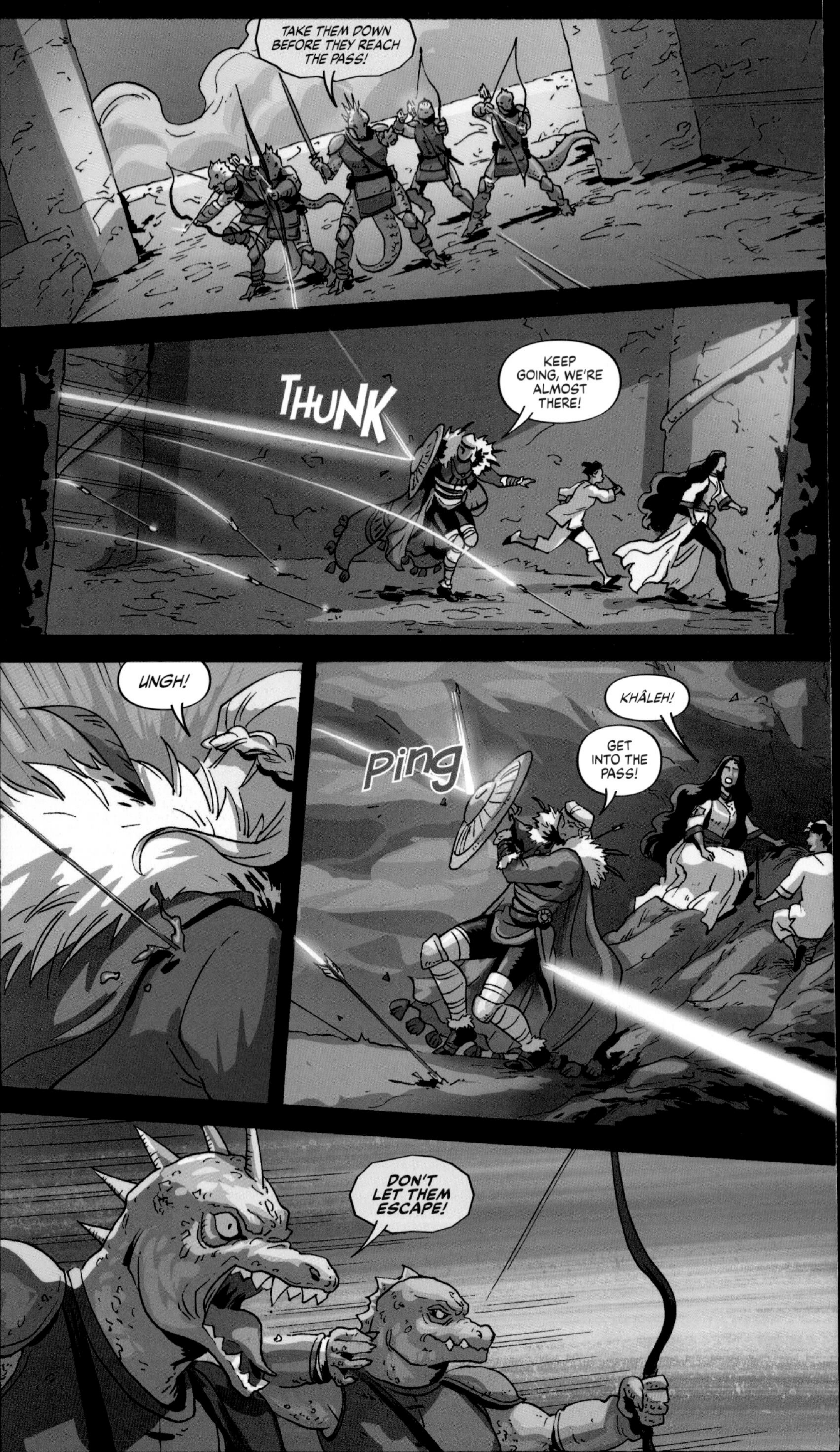
TAKE THEM DOWN BEFORE THEY REACH THE PASS!
THUNK
KEEP GOING, WE'RE ALMOST THERE!
UNGH!
ping
KHÂLEH!
GET INTO THE PASS!
DON'T LET THEM ESCAPE!

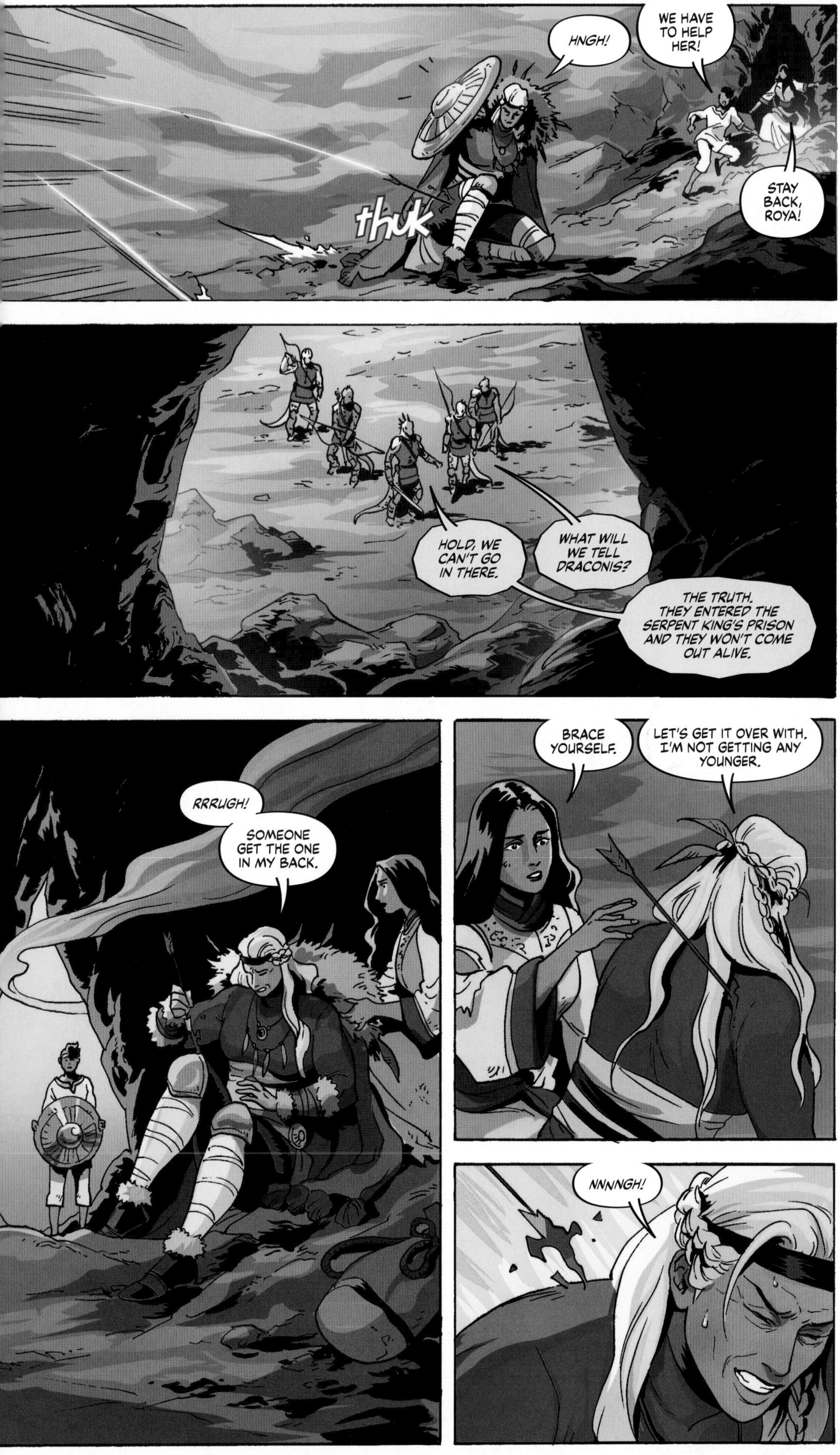
HNGH!
WE HAVE TO HELP HER!
STAY BACK, ROYA!
thuk
HOLD, WE CAN'T GO IN THERE.
WHAT WILL WE TELL DRACONIS?
THE TRUTH. THEY ENTERED THE SERPENT KING'S PRISON AND THEY WON'T COME OUT ALIVE.
RRRUGH!
SOMEONE GET THE ONE IN MY BACK.
BRACE YOURSELF.
LET'S GET IT OVER WITH. I'M NOT GETTING ANY YOUNGER.
NNNNGH!

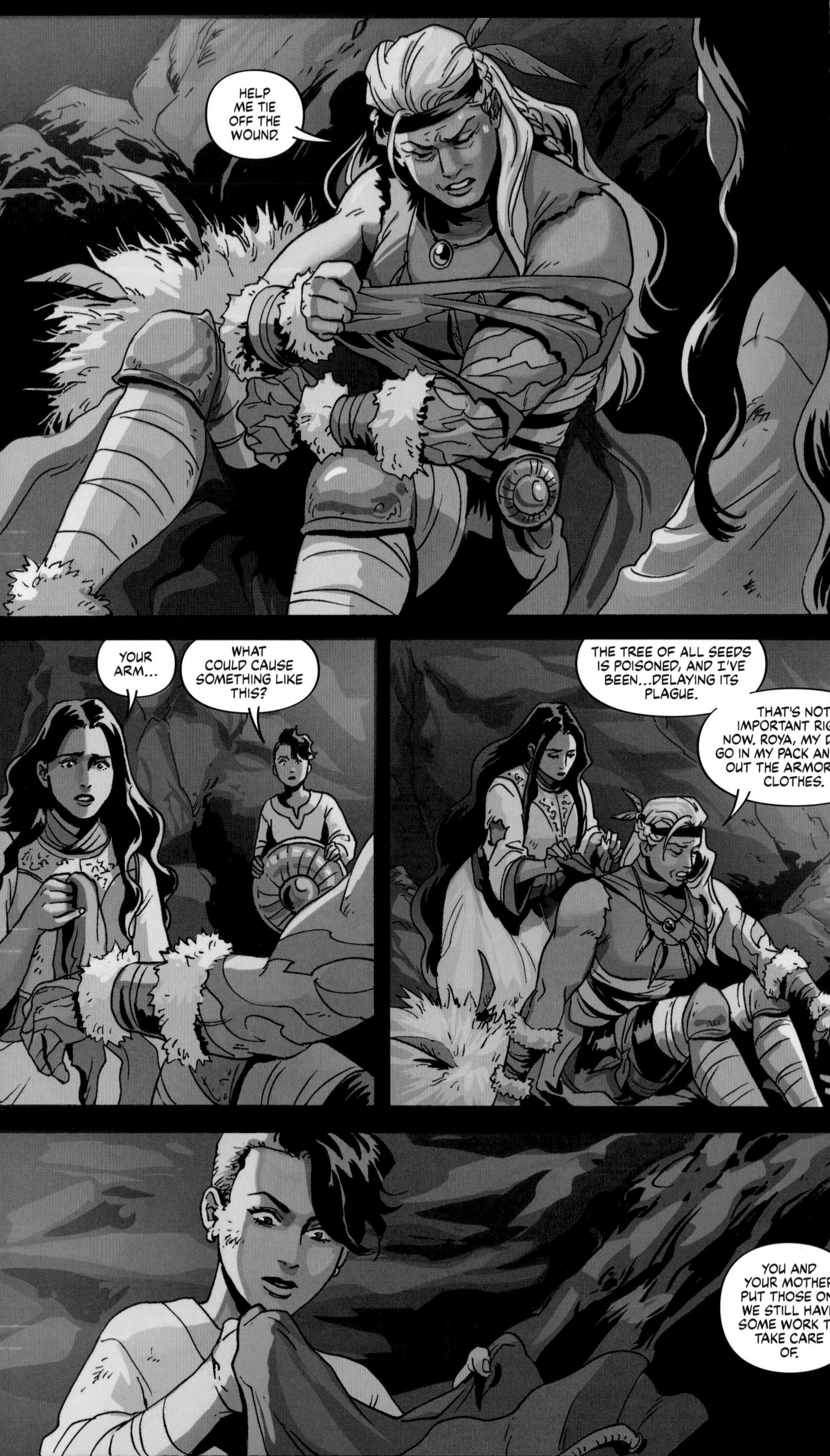
HELP ME TIE OFF THE WOUND.
YOUR ARM...
WHAT COULD CAUSE SOMETHING LIKE THIS?
THE TREE OF ALL SEEDS IS POISONED, AND I'VE BEEN...DELAYING ITS PLAGUE.
THAT'S NOT IMPORTANT RIG NOW. ROYA, MY D GO IN MY PACK AN OUT THE ARMOR CLOTHES.
YOU AND YOUR MOTHER PUT THOSE ON WE STILL HAV SOME WORK T TAKE CARE OF.

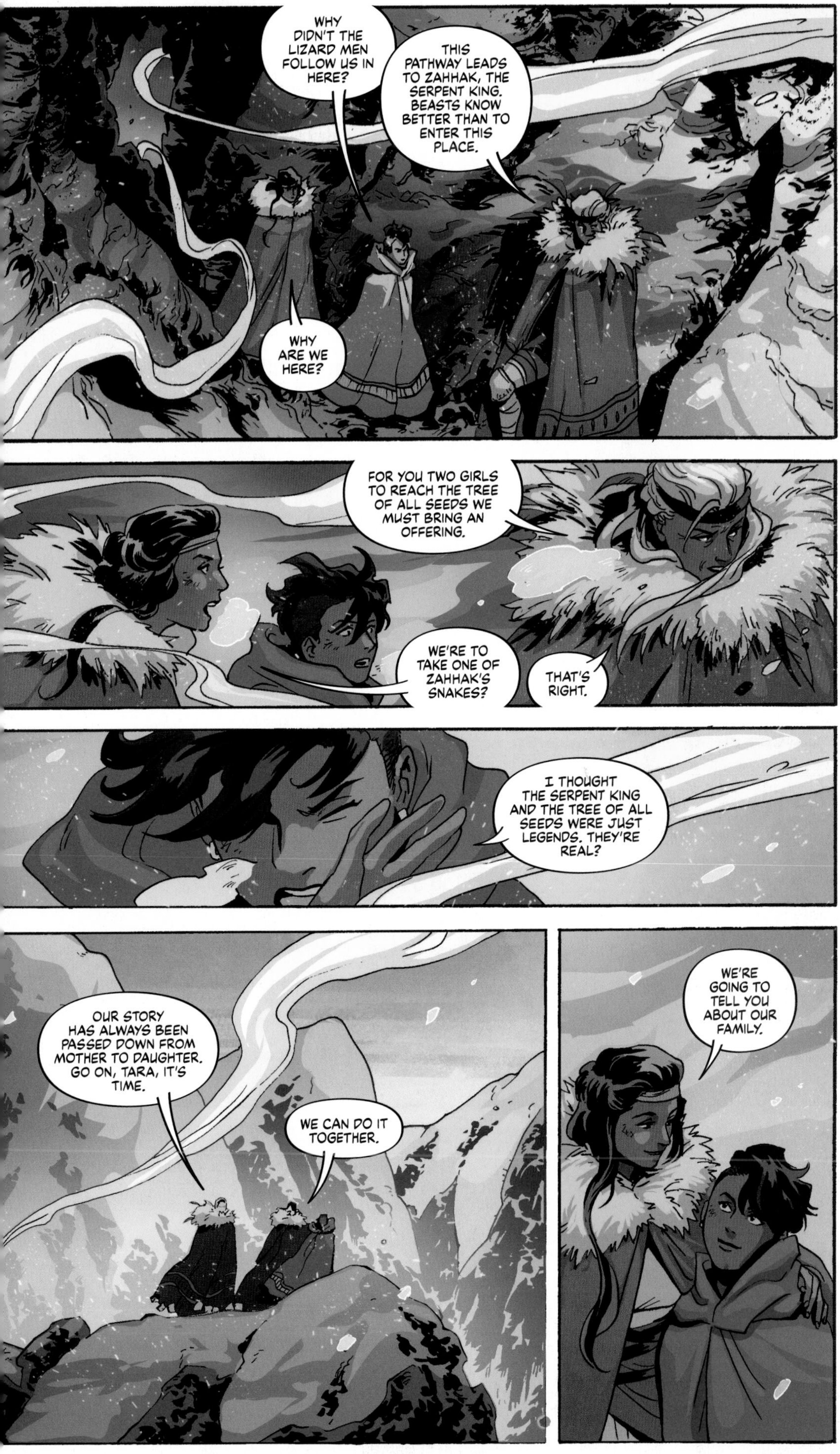
WHY DIDN'T THE LIZARD MEN FOLLOW US IN HERE?
THIS PATHWAY LEADS TO ZAHHAK, THE SERPENT KING. BEASTS KNOW BETTER THAN TO ENTER THIS PLACE.
WHY ARE WE HERE?
FOR YOU TWO GIRLS TO REACH THE TREE OF ALL SEEDS WE MUST BRING AN OFFERING.
WE'RE TO TAKE ONE OF ZAHHAK'S SNAKES?
THAT'S RIGHT.
I THOUGHT THE SERPENT KING AND THE TREE OF ALL SEEDS WERE JUST LEGENDS. THEY'RE REAL?
OUR STORY HAS ALWAYS BEEN PASSED DOWN FROM MOTHER TO DAUGHTER. GO ON, TARA, IT'S TIME.
WE CAN DO IT TOGETHER.
WE'RE GOING TO TELL YOU ABOUT OUR FAMILY.

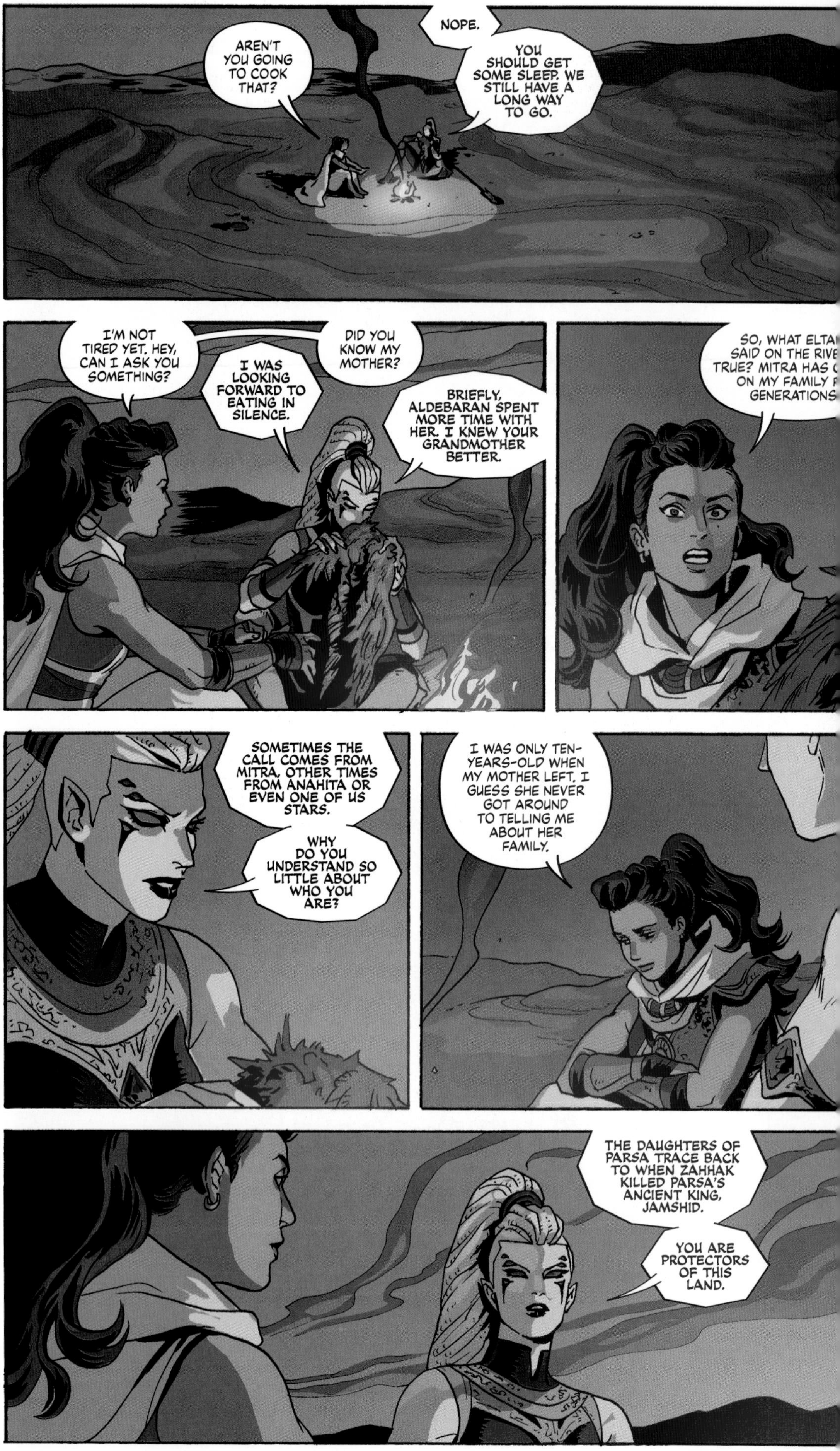
AREN'T YOU GOING TO COOK THAT?
NOPE.
YOU SHOULD GET SOME SLEEP. WE STILL HAVE A LONG WAY TO GO.
I'M NOT TIRED YET. HEY, CAN I ASK YOU SOMETHING?
DID YOU KNOW MY MOTHER?
I WAS LOOKING FORWARD TO EATING IN SILENCE.
BRIEFLY. ALDEBARAN SPENT MORE TIME WITH HER. I KNEW YOUR GRANDMOTHER BETTER.
SO, WHAT ELTA SAID ON THE RIVE TRUE? MITRA HAS ON MY FAMILY GENERATIONS
SOMETIMES THE CALL COMES FROM MITRA. OTHER TIMES FROM ANAHITA OR EVEN ONE OF US STARS.
WHY DO YOU UNDERSTAND SO LITTLE ABOUT WHO YOU ARE?
I WAS ONLY TEN-YEARS-OLD WHEN MY MOTHER LEFT. I GUESS SHE NEVER GOT AROUND TO TELLING ME ABOUT HER FAMILY.
THE DAUGHTERS OF PARSA TRACE BACK TO WHEN ZAHHAK KILLED PARSA'S ANCIENT KING, JAMSHID.
YOU ARE PROTECTORS OF THIS LAND.

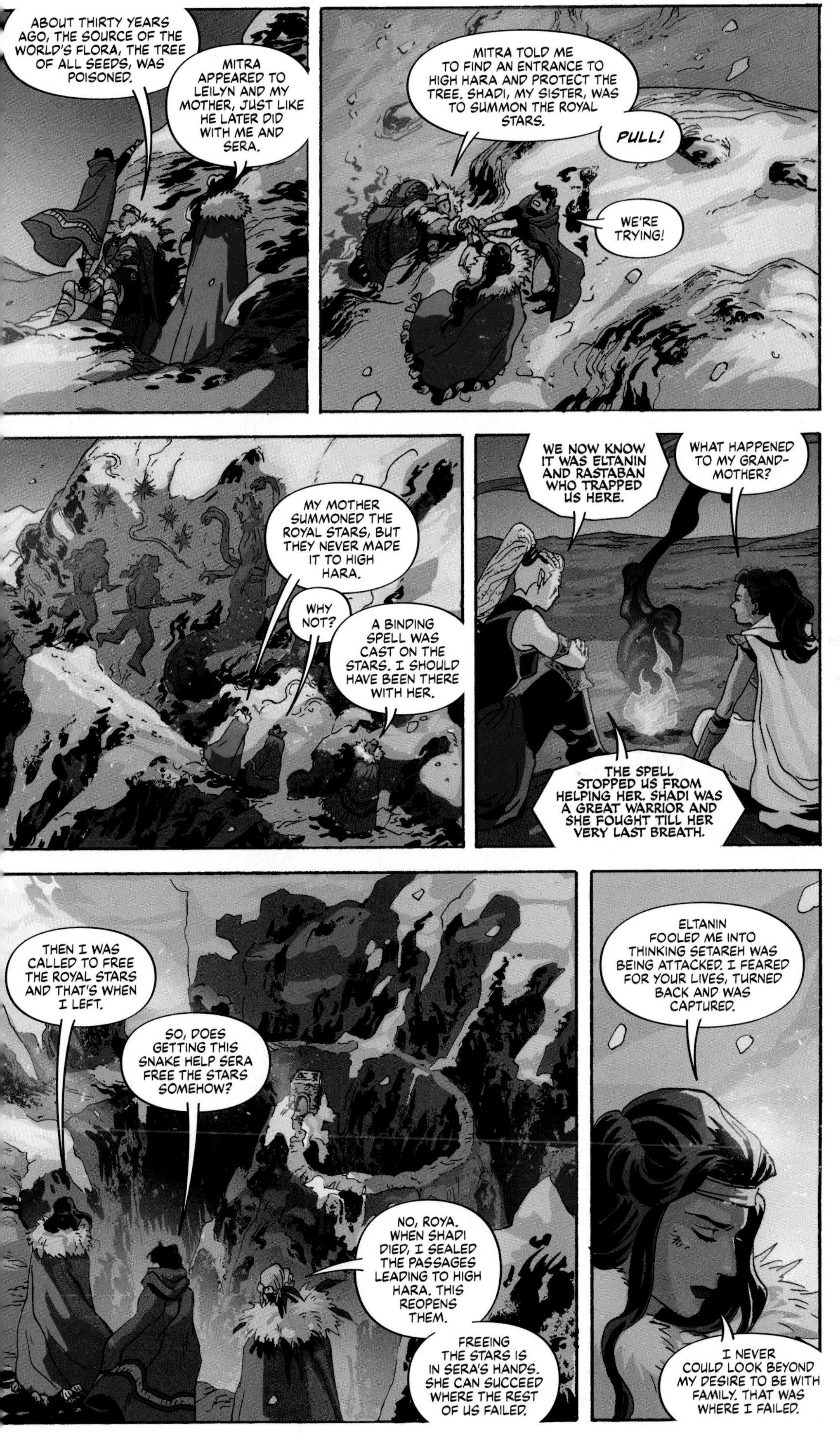
ABOUT THIRTY YEARS AGO, THE SOURCE OF THE WORLD'S FLORA, THE TREE OF ALL SEEDS, WAS POISONED.
MITRA APPEARED TO LEILYN AND MY MOTHER, JUST LIKE HE LATER DID WITH ME AND SERA.
MITRA TOLD ME TO FIND AN ENTRANCE TO HIGH HARA AND PROTECT THE TREE. SHADI, MY SISTER, WAS TO SUMMON THE ROYAL STARS.
PULL!
WE'RE TRYING!
MY MOTHER SUMMONED THE ROYAL STARS, BUT THEY NEVER MADE IT TO HIGH HARA.
WHY NOT?
A BINDING SPELL WAS CAST ON THE STARS. I SHOULD HAVE BEEN THERE WITH HER.
WE NOW KNOW IT WAS ELTANIN AND RASTABAN WHO TRAPPED US HERE.
WHAT HAPPENED TO MY GRAND-MOTHER?
THE SPELL STOPPED US FROM HELPING HER. SHADI WAS A GREAT WARRIOR AND SHE FOUGHT TILL HER VERY LAST BREATH.
THEN I WAS CALLED TO FREE THE ROYAL STARS AND THAT'S WHEN I LEFT.
SO, DOES GETTING THIS SNAKE HELP SERA FREE THE STARS SOMEHOW?
NO, ROYA. WHEN SHADI DIED, I SEALED THE PASSAGES LEADING TO HIGH HARA. THIS REOPENS THEM.
FREEING THE STARS IS IN SERA'S HANDS. SHE CAN SUCCEED WHERE THE REST OF US FAILED.
ELTANIN FOOLED ME INTO THINKING SETAREH WAS BEING ATTACKED. I FEARED FOR YOUR LIVES, TURNED BACK AND WAS CAPTURED.
I NEVER COULD LOOK BEYOND MY DESIRE TO BE WITH FAMILY. THAT WAS WHERE I FAILED.

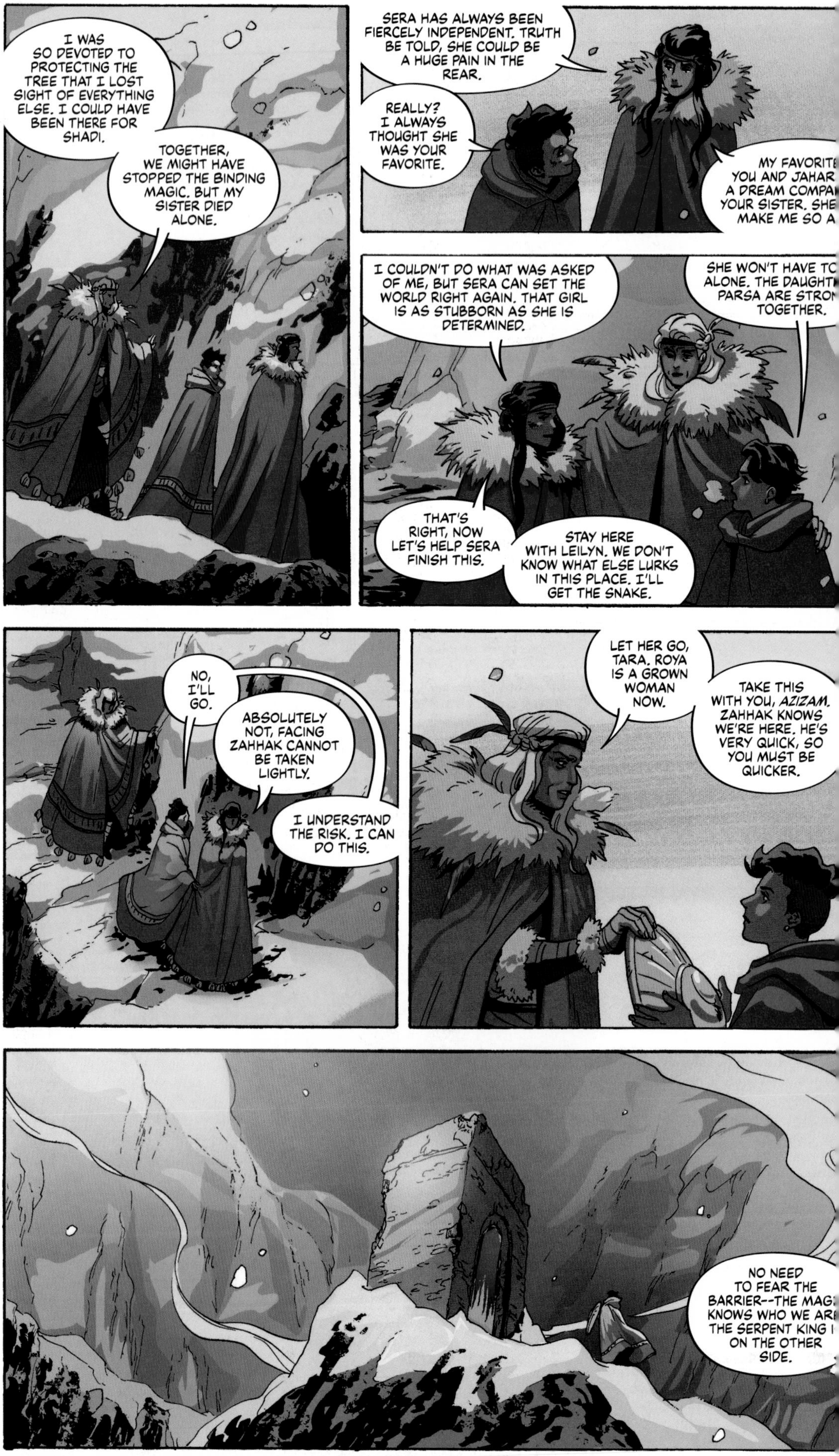
I WAS SO DEVOTED TO PROTECTING THE TREE THAT I LOST SIGHT OF EVERYTHING ELSE. I COULD HAVE BEEN THERE FOR SHADI.
TOGETHER, WE MIGHT HAVE STOPPED THE BINDING MAGIC. BUT MY SISTER DIED ALONE.
SERA HAS ALWAYS BEEN FIERCELY INDEPENDENT. TRUTH BE TOLD, SHE COULD BE A HUGE PAIN IN THE REAR.
REALLY? I ALWAYS THOUGHT SHE WAS YOUR FAVORITE.
MY FAVORITE YOU AND JAHAR A DREAM COMPA YOUR SISTER. SHE MAKE ME SO A
I COULDN'T DO WHAT WAS ASKED OF ME, BUT SERA CAN SET THE WORLD RIGHT AGAIN. THAT GIRL IS AS STUBBORN AS SHE IS DETERMINED.
SHE WON'T HAVE TO ALONE. THE DAUGHT PARSA ARE STRON TOGETHER.
THAT'S RIGHT, NOW LET'S HELP SERA FINISH THIS.
STAY HERE WITH LEILYN. WE DON'T KNOW WHAT ELSE LURKS IN THIS PLACE. I'LL GET THE SNAKE.
NO, I'LL GO.
ABSOLUTELY NOT, FACING ZAHHAK CANNOT BE TAKEN LIGHTLY.
I UNDERSTAND THE RISK. I CAN DO THIS.
LET HER GO, TARA. ROYA IS A GROWN WOMAN NOW.
TAKE THIS WITH YOU, *AZIZAM.* ZAHHAK KNOWS WE'RE HERE. HE'S VERY QUICK, SO YOU MUST BE QUICKER.
NO NEED TO FEAR THE BARRIER--THE MAG KNOWS WHO WE AR THE SERPENT KING I ON THE OTHER SIDE.

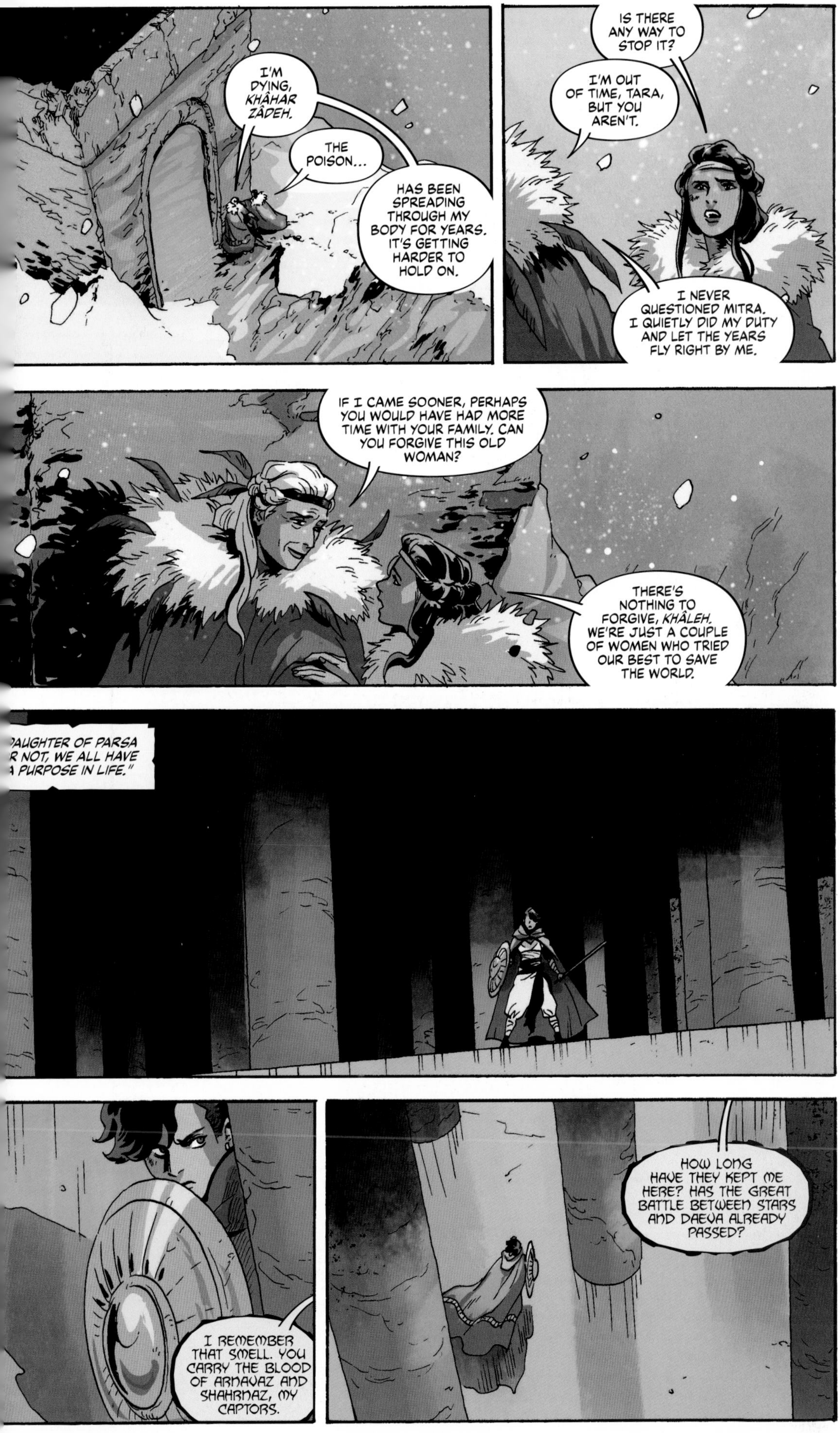
I'M DYING, *KHÂHAR ZÂDEH.*
THE POISON...
HAS BEEN SPREADING THROUGH MY BODY FOR YEARS. IT'S GETTING HARDER TO HOLD ON.
IS THERE ANY WAY TO STOP IT?
I'M OUT OF TIME, TARA, BUT YOU AREN'T.
I NEVER QUESTIONED MITRA. I QUIETLY DID MY DUTY AND LET THE YEARS FLY RIGHT BY ME.
IF I CAME SOONER, PERHAPS YOU WOULD HAVE HAD MORE TIME WITH YOUR FAMILY. CAN YOU FORGIVE THIS OLD WOMAN?
THERE'S NOTHING TO FORGIVE, *KHÂLEH.* WE'RE JUST A COUPLE OF WOMEN WHO TRIED OUR BEST TO SAVE THE WORLD.
DAUGHTER OF PARSA R NOT, WE ALL HAVE A PURPOSE IN LIFE."
I REMEMBER THAT SMELL. YOU CARRY THE BLOOD OF ARNAVAZ AND SHAHRNAZ, MY CAPTORS.
HOW LONG HAVE THEY KEPT ME HERE? HAS THE GREAT BATTLE BETWEEN STARS AND DAEVA ALREADY PASSED?

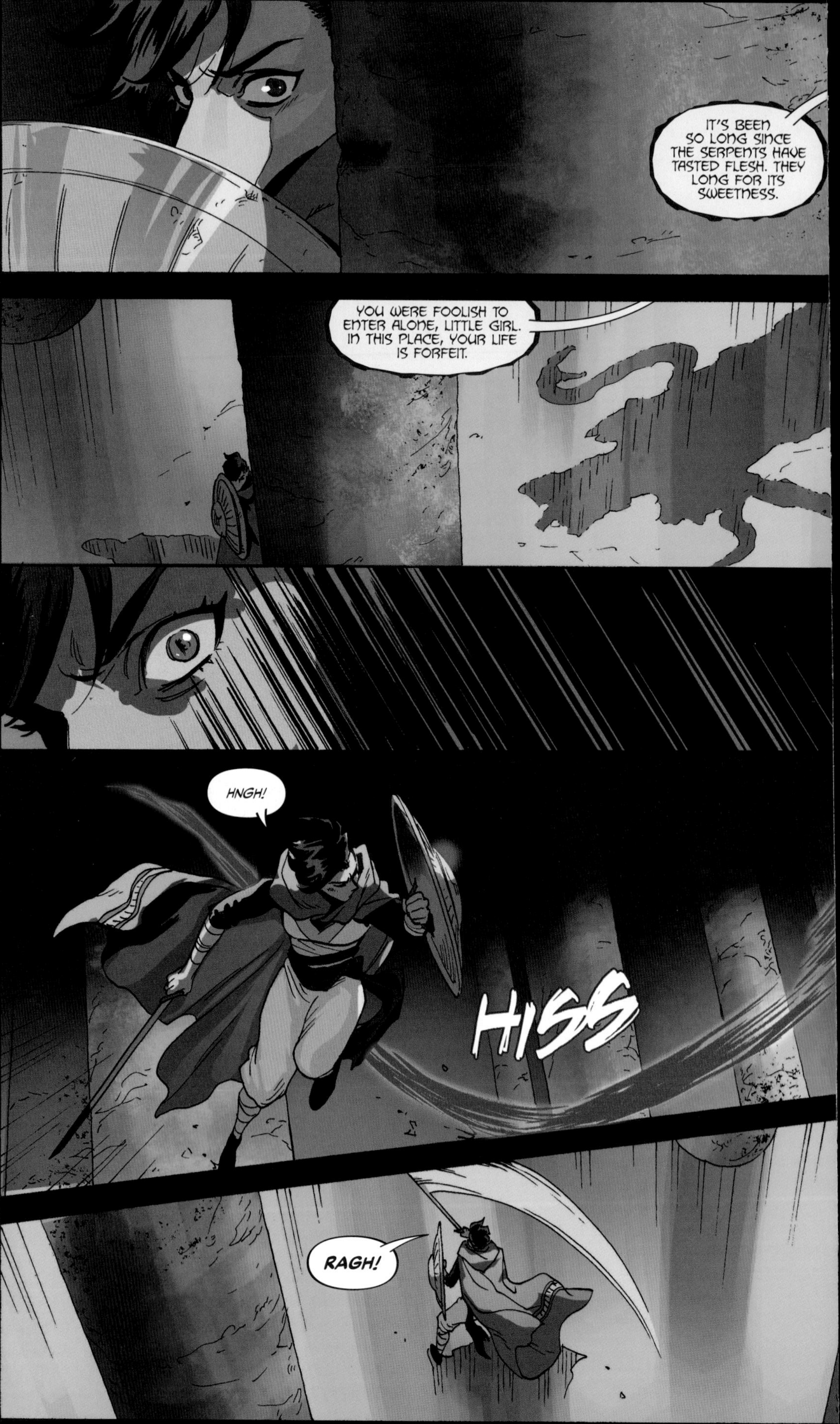
IT'S BEEN SO LONG SINCE THE SERPENTS HAVE TASTED FLESH. THEY LONG FOR ITS SWEETNESS.
YOU WERE FOOLISH TO ENTER ALONE, LITTLE GIRL. IN THIS PLACE, YOUR LIFE IS FORFEIT.
HNGH!
HISS
RAGH!

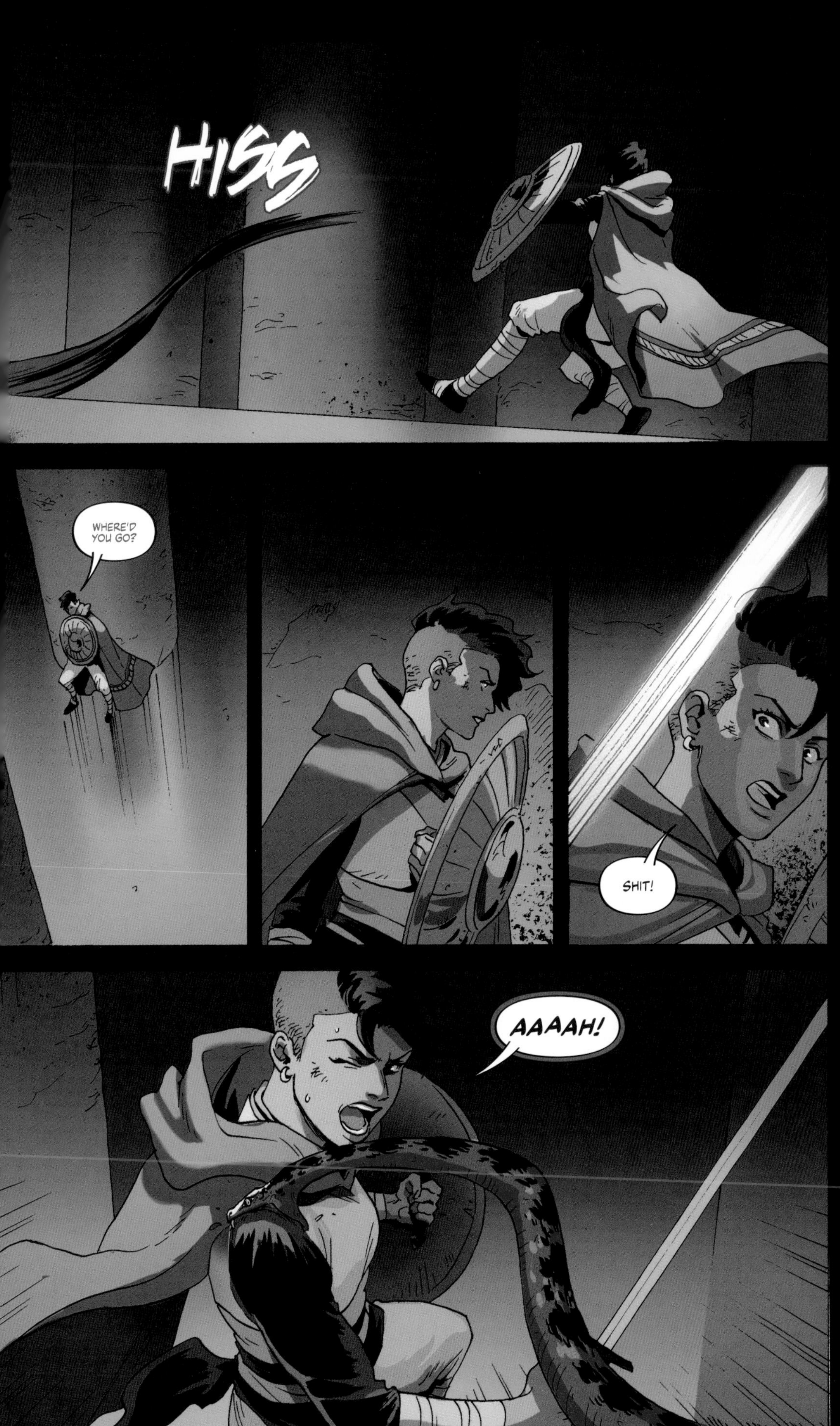
HISS
WHERE'D YOU GO?
SHIT!
AAAAH!

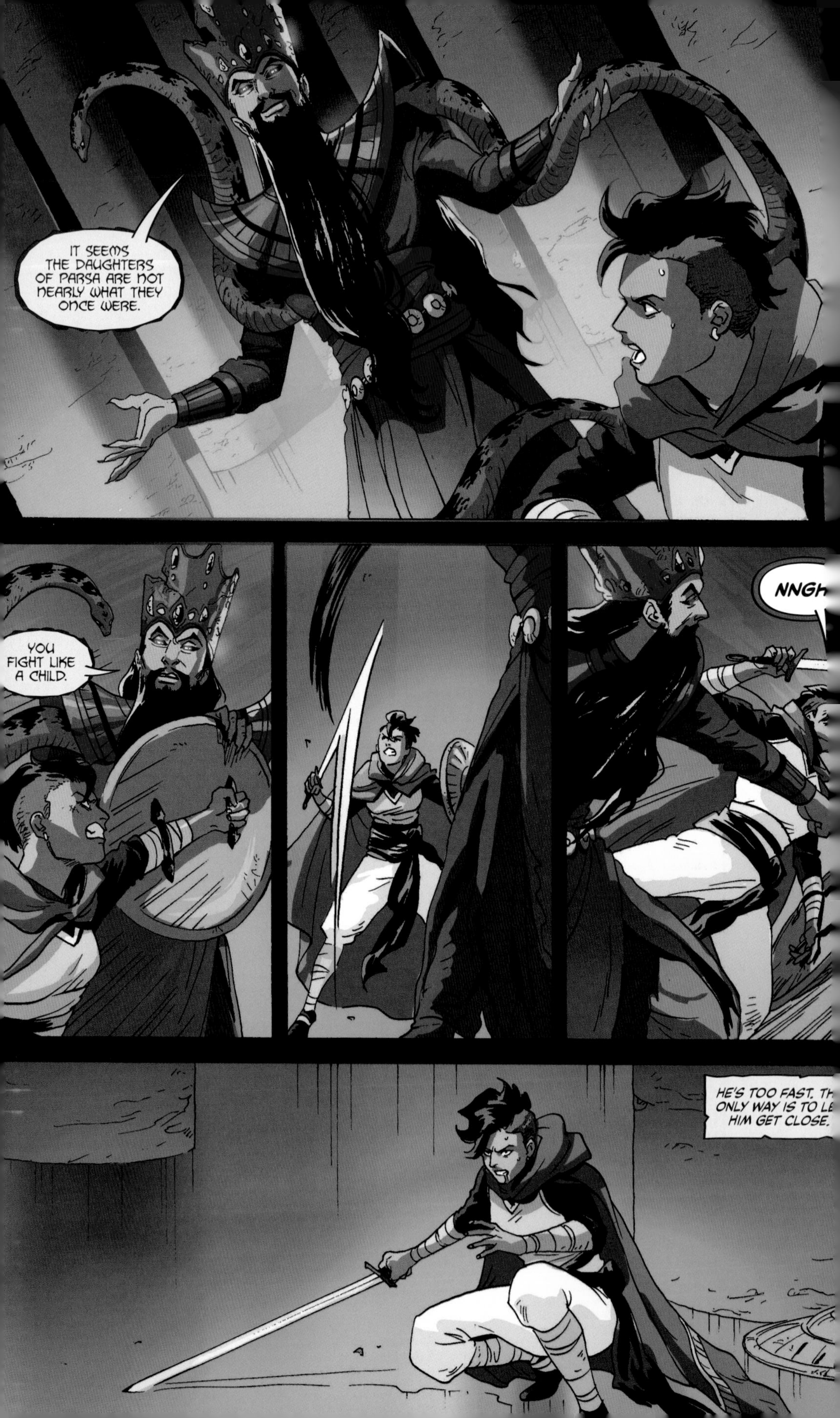
IT SEEMS THE DAUGHTERS OF PARSA ARE NOT NEARLY WHAT THEY ONCE WERE.
YOU FIGHT LIKE A CHILD.
NNGH
HE'S TOO FAST. TH ONLY WAY IS TO LE HIM GET CLOSE.

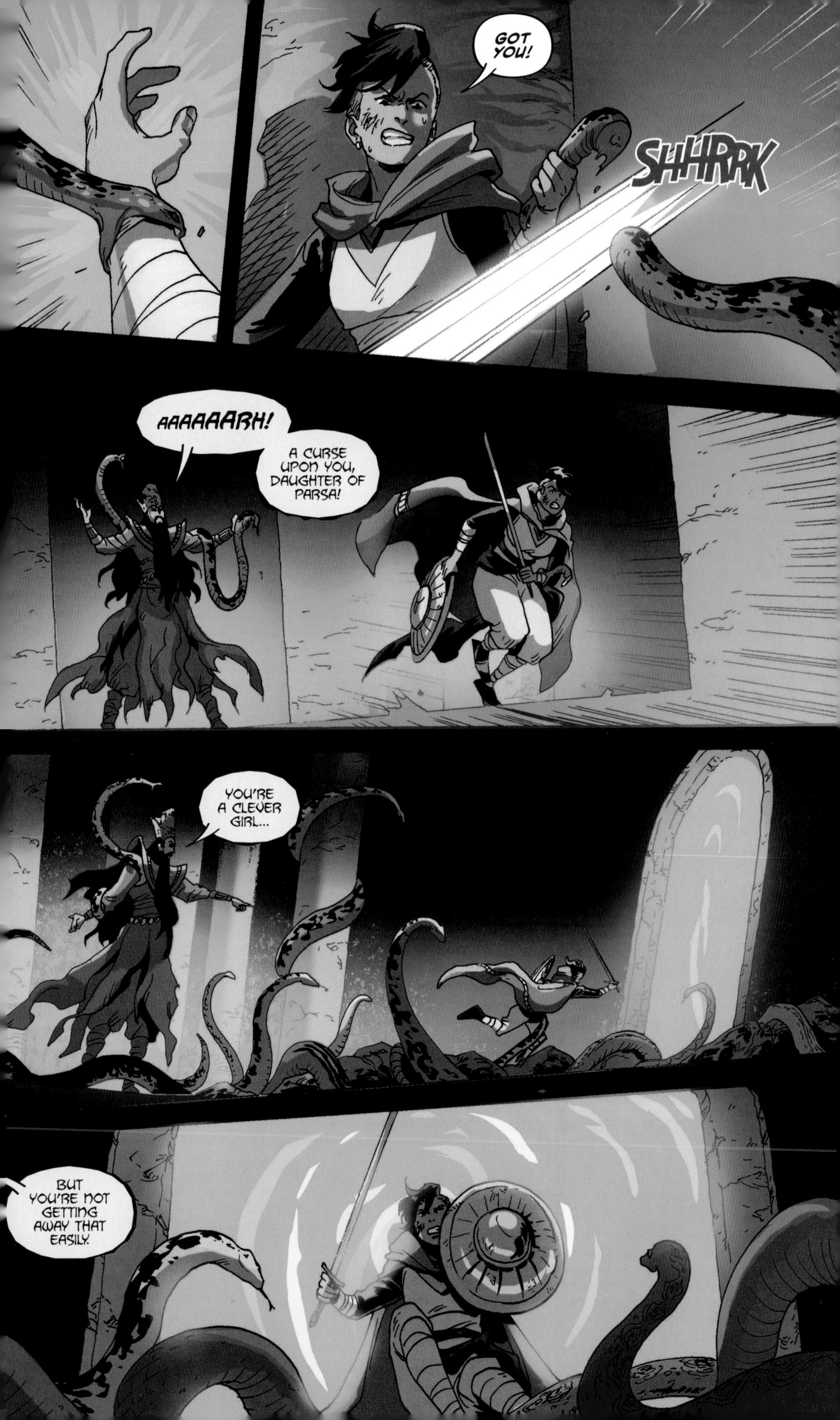

GOT YOU!
SHHRRK
AAAAAARH!
A CURSE UPON YOU, DAUGHTER OF PARSA!
YOU'RE A CLEVER GIRL...
BUT YOU'RE NOT GETTING AWAY THAT EASILY.

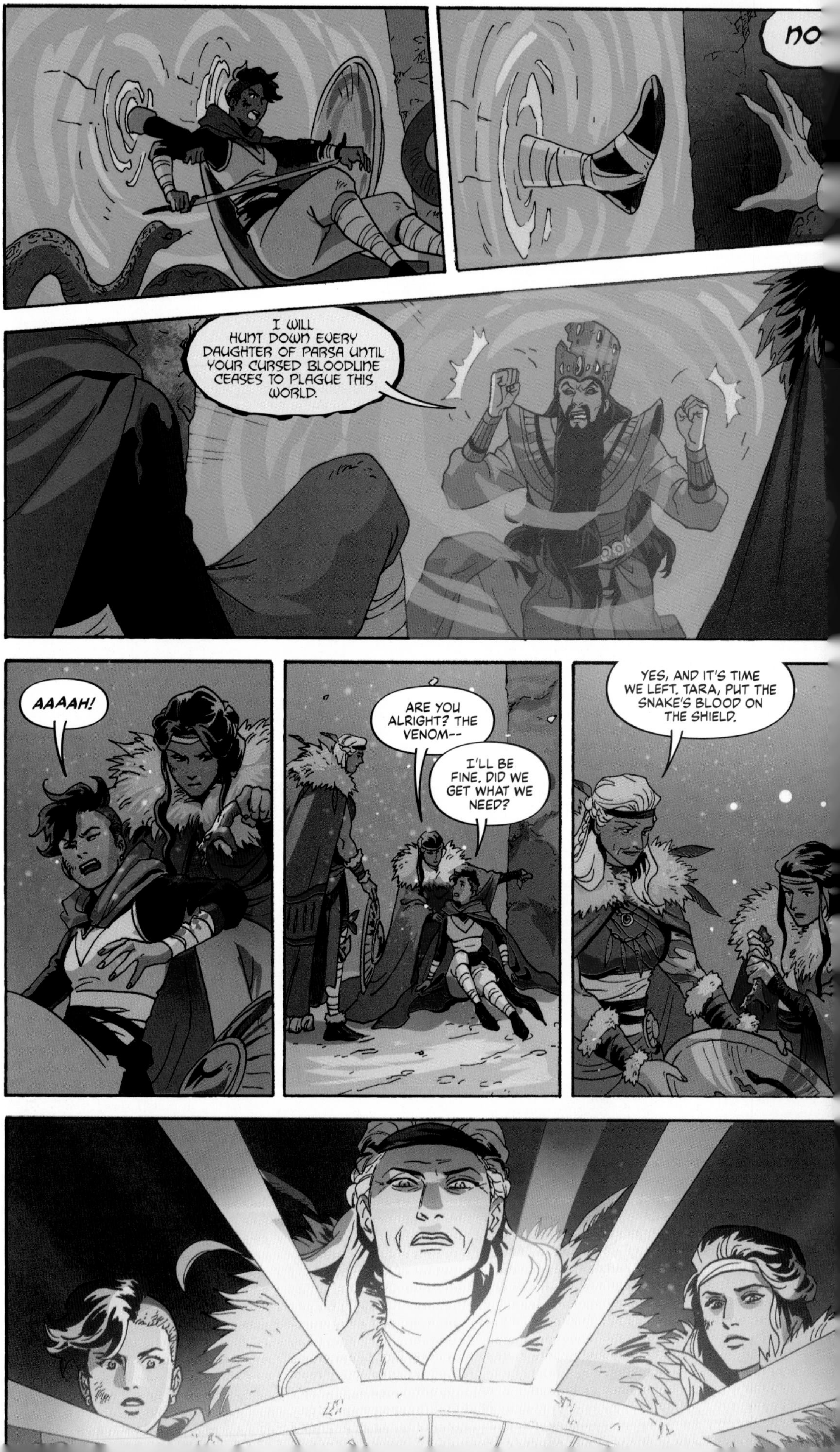
no
I WILL HUNT DOWN EVERY DAUGHTER OF PARSA UNTIL YOUR CURSED BLOODLINE CEASES TO PLAGUE THIS WORLD.
AAAAH!
ARE YOU ALRIGHT? THE VENOM--
I'LL BE FINE. DID WE GET WHAT WE NEED?
YES, AND IT'S TIME WE LEFT. TARA, PUT THE SNAKE'S BLOOD ON THE SHIELD.

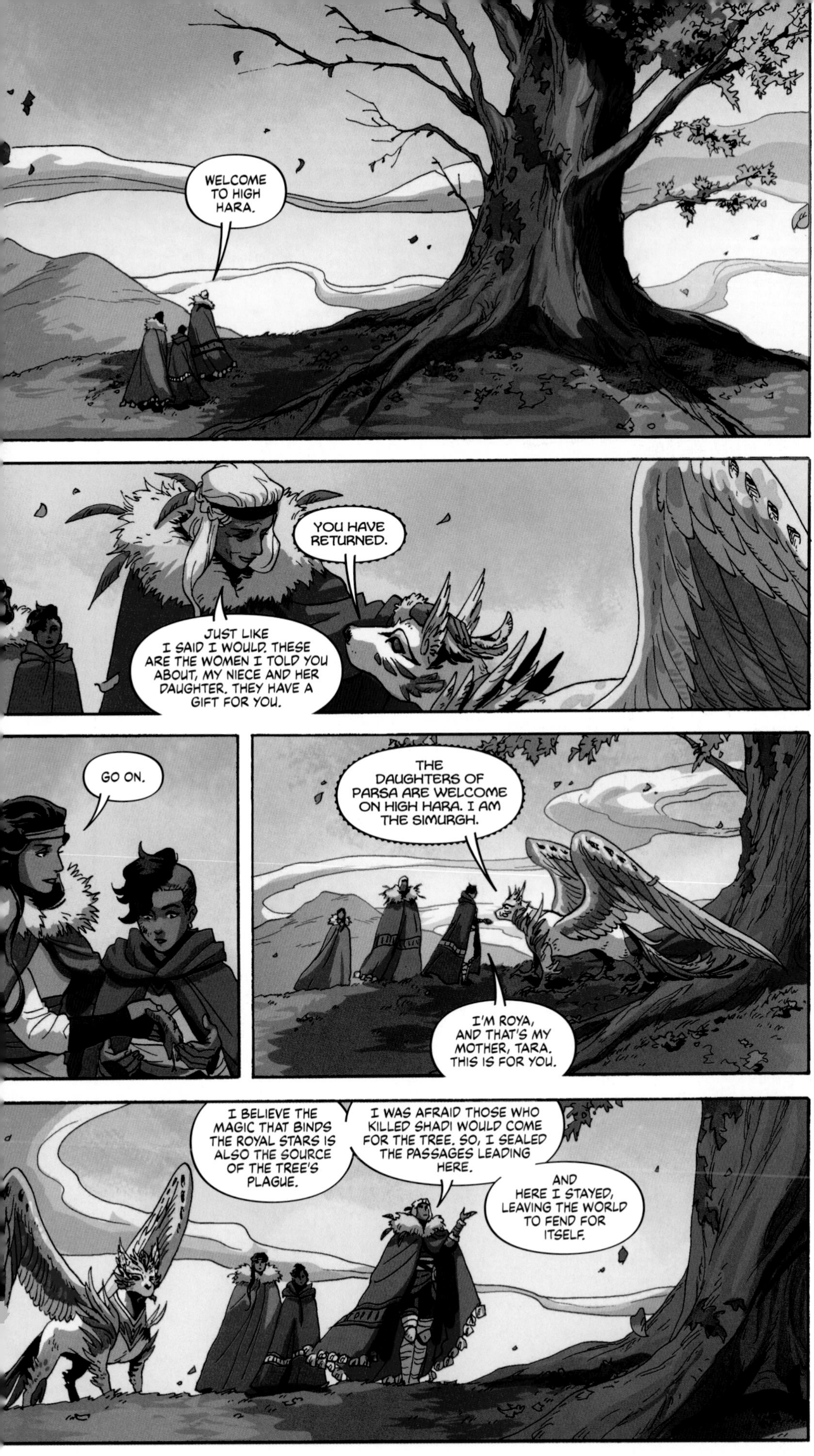
WELCOME TO HIGH HARA.
YOU HAVE RETURNED.
JUST LIKE I SAID I WOULD. THESE ARE THE WOMEN I TOLD YOU ABOUT, MY NIECE AND HER DAUGHTER. THEY HAVE A GIFT FOR YOU.
GO ON.
THE DAUGHTERS OF PARSA ARE WELCOME ON HIGH HARA. I AM THE SIMURGH.
I'M ROYA, AND THAT'S MY MOTHER, TARA. THIS IS FOR YOU.
I BELIEVE THE MAGIC THAT BINDS THE ROYAL STARS IS ALSO THE SOURCE OF THE TREE'S PLAGUE.
I WAS AFRAID THOSE WHO KILLED SHADI WOULD COME FOR THE TREE. SO, I SEALED THE PASSAGES LEADING HERE.
AND HERE I STAYED, LEAVING THE WORLD TO FEND FOR ITSELF.

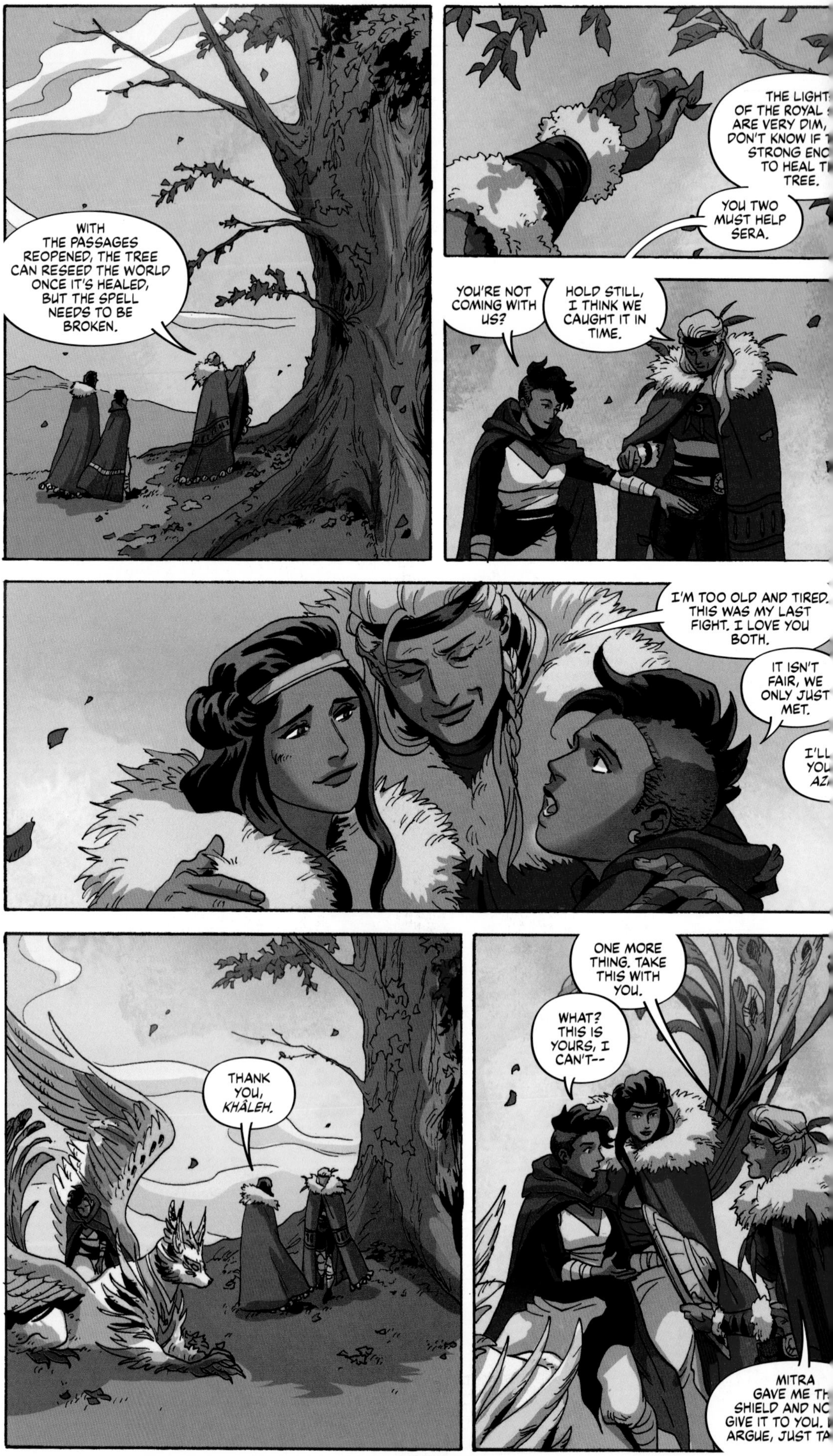

WITH THE PASSAGES REOPENED, THE TREE CAN RESEED THE WORLD ONCE IT'S HEALED, BUT THE SPELL NEEDS TO BE BROKEN.
THE LIGHT OF THE ROYAL ARE VERY DIM, DON'T KNOW IF STRONG ENC TO HEAL T TREE.
YOU TWO MUST HELP SERA.
YOU'RE NOT COMING WITH US?
HOLD STILL, I THINK WE CAUGHT IT IN TIME.
I'M TOO OLD AND TIRED. THIS WAS MY LAST FIGHT. I LOVE YOU BOTH.
IT ISN'T FAIR, WE ONLY JUST MET.
I'LL YOU
THANK YOU, KHÂLEH.
ONE MORE THING. TAKE THIS WITH YOU.
WHAT? THIS IS YOURS, I CAN'T--
MITRA GAVE ME TH SHIELD AND NO GIVE IT TO YOU. ARGUE, JUST TA

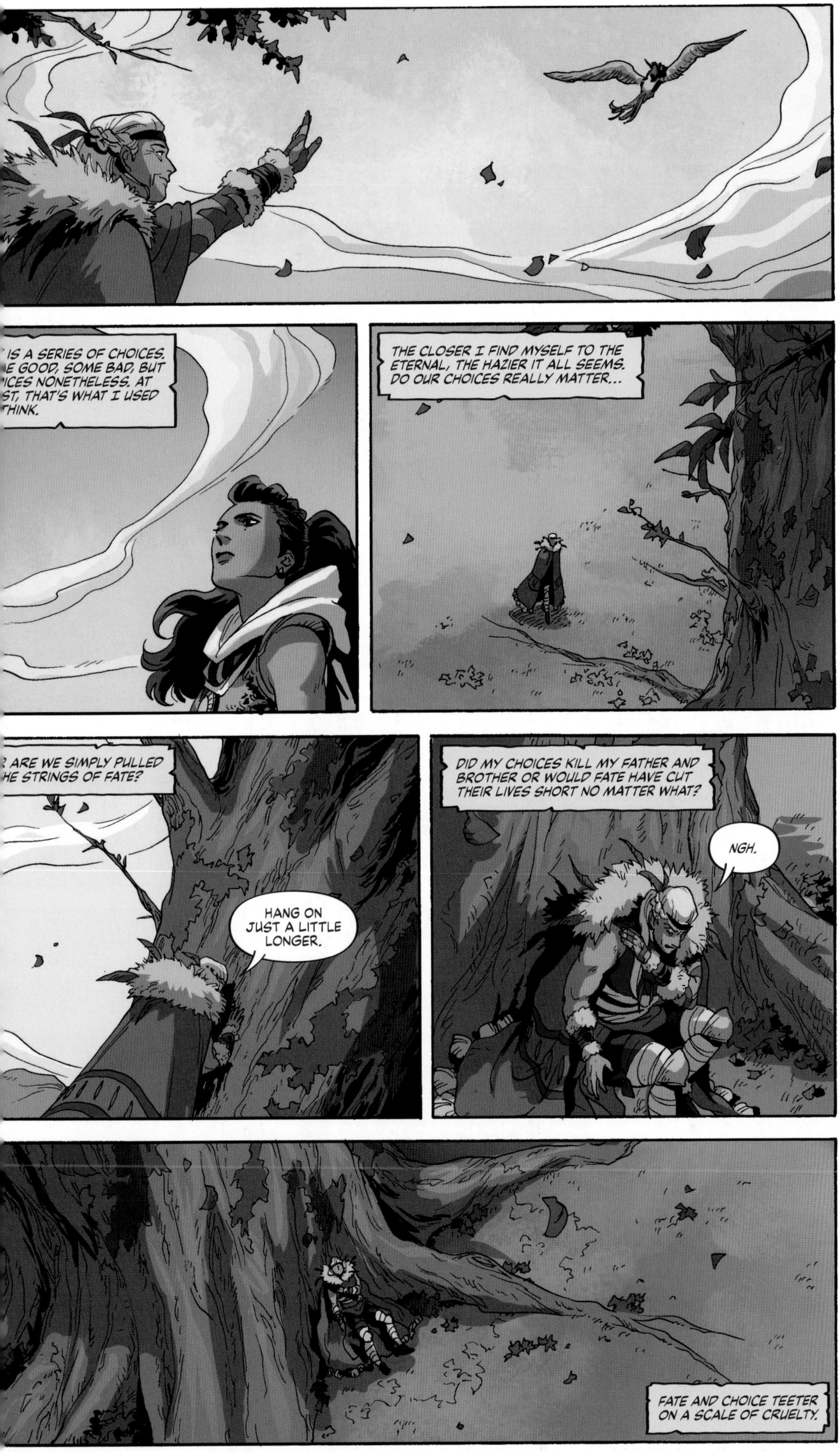
IS A SERIES OF CHOICES. E GOOD, SOME BAD, BUT ICES NONETHELESS. AT ST, THAT'S WHAT I USED THINK.
THE CLOSER I FIND MYSELF TO THE ETERNAL, THE HAZIER IT ALL SEEMS. DO OUR CHOICES REALLY MATTER...
ARE WE SIMPLY PULLED HE STRINGS OF FATE?
HANG ON JUST A LITTLE LONGER.
DID MY CHOICES KILL MY FATHER AND BROTHER OR WOULD FATE HAVE CUT THEIR LIVES SHORT NO MATTER WHAT?
NGH.
FATE AND CHOICE TEETER ON A SCALE OF CRUELTY.

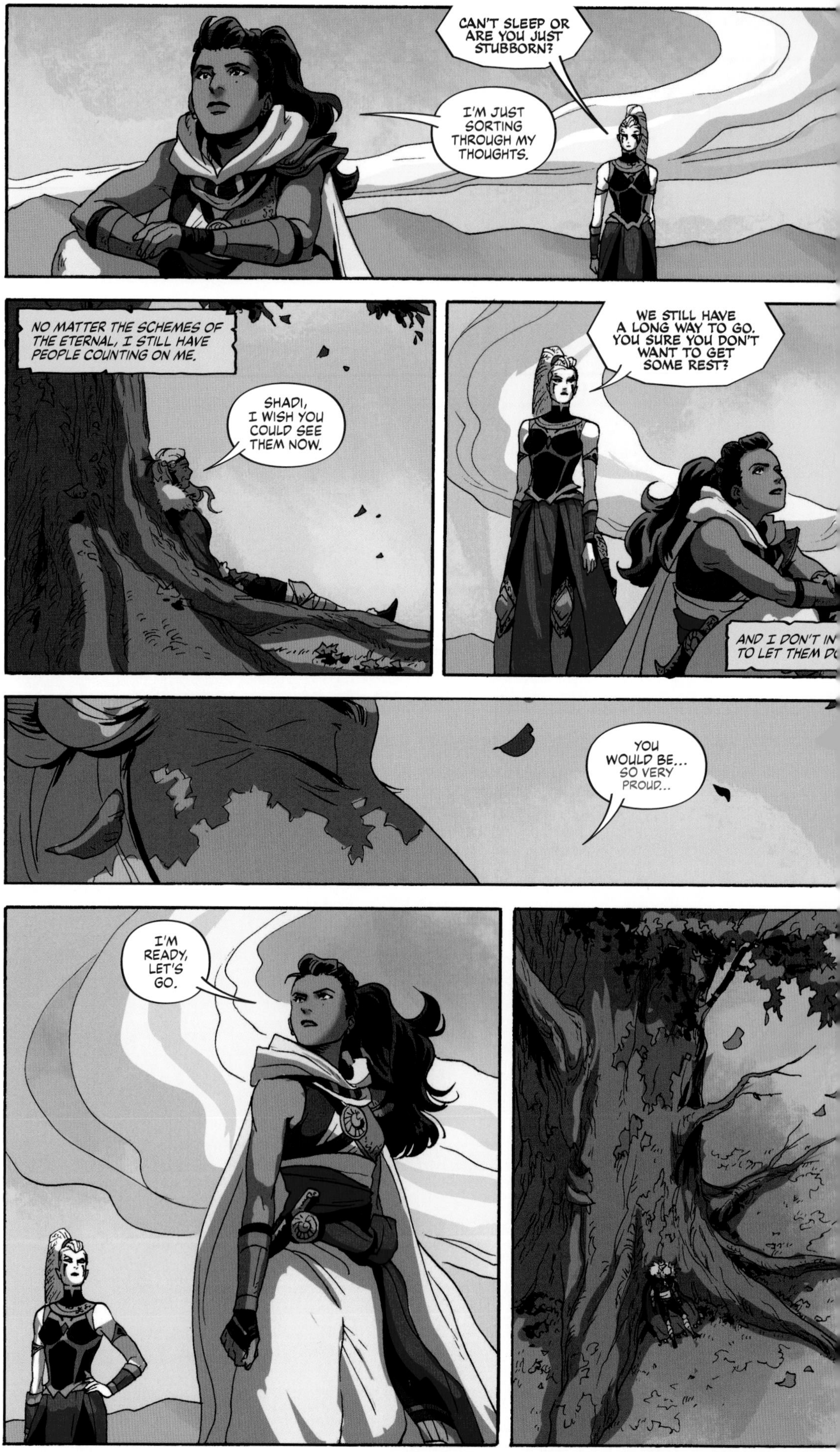
CAN'T SLEEP OR ARE YOU JUST STUBBORN?
I'M JUST SORTING THROUGH MY THOUGHTS.
NO MATTER THE SCHEMES OF THE ETERNAL, I STILL HAVE PEOPLE COUNTING ON ME.
SHADI, I WISH YOU COULD SEE THEM NOW.
WE STILL HAVE A LONG WAY TO GO. YOU SURE YOU DON'T WANT TO GET SOME REST?
AND I DON'T IN
TO LET THEM DO
YOU WOULD BE... SO VERY PROUD...
I'M READY, LET'S GO.

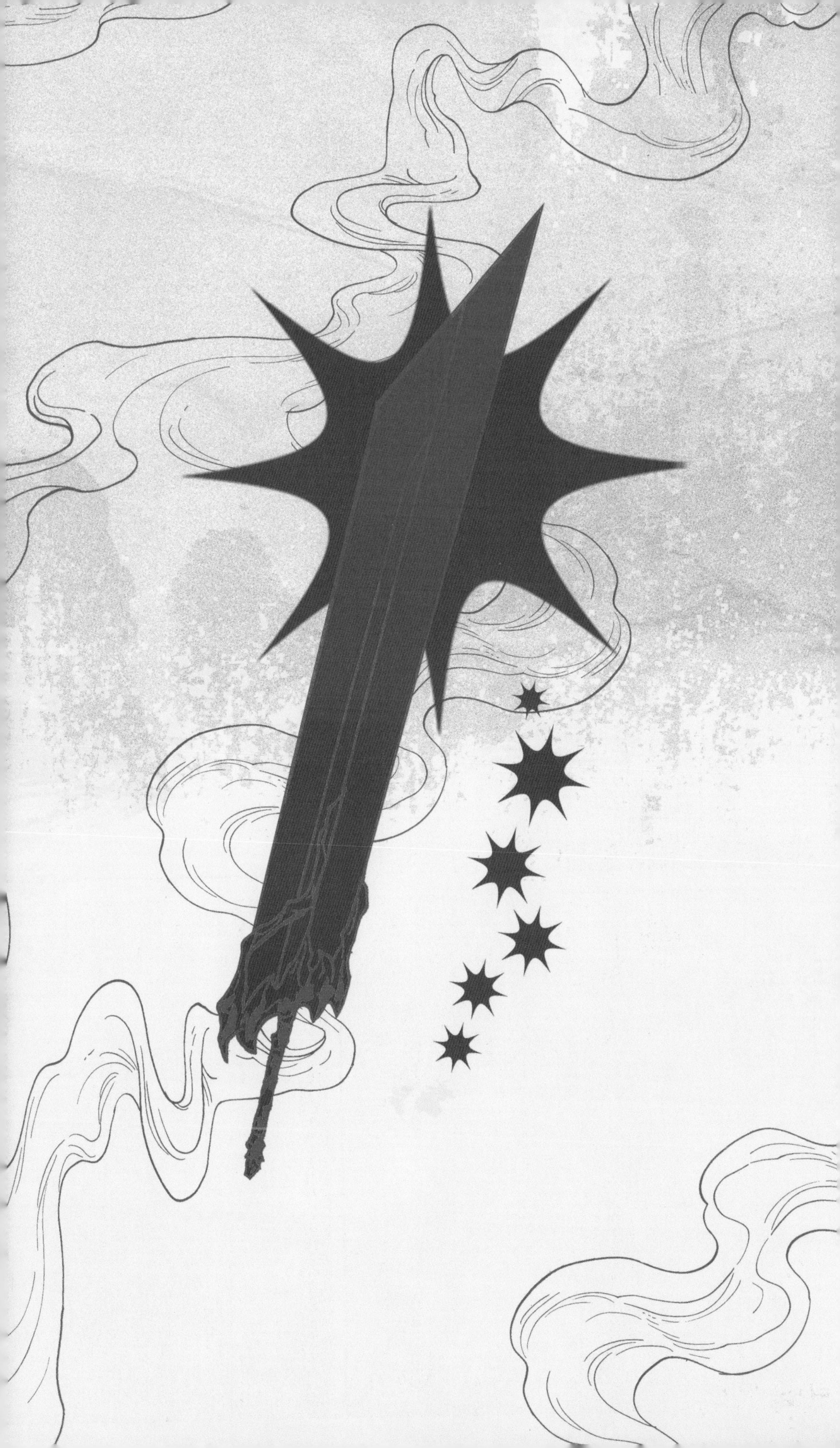

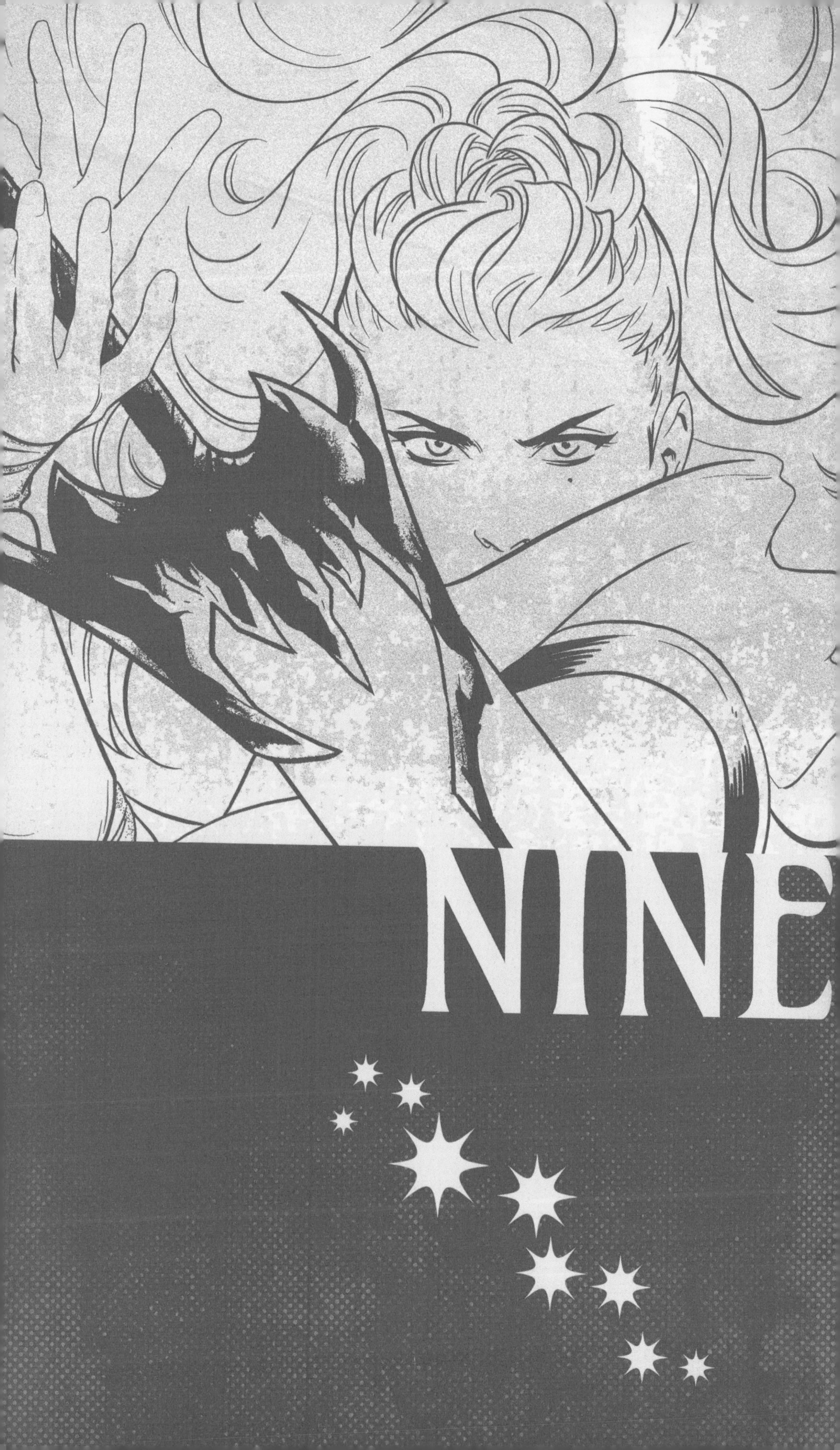

NINE

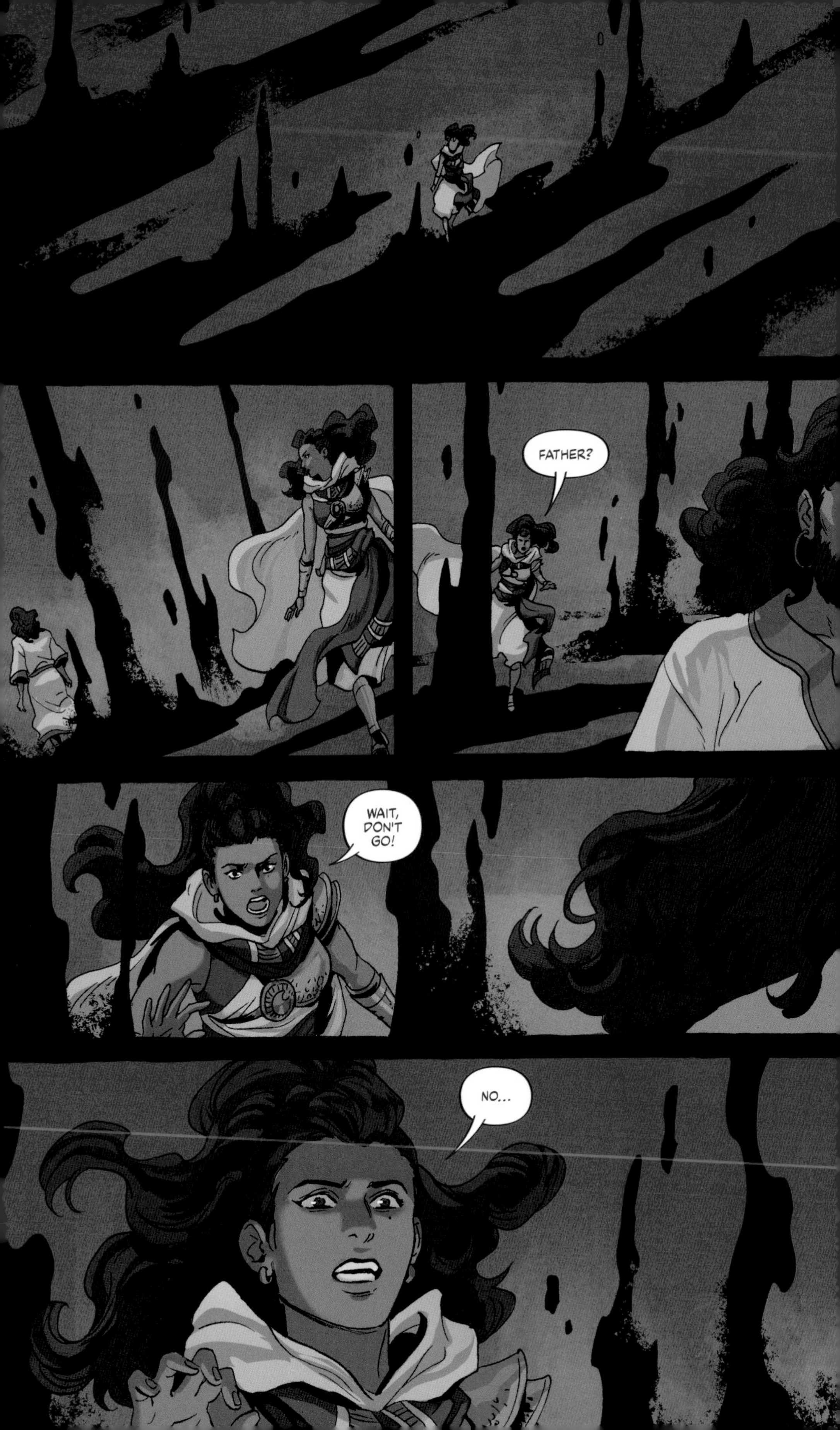
FATHER?
WAIT, DON'T GO!
NO...

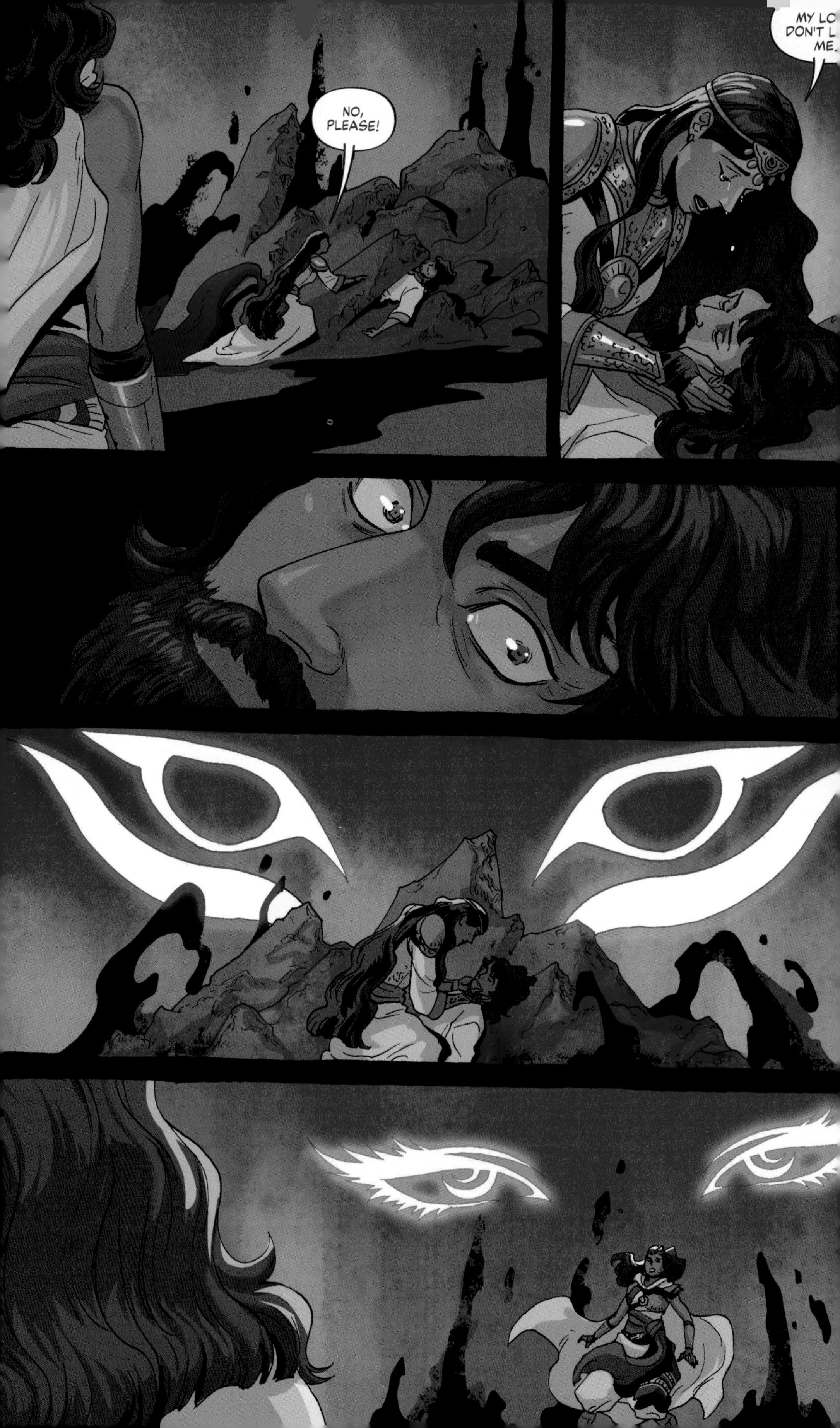
NO, PLEASE!
MY LO DON'T L ME.

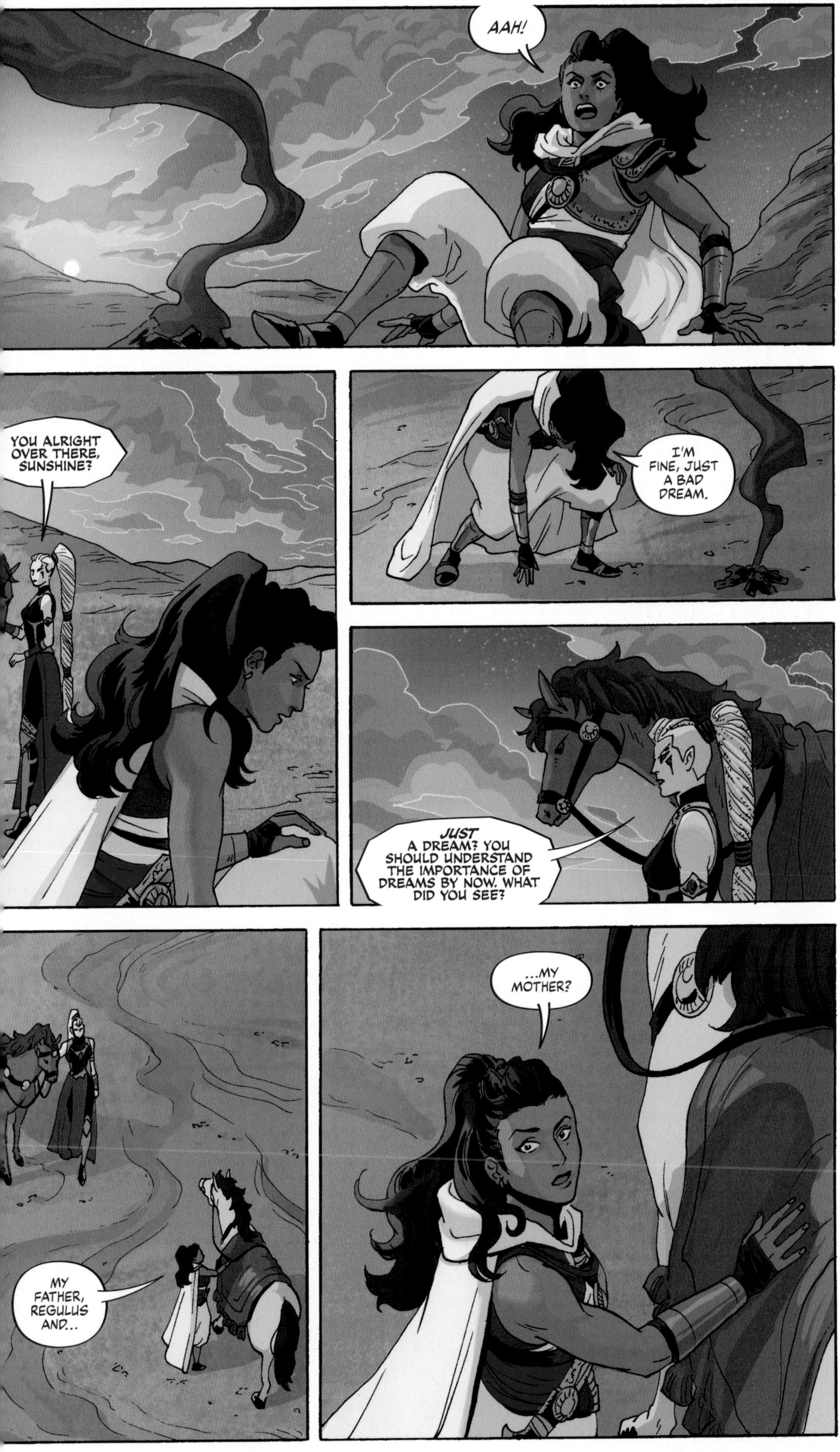
AAH!
YOU ALRIGHT OVER THERE, SUNSHINE?
I'M FINE, JUST A BAD DREAM.
JUST A DREAM? YOU SHOULD UNDERSTAND THE IMPORTANCE OF DREAMS BY NOW. WHAT DID YOU SEE?
MY FATHER, REGULUS AND...
...MY MOTHER?

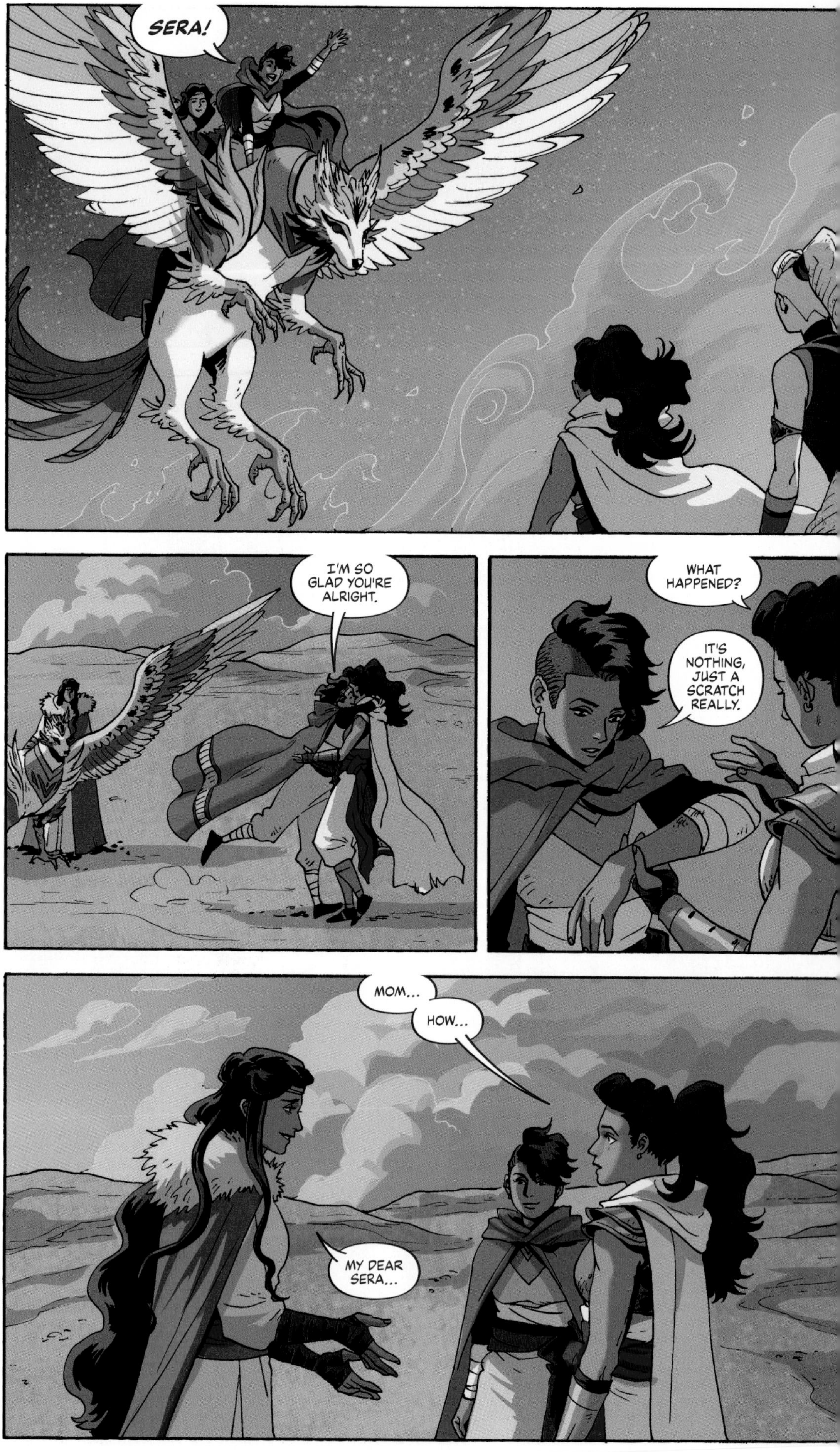
SERA!
I'M SO GLAD YOU'RE ALRIGHT.
WHAT HAPPENED?
IT'S NOTHING, JUST A SCRATCH REALLY.
MOM...
HOW...
MY DEAR SERA...

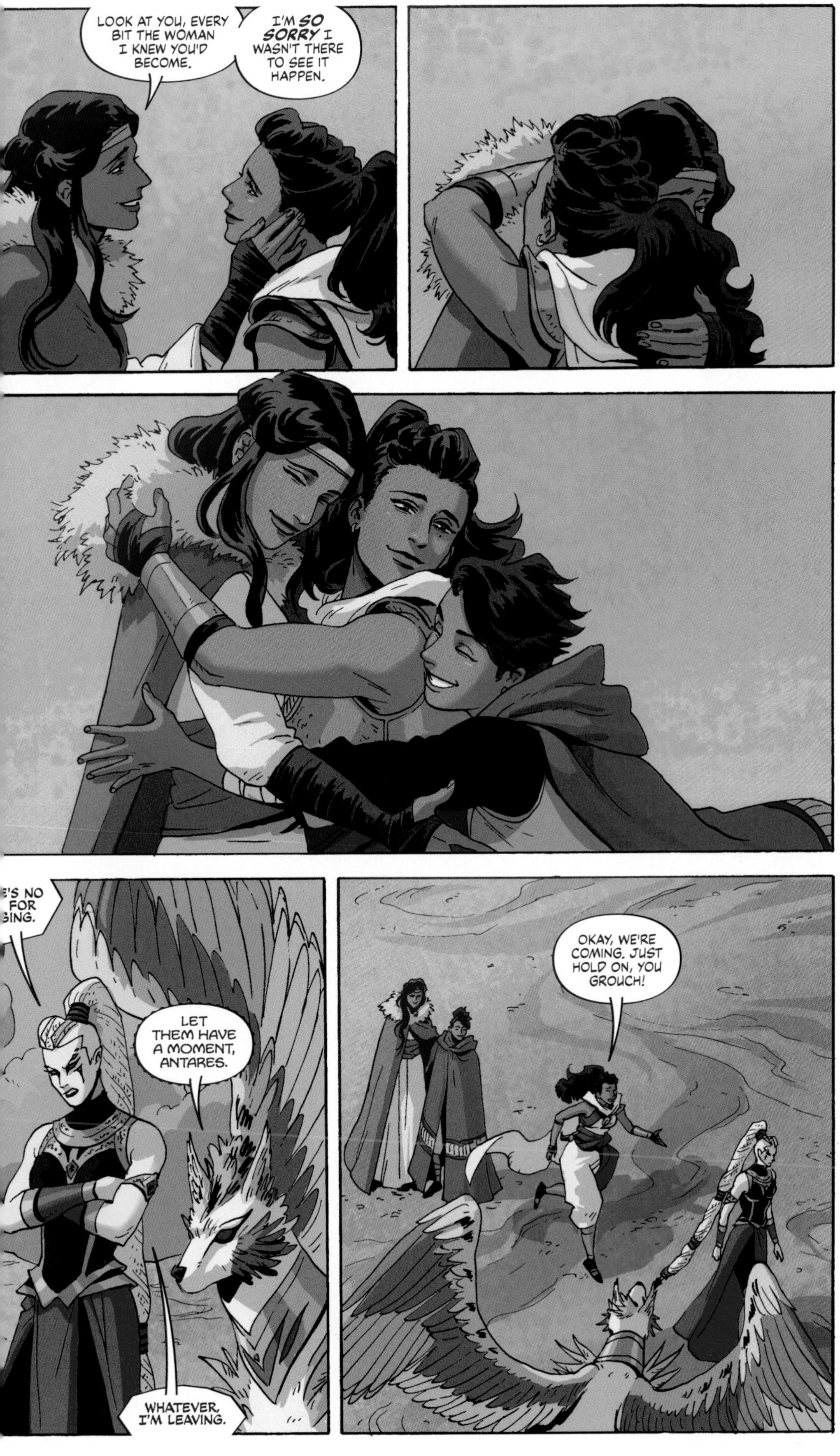
LOOK AT YOU, EVERY BIT THE WOMAN I KNEW YOU'D BECOME.
I'M SO SORRY I WASN'T THERE TO SEE IT HAPPEN.
E'S NO FOR GING.
LET THEM HAVE A MOMENT, ANTARES.
WHATEVER, I'M LEAVING.
OKAY, WE'RE COMING. JUST HOLD ON, YOU GROUCH!

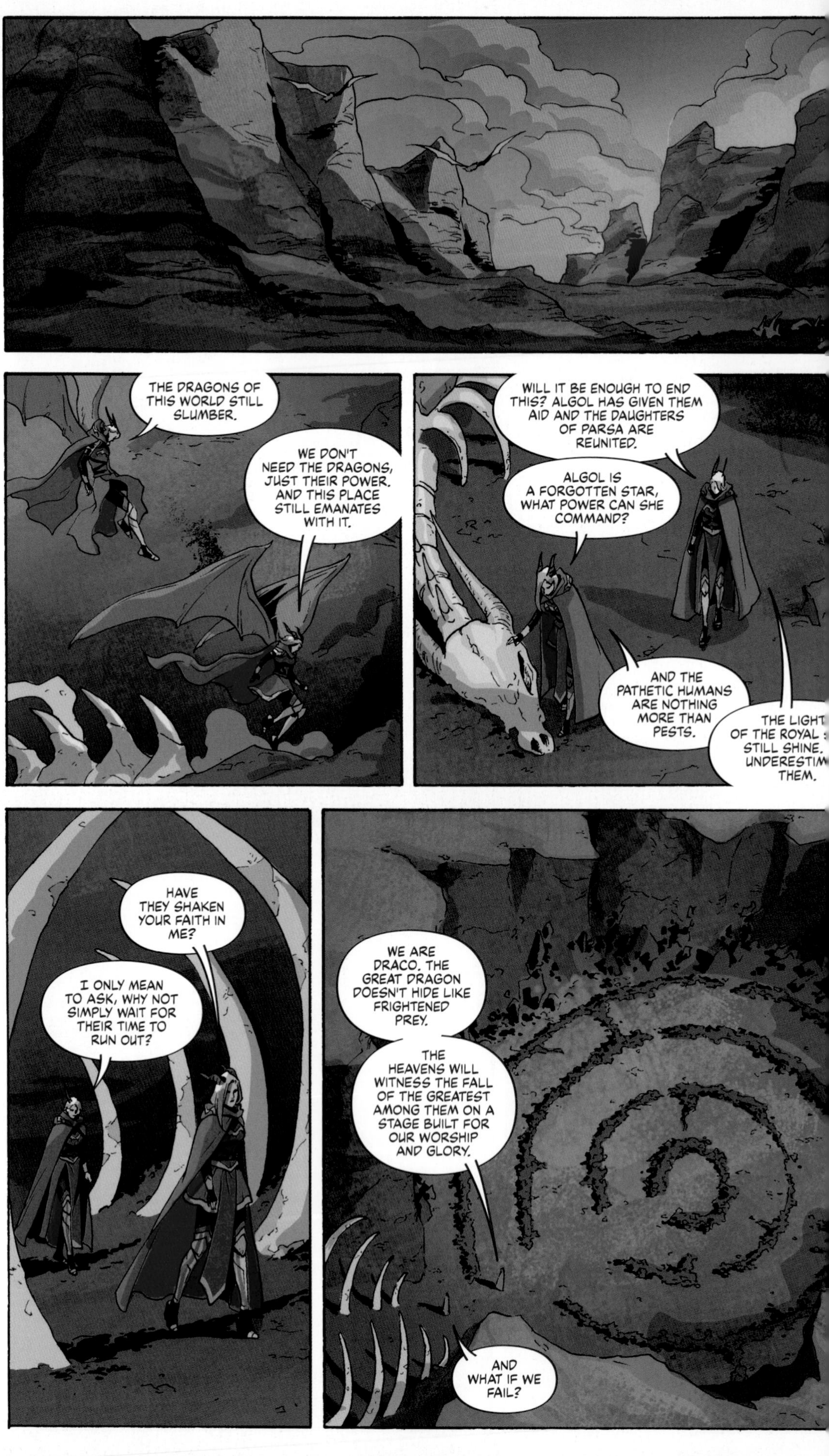
THE DRAGONS OF THIS WORLD STILL SLUMBER.
WE DON'T NEED THE DRAGONS, JUST THEIR POWER. AND THIS PLACE STILL EMANATES WITH IT.
WILL IT BE ENOUGH TO END THIS? ALGOL HAS GIVEN THEM AID AND THE DAUGHTERS OF PARSA ARE REUNITED.
ALGOL IS A FORGOTTEN STAR, WHAT POWER CAN SHE COMMAND?
AND THE PATHETIC HUMANS ARE NOTHING MORE THAN PESTS.
THE LIGHT OF THE ROYAL STILL SHINE. UNDERESTIM THEM.
HAVE THEY SHAKEN YOUR FAITH IN ME?
I ONLY MEAN TO ASK, WHY NOT SIMPLY WAIT FOR THEIR TIME TO RUN OUT?
WE ARE DRACO. THE GREAT DRAGON DOESN'T HIDE LIKE FRIGHTENED PREY.
THE HEAVENS WILL WITNESS THE FALL OF THE GREATEST AMONG THEM ON A STAGE BUILT FOR OUR WORSHIP AND GLORY.
AND WHAT IF WE FAIL?

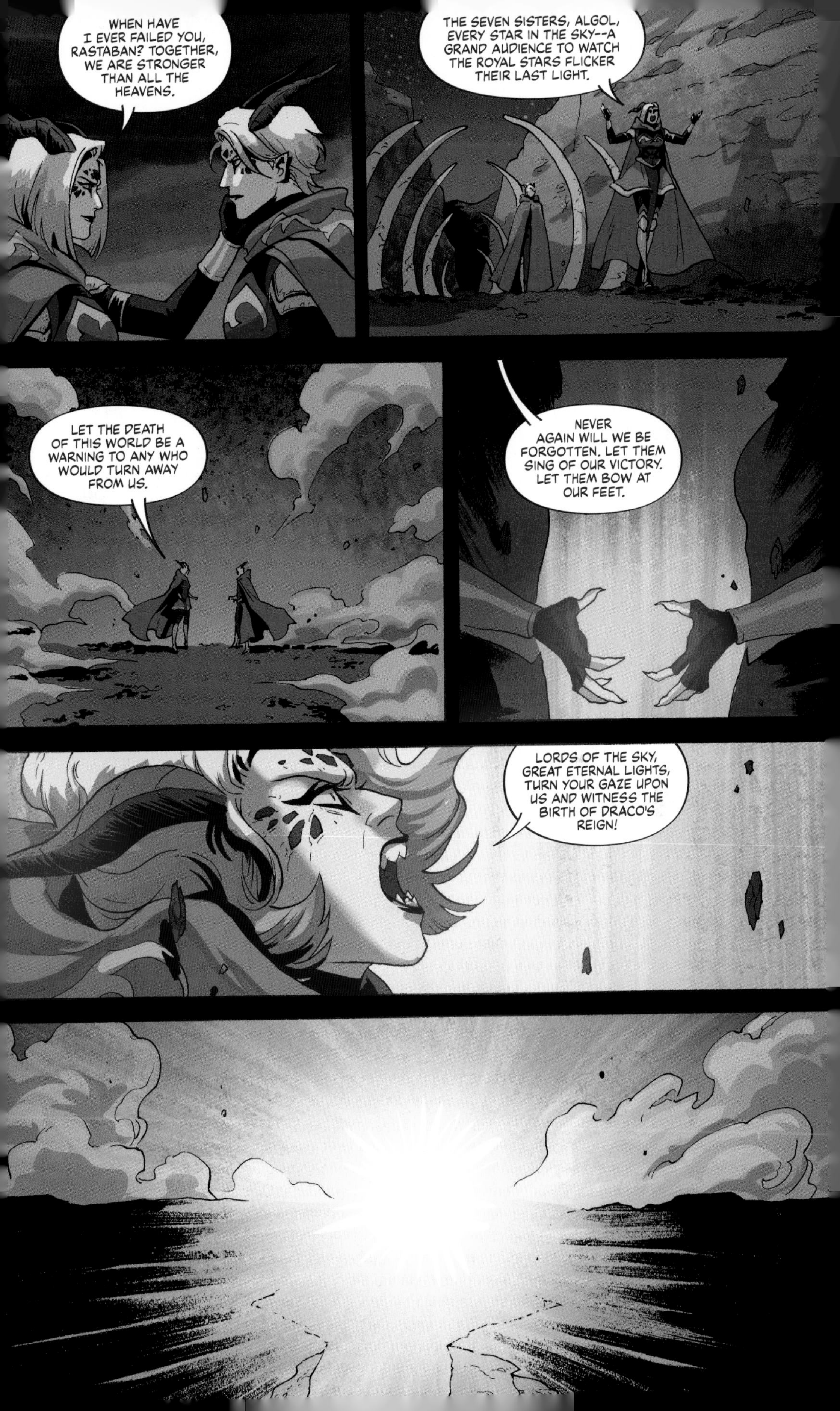
WHEN HAVE I EVER FAILED YOU, RASTABAN? TOGETHER, WE ARE STRONGER THAN ALL THE HEAVENS.
THE SEVEN SISTERS, ALGOL, EVERY STAR IN THE SKY--A GRAND AUDIENCE TO WATCH THE ROYAL STARS FLICKER THEIR LAST LIGHT.
LET THE DEATH OF THIS WORLD BE A WARNING TO ANY WHO WOULD TURN AWAY FROM US.
NEVER AGAIN WILL WE BE FORGOTTEN. LET THEM SING OF OUR VICTORY. LET THEM BOW AT OUR FEET.
LORDS OF THE SKY, GREAT ETERNAL LIGHTS, TURN YOUR GAZE UPON US AND WITNESS THE BIRTH OF DRACO'S REIGN!

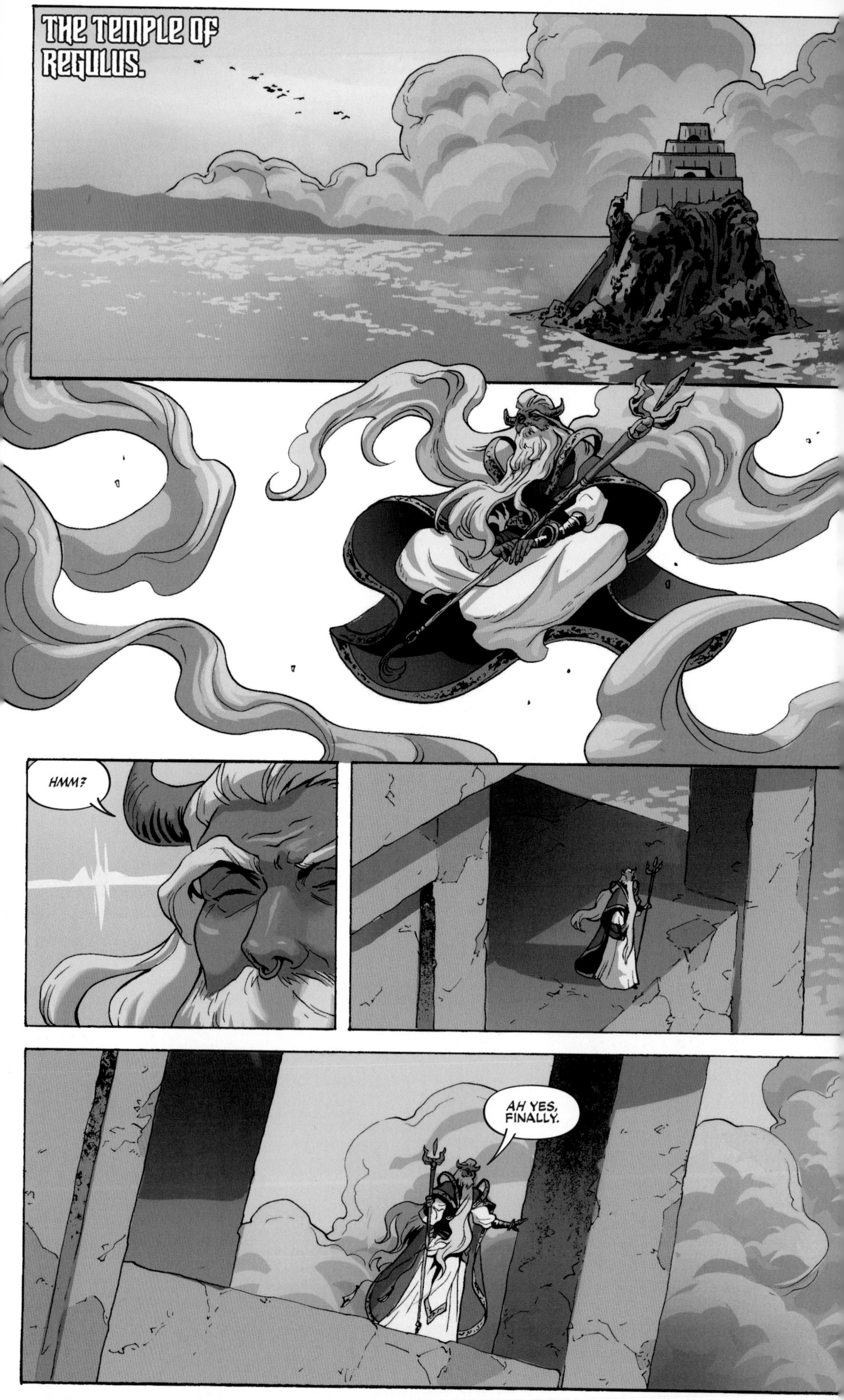
THE TEMPLE OF REGULUS.
HMM?
AH YES, FINALLY.

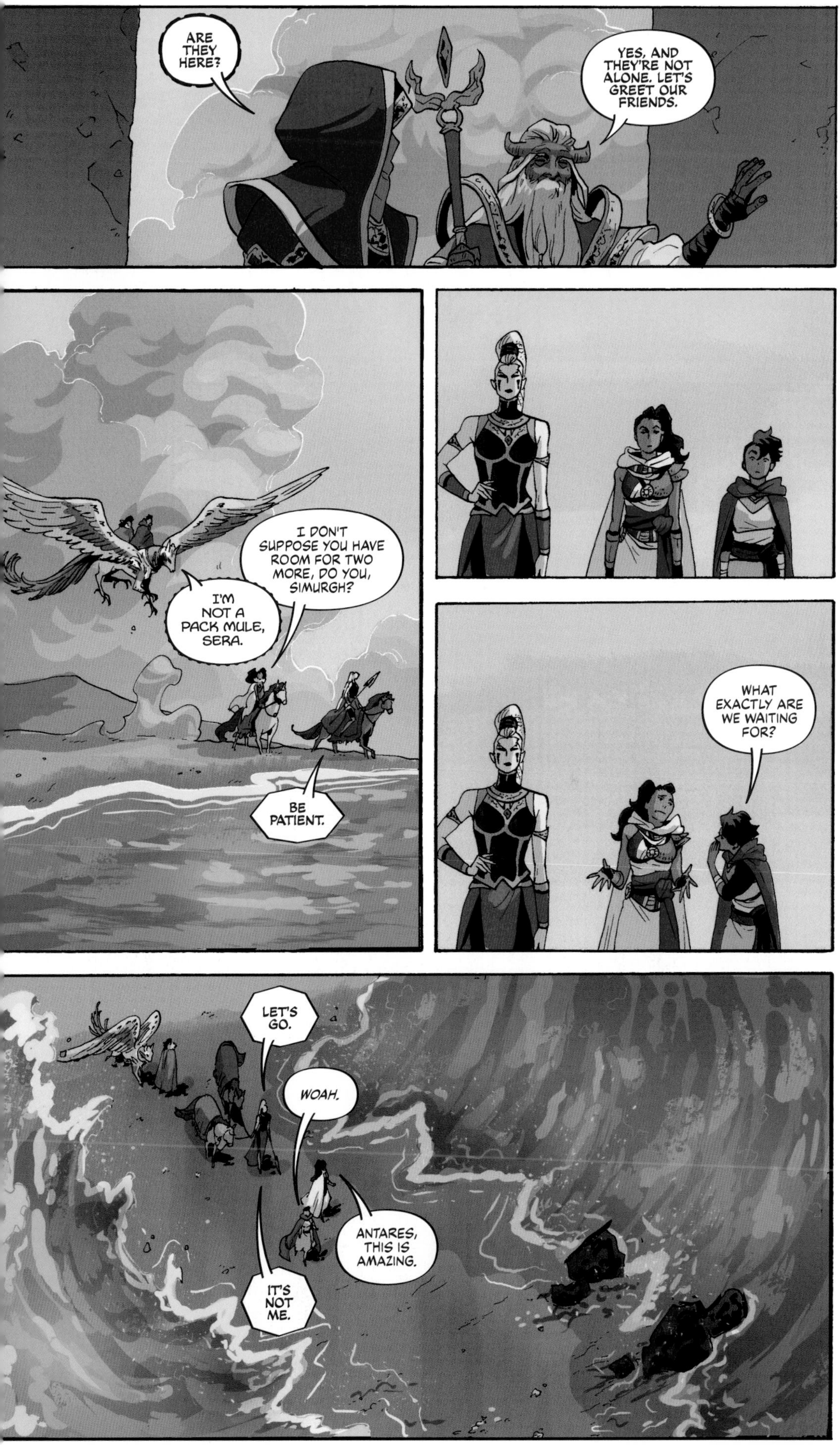
ARE THEY HERE?
YES, AND THEY'RE NOT ALONE. LET'S GREET OUR FRIENDS.
I DON'T SUPPOSE YOU HAVE ROOM FOR TWO MORE, DO YOU, SIMURGH?
I'M NOT A PACK MULE, SERA.
BE PATIENT.
WHAT EXACTLY ARE WE WAITING FOR?
LET'S GO.
WOAH.
ANTARES, THIS IS AMAZING.
IT'S NOT ME.

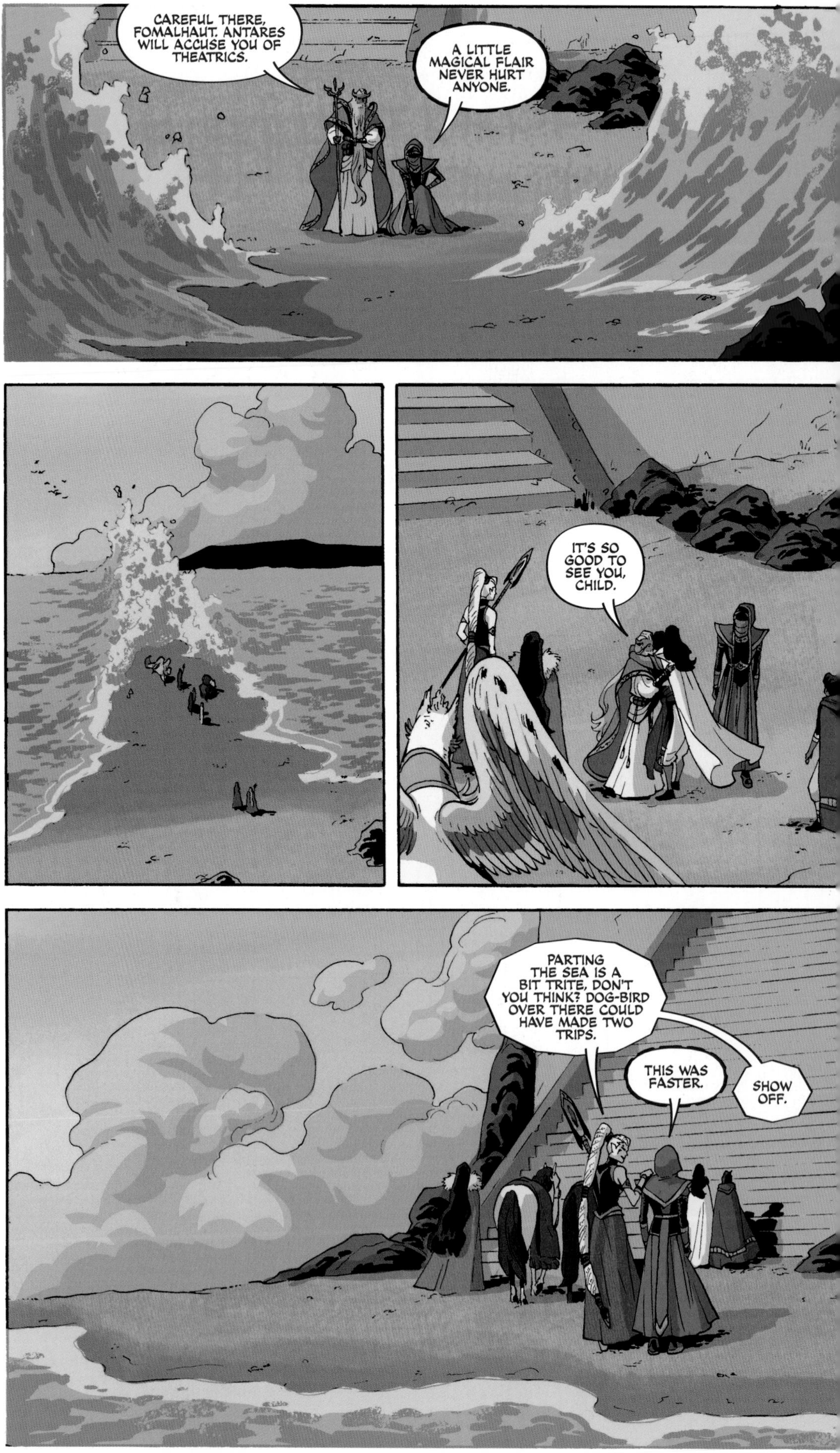
CAREFUL THERE, FOMALHAUT. ANTARES WILL ACCUSE YOU OF THEATRICS.
A LITTLE MAGICAL FLAIR NEVER HURT ANYONE.
IT'S SO GOOD TO SEE YOU, CHILD.
PARTING THE SEA IS A BIT TRITE, DON'T YOU THINK? DOG-BIRD OVER THERE COULD HAVE MADE TWO TRIPS.
THIS WAS FASTER.
SHOW OFF.

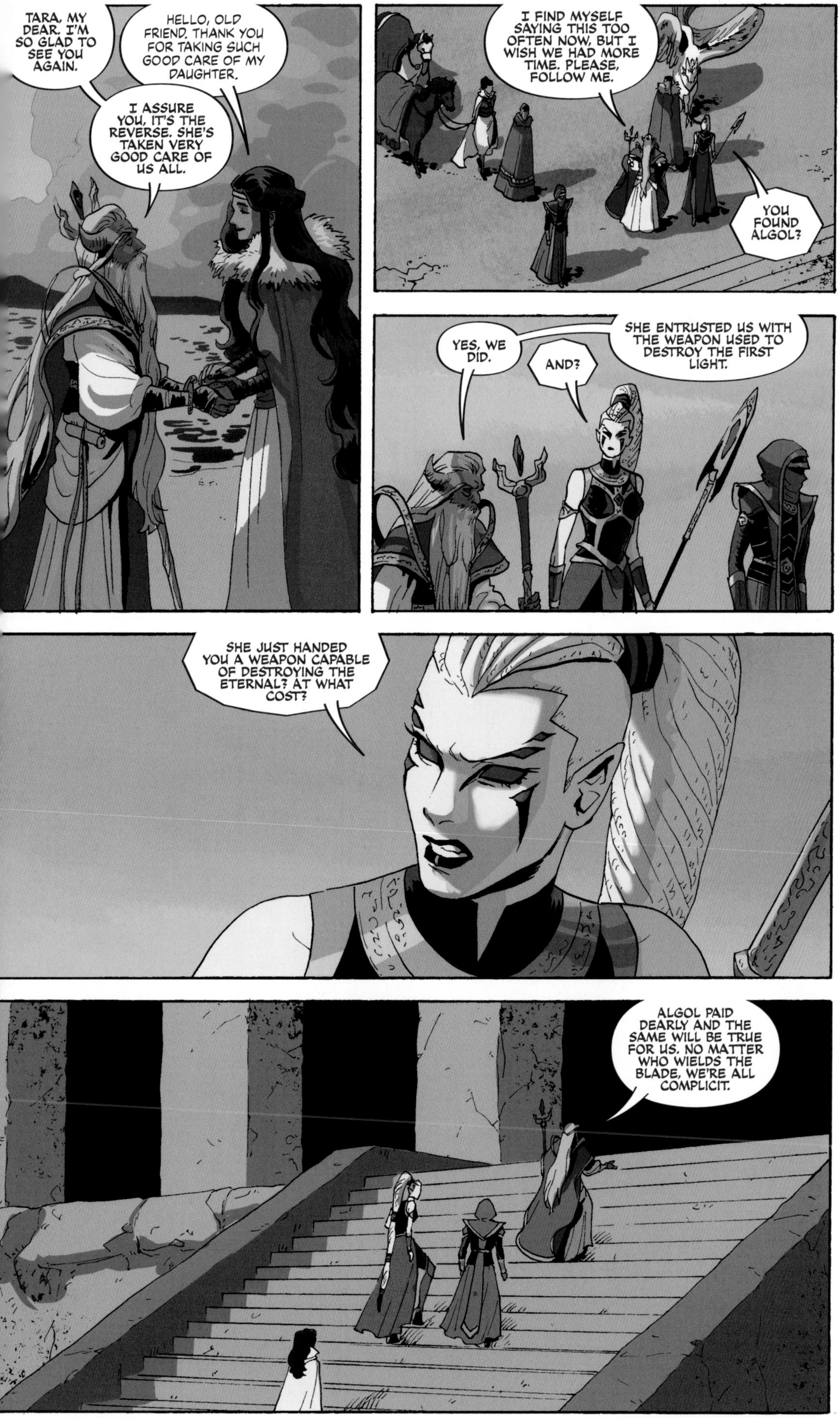
TARA, MY DEAR. I'M SO GLAD TO SEE YOU AGAIN.
HELLO, OLD FRIEND. THANK YOU FOR TAKING SUCH GOOD CARE OF MY DAUGHTER.
I ASSURE YOU, IT'S THE REVERSE. SHE'S TAKEN VERY GOOD CARE OF US ALL.
I FIND MYSELF SAYING THIS TOO OFTEN NOW, BUT I WISH WE HAD MORE TIME. PLEASE, FOLLOW ME.
YOU FOUND ALGOL?
YES, WE DID.
AND?
SHE ENTRUSTED US WITH THE WEAPON USED TO DESTROY THE FIRST LIGHT.
SHE JUST HANDED YOU A WEAPON CAPABLE OF DESTROYING THE ETERNAL? AT WHAT COST?
ALGOL PAID DEARLY AND THE SAME WILL BE TRUE FOR US. NO MATTER WHO WIELDS THE BLADE, WE'RE ALL COMPLICIT.

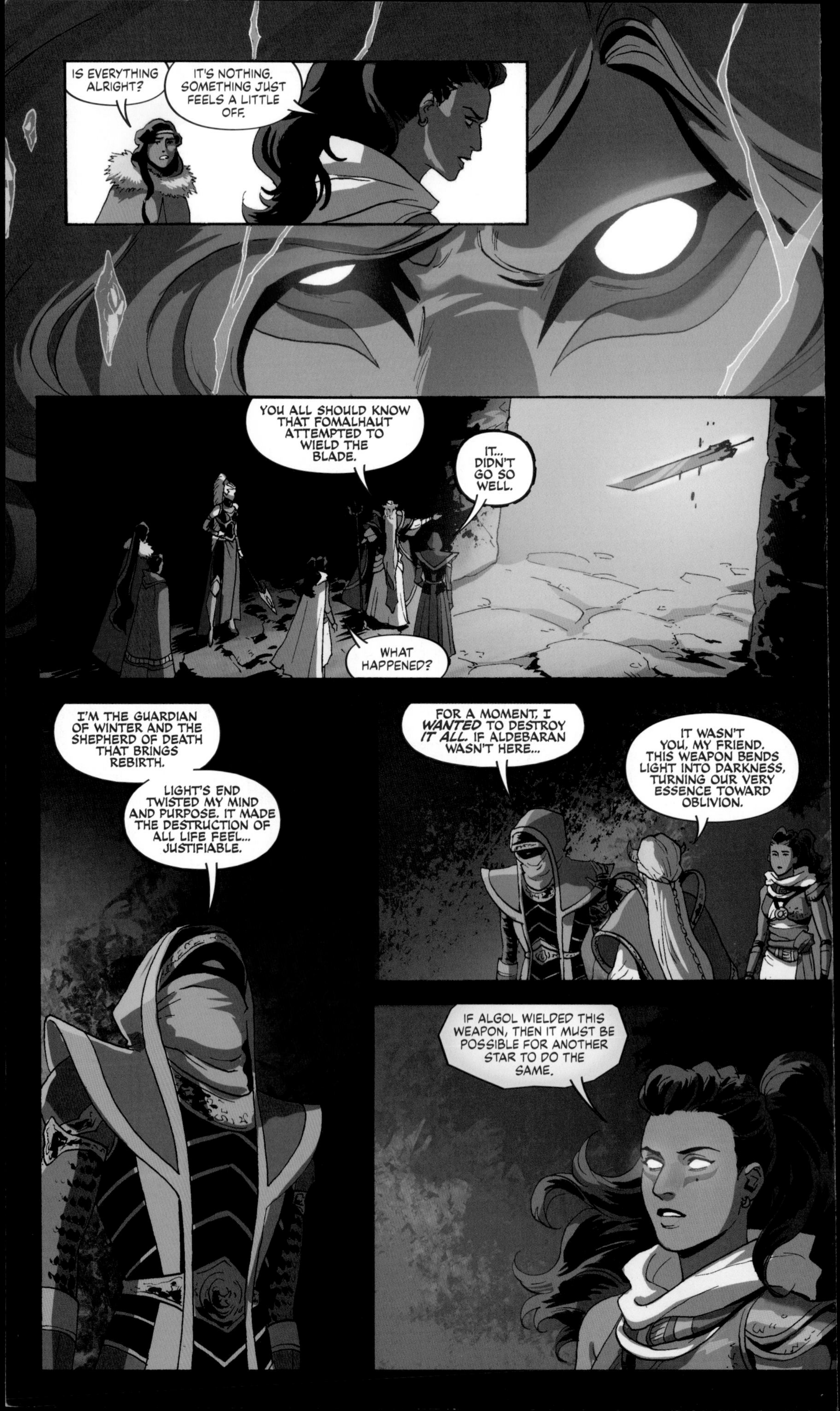
IS EVERYTHING ALRIGHT?
IT'S NOTHING. SOMETHING JUST FEELS A LITTLE OFF.
YOU ALL SHOULD KNOW THAT FOMALHAUT ATTEMPTED TO WIELD THE BLADE.
IT... DIDN'T GO SO WELL.
WHAT HAPPENED?
I'M THE GUARDIAN OF WINTER AND THE SHEPHERD OF DEATH THAT BRINGS REBIRTH.
LIGHT'S END TWISTED MY MIND AND PURPOSE. IT MADE THE DESTRUCTION OF ALL LIFE FEEL... JUSTIFIABLE.
FOR A MOMENT, I *WANTED* TO DESTROY *IT ALL*. IF ALDEBARAN WASN'T HERE...
IT WASN'T YOU, MY FRIEND. THIS WEAPON BENDS LIGHT INTO DARKNESS, TURNING OUR VERY ESSENCE TOWARD OBLIVION.
IF ALGOL WIELDED THIS WEAPON, THEN IT MUST BE POSSIBLE FOR ANOTHER STAR TO DO THE SAME.

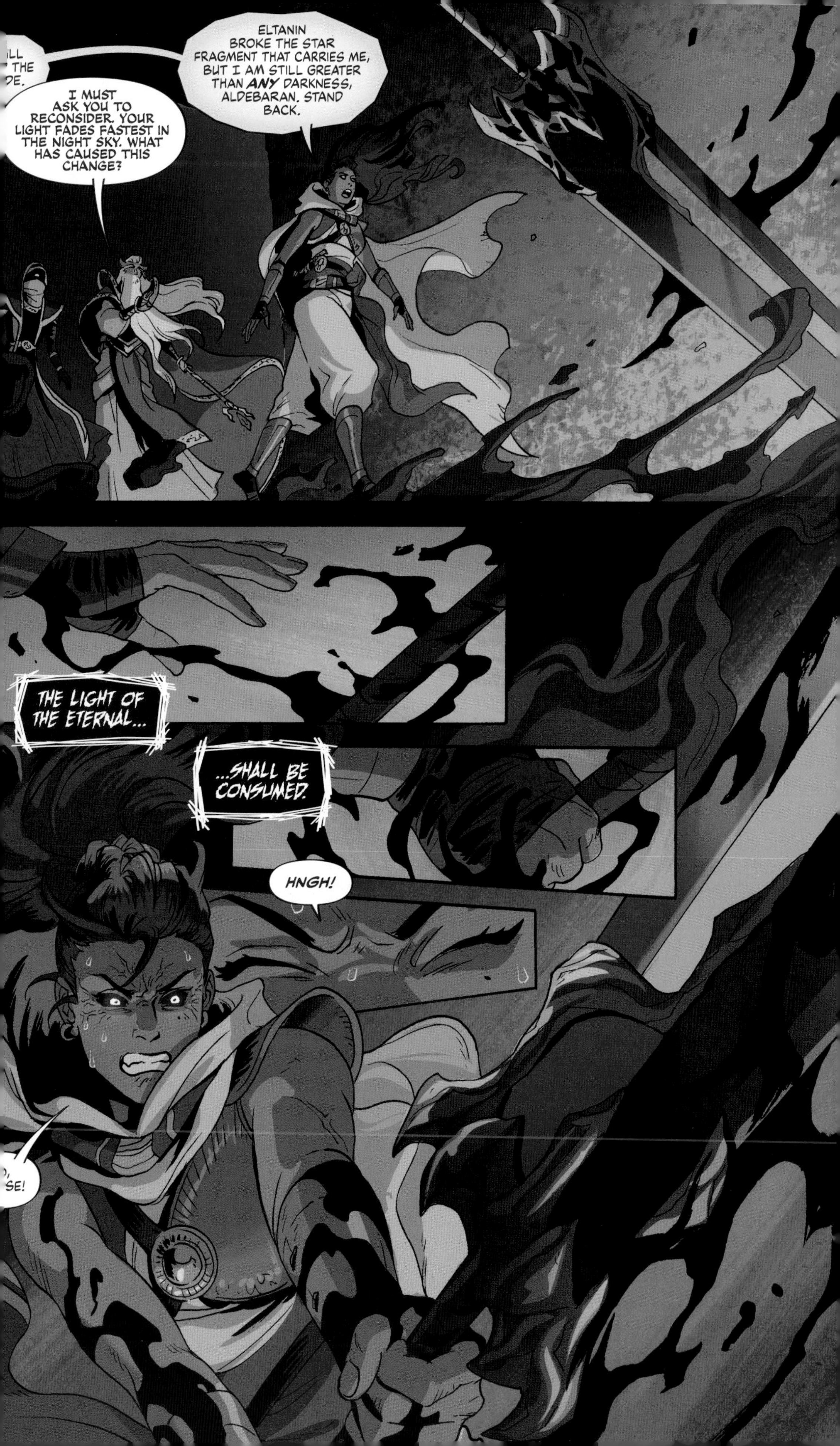
I MUST ASK YOU TO RECONSIDER. YOUR LIGHT FADES FASTEST IN THE NIGHT SKY. WHAT HAS CAUSED THIS CHANGE?
ELTANIN BROKE THE STAR FRAGMENT THAT CARRIES ME, BUT I AM STILL GREATER THAN ANY DARKNESS, ALDEBARAN. STAND BACK.
THE LIGHT OF THE ETERNAL...
...SHALL BE CONSUMED.
HNGH!

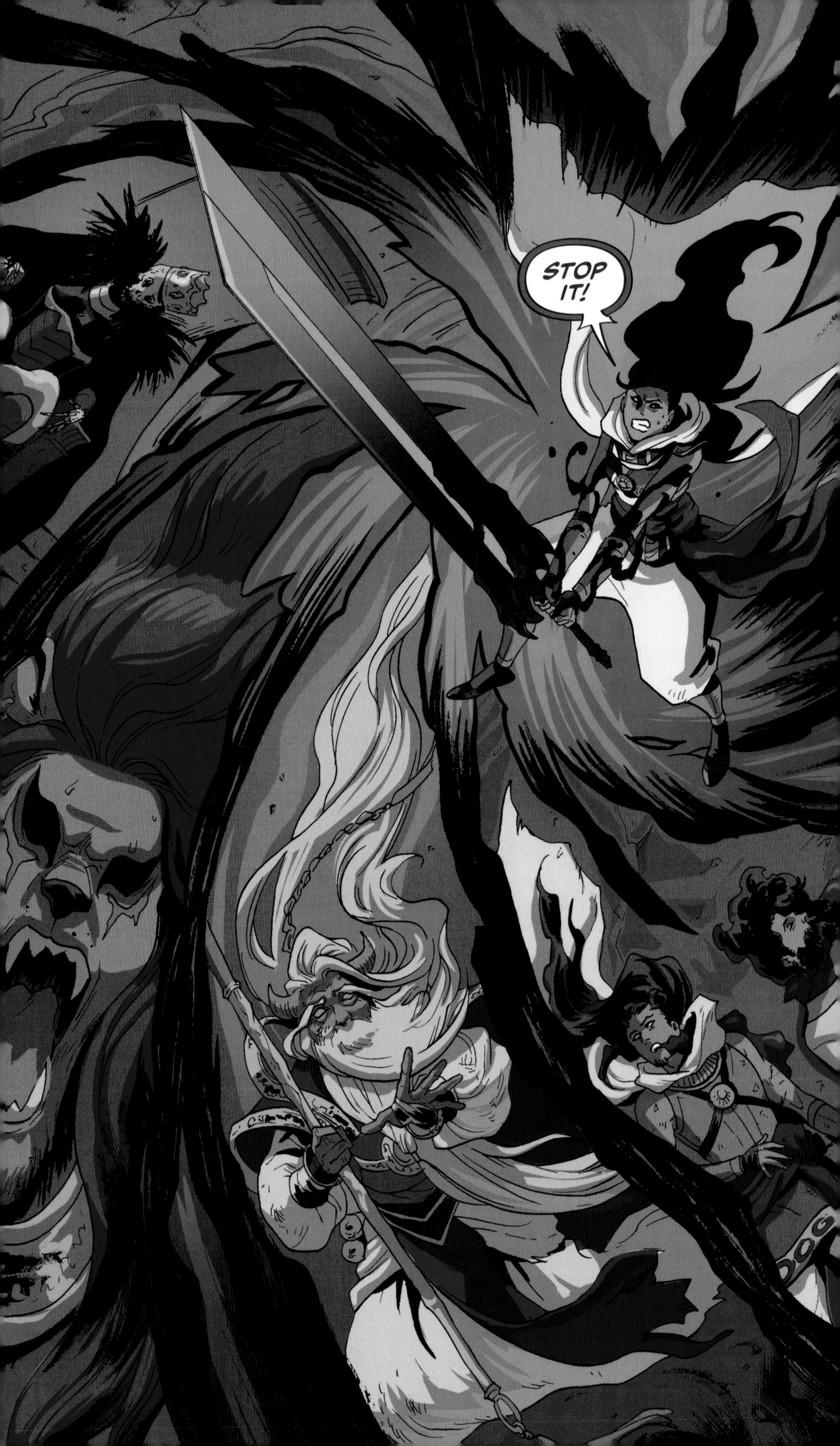
STOP IT!

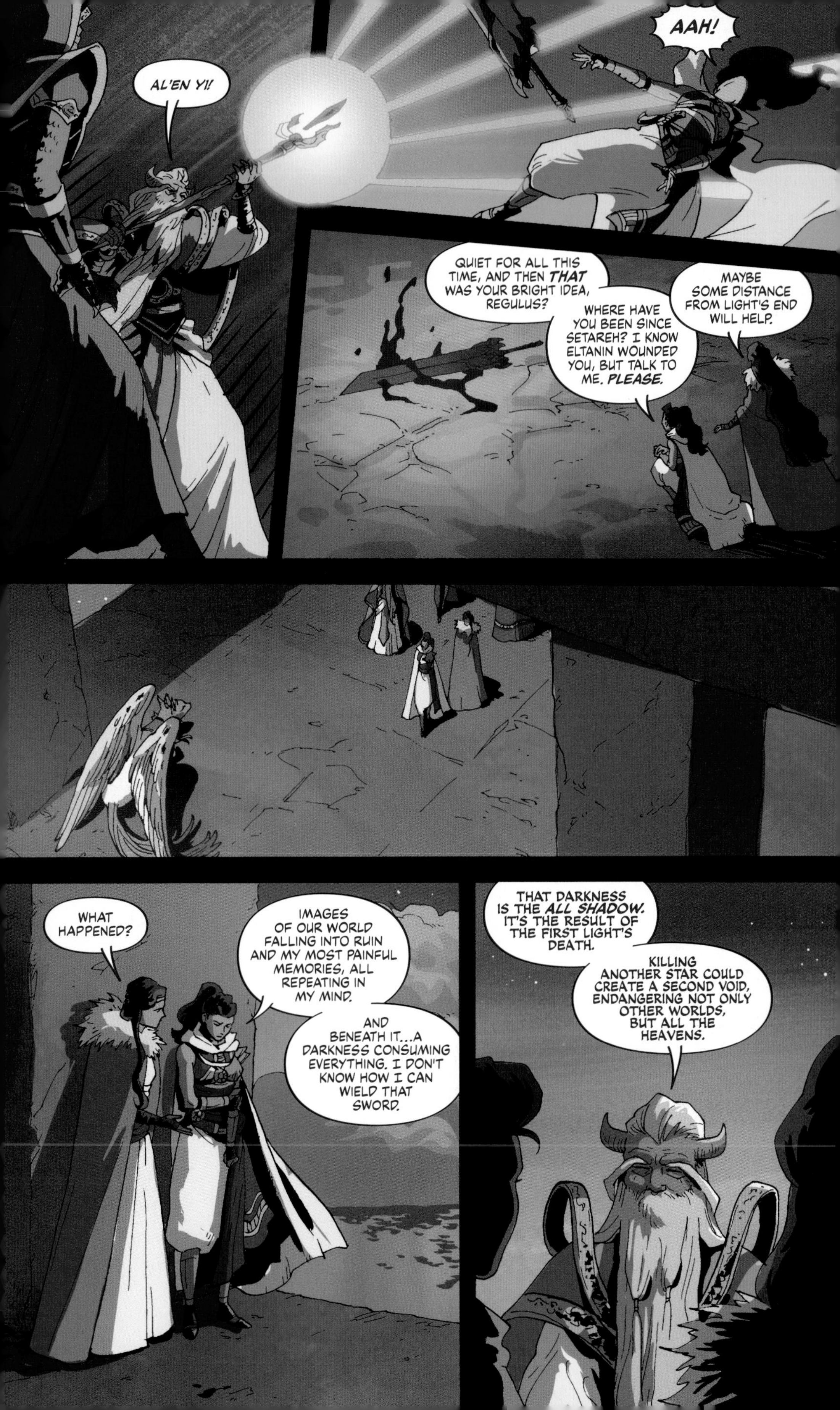
AAH!
AL'EN YI!
QUIET FOR ALL THIS TIME, AND THEN THAT WAS YOUR BRIGHT IDEA, REGULUS?
WHERE HAVE YOU BEEN SINCE SETAREH? I KNOW ELTANIN WOUNDED YOU, BUT TALK TO ME. PLEASE.
MAYBE SOME DISTANCE FROM LIGHT'S END WILL HELP.
WHAT HAPPENED?
IMAGES OF OUR WORLD FALLING INTO RUIN AND MY MOST PAINFUL MEMORIES, ALL REPEATING IN MY MIND.
AND BENEATH IT...A DARKNESS CONSUMING EVERYTHING. I DON'T KNOW HOW I CAN WIELD THAT SWORD.
THAT DARKNESS IS THE ALL SHADOW. IT'S THE RESULT OF THE FIRST LIGHT'S DEATH.
KILLING ANOTHER STAR COULD CREATE A SECOND VOID, ENDANGERING NOT ONLY OTHER WORLDS, BUT ALL THE HEAVENS.

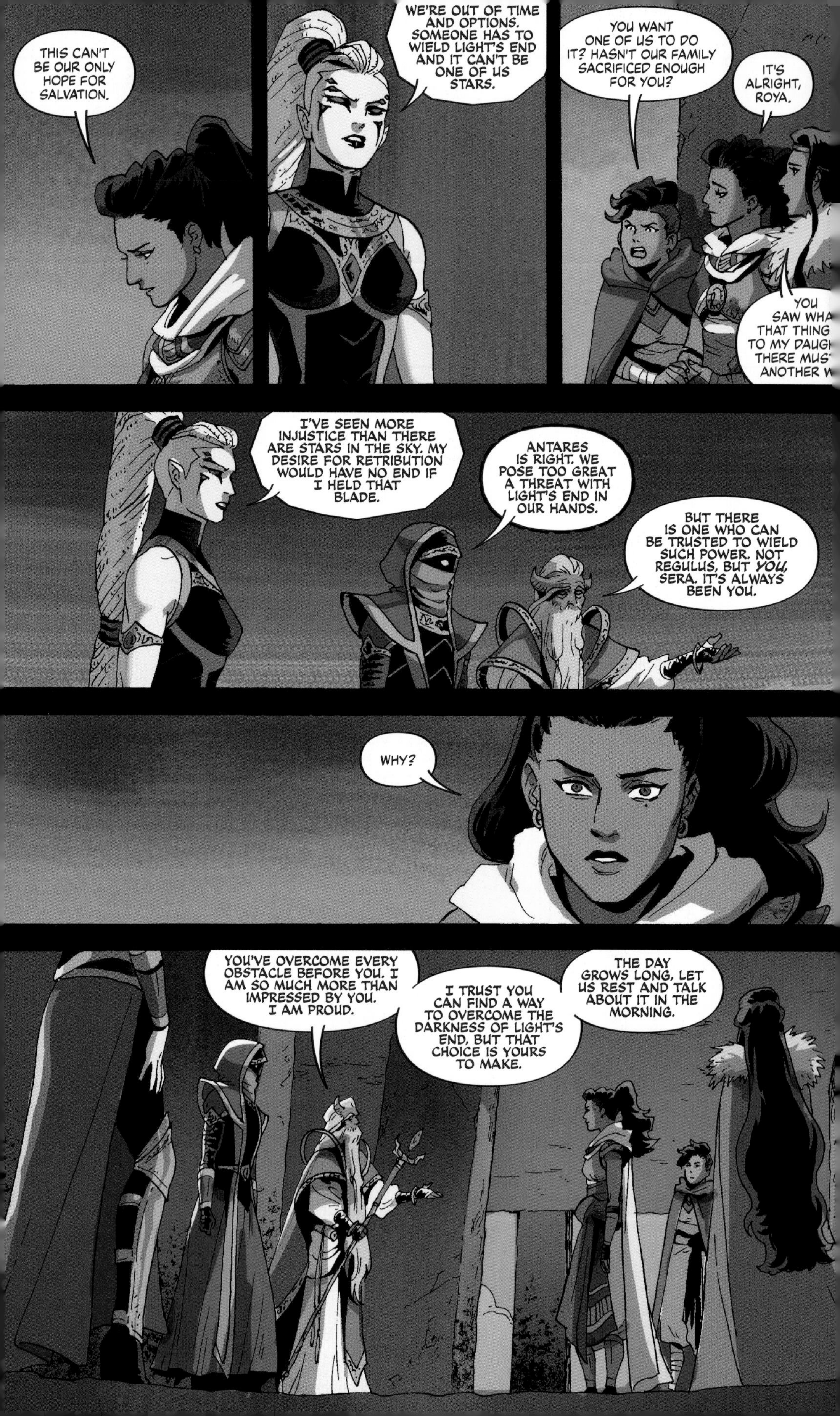
THIS CAN'T BE OUR ONLY HOPE FOR SALVATION.
WE'RE OUT OF TIME AND OPTIONS. SOMEONE HAS TO WIELD LIGHT'S END AND IT CAN'T BE ONE OF US STARS.
YOU WANT ONE OF US TO DO IT? HASN'T OUR FAMILY SACRIFICED ENOUGH FOR YOU?
IT'S ALRIGHT, ROYA.
YOU SAW WHA THAT THING TO MY DAUGH THERE MUS ANOTHER W
I'VE SEEN MORE INJUSTICE THAN THERE ARE STARS IN THE SKY. MY DESIRE FOR RETRIBUTION WOULD HAVE NO END IF I HELD THAT BLADE.
ANTARES IS RIGHT. WE POSE TOO GREAT A THREAT WITH LIGHT'S END IN OUR HANDS.
BUT THERE IS ONE WHO CAN BE TRUSTED TO WIELD SUCH POWER. NOT REGULUS, BUT *YOU*, SERA. IT'S ALWAYS BEEN YOU.
WHY?
YOU'VE OVERCOME EVERY OBSTACLE BEFORE YOU. I AM SO MUCH MORE THAN IMPRESSED BY YOU. I AM PROUD.
I TRUST YOU CAN FIND A WAY TO OVERCOME THE DARKNESS OF LIGHT'S END, BUT THAT CHOICE IS YOURS TO MAKE.
THE DAY GROWS LONG, LET US REST AND TALK ABOUT IT IN THE MORNING.

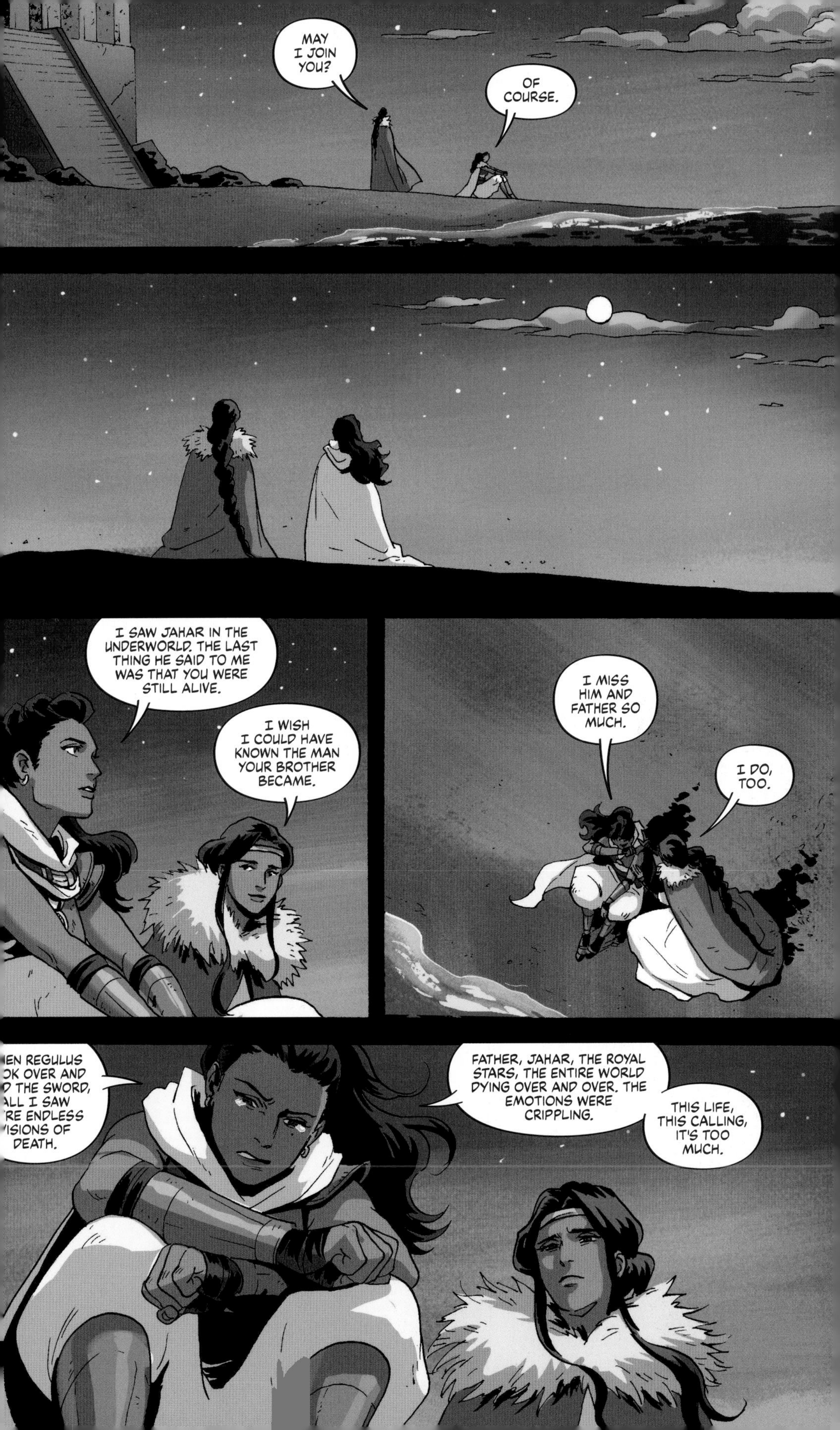
MAY I JOIN YOU?
OF COURSE.
I SAW JAHAR IN THE UNDERWORLD. THE LAST THING HE SAID TO ME WAS THAT YOU WERE STILL ALIVE.
I WISH I COULD HAVE KNOWN THE MAN YOUR BROTHER BECAME.
I MISS HIM AND FATHER SO MUCH.
I DO, TOO.
EN REGULUS OK OVER AND D THE SWORD, ALL I SAW RE ENDLESS VISIONS OF DEATH.
FATHER, JAHAR, THE ROYAL STARS, THE ENTIRE WORLD DYING OVER AND OVER. THE EMOTIONS WERE CRIPPLING.
THIS LIFE, THIS CALLING, IT'S TOO MUCH.

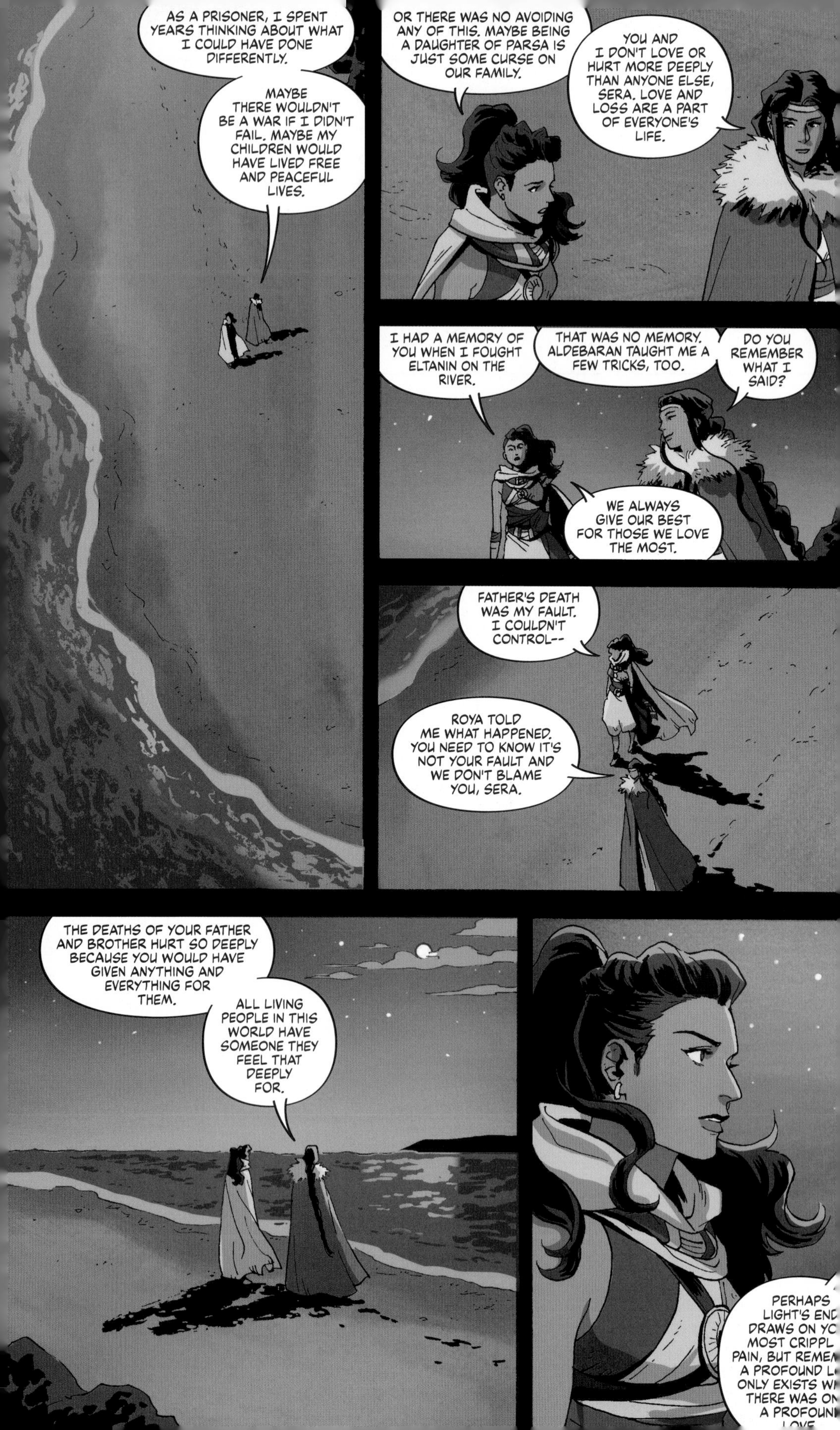

AS A PRISONER, I SPENT YEARS THINKING ABOUT WHAT I COULD HAVE DONE DIFFERENTLY.
MAYBE THERE WOULDN'T BE A WAR IF I DIDN'T FAIL. MAYBE MY CHILDREN WOULD HAVE LIVED FREE AND PEACEFUL LIVES.
OR THERE WAS NO AVOIDING ANY OF THIS. MAYBE BEING A DAUGHTER OF PARSA IS JUST SOME CURSE ON OUR FAMILY.
YOU AND I DON'T LOVE OR HURT MORE DEEPLY THAN ANYONE ELSE, SERA. LOVE AND LOSS ARE A PART OF EVERYONE'S LIFE.
I HAD A MEMORY OF YOU WHEN I FOUGHT ELTANIN ON THE RIVER.
THAT WAS NO MEMORY. ALDEBARAN TAUGHT ME A FEW TRICKS, TOO.
DO YOU REMEMBER WHAT I SAID?
WE ALWAYS GIVE OUR BEST FOR THOSE WE LOVE THE MOST.
FATHER'S DEATH WAS MY FAULT. I COULDN'T CONTROL--
ROYA TOLD ME WHAT HAPPENED. YOU NEED TO KNOW IT'S NOT YOUR FAULT AND WE DON'T BLAME YOU, SERA.
THE DEATHS OF YOUR FATHER AND BROTHER HURT SO DEEPLY BECAUSE YOU WOULD HAVE GIVEN ANYTHING AND EVERYTHING FOR THEM.
ALL LIVING PEOPLE IN THIS WORLD HAVE SOMEONE THEY FEEL THAT DEEPLY FOR.
PERHAPS LIGHT'S END DRAWS ON YO MOST CRIPPL PAIN, BUT REMEM A PROFOUND L ONLY EXISTS WI THERE WAS ON A PROFOUN

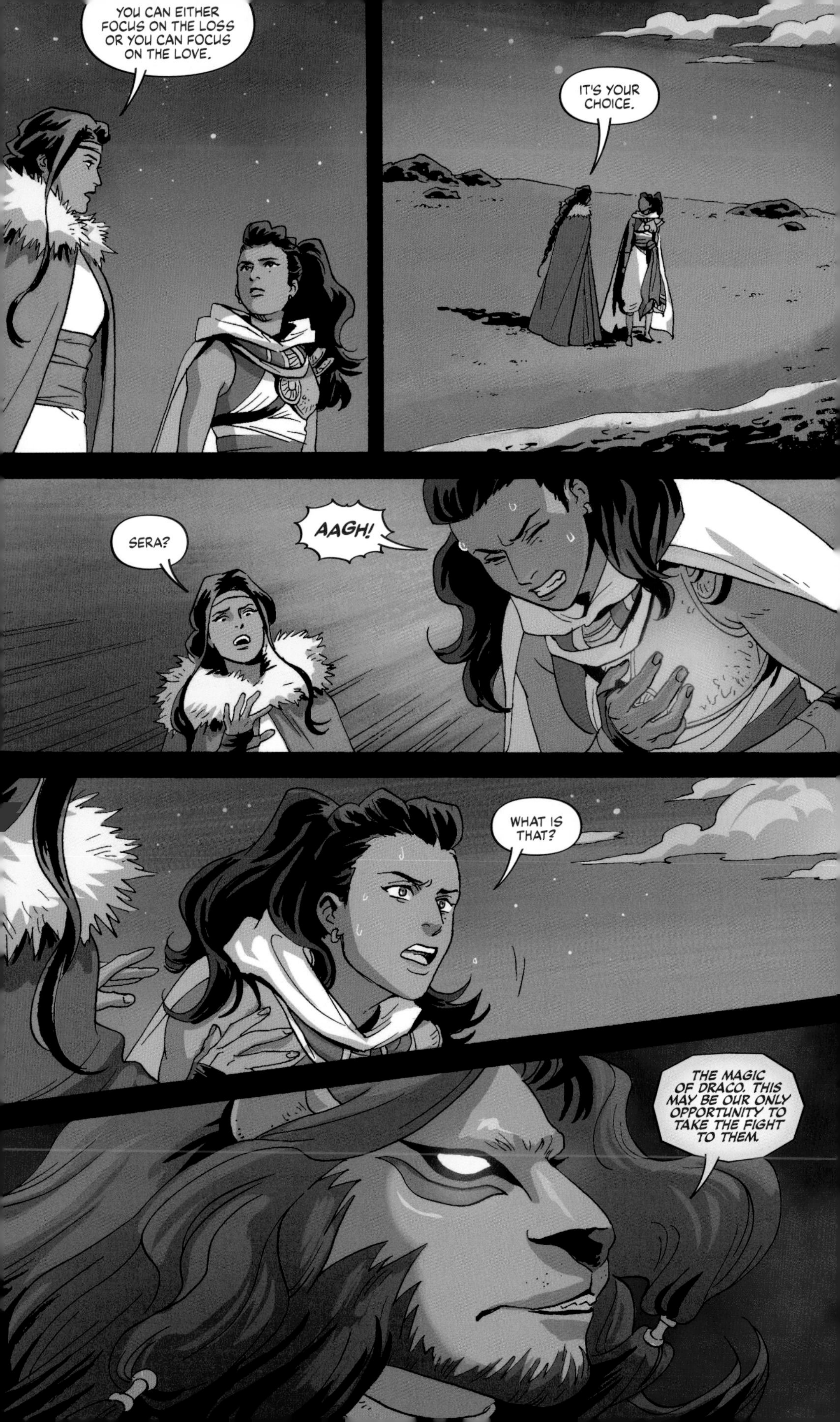
YOU CAN EITHER FOCUS ON THE LOSS OR YOU CAN FOCUS ON THE LOVE.
IT'S YOUR CHOICE.
SERA?
AAGH!
WHAT IS THAT?
THE MAGIC OF DRACO. THIS MAY BE OUR ONLY OPPORTUNITY TO TAKE THE FIGHT TO THEM.

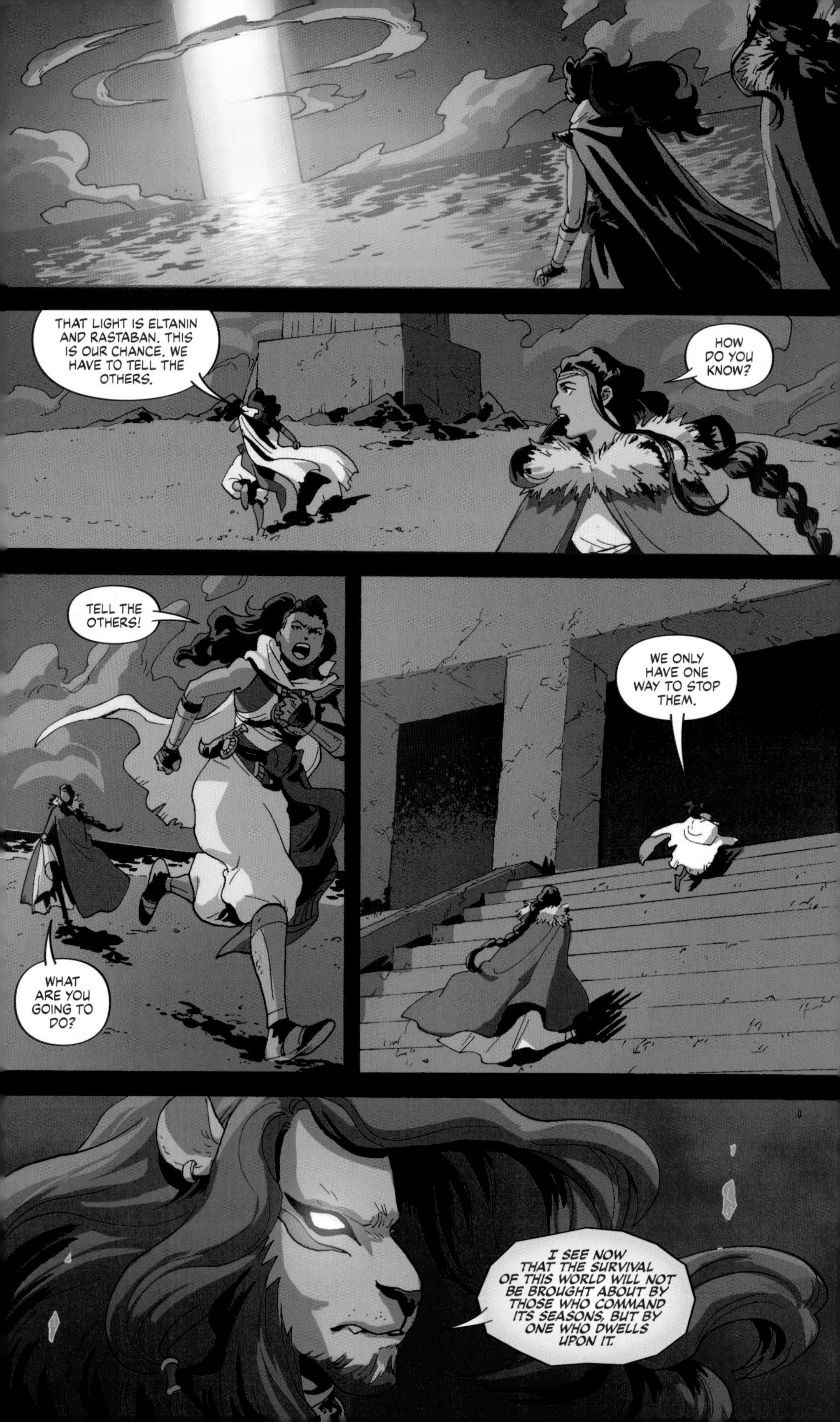
THAT LIGHT IS ELTANIN AND RASTABAN. THIS IS OUR CHANCE. WE HAVE TO TELL THE OTHERS.
HOW DO YOU KNOW?
TELL THE OTHERS!
WHAT ARE YOU GOING TO DO?
WE ONLY HAVE ONE WAY TO STOP THEM.
I SEE NOW THAT THE SURVIVAL OF THIS WORLD WILL NOT BE BROUGHT ABOUT BY THOSE WHO COMMAND ITS SEASONS, BUT BY ONE WHO DWELLS UPON IT.

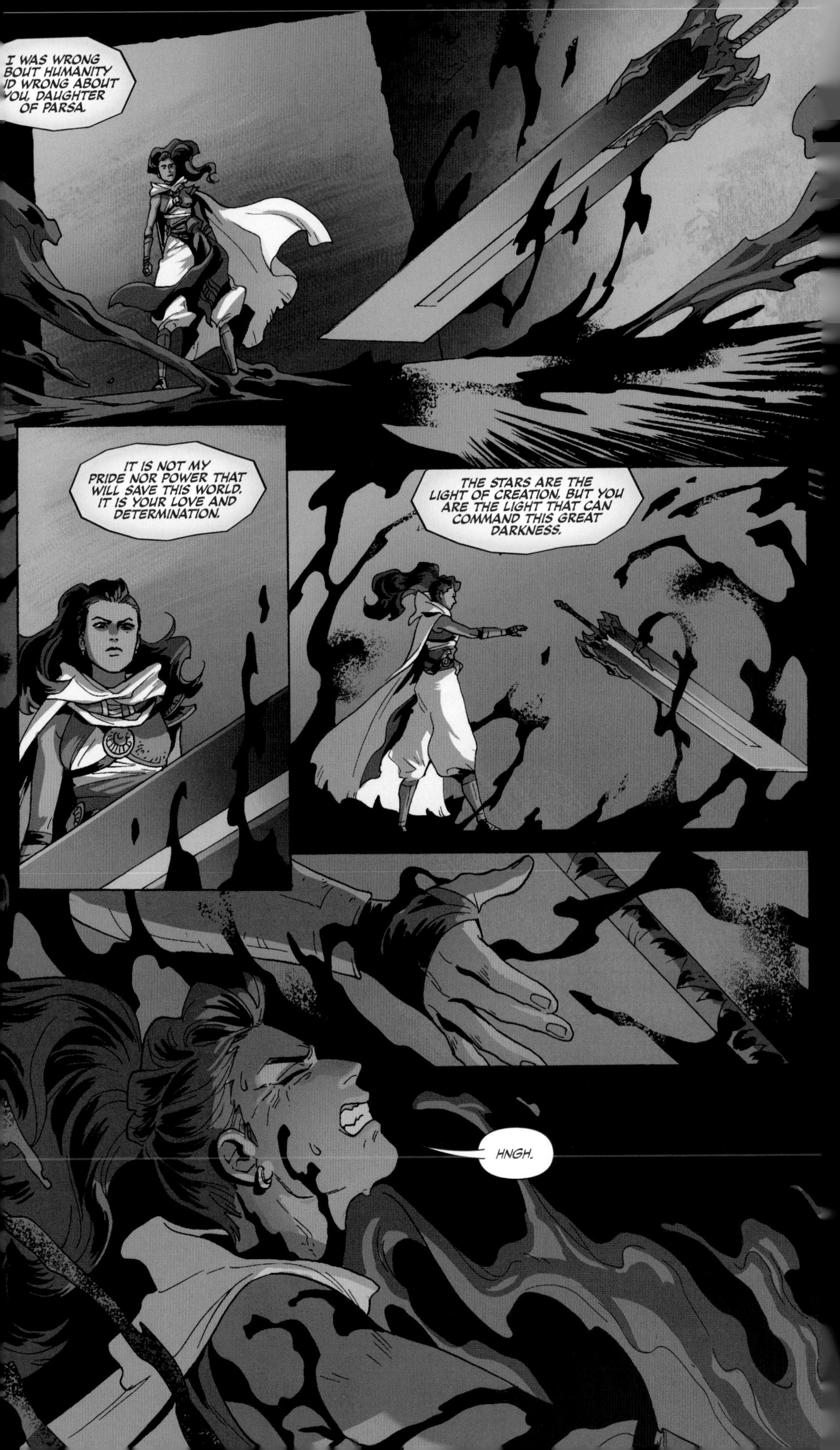
I WAS WRONG
BOUT HUMANITY
ID WRONG ABOUT
YOU, DAUGHTER
OF PARSA.
IT IS NOT MY PRIDE NOR POWER THAT WILL SAVE THIS WORLD. IT IS YOUR LOVE AND DETERMINATION.
THE STARS ARE THE LIGHT OF CREATION, BUT YOU ARE THE LIGHT THAT CAN COMMAND THIS GREAT DARKNESS.
HNGH.

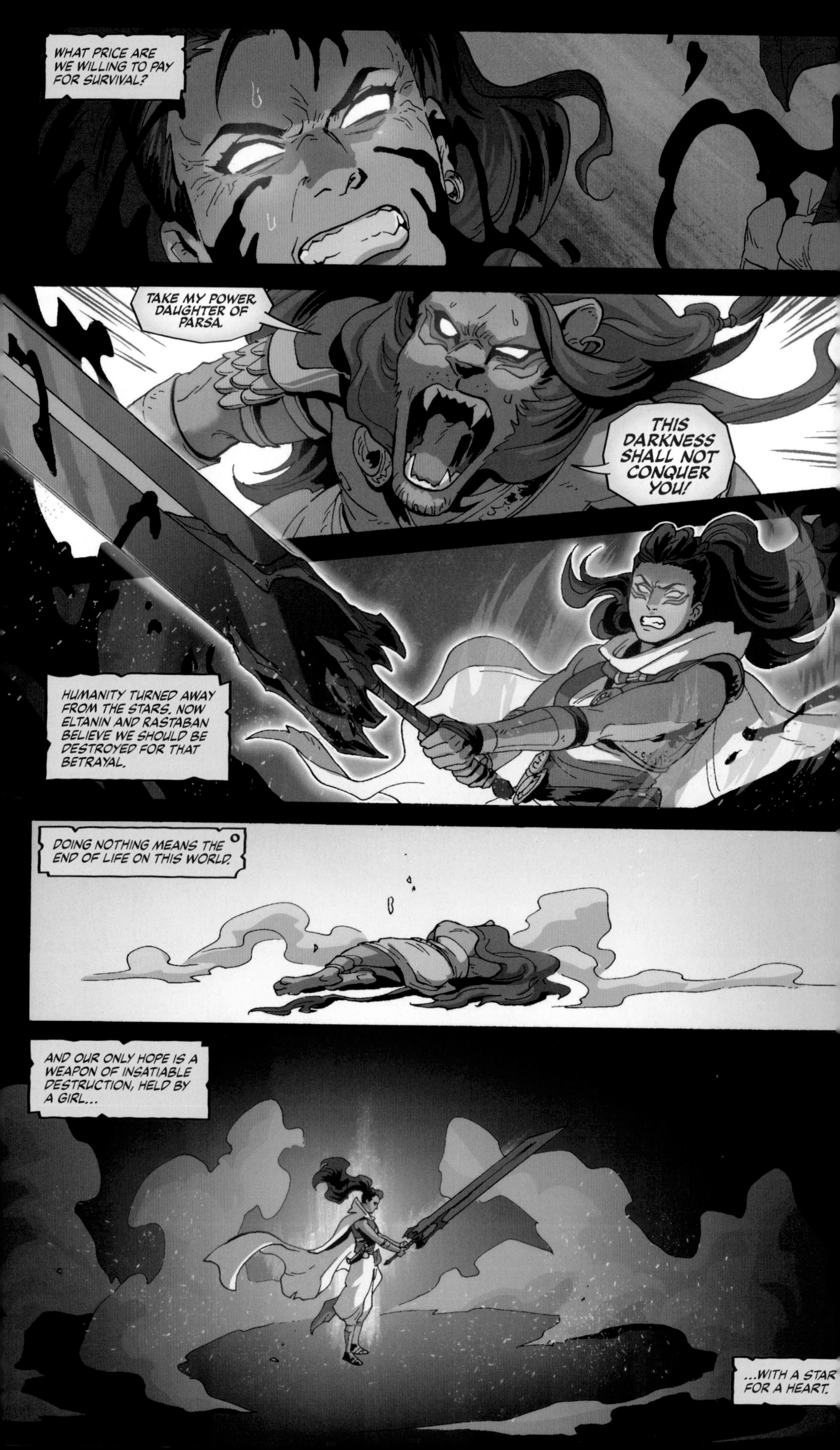
WHAT PRICE ARE WE WILLING TO PAY FOR SURVIVAL?
TAKE MY POWER, DAUGHTER OF PARSA.
THIS DARKNESS SHALL NOT CONQUER YOU!
HUMANITY TURNED AWAY FROM THE STARS. NOW ELTANIN AND RASTABAN BELIEVE WE SHOULD BE DESTROYED FOR THAT BETRAYAL.
DOING NOTHING MEANS THE END OF LIFE ON THIS WORLD.
AND OUR ONLY HOPE IS A WEAPON OF INSATIABLE DESTRUCTION, HELD BY A GIRL...
...WITH A STAR FOR A HEART.

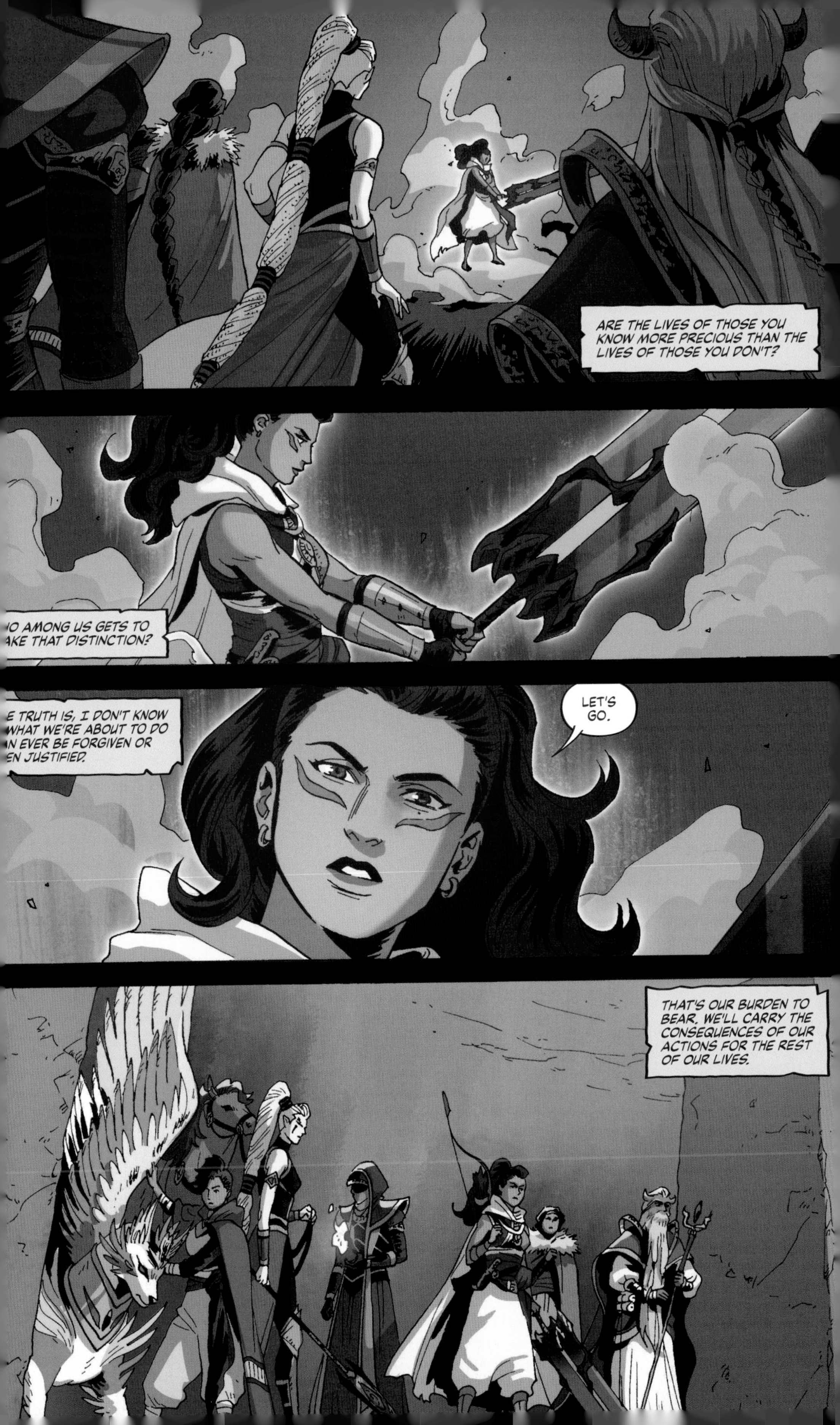

ARE THE LIVES OF THOSE YOU KNOW MORE PRECIOUS THAN THE LIVES OF THOSE YOU DON'T?
O AMONG US GETS TO AKE THAT DISTINCTION?
E TRUTH IS, I DON'T KNOW WHAT WE'RE ABOUT TO DO N EVER BE FORGIVEN OR EN JUSTIFIED.
LET'S GO.
THAT'S OUR BURDEN TO BEAR. WE'LL CARRY THE CONSEQUENCES OF OUR ACTIONS FOR THE REST OF OUR LIVES.

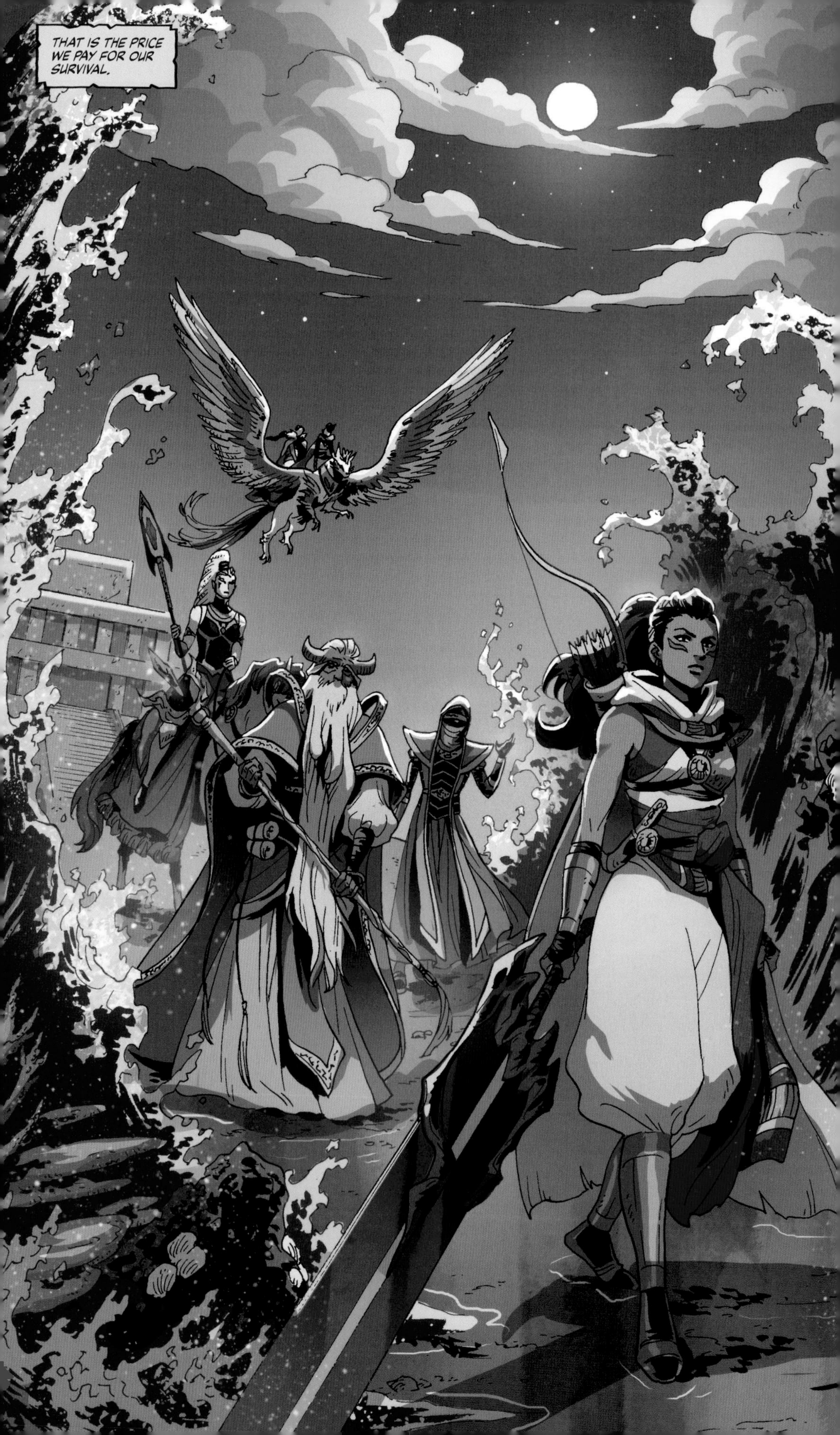
THAT IS THE PRICE WE PAY FOR OUR SURVIVAL.

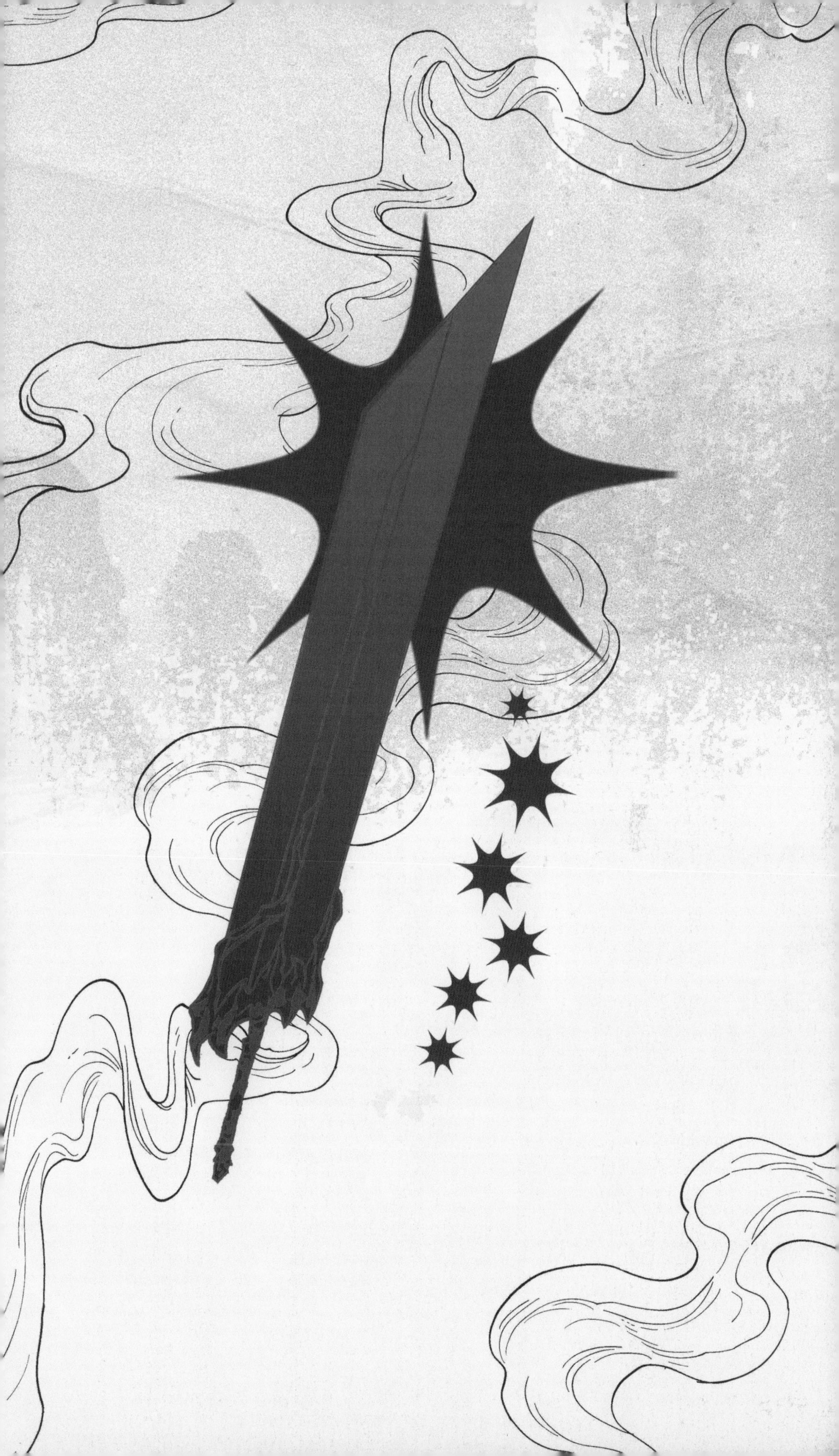

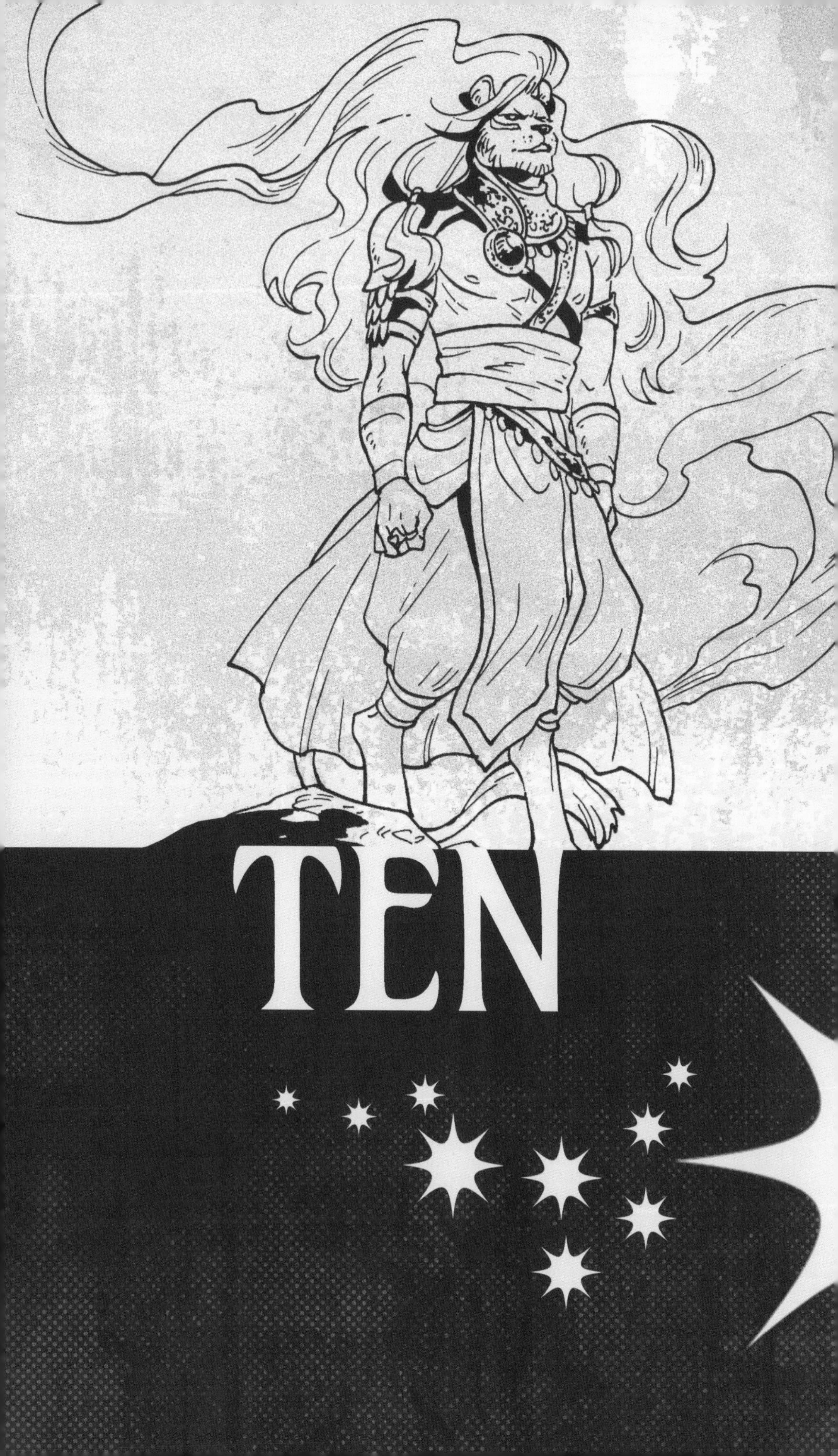

TEN

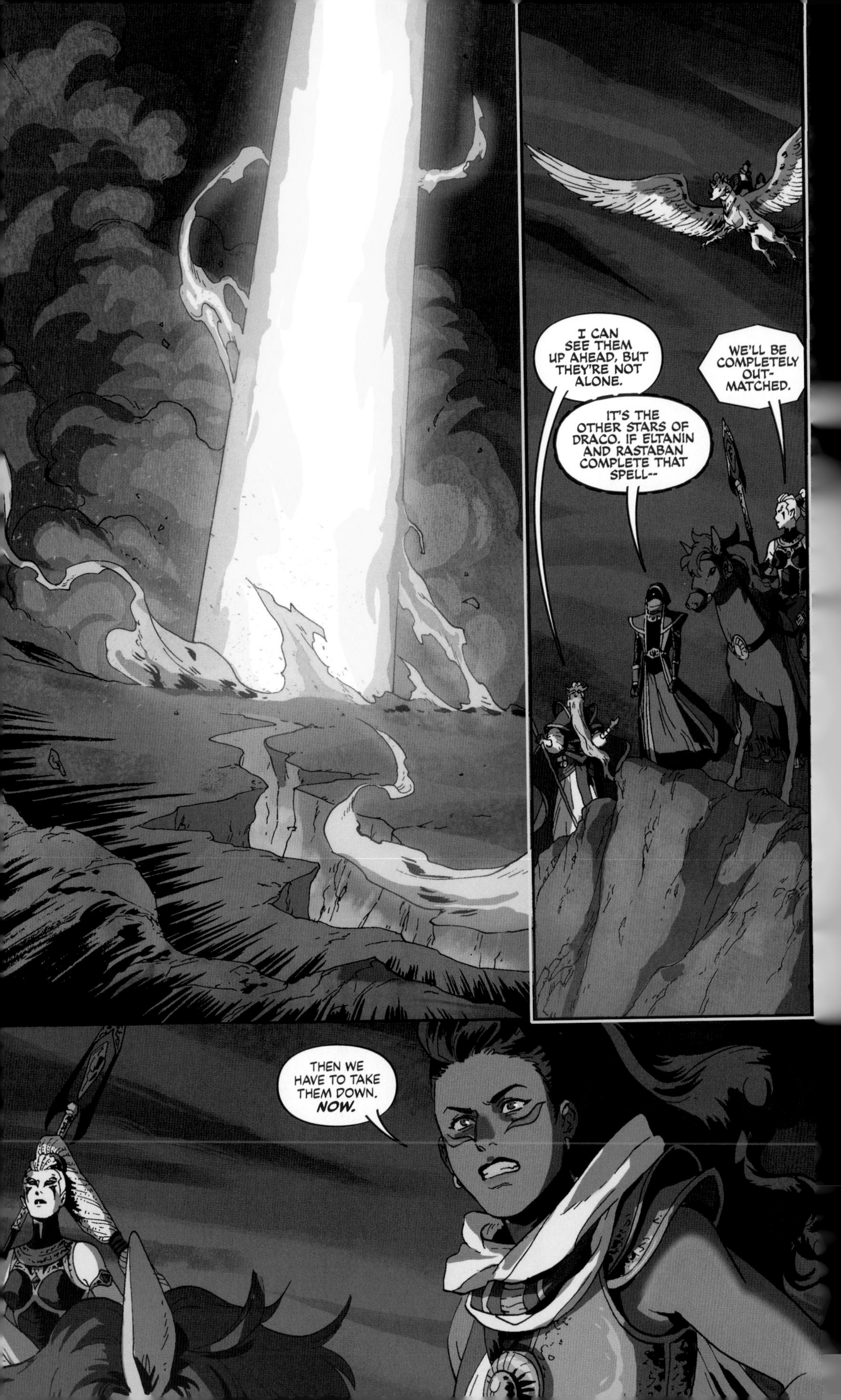
I CAN SEE THEM UP AHEAD, BUT THEY'RE NOT ALONE.
IT'S THE OTHER STARS OF DRACO. IF ELTANIN AND RASTABAN COMPLETE THAT SPELL--
WE'LL BE COMPLETELY OUT-MATCHED.
THEN WE HAVE TO TAKE THEM DOWN. *NOW.*

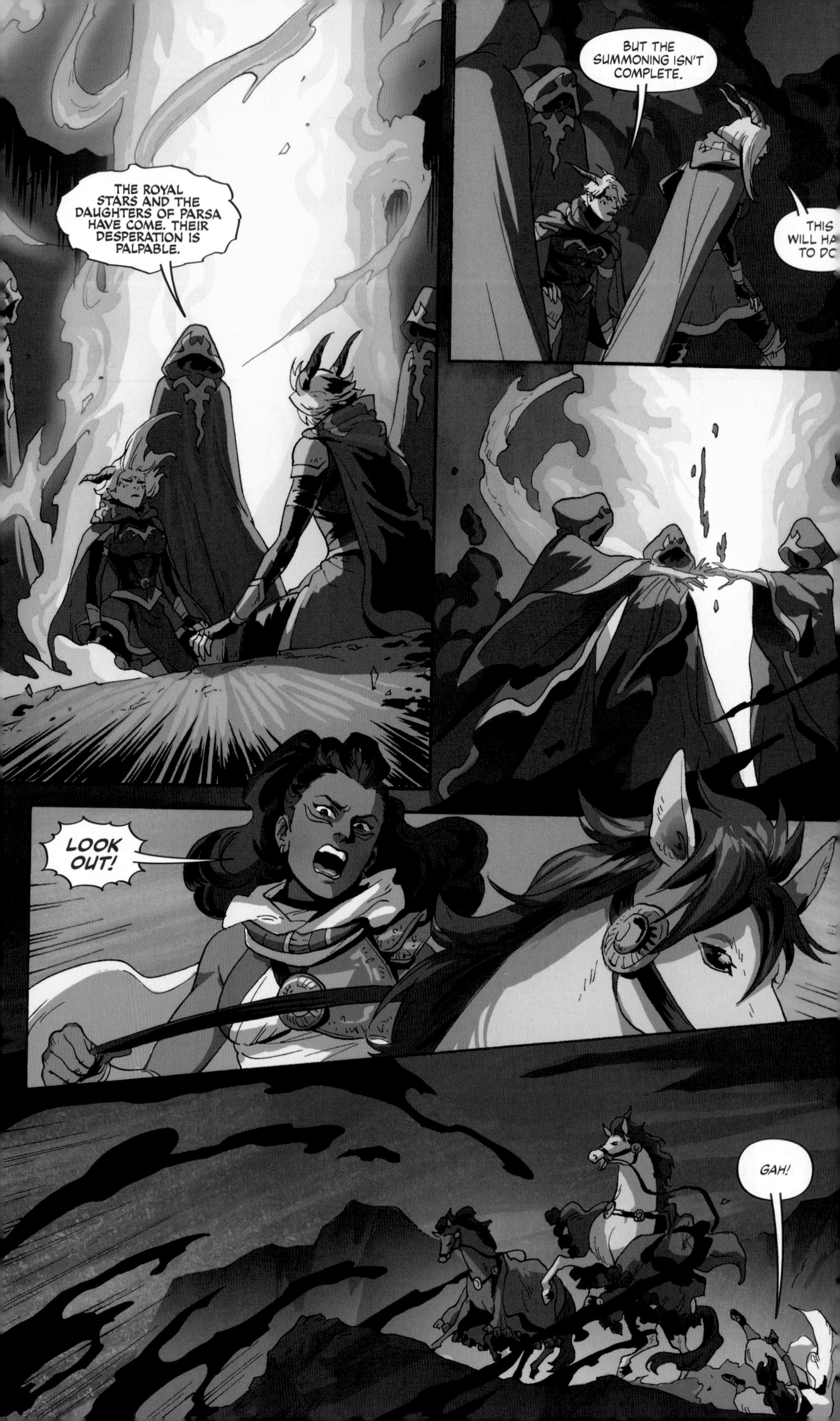
THE ROYAL STARS AND THE DAUGHTERS OF PARSA HAVE COME. THEIR DESPERATION IS PALPABLE.
BUT THE SUMMONING ISN'T COMPLETE.
THIS WILL HA TO DO
LOOK OUT!
GAH!

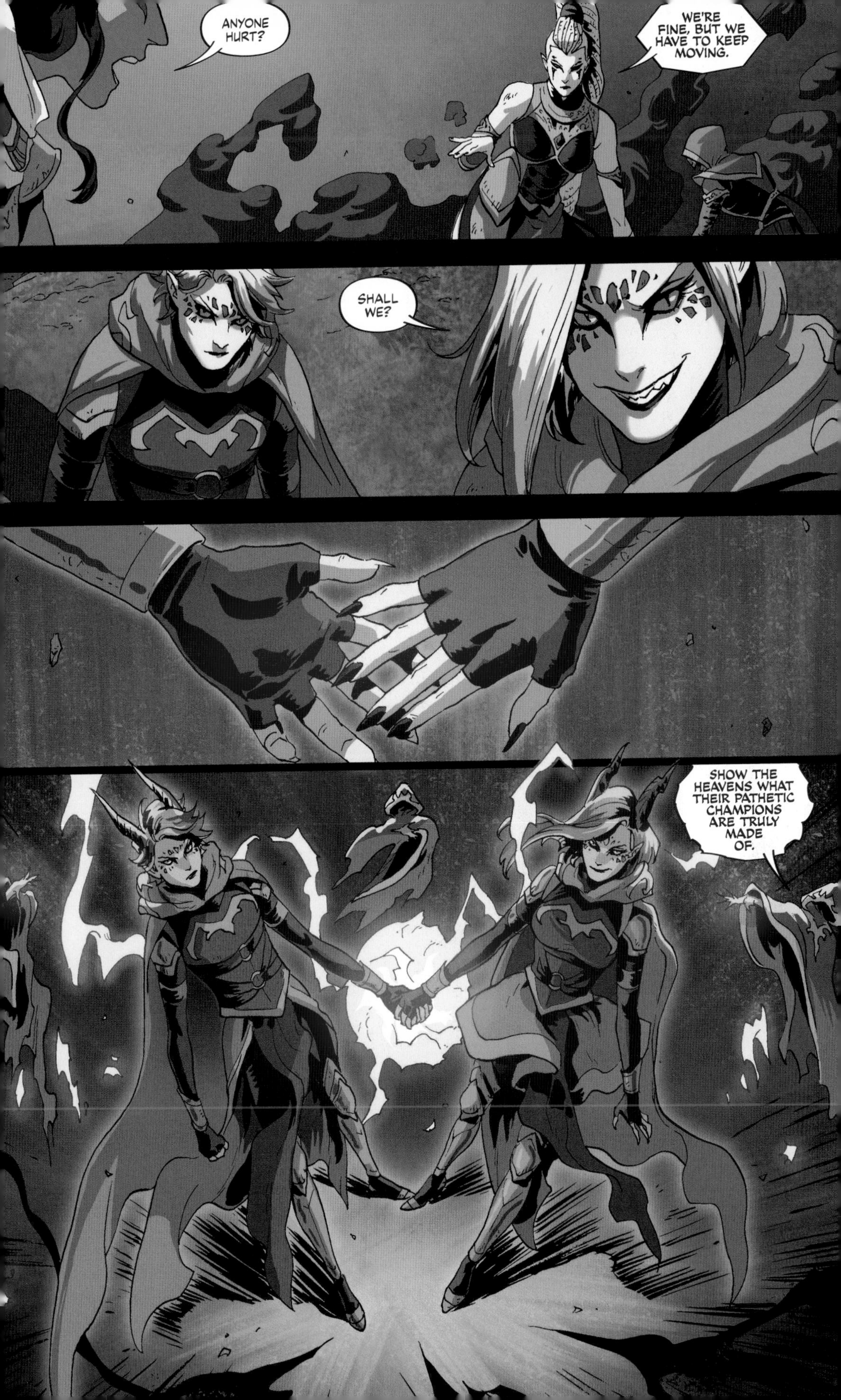
ANYONE HURT?
WE'RE FINE, BUT WE HAVE TO KEEP MOVING.
SHALL WE?
SHOW THE HEAVENS WHAT THEIR PATHETIC CHAMPIONS ARE TRULY MADE OF.

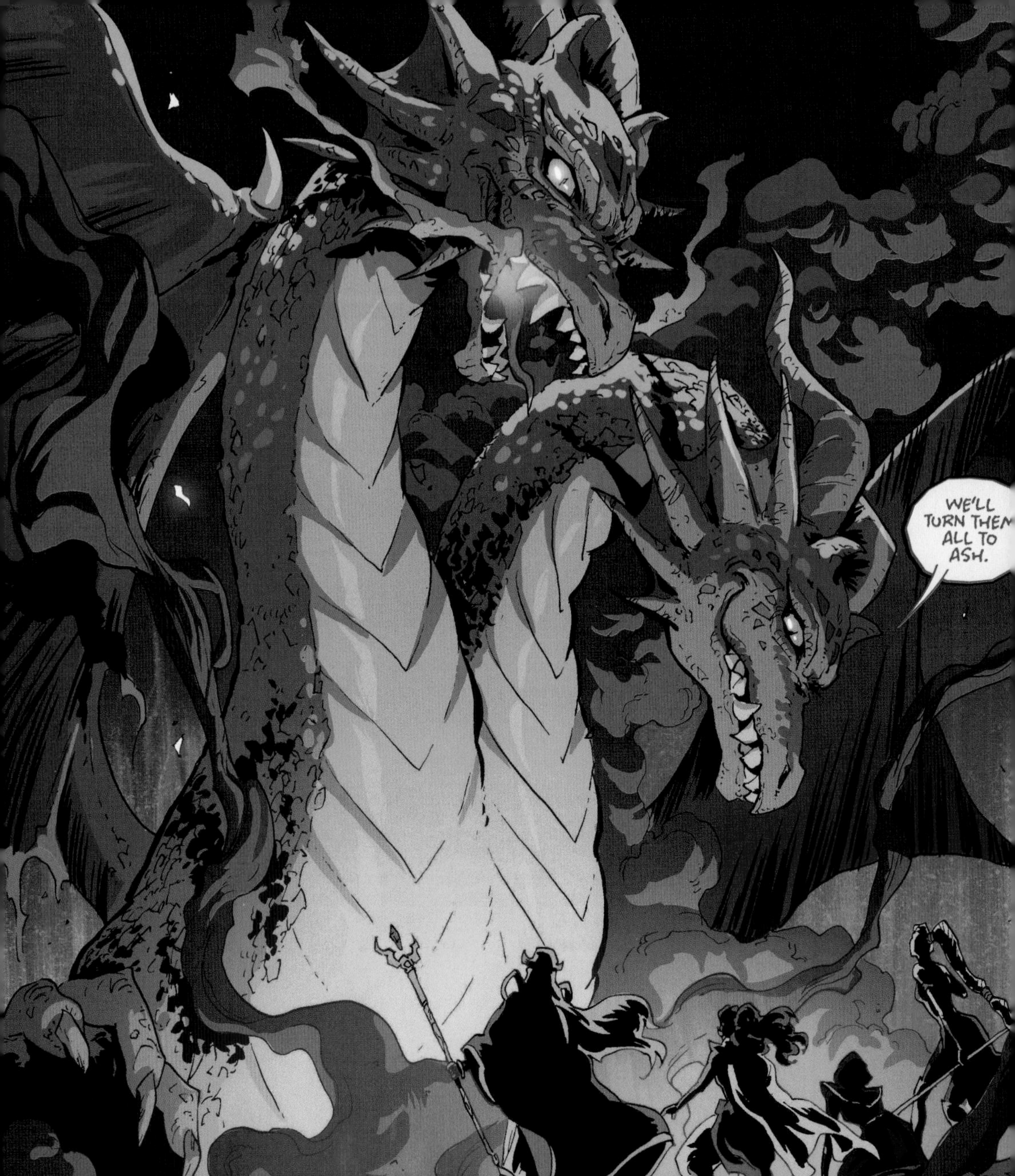
WE'LL TURN THEM ALL TO ASH.

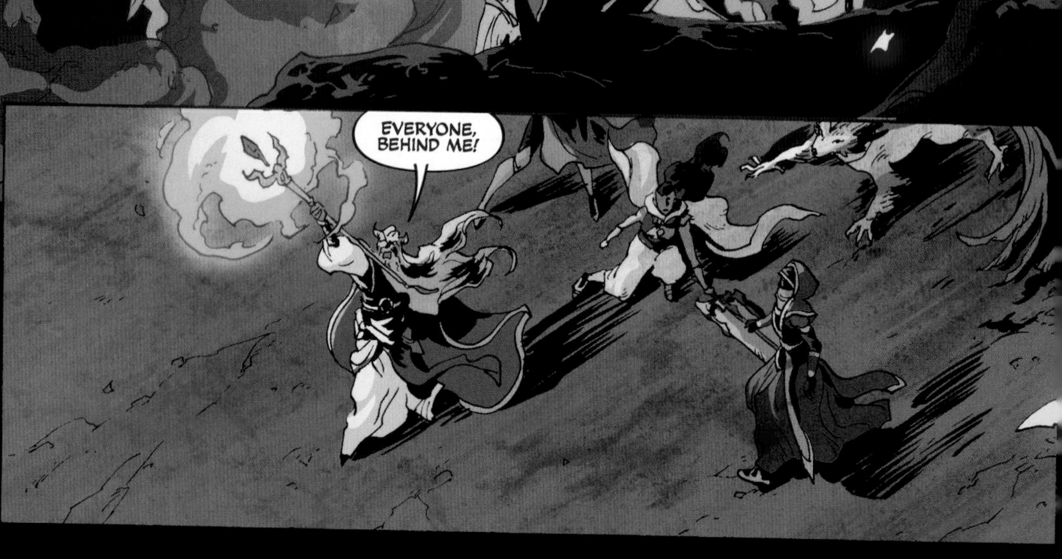
EVERYONE, BEHIND ME!

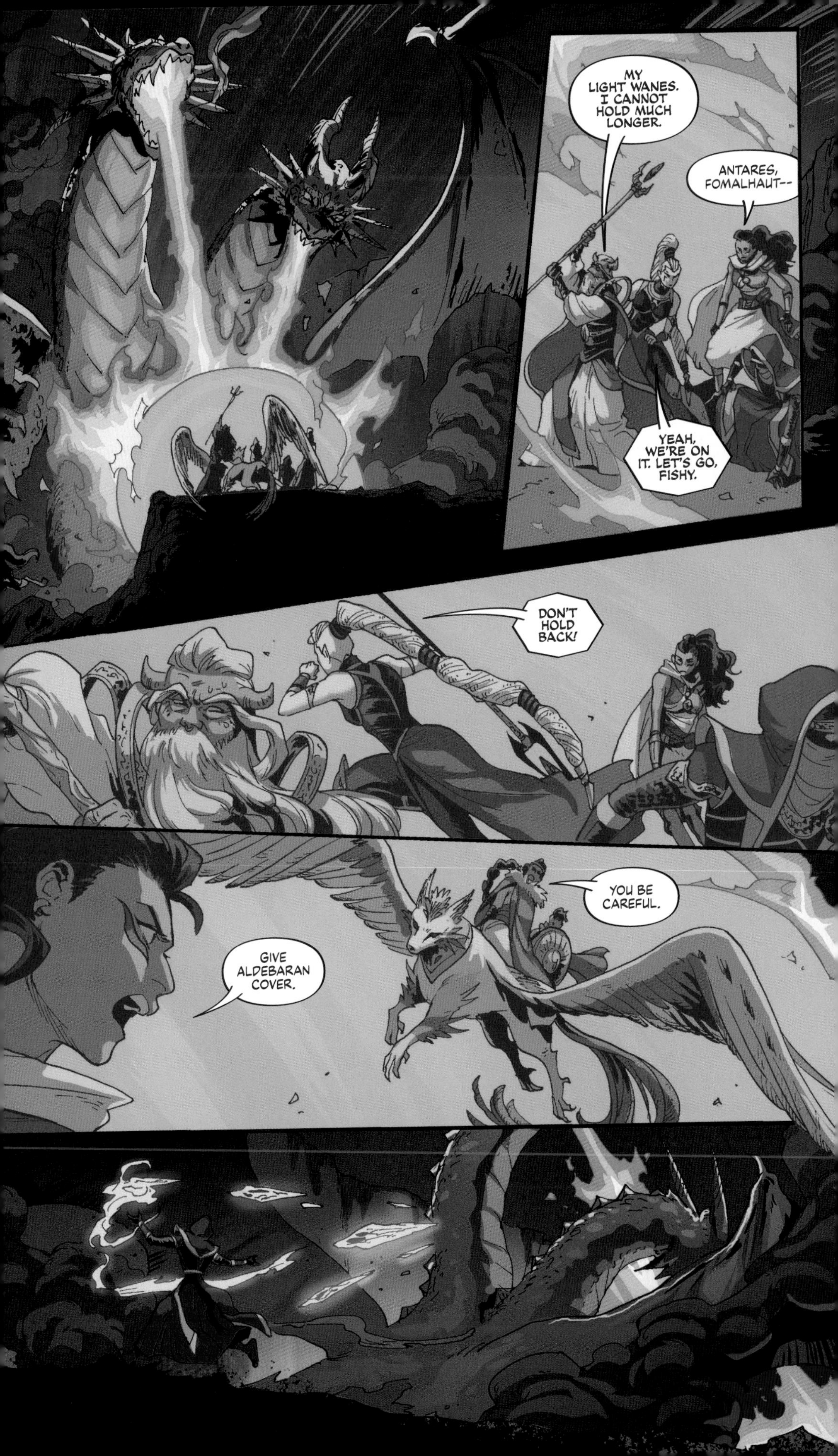
MY LIGHT WANES. I CANNOT HOLD MUCH LONGER.
ANTARES, FOMALHAUT--
YEAH, WE'RE ON IT. LET'S GO, FISHY.
DON'T HOLD BACK!
YOU BE CAREFUL.
GIVE ALDEBARAN COVER.

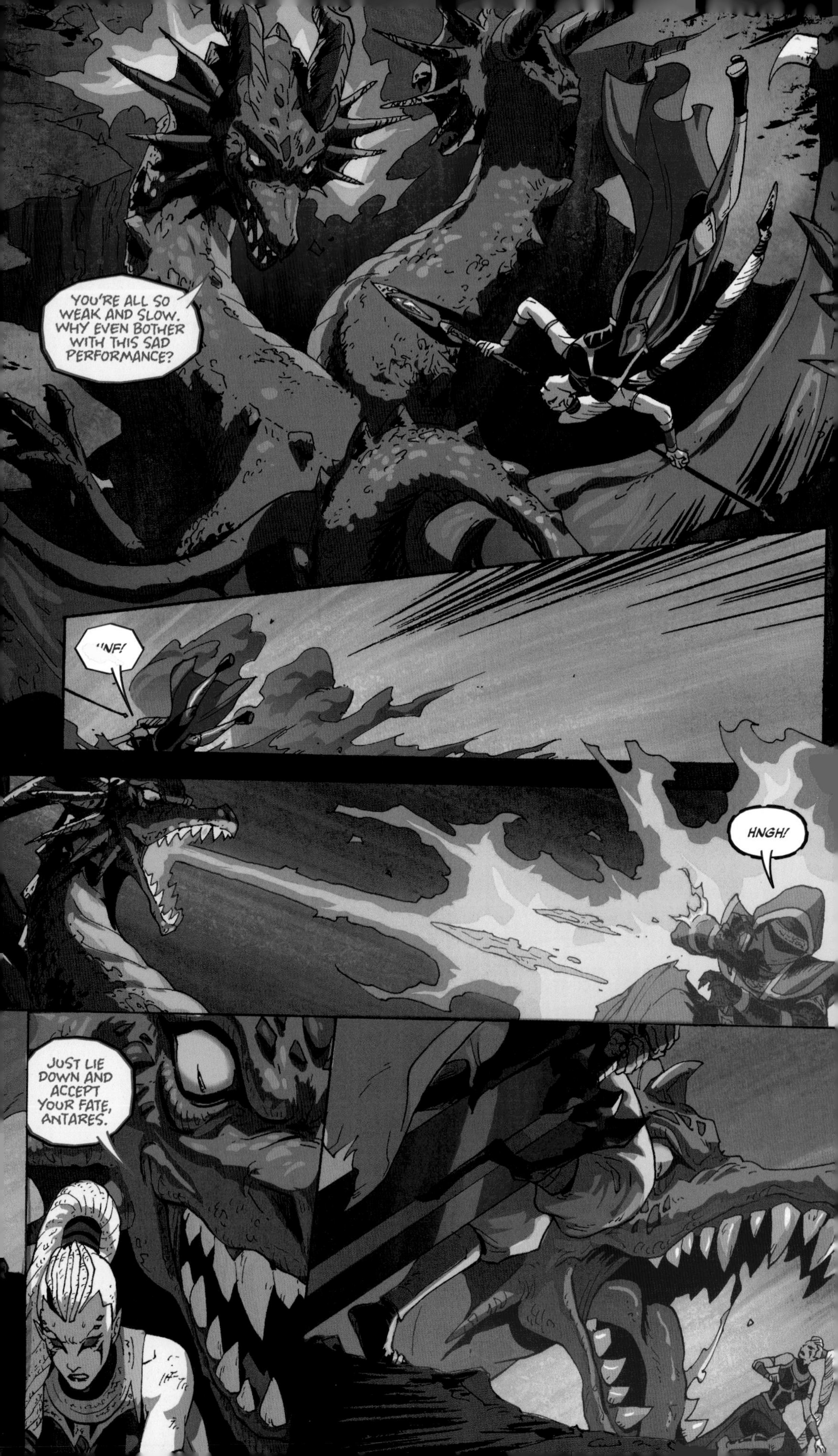
YOU'RE ALL SO WEAK AND SLOW. WHY EVEN BOTHER WITH THIS SAD PERFORMANCE?
UNF!
HNGH!
JUST LIE DOWN AND ACCEPT YOUR FATE, ANTARES.

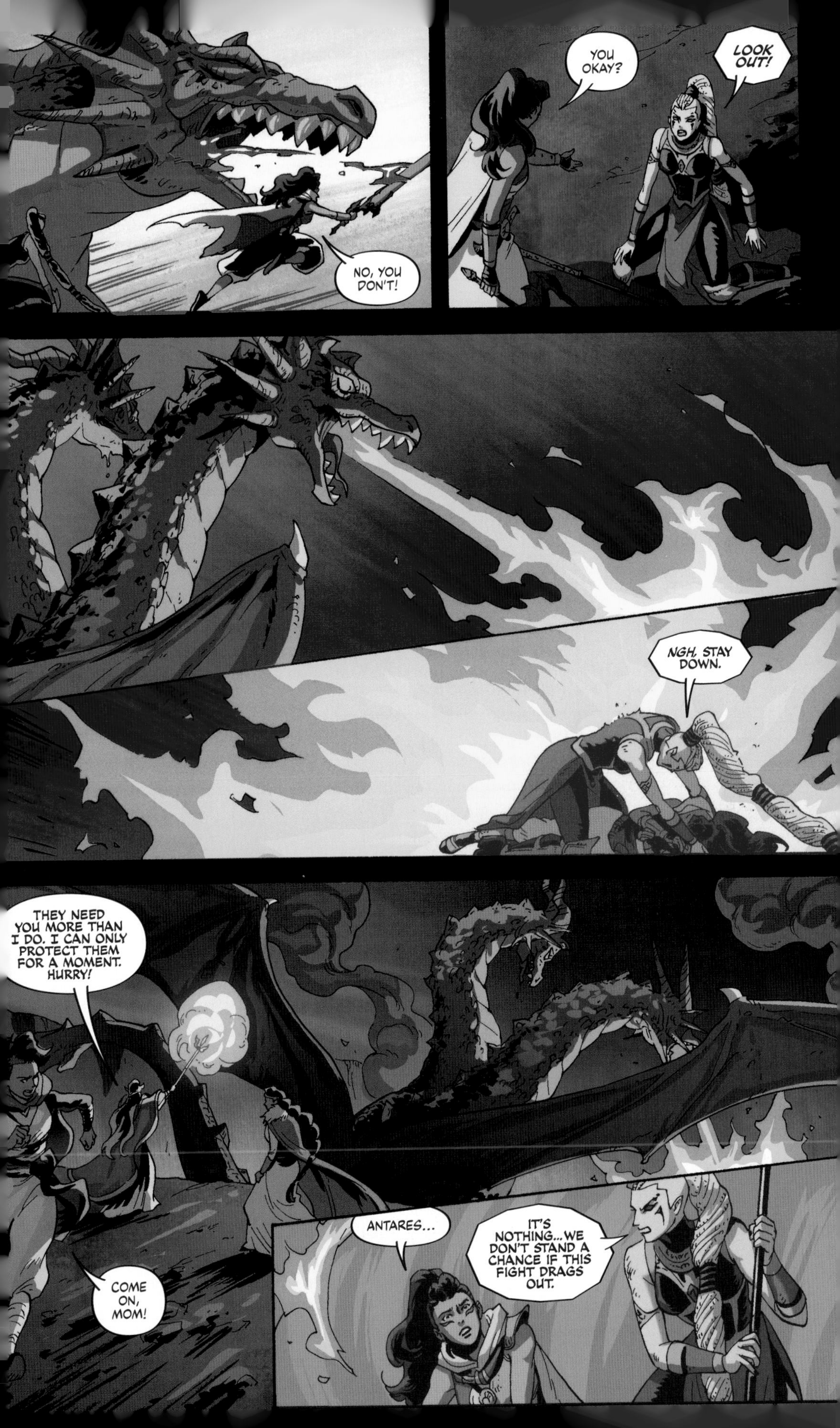
NO, YOU DON'T!
YOU OKAY?
LOOK OUT!
NGH, STAY DOWN.
THEY NEED YOU MORE THAN I DO. I CAN ONLY PROTECT THEM FOR A MOMENT. HURRY!
COME ON, MOM!
ANTARES...
IT'S NOTHING...WE DON'T STAND A CHANCE IF THIS FIGHT DRAGS OUT.

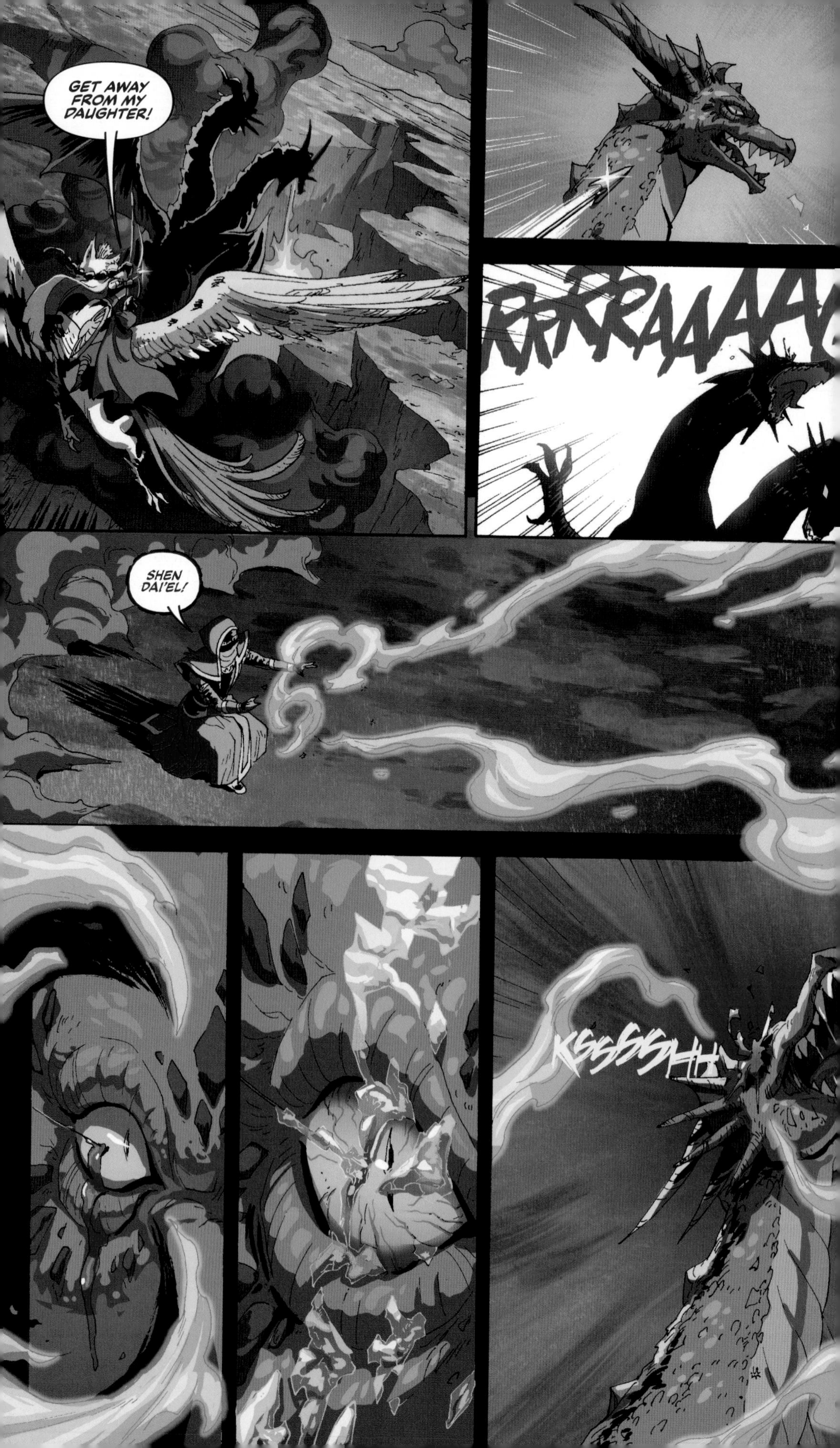
GET AWAY FROM MY DAUGHTER!
RRRRAAAAA
SHEN DAI'EL!
KSSSSSHH

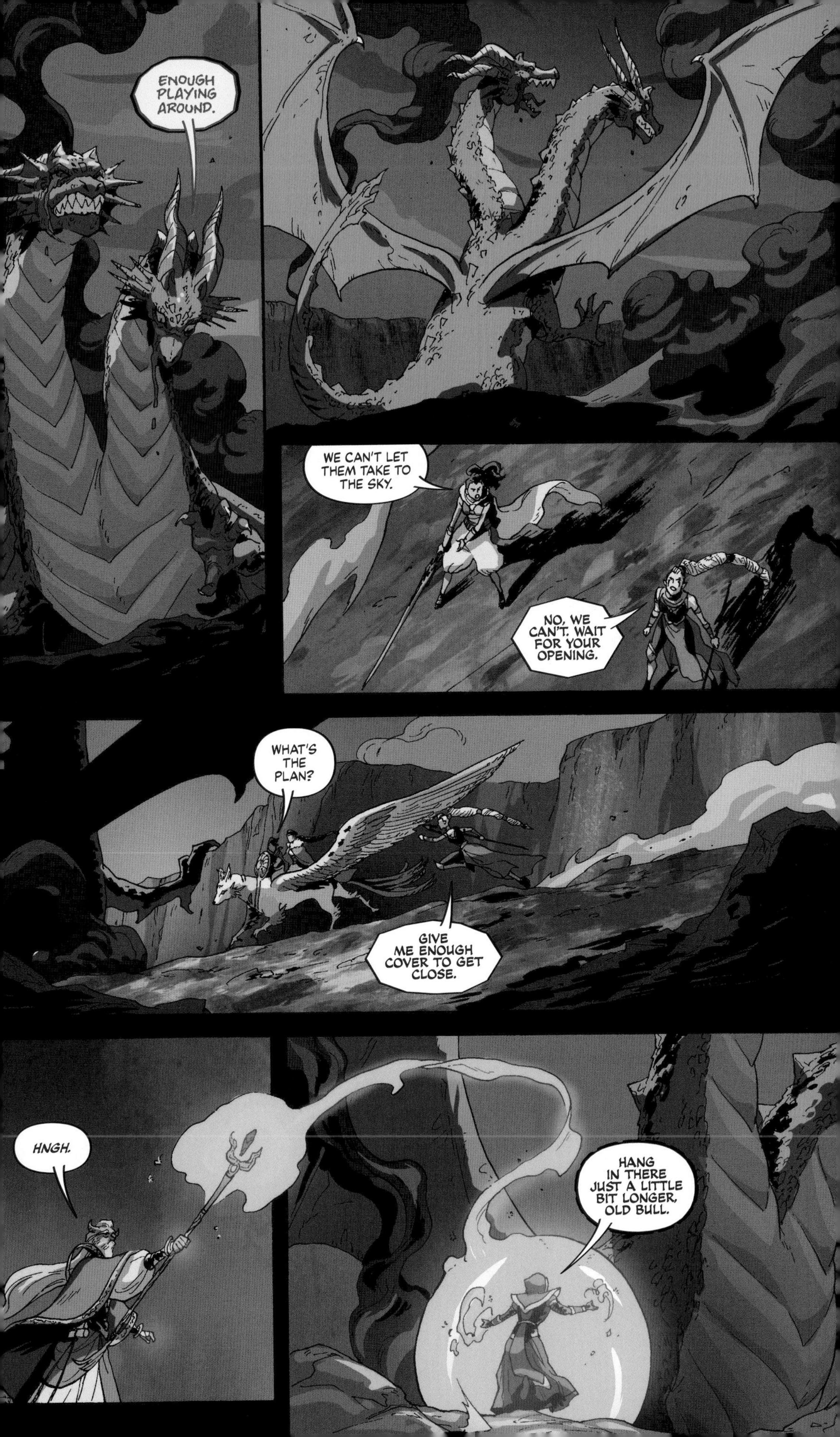
ENOUGH PLAYING AROUND.
WE CAN'T LET THEM TAKE TO THE SKY.
NO, WE CAN'T. WAIT FOR YOUR OPENING.
WHAT'S THE PLAN?
GIVE ME ENOUGH COVER TO GET CLOSE.
HNGH.
HANG IN THERE JUST A LITTLE BIT LONGER, OLD BULL.

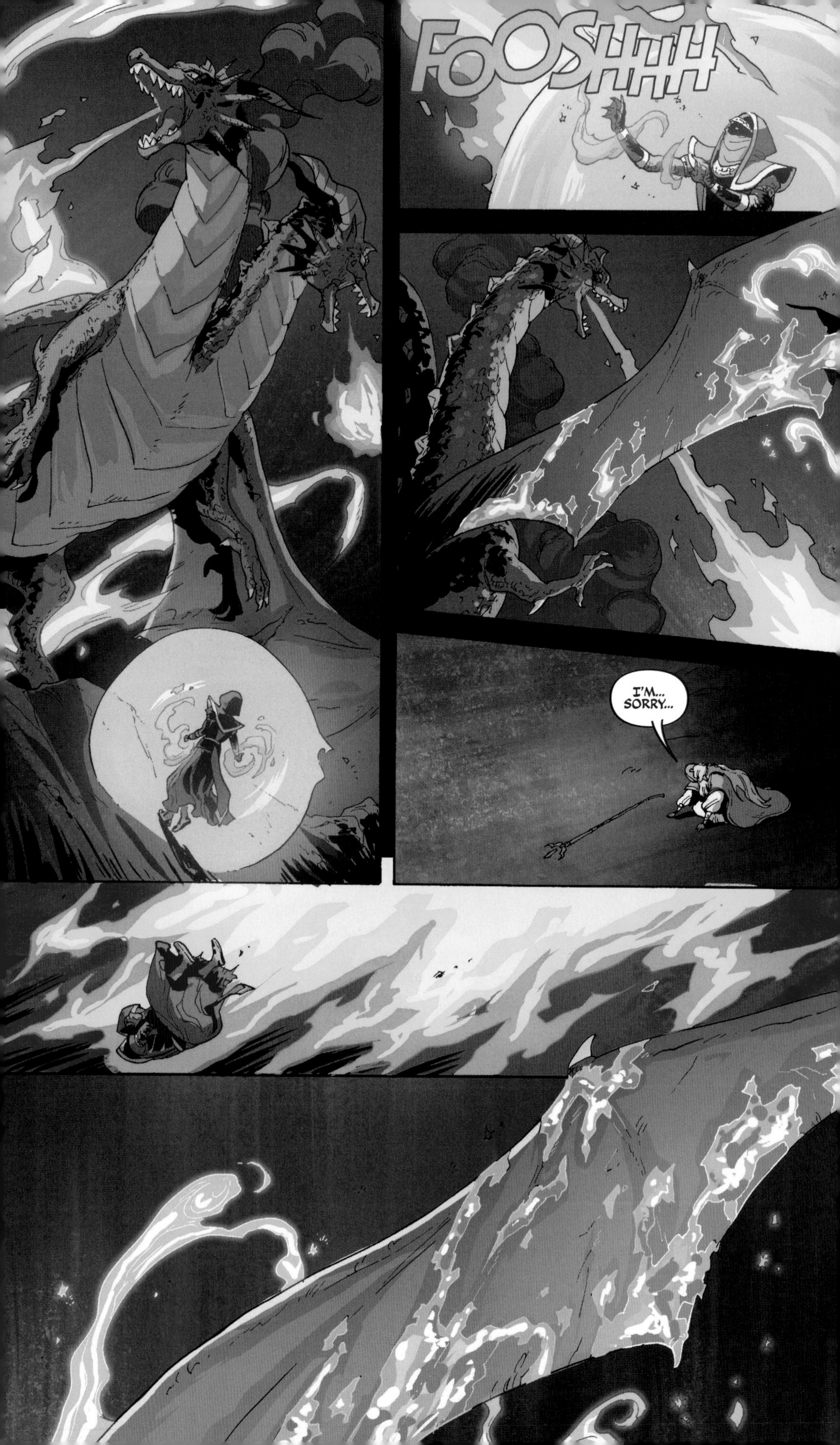
FOOSHHHH
I'M... SORRY...

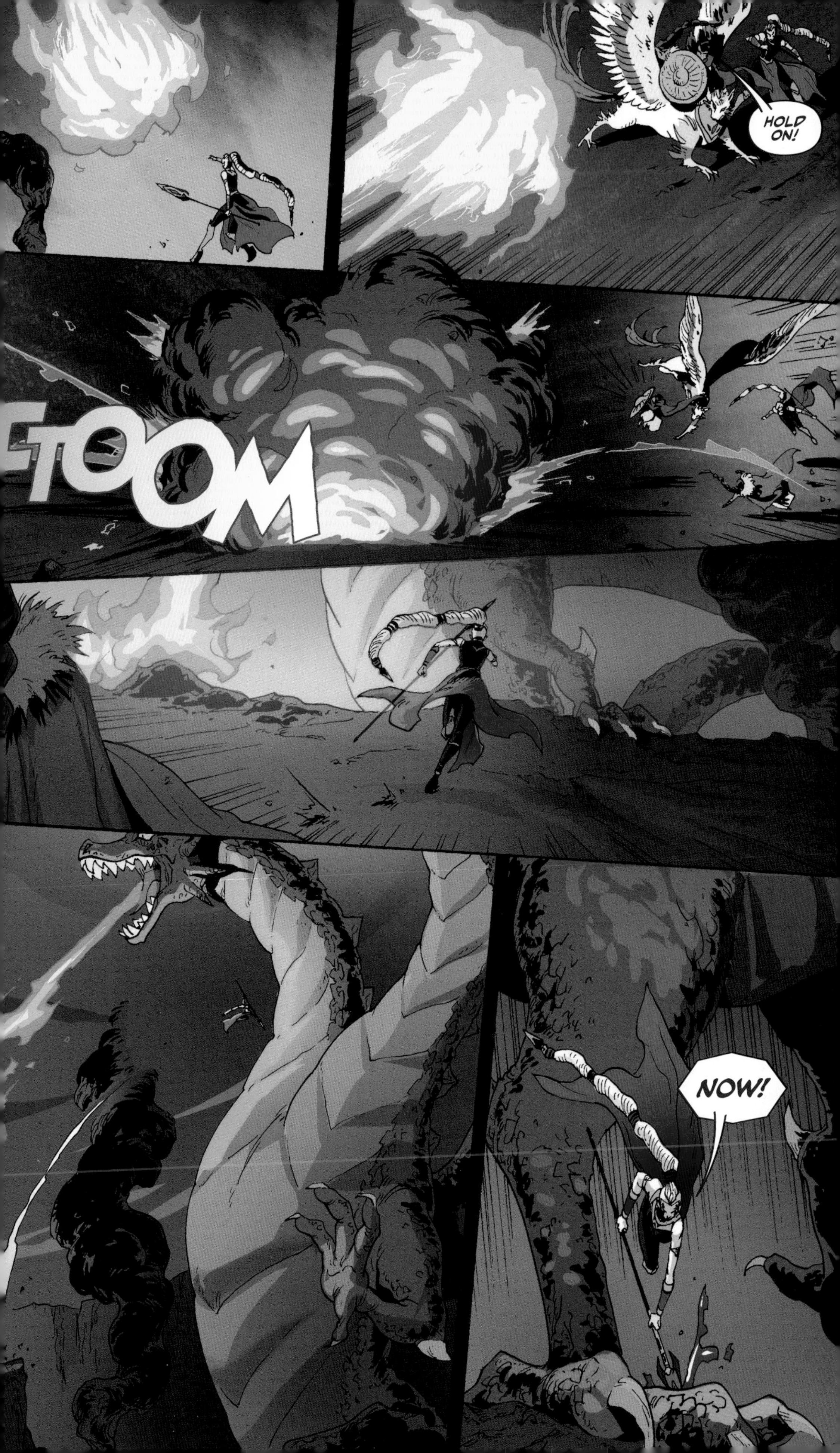
HOLD ON!
TOOM
NOW!

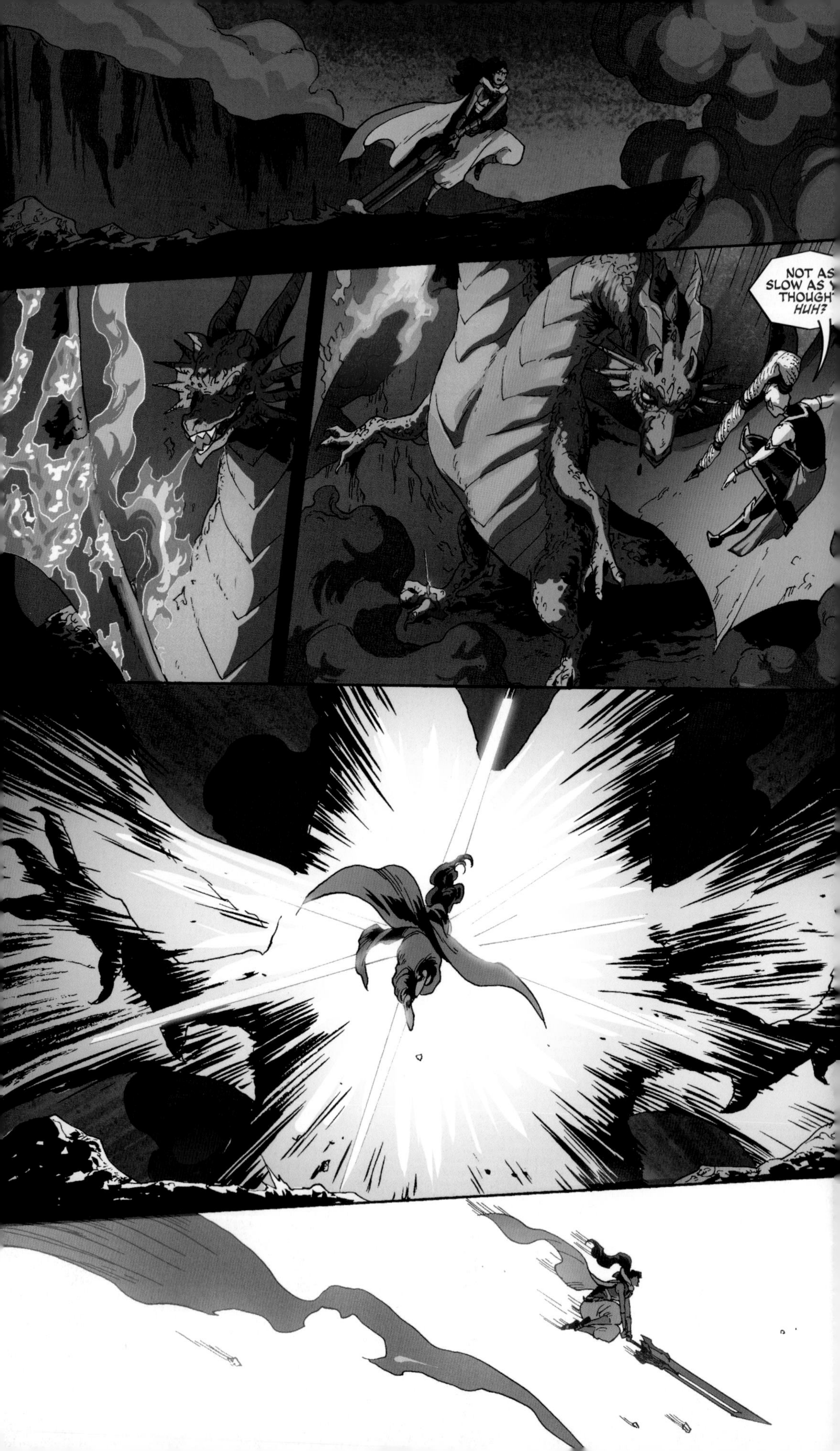
NOT AS SLOW AS THOUGH HUH?

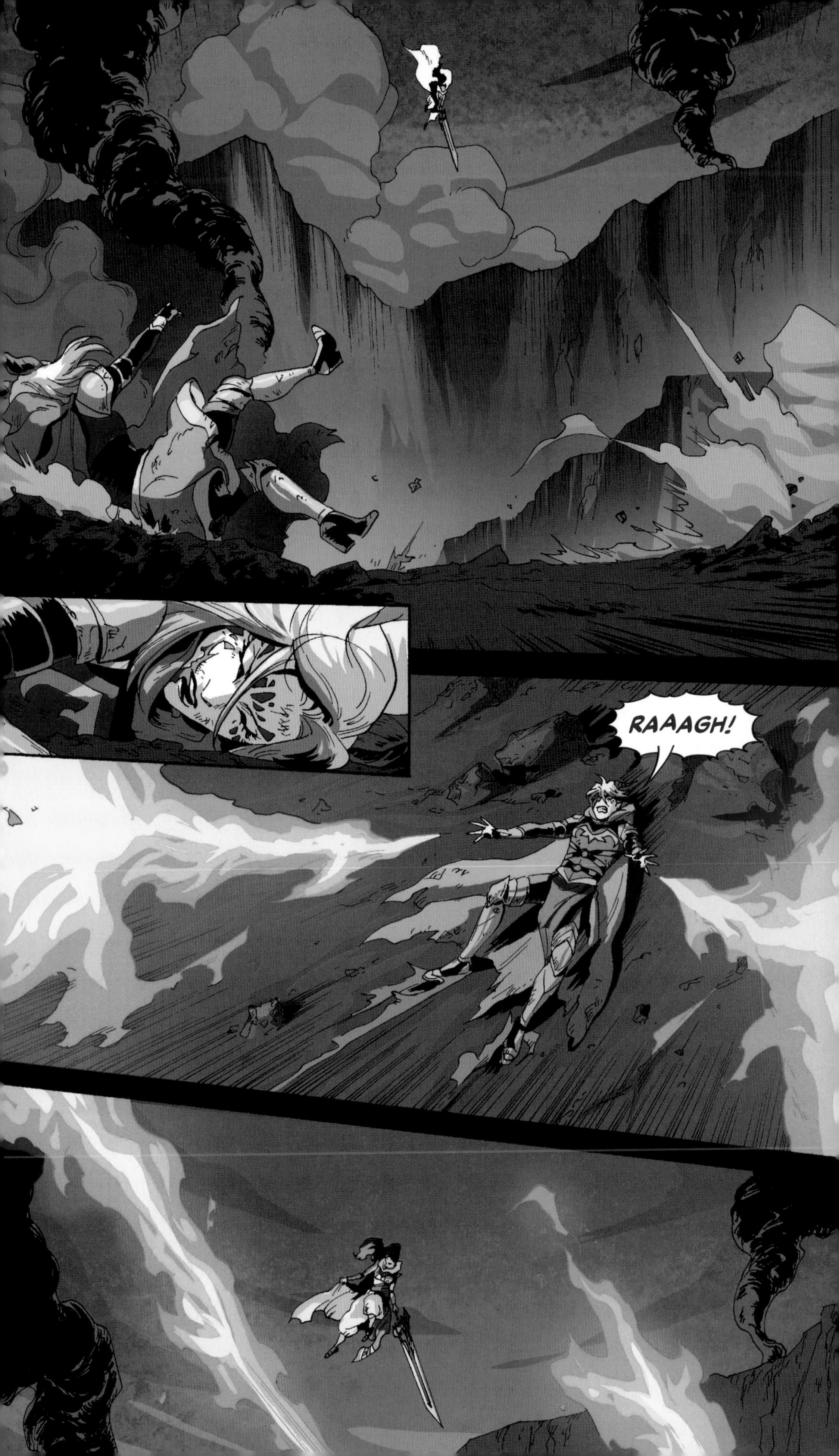
RAAAGH!

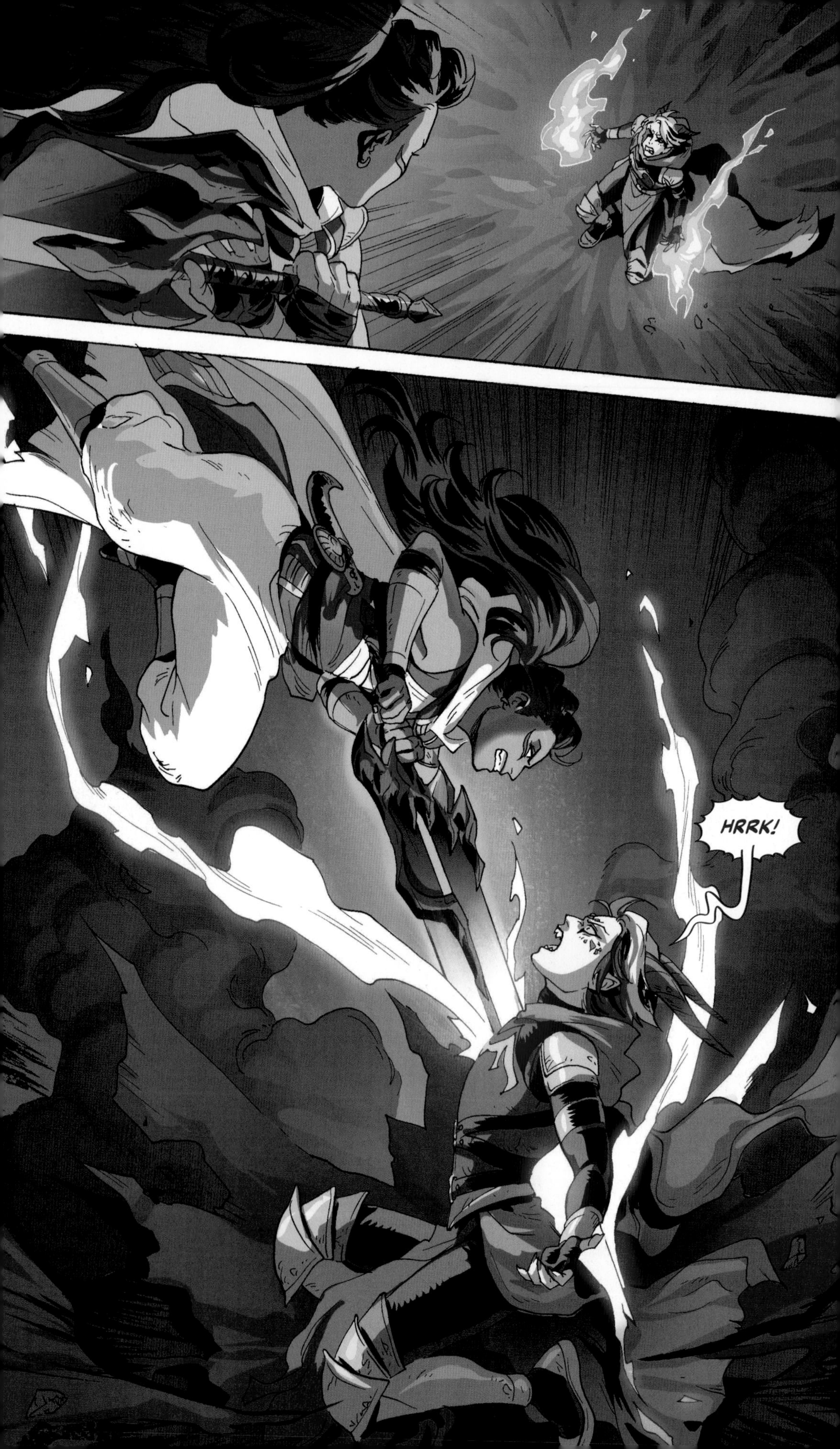
HRRK!

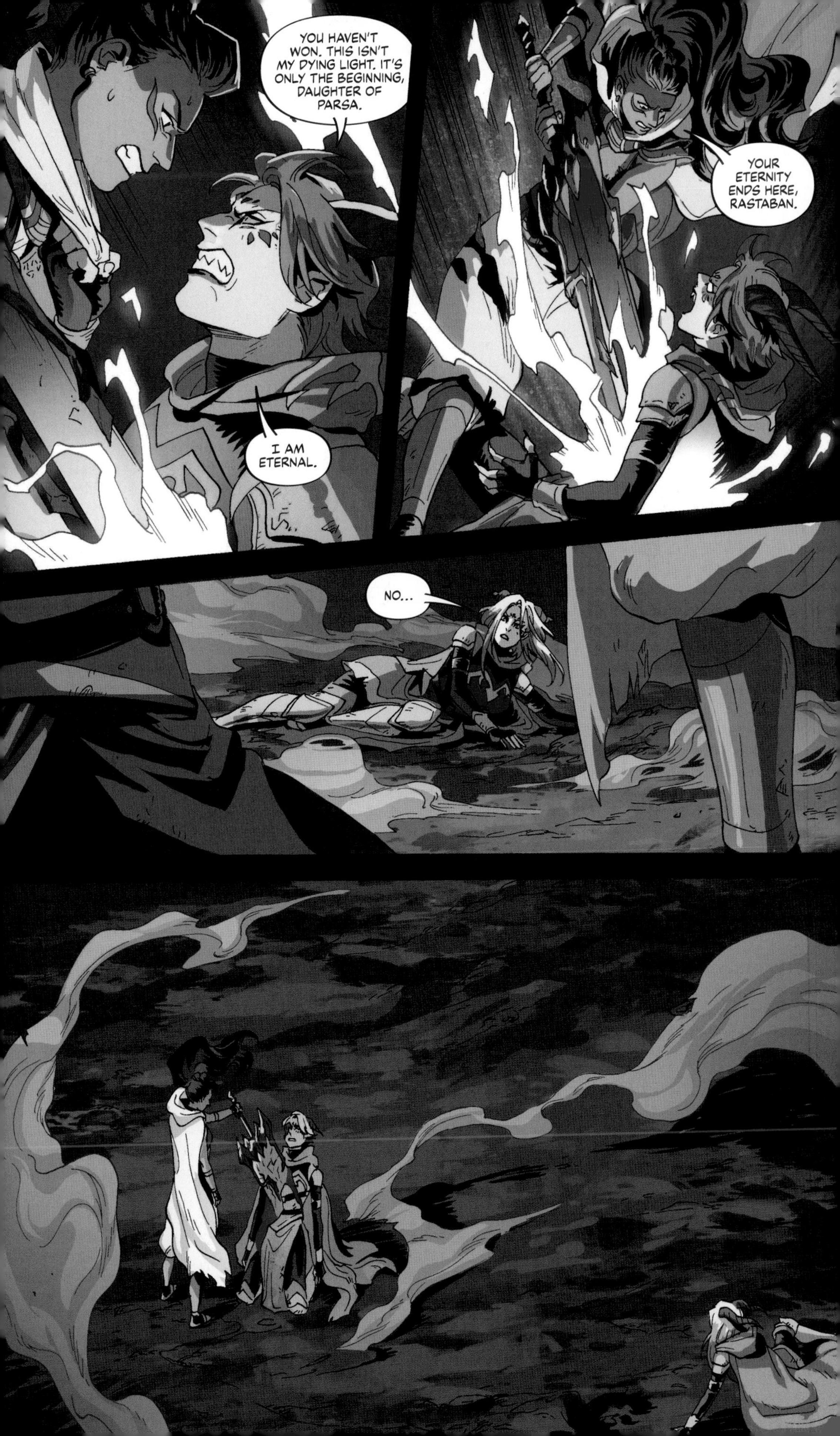

YOU HAVEN'T WON. THIS ISN'T MY DYING LIGHT. IT'S ONLY THE BEGINNING, DAUGHTER OF PARSA.
I AM ETERNAL.
YOUR ETERNITY ENDS HERE, RASTABAN.
NO...

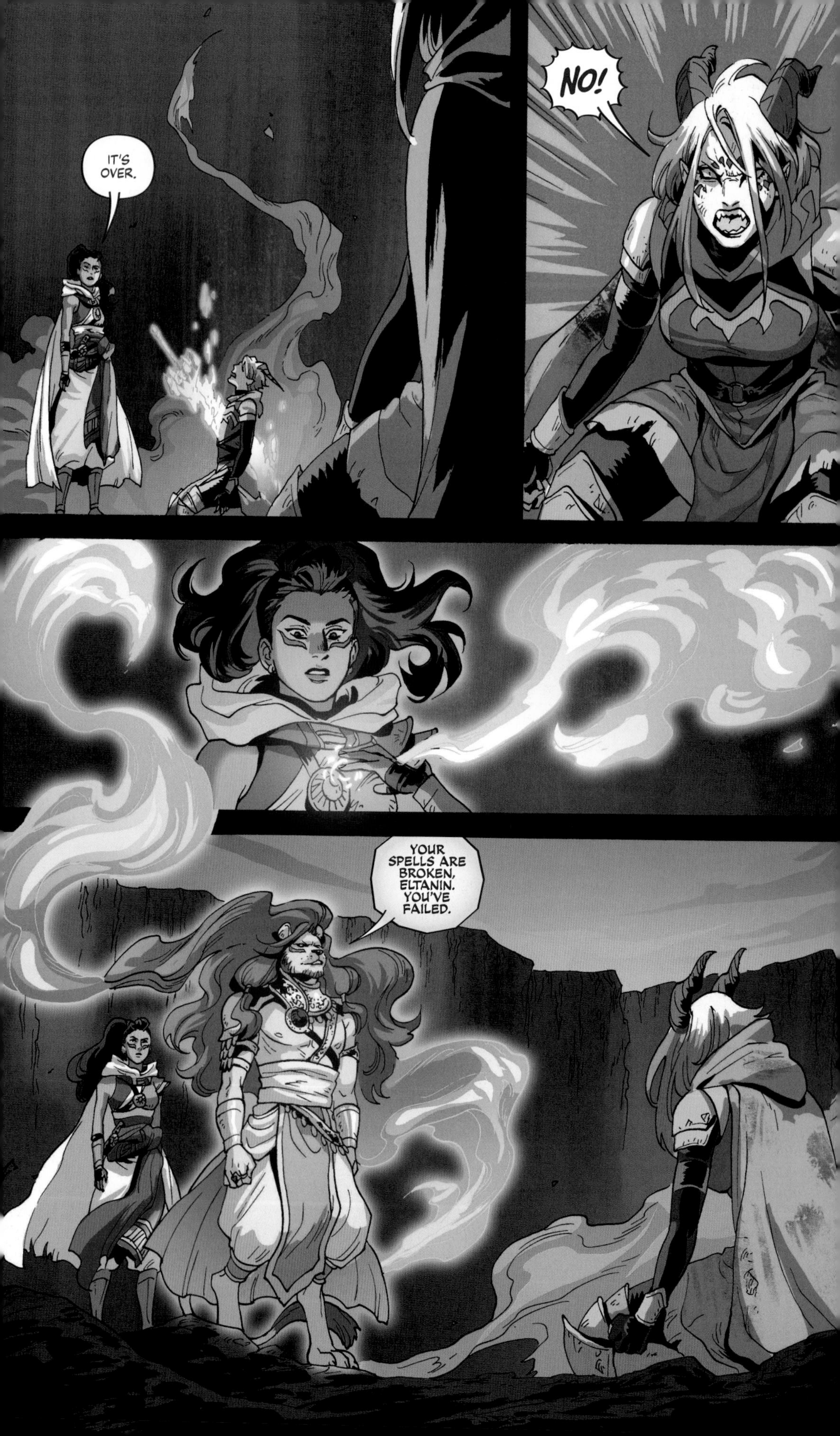
IT'S OVER.
NO!
YOUR SPELLS ARE BROKEN, ELTANIN. YOU'VE FAILED.

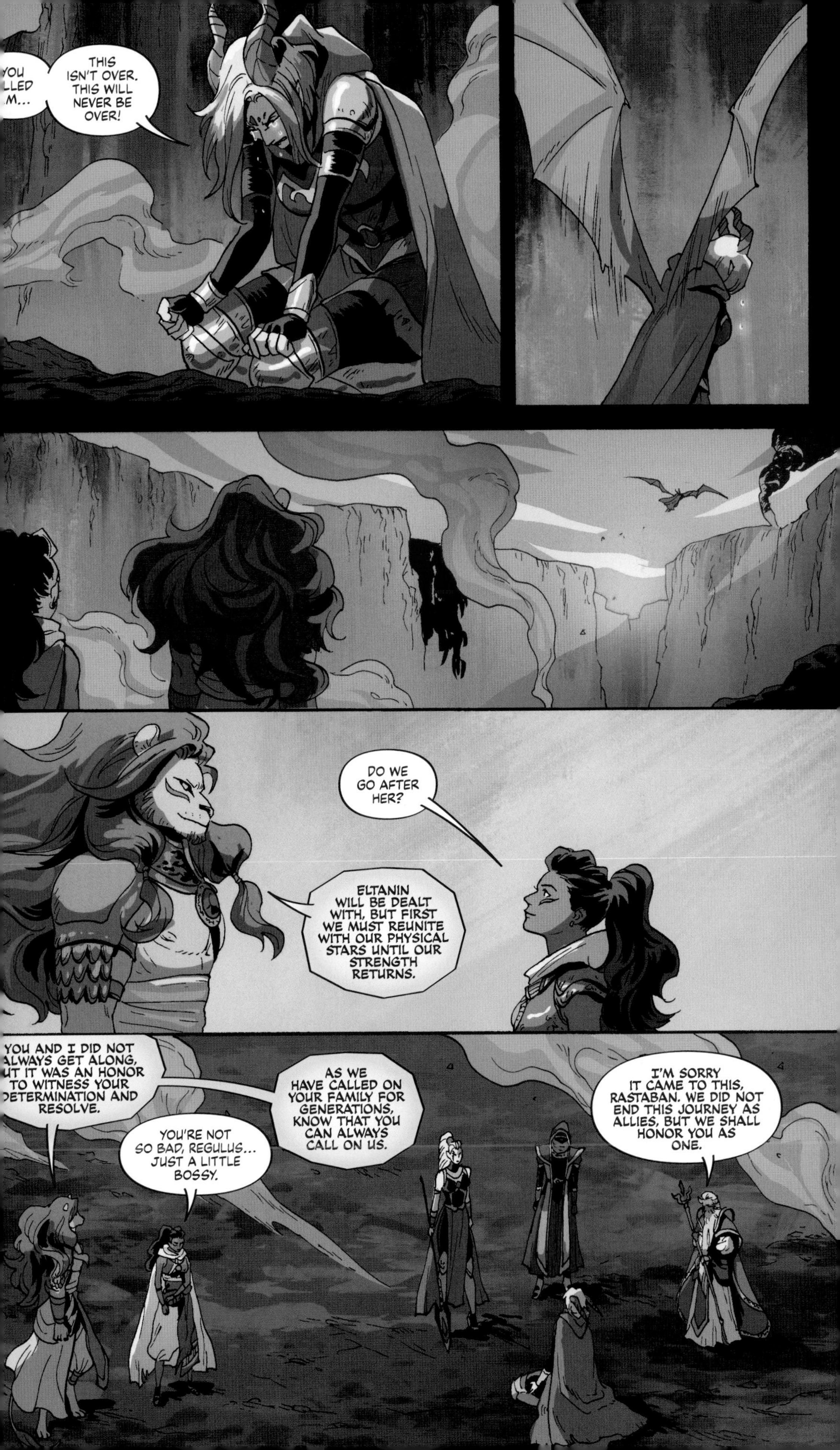
YOU LLED M...
THIS ISN'T OVER. THIS WILL NEVER BE OVER!
DO WE GO AFTER HER?
ELTANIN WILL BE DEALT WITH, BUT FIRST WE MUST REUNITE WITH OUR PHYSICAL STARS UNTIL OUR STRENGTH RETURNS.
YOU AND I DID NOT LWAYS GET ALONG, UT IT WAS AN HONOR TO WITNESS YOUR ETERMINATION AND RESOLVE.
YOU'RE NOT SO BAD, REGULUS... JUST A LITTLE BOSSY.
AS WE HAVE CALLED ON YOUR FAMILY FOR GENERATIONS, KNOW THAT YOU CAN ALWAYS CALL ON US.
I'M SORRY IT CAME TO THIS, RASTABAN. WE DID NOT END THIS JOURNEY AS ALLIES, BUT WE SHALL HONOR YOU AS ONE.

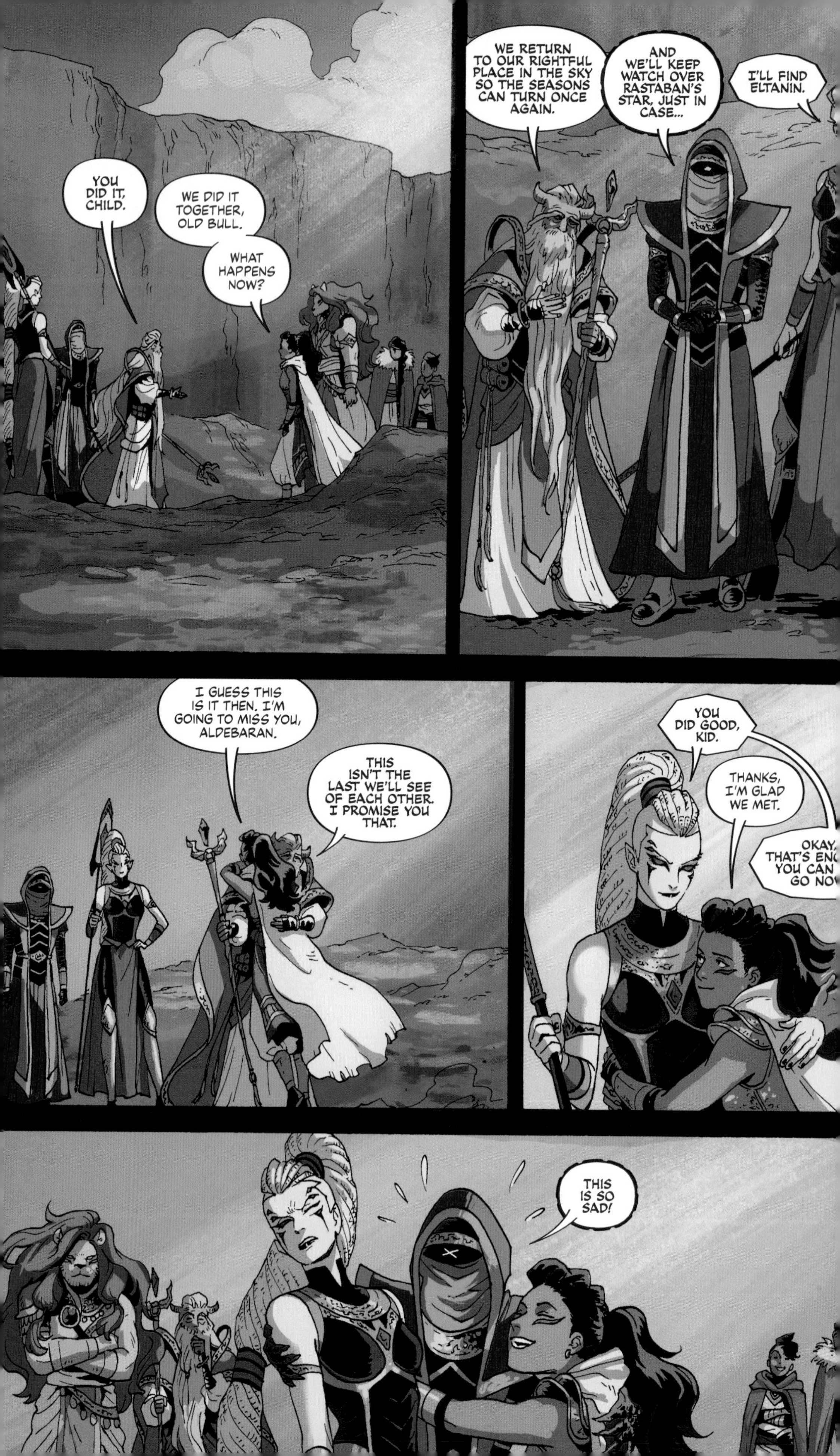
YOU DID IT, CHILD.
WE DID IT TOGETHER, OLD BULL.
WHAT HAPPENS NOW?
WE RETURN TO OUR RIGHTFUL PLACE IN THE SKY SO THE SEASONS CAN TURN ONCE AGAIN.
AND WE'LL KEEP WATCH OVER RASTABAN'S STAR, JUST IN CASE...
I'LL FIND ELTANIN.
I GUESS THIS IS IT THEN. I'M GOING TO MISS YOU, ALDEBARAN.
THIS ISN'T THE LAST WE'LL SEE OF EACH OTHER. I PROMISE YOU THAT.
YOU DID GOOD, KID.
THANKS, I'M GLAD WE MET.
THIS IS SO SAD!

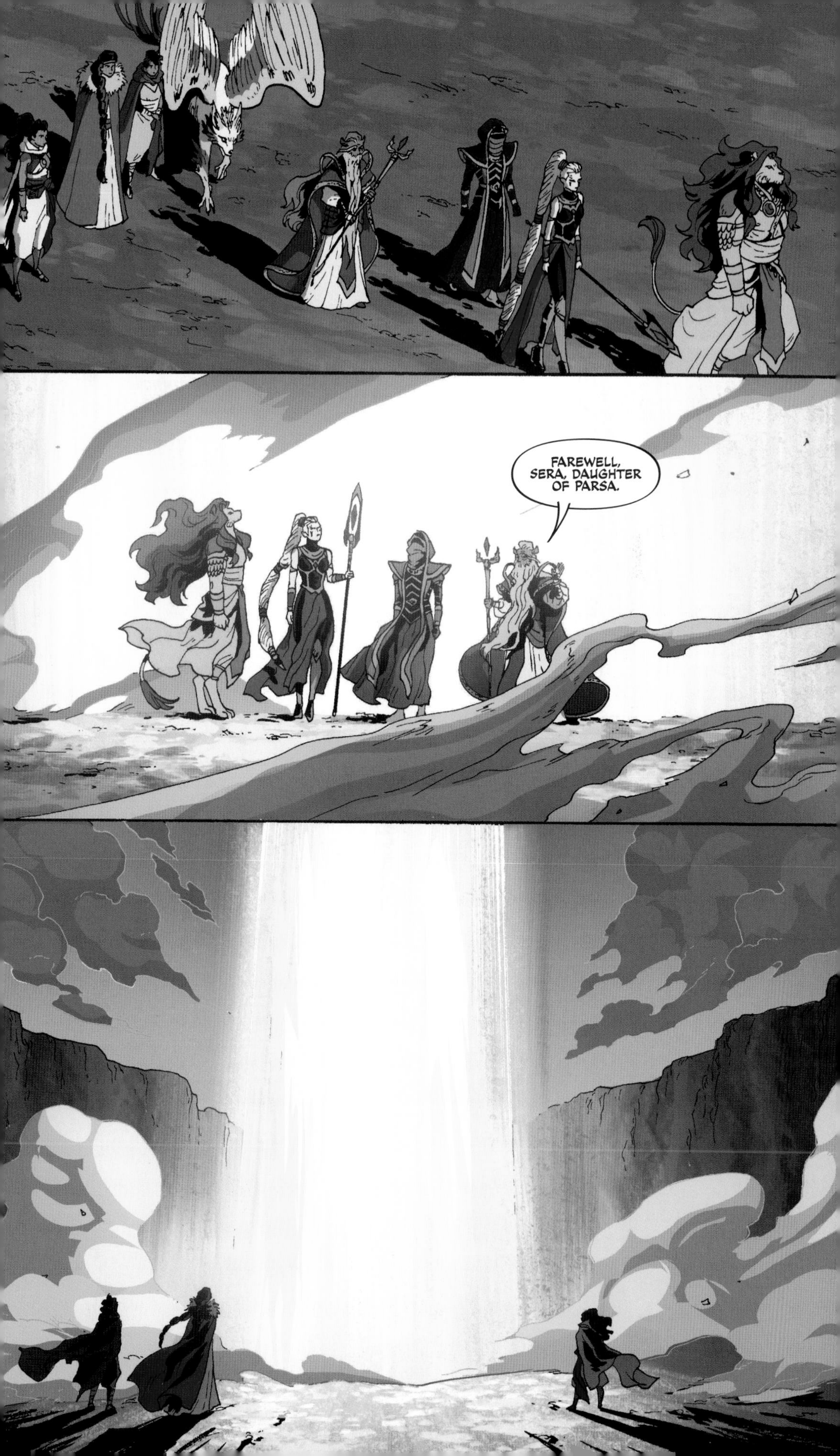
FAREWELL, SERA, DAUGHTER OF PARSA.

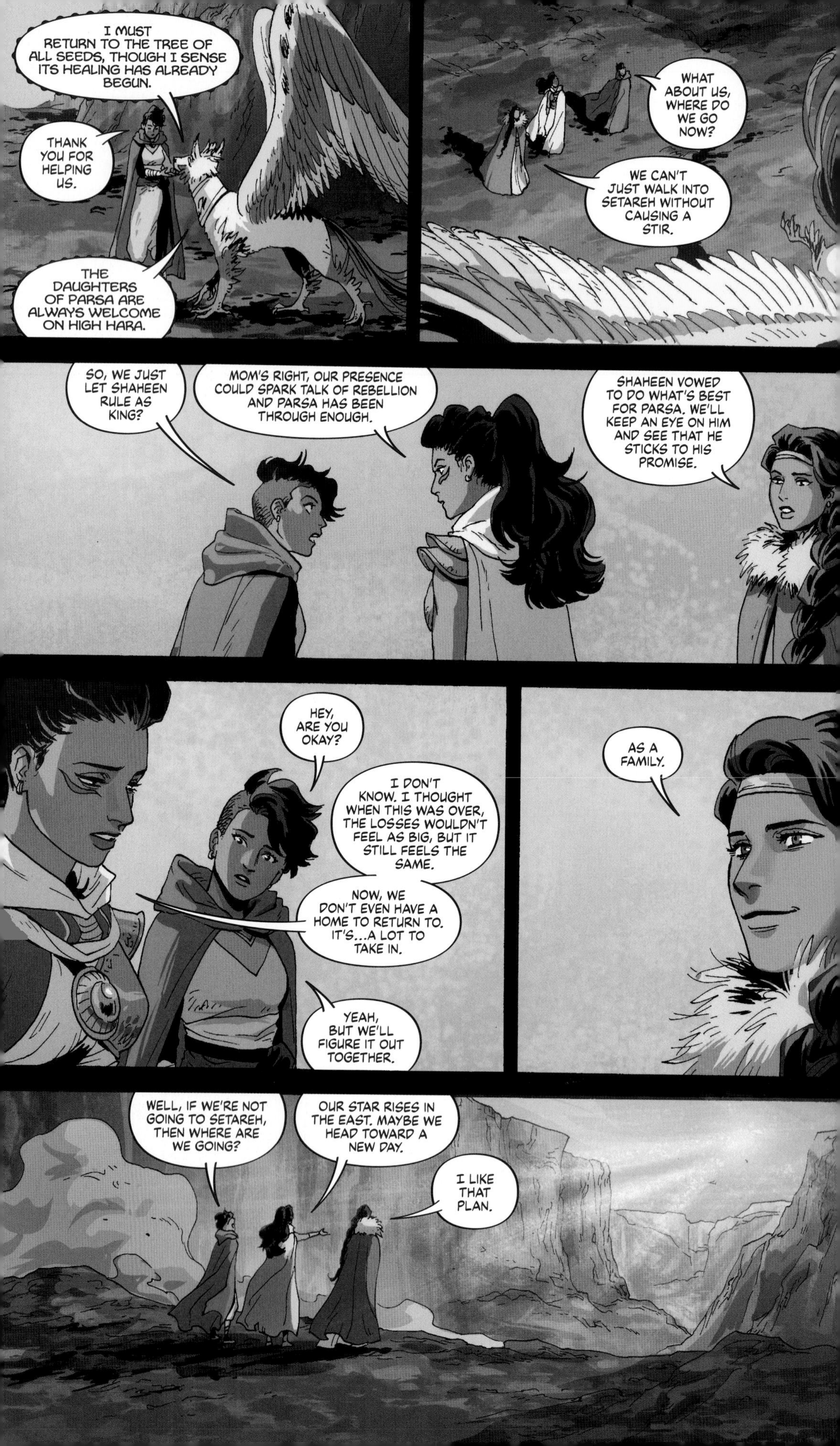
I MUST RETURN TO THE TREE OF ALL SEEDS, THOUGH I SENSE ITS HEALING HAS ALREADY BEGUN.
THANK YOU FOR HELPING US.
THE DAUGHTERS OF PARSA ARE ALWAYS WELCOME ON HIGH HARA.
WHAT ABOUT US, WHERE DO WE GO NOW?
WE CAN'T JUST WALK INTO SETAREH WITHOUT CAUSING A STIR.
SO, WE JUST LET SHAHEEN RULE AS KING?
MOM'S RIGHT, OUR PRESENCE COULD SPARK TALK OF REBELLION AND PARSA HAS BEEN THROUGH ENOUGH.
SHAHEEN VOWED TO DO WHAT'S BEST FOR PARSA. WE'LL KEEP AN EYE ON HIM AND SEE THAT HE STICKS TO HIS PROMISE.
HEY, ARE YOU OKAY?
I DON'T KNOW. I THOUGHT WHEN THIS WAS OVER, THE LOSSES WOULDN'T FEEL AS BIG, BUT IT STILL FEELS THE SAME.
NOW, WE DON'T EVEN HAVE A HOME TO RETURN TO. IT'S...A LOT TO TAKE IN.
YEAH, BUT WE'LL FIGURE IT OUT TOGETHER.
AS A FAMILY.
WELL, IF WE'RE NOT GOING TO SETAREH, THEN WHERE ARE WE GOING?
OUR STAR RISES IN THE EAST. MAYBE WE HEAD TOWARD A NEW DAY.
I LIKE THAT PLAN.

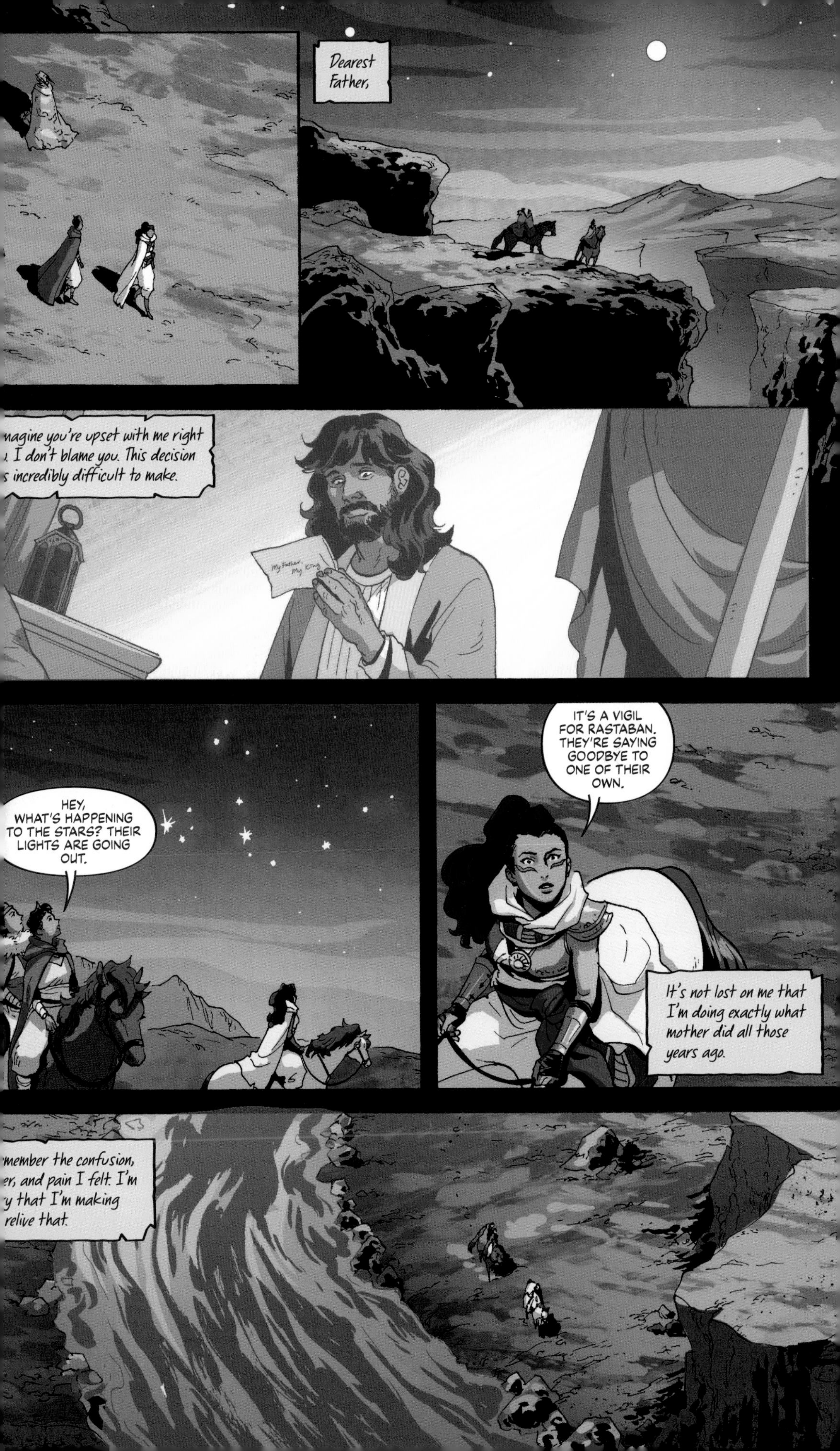
Dearest Father,
nagine you're upset with me right
. I don't blame you. This decision
s incredibly difficult to make.
My Father, My King
HEY, WHAT'S HAPPENING TO THE STARS? THEIR LIGHTS ARE GOING OUT.
IT'S A VIGIL FOR RASTABAN. THEY'RE SAYING GOODBYE TO ONE OF THEIR OWN.
It's not lost on me that I'm doing exactly what mother did all those years ago.
member the confusion,
er, and pain I felt. I'm
y that I'm making
relive that.

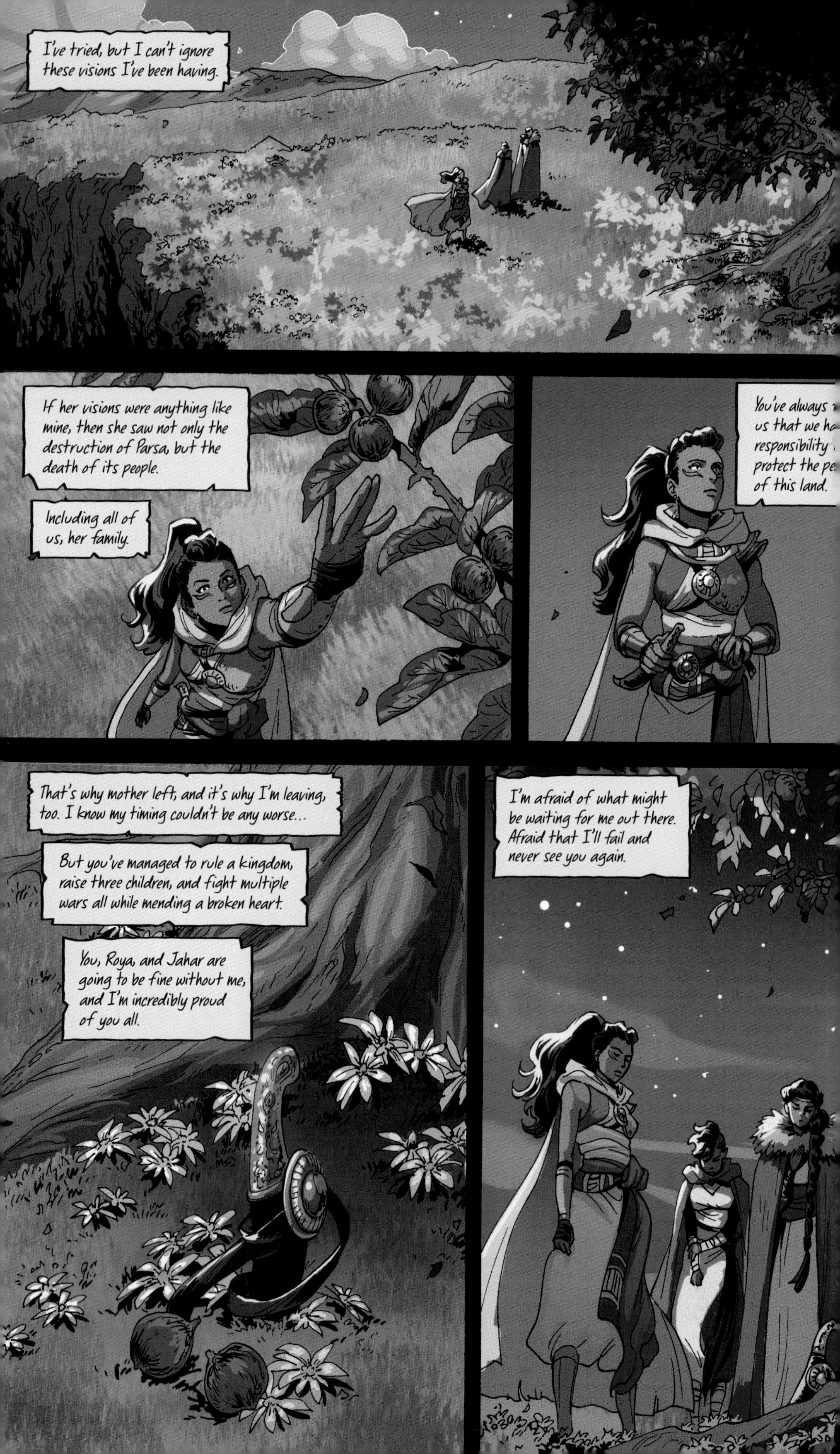

I've tried, but I can't ignore these visions I've been having.
If her visions were anything like mine, then she saw not only the destruction of Parsa, but the death of its people.
Including all of us, her family.
You've always
us that we ha
responsibility
protect the pe
of this land.
That's why mother left, and it's why I'm leaving, too. I know my timing couldn't be any worse...
But you've managed to rule a kingdom, raise three children, and fight multiple wars all while mending a broken heart.
You, Roya, and Jahar are going to be fine without me, and I'm incredibly proud of you all.
I'm afraid of what might be waiting for me out there. Afraid that I'll fail and never see you again.

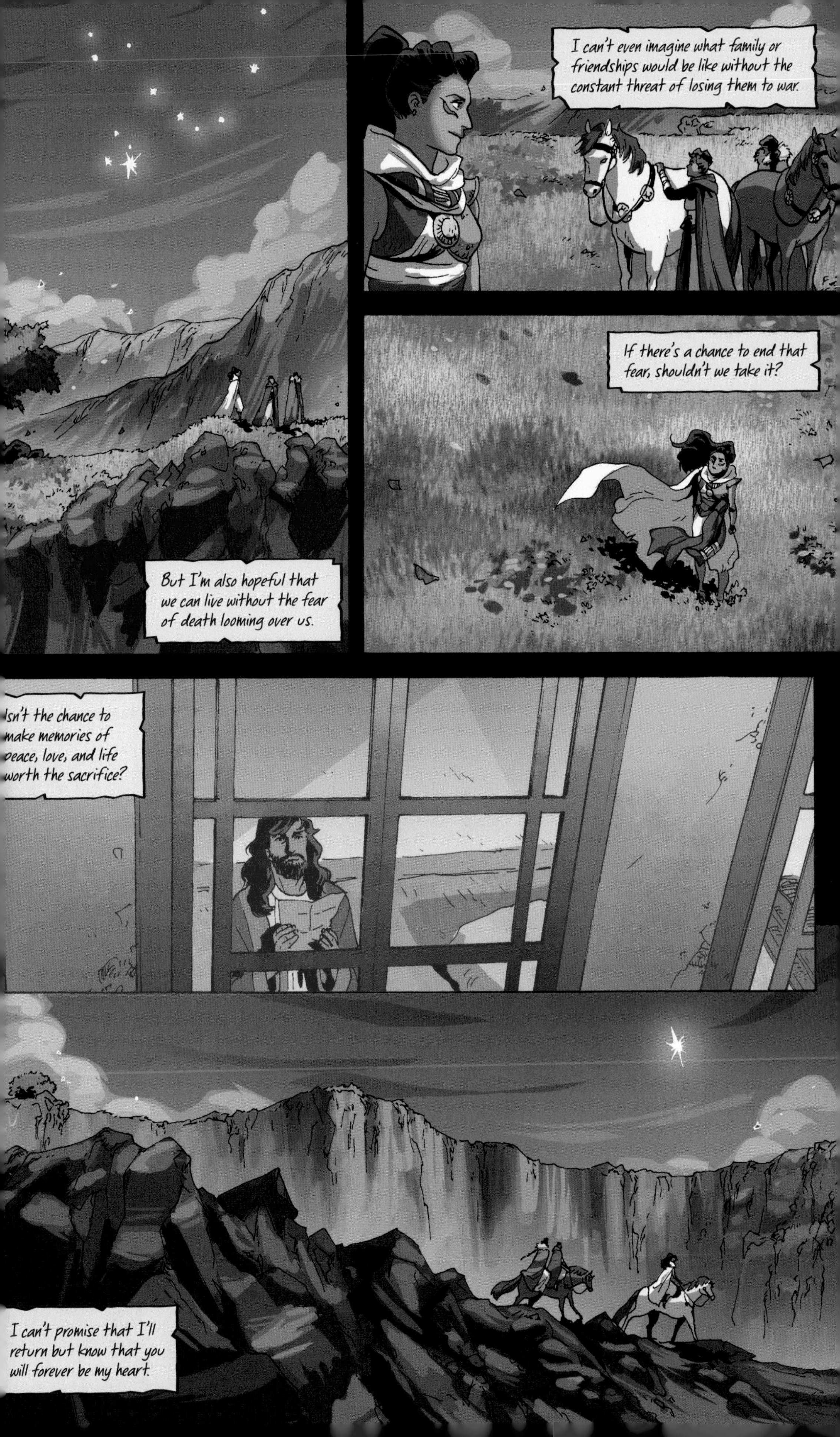
I can't even imagine what family or friendships would be like without the constant threat of losing them to war.
But I'm also hopeful that we can live without the fear of death looming over us.
If there's a chance to end that fear, shouldn't we take it?
Isn't the chance to make memories of peace, love, and life worth the sacrifice?
I can't promise that I'll return but know that you will forever be my heart.

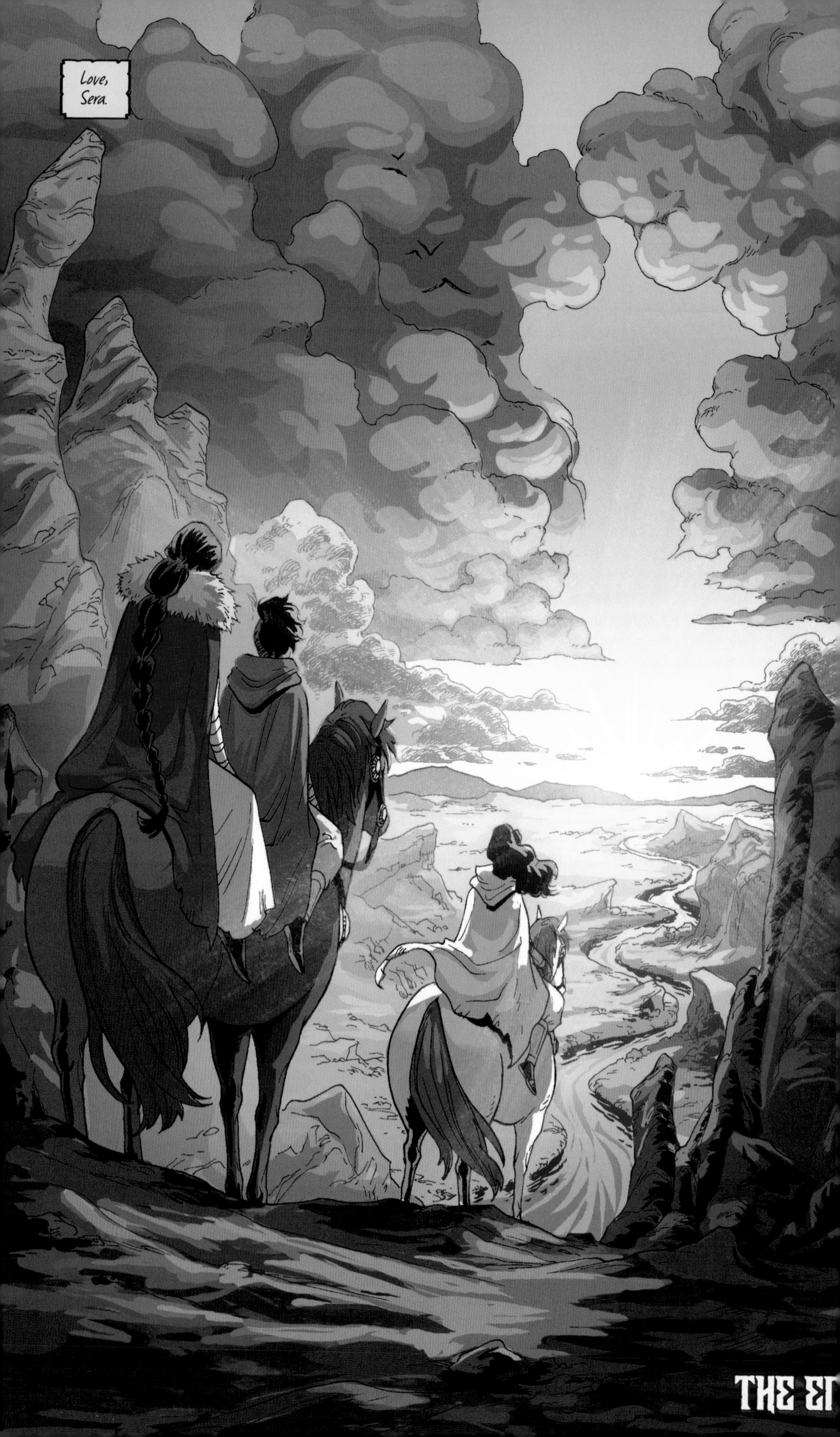

Love,
Sera.
THE EI

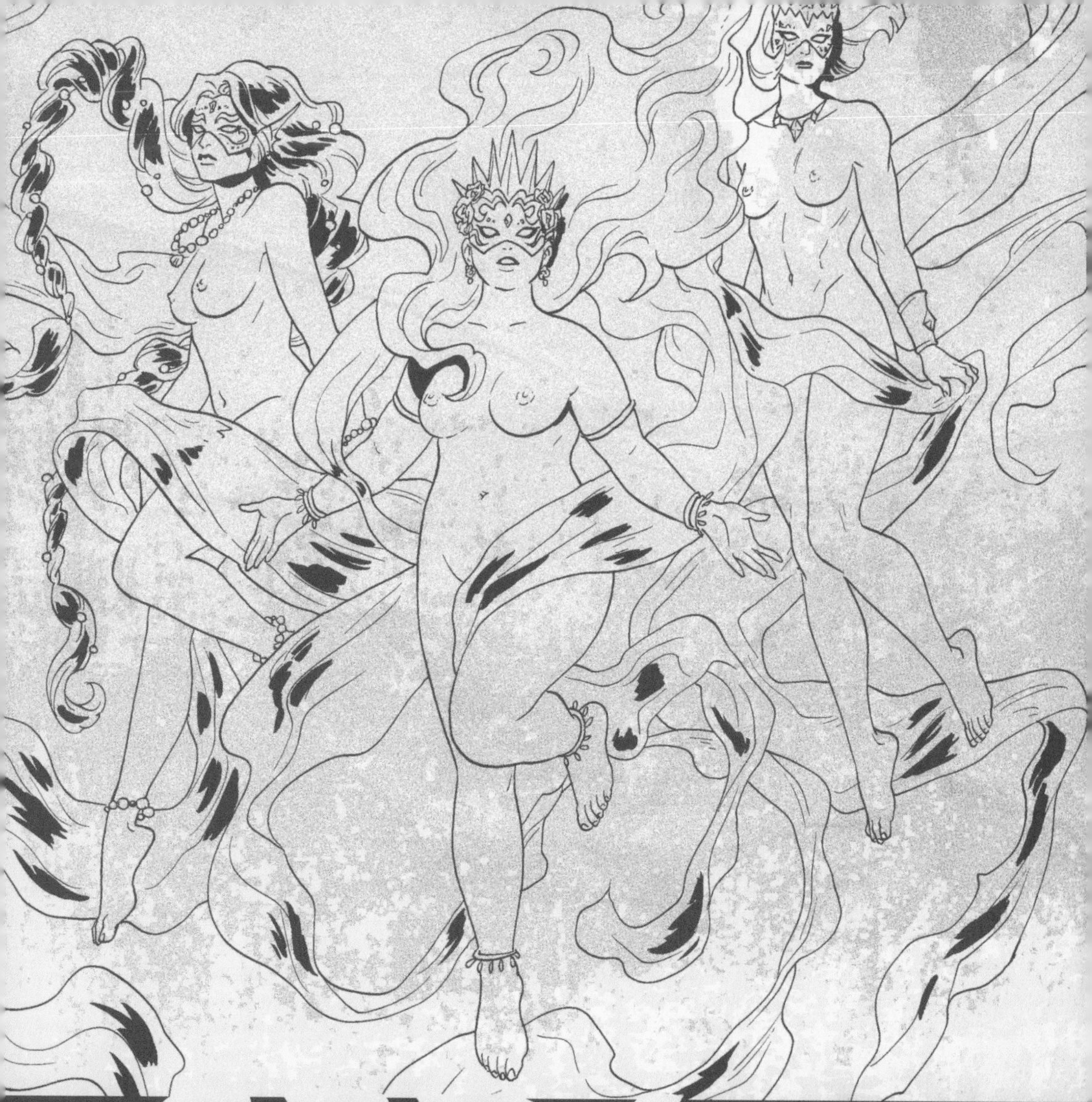

SERA &
THE ART OF AUDREY MOK

WITH EXCLUSIVE COVERS BY

NATASHA ALTERICI

KRIS ANKA

JEN BARTEL

IRENE KOH

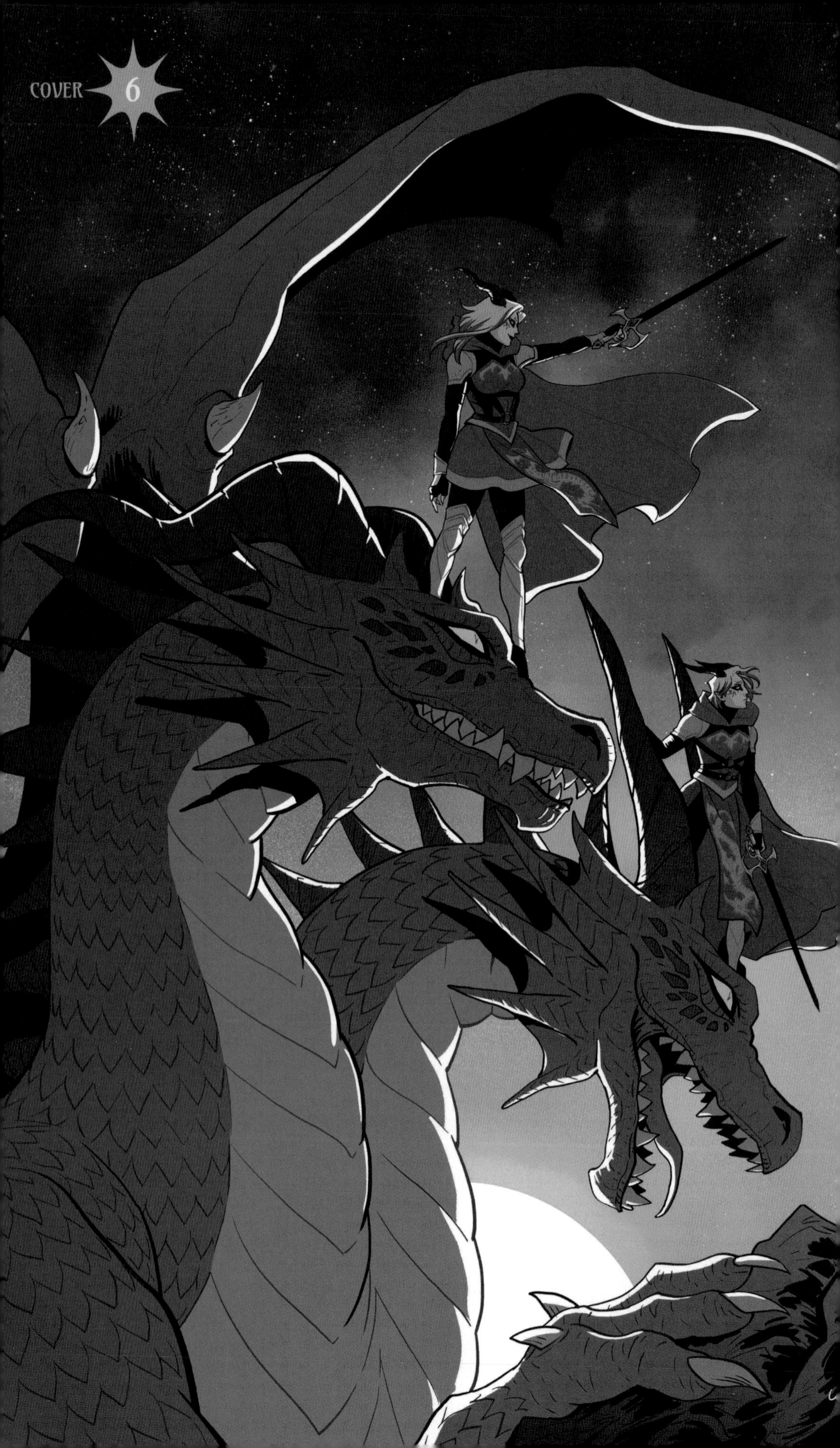
COVER 6

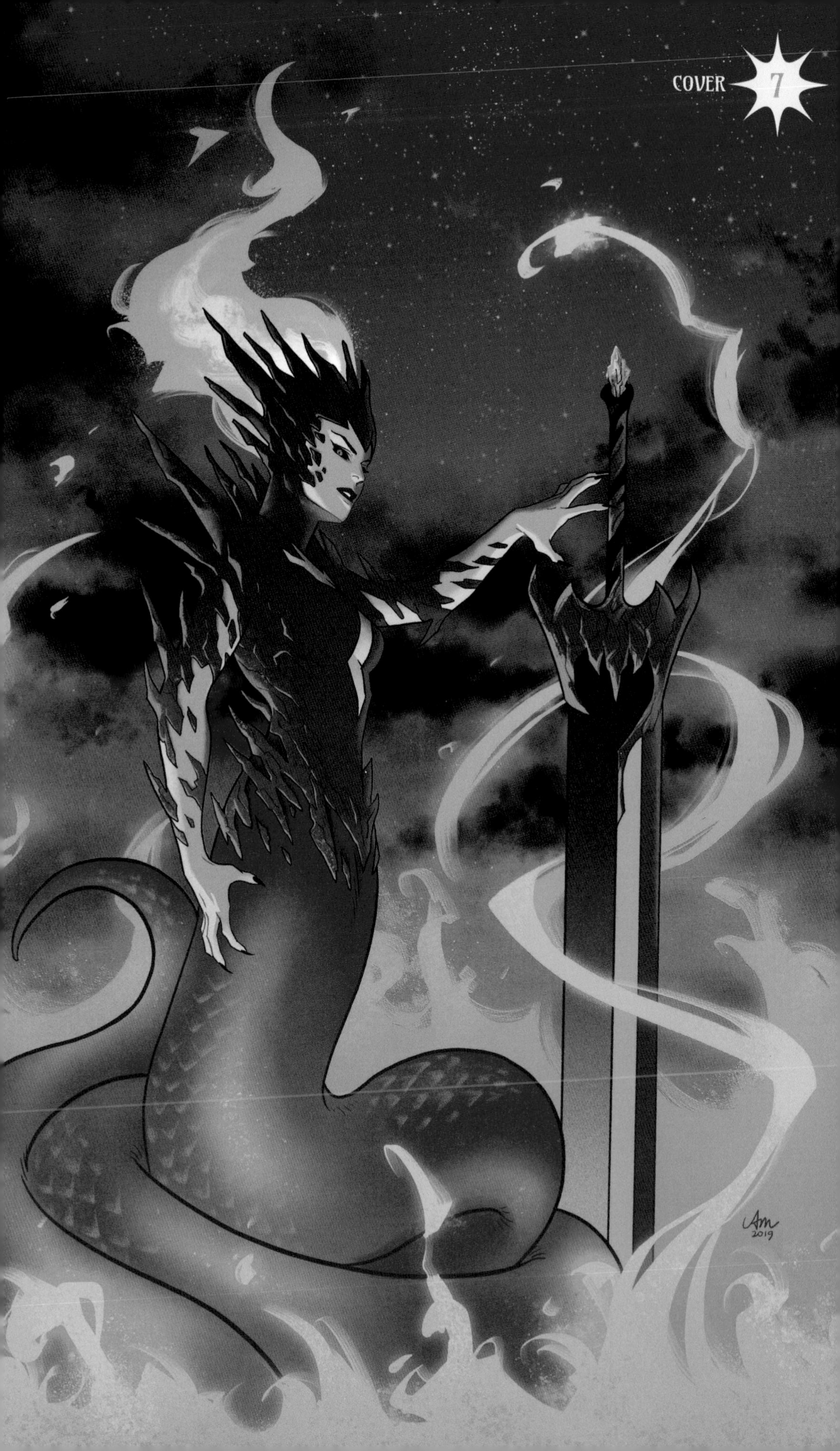
COVER 7
Am
2019

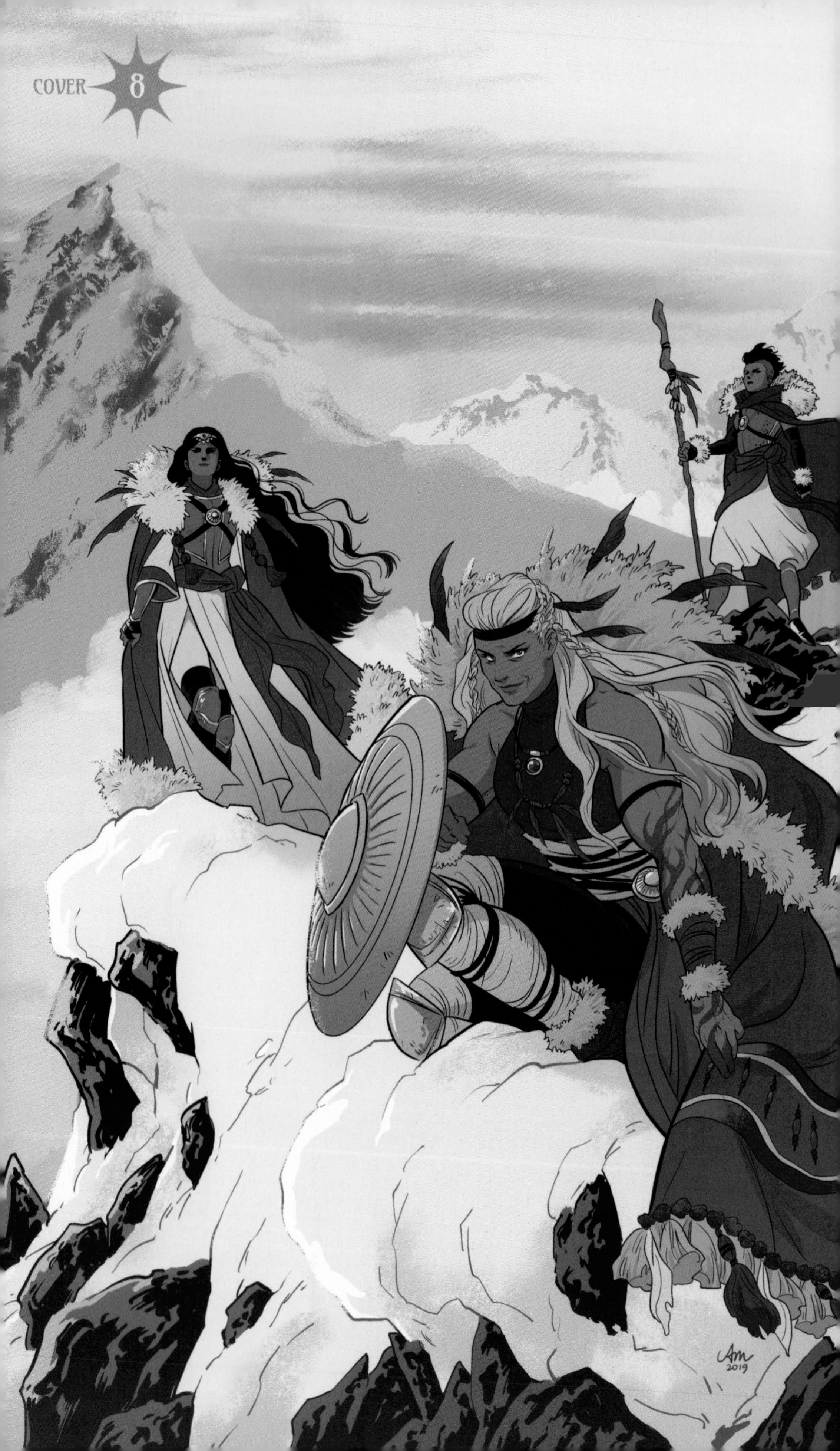
COVER 8
Am 2019

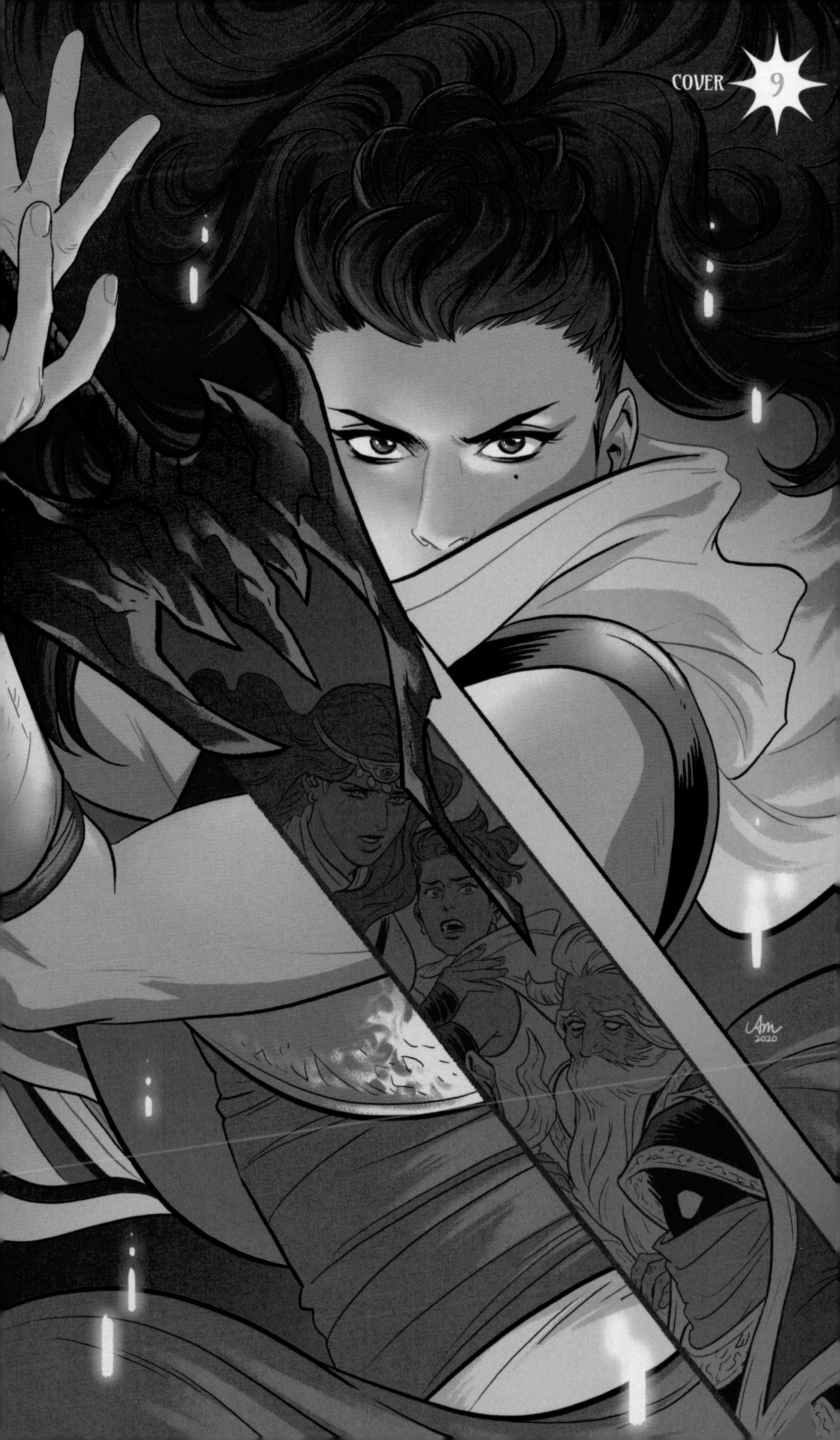
COVER 9
Am
2020

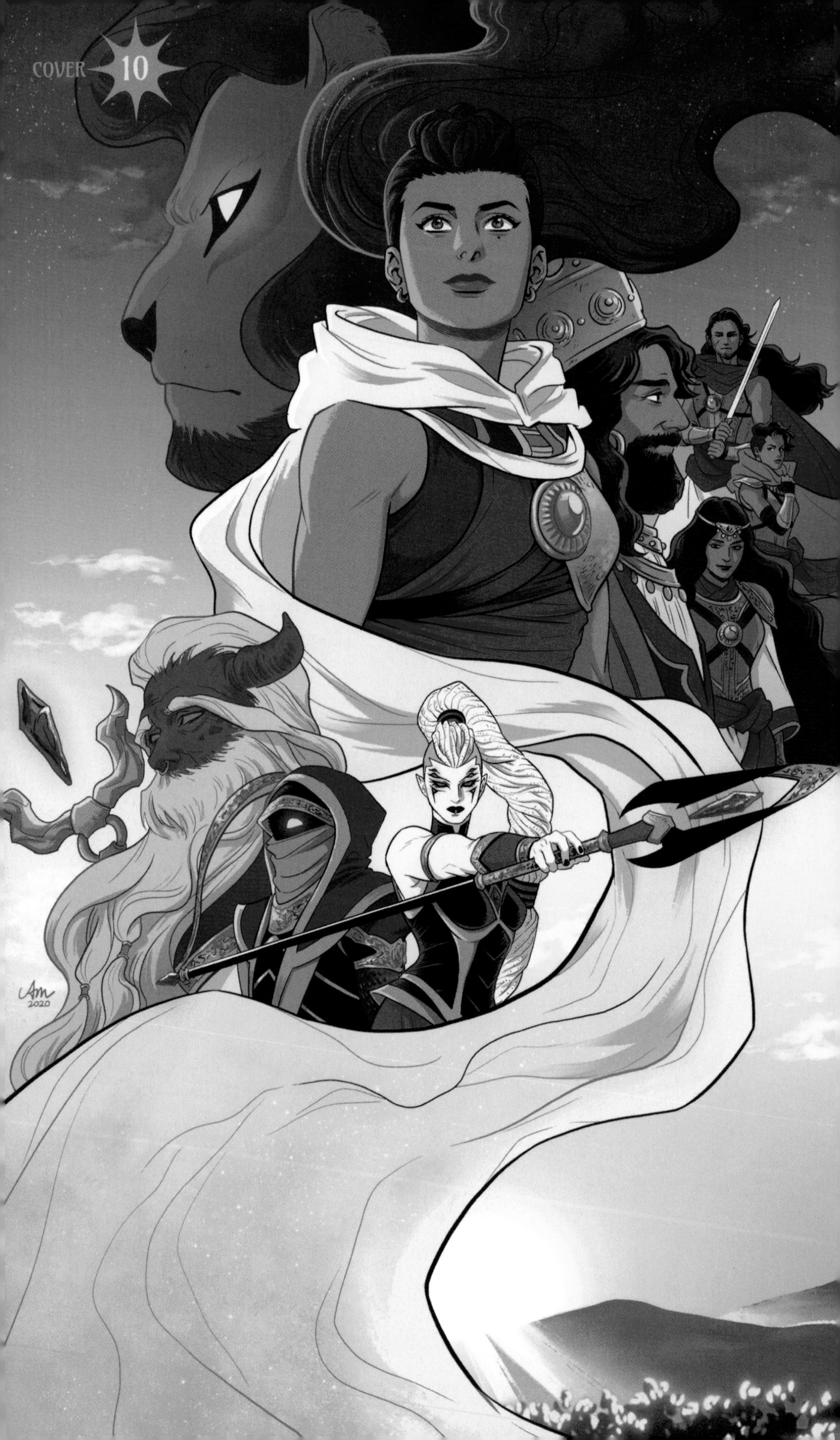
COVER 10
Am
2020

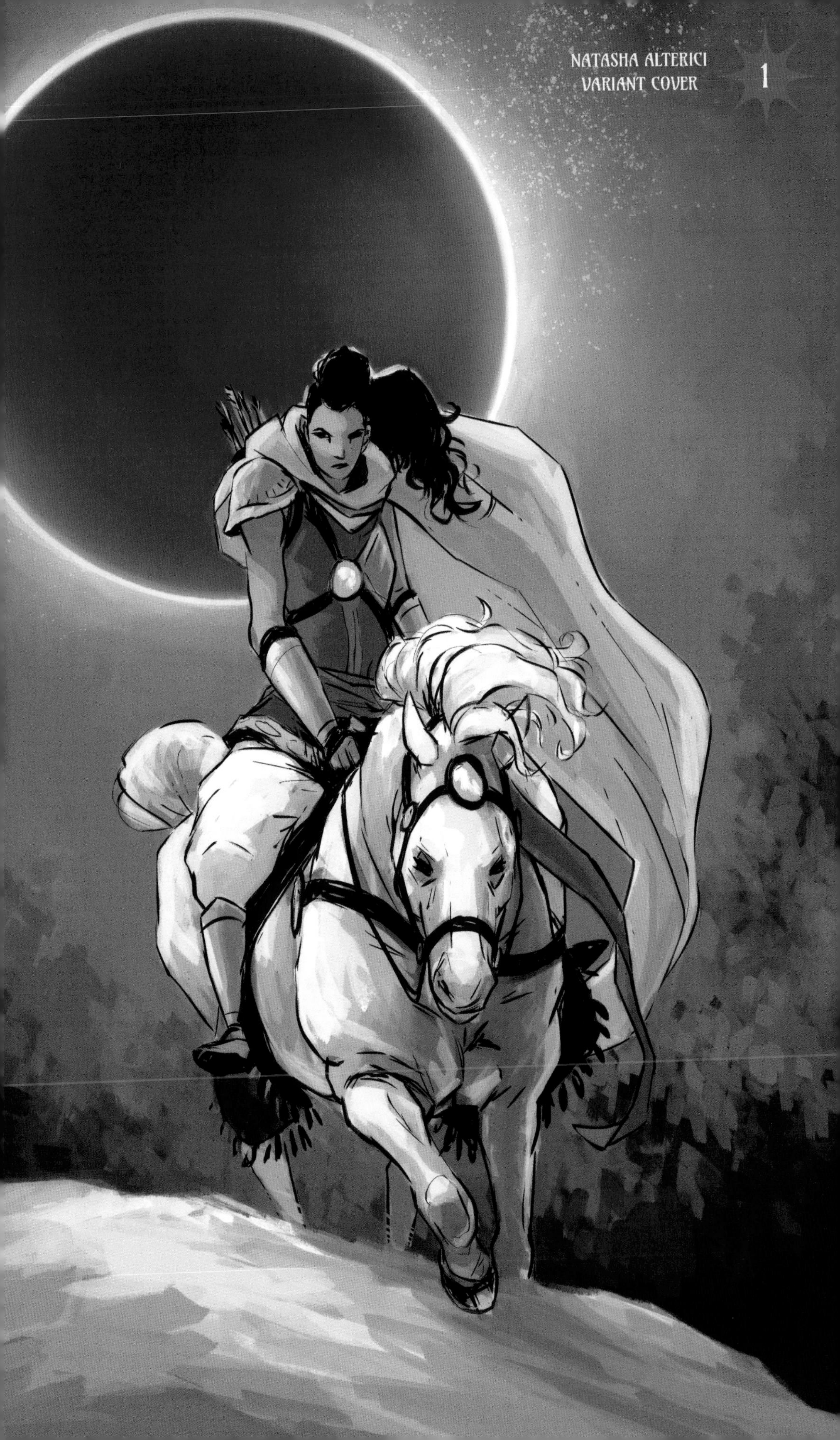
NATASHA ALTERICI
VARIANT COVER
1

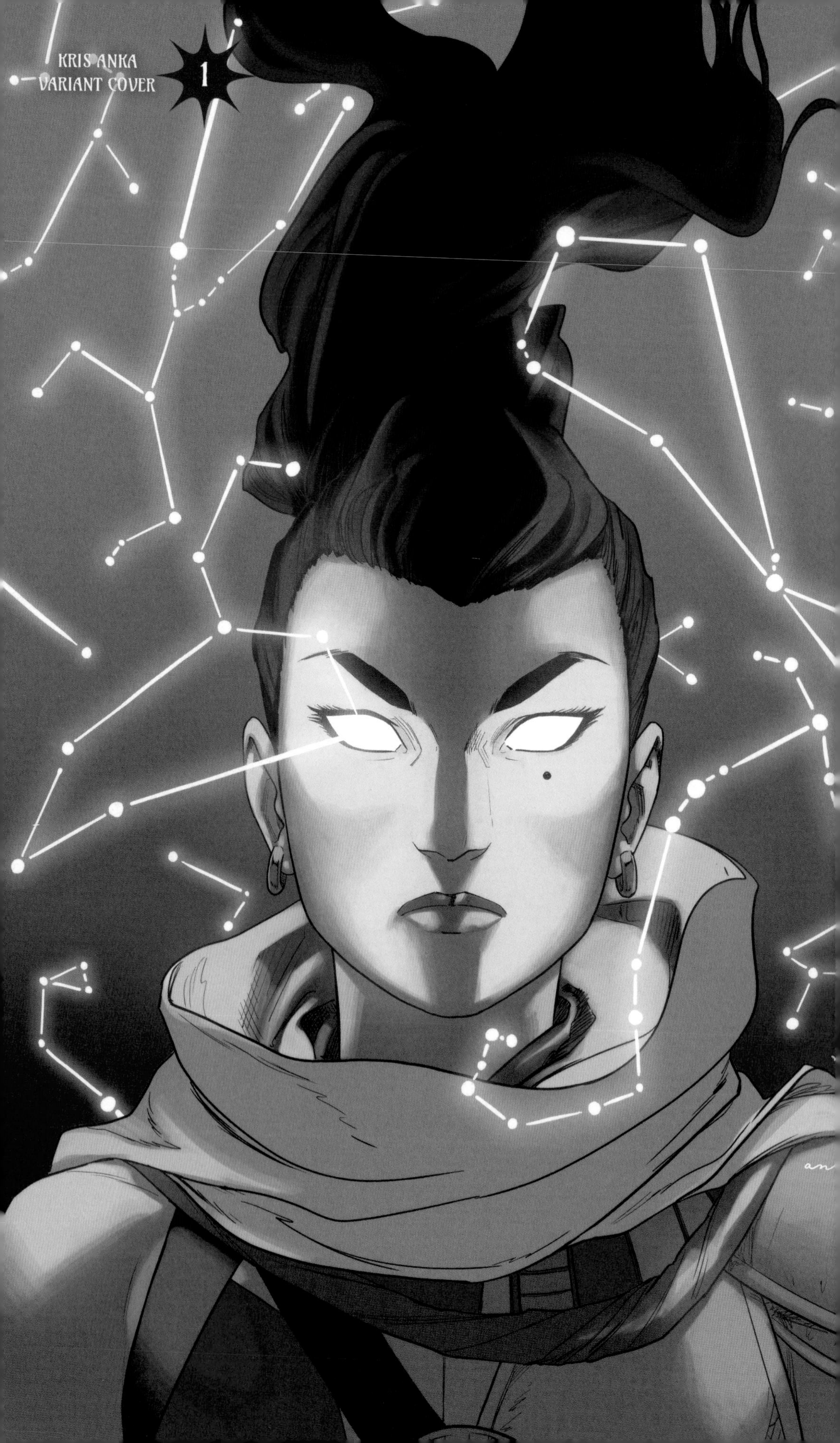

KRIS ANKA
VARIANT COVER
1

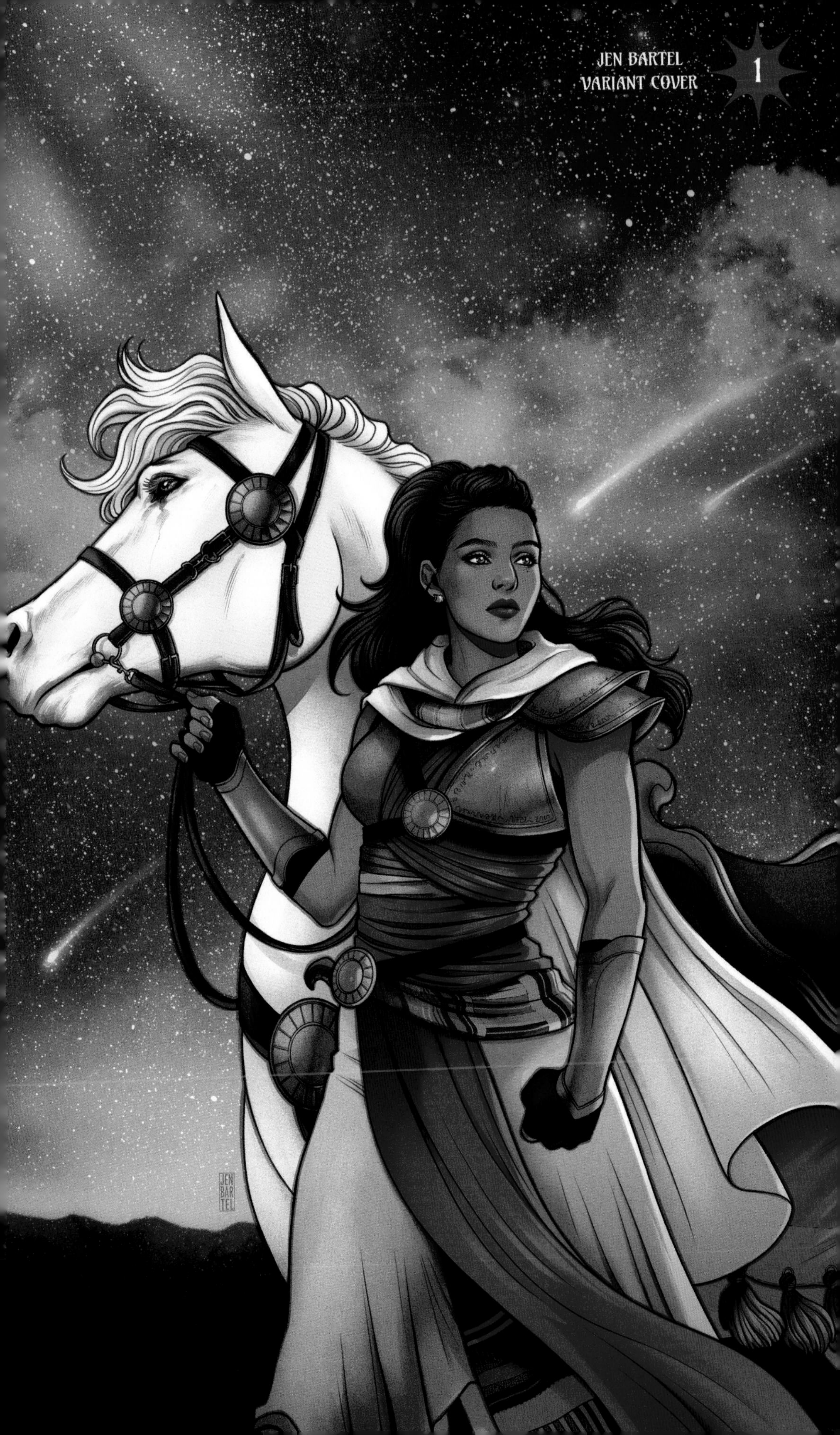
JEN BARTEL
VARIANT COVER
1
JEN
BAR
TEL

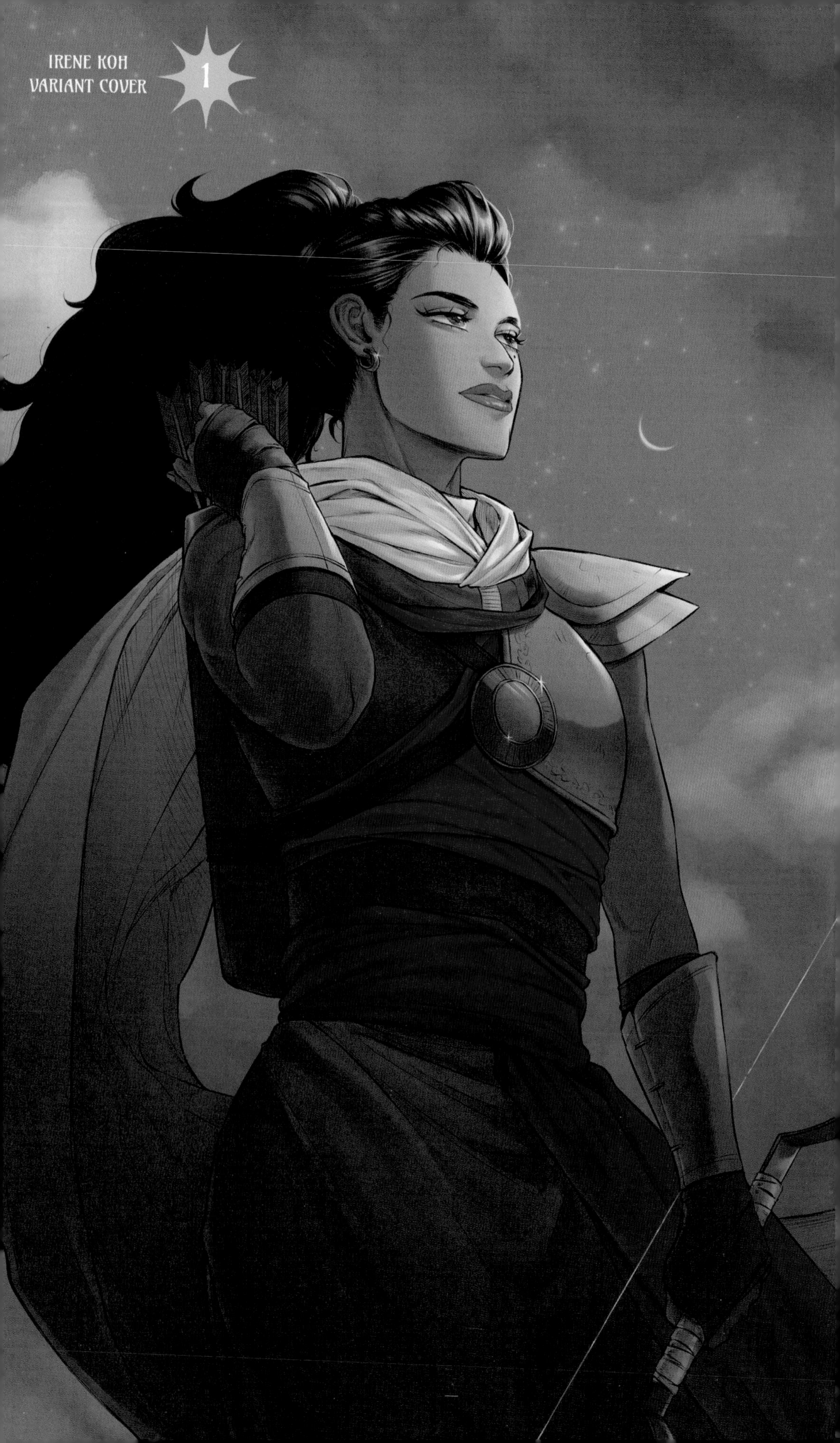
IRENE KOH
VARIANT COVER
1